Legacy of Dreams

Dan Vanderburg

Darlene -
Happy Birthday
Dan Vanderburg

Printed in the United States of America.

ISBN:152344732X
ISBN-13:978-1523447329

Dedication

This book is dedicated to the memory of my ancestors, the William W. Bell family of Fannin County, Texas who lived their lives on the Texas frontier in the days after the Texas revolution with Mexico. They and their neighbors helped build the Republic of Texas.

Acknowledgments

Tina Vanderburg, Shannon Twitty and Vicki Risinger:
Thank you for the encouragement and support you have given me to complete this book. Tina, thank you especially for all the technical help and hours of support you have given me.

Southwestern Writers Association, Tucson AZ:
Thanks to all the officers and members who know what it's like to do what we do. You are a wonderful network of talented, creative people.

Heritage Highlands Writers Group, Marana AZ:
What a great bunch of irreverent, tell-it-like-it-is soul mates. Thanks for all the laughs, tears and insightful criticisms. It was a joy reading your work every week but a challenge to find things to critique. You are all so talented.

Harvey Stanbrough: Author, Editor, Publisher and Writing Guru.
Harvey, you are the greatest. I learned so much from you. You have such a wealth of knowledge about getting the words right. With so many words to choose from, you can find the absolute best way of saying it.

Debbie Grayson Lincoln, Texas Artist:
Debbie, it has been such a rewarding experience working with you. It was so easy for us to come together with a common vision for what the cover art was to be. You have a way of taking the reality of the image far beyond the expectation.

PROLOGUE

SUMMER, 1879, VIRGINIA POINT, TEXAS

Will Bowman's eyes flew open to the crash of thunder. The lightning flickering beyond the windows illuminated puddles of water beginning to form on the window sill as the rain blew in between the flapping, white lace curtains. He quietly pulled himself from bed so as not to disturb his sleeping wife and groped his way across the room. His wrinkled but still strong features flickered in the reflection on the glass from the almost constant lightning as he pulled the curtains aside and closed the window.

Just how bad is this going to be? He thought, squinting out into the night. *Is there a tornado out there? Should I take them to the cellar?*

Bending closer to the window, barefoot and in his nightshirt, the seventy-one year old man strained to see beyond the rivulets of water flowing down the glass. He squinted at the silhouettes of live oak trees dotting the prairie beyond the yard as the lightning flashed. How *many times have I viewed this scene in all kinds of weather? Hundreds? Maybe thousands?*

A shiver went through him as he remembered the times years earlier when he and Jeff survived nights much like this in their old surveying tent. They'd spent so many cold, wet, and sometimes freezing nights trying to find a warm spot under the blankets. *We just waited out the night. But the good days and nights far outnumbered the bad.*

Still leaning on the window frame and gazing out at the storm, he listened to the rhythm of raindrops on the roof, against the window, and in the puddles in the yard. The sounds brought more memories. *Has it really been fifty years?* He shook his head. *Fifty years since that day in Virginia when I told Papa I was coming to Texas. So much has happened. So much hardship and sacrifice.* A smile crept across his face. *But so much satisfaction.*

A flash of lightning in the trees a mile north of the house jolted the old man back to the present. The massive white glow was soon followed by a shattering boom that rattled the windows.

A strange, uncontrollable shudder trembled its way through Will. He grabbed the window frame to steady himself. *What the?*

He didn't see the details of the lightning striking the ancient oak tree. He didn't see the thick trunk shatter and fall away or the gnarled branches explode from the pressure as its sap instantaneously boiled off. Nor did he see the long-held secret that was finally revealed by the storm's fury that night.

Chapter 1

Spring, 1829, Western Virginia
Fifty Years Earlier

The two men led their horses as they walked along the edge of the cotton field. The older man watched the Negro workers, scattered among the furrows, hoeing weeds from the Virginia dirt between the young cotton plants. The older man occasionally glanced at his son walking beside him. The young man looked to be in deep thought. Henry Bowman was worried about his youngest son. It was against Will's nature to be as quiet and serious as he had been lately.

"Working on a problem, Son?"

"What?" Will looked up from the dirt.

"I asked if you had a problem. You've been awfully preoccupied lately. Women problems?"

"No, Papa. Nothing like that."

Will Bowman did have something on his mind. He'd been thinking it over for a month, ever since he'd received the letter. It was time to share his decision with his family and act on his plan.

Henry was pleased when Will suggested they ride out together and check the crops that sunny, spring morning. Henry had spent little time with his youngest son in the last several years. Will had been away at school most of the time. Since he'd graduated from the academy, he was frequently away in other parts of the state working on surveying projects.

The old man continued to steal sideways glances at Will while they walked. He'd come to realize how much Will had matured in the last few years.

Now twenty-one years old, he was a slender young man but built with a strong frame. He stood at six-feet, two and was taller than his father. It wouldn't have surprised Henry if his good-looking, blue eyed son *was* brooding because he was in love. He'd noticed several young women glancing approvingly at Will when he, Will and Taylor, one of his older sons, were in Roanoke for supplies a few weeks earlier. Henry reflected, *come to think of it, that's about how long Will's been acting a little preoccupied.*

Will broke the silence. "Papa, why did you decide to put your roots down here?"

"What do you mean, Son?"

"What made you decide to settle way out here in western Virginia when you did? Wasn't it still wild out here then?"

Henry stopped walking and looked at Will. The horses grazed on the fresh grass at the end of the cotton rows. "Why did I settle out here?" He took off his hat off and scratched his head as he thought back. "Several reasons, I guess." He smiled as he remembered. "I was determined to build a good life for the family I hoped to have some day. I knew it wouldn't be easy, but I was young, strong, and full of ambition. Wanted to have a place where I'd have room to spread out and be my own man. Besides, the price was right." He winked at Will and his smile widened, wrinkling his cheek. "I was lucky enough to find a good woman that would have me. Your mother wanted this kind of life too. Didn't start out with any help, either. Wasn't able to get any help for several years. A strong team of mules is all we had in the beginning. When your brothers started coming along and your mother couldn't help in the fields, it was just me and the mules 'til I could afford some help. Anyway, why are you asking something like that? Son, what's on your mind?"

"I'm . . . I'm just thinking about a lot of things right now."

"What kind of things?"

Well hesitated a moment before continuing. "Remember when we were in Roanoke a couple of weeks ago?"

"Yeah."

"Well, I picked up a letter from a fellow named Austin. He's been commissioned by the government of Mexico to develop colonization in Texas. He's the son of the man Uncle John told us about when he was visiting here that winter, six or seven years ago. A lot of settlers are moving out there now, taking advantage of the Mexican land grants." Will removed his hat and fingered the brim for a moment before looking at his father again. "Fact is, he wants me to come to Texas too, and claim a Mexican land grant for myself and do surveying for immigrants moving into the area."

Henry stared at his son, the smile was gone from his face. He knew people were moving to Texas and had a good idea what it was like there. He remembered the visit from his wife's brother, John Bell, one of the first American settlers in Texas, and he'd received several letters over the years from John describing that part of the country and their way of life.

Henry expected Will to eventually assume his place on the family plantation like his brothers. Now his youngest son was talking about leaving family and home and moving across the continent to a wilderness filled with uncertainty and possible danger. As much as Henry wanted to discourage him, raising Will and his brothers had taught him to be patient.

Will continued. "The Mexican government is offering land grants of over a thousand acres for a single man and over forty-five hundred acres to men with families. With all the immigration and settlement that's going on, there's a tremendous amount of work for surveyors and not near enough certified people to do it. I'll not only have an opportunity to select my own land, but I can make a good living with my surveying."

Henry looked at the ground and shook his head, then looked back up at Will. "Son, I don't doubt there's plenty of opportunity, but from what I understand, there are also plenty of chances for things to go sour. What about the Mexican government? How stable is it? What about the Indians? We've both heard what those murdering savages can do. There's no militia out there. Why, that country's so big from what I hear, you might travel for weeks without seeing another human being. Not a civilized one, anyway."

Henry put his hands on Will's shoulders. "Son, I've worked my entire life to provide a better way for my children so you'd be spared some of the difficulty I had when I was young. I expanded this place over the years so you all could have a reasonable share. I've tried to give you a good foundation. I've taught you, and I've sent you away for schooling to become an educated man with military training. I've raised you to be a Southern gentleman. Now you want to turn your back on all of it and travel a thousand miles into the wilderness and start from scratch?" Henry released Will and his arms sagged to his sides. He gazed at the ground, sucked air between his teeth and sighed. He looked at Will again and slowly shook his head. "Son, I just don't know."

"It's not that I want to turn my back on everything you've done, Papa. I just want to earn my own. If anybody can understand that, you can. Yes sir, you taught me to stand on my own two feet — to stand up for what I believe." Will hesitated, and looked his father in the eyes. "I *believe* in this, Papa. I believe this new country will provide an opportunity for me that I could never realize here." He looked across the fields for a moment, then back at his father. "I don't know exactly what I have to offer Texas except my surveying skills, but I have the determination, ambition, and desire to contribute whatever I can to help it develop from a colony into whatever it will become. You prepared me well, Papa. I'm not afraid to face the unknown. I'm young, like you were when you started out here. I've got a vision of what I want for my family one of these days. And like you, I'm willing to take a risk and work hard for it."

Will paused again, glancing across the fields, then met his father's gaze. "Papa, I really appreciate what you've done for me, and I love you for it, but this is what I have to do. I want someday to have the same pride and satisfaction that you have now. I want to know that whatever level of success I may achieve, I accomplished it on my own, by my own wits and ability. I've set my course — but I really do want your blessing to do it."

Henry returned Will's gaze with a look of pride and sorrow on his lined face. He saw so much of himself in his son's blue eyes. He hesitated a moment, then nodded. "I do understand how you feel, Son. Give me some time to think on it." Henry reached for his saddle horn and pulled himself into his saddle. "Let's sleep on it tonight and see how it looks in the morning."

They rode quietly back to the big house for lunch. Both were too caught up in their own thoughts for further conversation.

Breaking the news to his father relieved Will of a burden he had carried since he'd first started thinking about venturing out on his own. He had known for some time that he wanted to define his own destiny. He just hadn't known which direction to follow until he'd received the letter from Austin.

He loved his family and felt an obligation to follow his father's plan, but a stronger desire urged him to follow his heart. He knew if he fulfilled his family's expectations by settling on his father's farm, he would miss what he considered the opportunity and adventure of a lifetime. He wanted a home and family some day, but there was much he needed to accomplish first. The invitation to Texas was just what he'd been looking for.

Many experiences in Will's life had prepared him for this decision. Although Henry Bowman and all of his sons were considered gentlemen, he'd seen to it that all of his sons knew how to live off the land. Will had been trained to hunt and shoot as soon as he could hold his father's rifle. He could distinguish useful plants from those that were harmful, and knew how to find water where there appeared to be none. He'd prepared many animals for the table and knew how to use their hides.

Will was also a good farmer. He could get the most from the land and felt a deep satisfaction from seeing the seeds of his labor come to fruition at harvest time. He had experienced exhausting labor first hand and considered himself the better for it. Now he was ready to take those skills to Texas.

Will remembered as a young teenager sitting by the fireside during his uncle's visit, listening to stories of Texas. Uncle John spoke of a land so vast it seemed endless. Most of it was still unexplored by white men. He talked of black land so rich that cotton produced a yield over twice what a good farmer could expect in Virginia. He said there was wildlife in abundance. Scattered herds of wild horses and cattle ran free. Hundreds of thousands of buffalo covered the plains. Deer, turkey, and wild hogs were so plentiful there would always be meat for the table.

He also spoke of the dangers of everyday living in that part of the country. The Indian conflict was not so threatening in the southern part of the territory but the Comanches to the north and west were hostile and occasionally raided the scattered Mexican settlements.

Uncle John had painted an exciting picture of the new frontier and planted a seed of adventure in young Will's mind.

Will did his homework after receiving Austin's letter. He made several trips to Roanoke to research newspaper articles regarding the current state of affairs in Texas. He learned that there had been many changes in Mexico since John's visit to Virginia. After winning its independence from Spain, Mexico was limited in what a struggling, sometimes politically unstable new country could accomplish. It was short on cash but long on millions of acres of unclaimed, untamed land.

He also learned that after Moses Austin's death, Stephen Austin had successfully continued his father's work by obtaining permission to develop colonies in northeastern Mexico, which included Texas. Several land grants had been issued by the Mexican government to commissioners — or impresarios, as they were called, including Austin. They agreed to attract large numbers of families into their grant for settlement in exchange for huge grants of land for themselves.

Will felt well informed and secure with his decision. He just hoped his father and the rest of his family would share his enthusiasm.

Chapter 2

Jessie, the house keeper, sent the two girls outside just before noon to wait for the men to come home for lunch. Fourteen year old Mary, the youngest of the Bowman household, had played all morning with Anna Thompson. Anna was staying with the Bowman family while her mother and father were away in Richmond. Mary loved to have girlfriends her own age stay with her for several days at a time. Henry encouraged the guests as they gave Mary her only chance, aside from school, to have female companionship besides Jessie, the house slave.

Mary and Anna were as opposite in appearance as they were alike in behavior. Mary was fair, blond, and freckled, where Anna had a slightly darker complexion and dark, wavy hair. Mary, at an awkward stage in her development, seemed to be all arms and legs. Anna, just shy of her fifteenth birthday had started to mature. Both girls had blue eyes, but Anna's, framed by long, dark lashes were a strikingly beautiful blue-gray. It was obvious that both girls would be beauties soon, but neither was concerned with her looks that morning. They were more interested in making mischief for Will Bowman.

Will was Mary's favorite brother because he was the closest to her in age. Though seven years older, he frequently took time to indulge his sister and interact with her friends.

The men usually dismounted in the shade of the large apple tree at the side of the plantation house where Jefferson met them to take the horses to the barn. The girls decided to climb the tree and wait for the men. Their initial intention was to simply hide from the men when they rode into the yard. However, the small, green apples in the tree inspired more mischief. They began gathering apples in their long, full skirts until each had collected a good sized arsenal.

Soon Henry and Will turned their horses under the tree as

expected and called for Jefferson. The girls waited eagerly for just the right moment. As Will strode under the tree, they released their ammunition. Will's hat and shoulders took most of the barrage. It wasn't hard to detect the culprits from their giggling in the tree. Mary had to grab Anna to keep her from falling from her perch, she was laughing so hard. Will took the joke well as he always did. He and Henry joined in the laughter, but he warned the girls as he laughed, “You two had better watch out; you might get paid back when you least expect it.”

Anna had other reasons for visiting the Bowman plantation that she wouldn't even admit to Mary. She had been attracted to Will Bowman far as long as she could remember. Recently, since he returned from the military academy so mature and self-assured, her feelings toward him had intensified with her developing young womanhood. Now, as he encircled her waist with his hands and easily lifted her from the low-hanging tree limb, she peered at him through her long, dark lashes and felt her cheeks burn.

Although she was becoming a young woman, she was still a child in Will's eyes. He swatted at both of them with his hat as they ran away. He called after them, “You girls shouldn't be deviling men going about their business.”

Their merriment was interrupted by Jessie ringing the dinner bell on the side porch to summon the Bowman family to their noonday meal. Jessie had prepared lunch for the Bowmans as she did every day for the last fourteen years since Mrs. Bowman died giving birth to Mary. After Henry lost his wife, he bought Jessie, Amos, and their son, Jefferson from a neighbor who was moving west.

Will was just seven years old when the new slaves arrived. Jessie tended to the baby, cleaned the house, took care of everyone's clothes and kept the family well fed. Amos and Jefferson provided food for the Bowman plantation and cultivated the vegetable gardens and orchards. The quality and taste of their fruits and vegetables gave testimony to the care they spent working the crops. They were also responsible for the livestock that supplied the table. The beefsteaks, roasts, ribs and chops were always juicy and flavorful. Amos' sausage and ham were almost as legendary as Jessie's fried chicken.

As Jefferson grew toward manhood, he was trained as a blacksmith. He also cared for the saddle horses, mules, and oxen. Amos and Jessie took pride in their work and taught Jefferson the satisfaction of good workmanship.

The Bowmans treated all of their people well, but Jessie, Amos, and Jefferson felt a special relationship with their masters. Those feelings were reflected in the quality of their work, their positive attitude, and their loyalty to the family.

Jefferson was the same age as Will, so it was natural for Will and Jeff, as Will called him, to be childhood playmates. When Jefferson wasn't working with his father or training under the instruction of Will's brothers, he and Will explored the valleys and creeks around the plantation together. It wasn't unusual for them to bring home fish for supper after an afternoon at the fishing hole.

As teenagers, Will often took Jefferson hunting with him after chores were done. Although it was frowned upon, if not forbidden, to allow a slave to handle firearms, Will ignored common practice and taught Jefferson to use the Tennessee long rifle. After some practice, Jeff became as adept a marksman as Will.

Like Will, Jefferson grew to become a tall man but was more muscular than Will with handsome, broad features and a bright smile. He had his own place in the cabin with his parents; a little alcove that was divided from the rest of the cabin by a curtain with a comfortable feather bed in the corner. He enjoyed plenty of good food that Jessie brought from the big house every night.

Jefferson felt content with his way of life. He'd been born into slavery. It was all he knew. Occasionally, though, he wondered what freedom would be like. He learned things quickly and wanted so much to be able to learn more. He enjoyed using his mind to design tools that he made with his forge and anvil and also to repair the farm equipment. But he knew he'd never learn to read and write. He thought there must be a law somewhere that said black folks couldn’t be taught to read and write. He didn't know if it was written law or not, but he knew that white people didn't want their slaves to learn anything other than what they could do with their hands.

Chapter 3

Henry didn't sleep much the night after Will outlined his plan. He lay awake thinking of Will's dream to help open the Texas frontier. Certainly, the opportunity for success and even wealth existed, but Henry couldn't help but feel protective toward his youngest boy. Will had always been his favorite son because he had been the baby for so many years before Mary came along.

Finally, before dawn, Henry made his decision and developed a plan for setting it in motion. He was up and dressed as Jessie started brewing coffee. He had a quick, early breakfast in the kitchen. He looked over his breakfast plate at Jessie. "Jessie, tell Jefferson to saddle my horse while I'm having my coffee. And another thing, I want you to plan a big supper for tonight. I'm going to have the whole family in. Fix up one of your extra-special suppers — roast beef and fried chicken with all your extras."

"Yes sir, but what—"

"I'll tell you later. Just fix it up special for the family."

"Yes sir."

Henry met Jefferson in the barn yard, waiting with the saddled bay gelding. He swung into the saddle. "Jefferson, tell all my sons that I want them and their wives to have dinner at the big house tonight."

"Yes sir."

"Oh, yeah, there's one other thing. I want you, Amos, and Jessie in the parlor at five o'clock this afternoon. There's something I need to discuss with you."

"Yes sir." A look of confusion crowded Jefferson's face He watched the master ride out of the barn lot and down the trail toward the road to Roanoke. *Now why would Mister Henry want to meet with us this evening?*

It was rare that the entire family came together at the same time except for holiday dinners unless there was a family crisis. Will's brothers discussed the purpose of the get-together during the day but couldn't determine a reason for the unexpected "mystery" dinner. The market conditions for cotton continued to look good with the European mills and the new mills being developed up North. The government was stable. The farm was in good shape. The weather had cooperated so far this season. If it held, they would reap a good crop and turn a nice profit. They had a well-rounded field crew with a total of fourteen slaves, including children. No one could understand the reason for the special occasion. No one except Will.

Will knew what the meeting was about, but he didn't know what turn his father would take. *Is he calling the dinner to announce his support of my immigration to Texas or to announce the restructuring of the family business to include me in the day-to-day operation?*

Just talking to his father about his plans made Will more resolute. He didn't want to have a scene with his father, especially in front of his whole family, but his decision had been made.

The house was abuzz with activity in preparation for the special family gathering. Jessie enlisted the girls' help with the housework. They dusted and aired the house while Amos and Jefferson scrubbed the floors.

Mary and Anna set the table in the spacious dining room with Mary's mother's fine china and the silver Henry bought for his wife on their fifteenth wedding anniversary. Mary liked to set a fancy table, even when it was just for herself and her father. Mary's mother's things were now hers and she enjoyed the role of mistress of the house.

Henry returned from town by early afternoon. After a short nap, he freshened up, dressed for dinner and was in the parlor at 5 o'clock. When Amos, Jessie and Jefferson approached the door, he was standing with his hands clasped behind his back, looking out the window at the meadow beyond the wide front porch. He turned to face the family in the center of the room. "Come in and close the door." Amos and Jefferson stood uncomfortably with their hats in their hands, Jefferson turning his nervously. Jessie clasped her hands at her ample bosom as wrinkled worry lines formed across her brow.

"I'm not going to beat around the bush about why I called you in," Henry said. "This has to do with Will, but it also has to do with Jefferson."

Jefferson lifted his gaze from the polished floor to follow every word more carefully.

"Will has decided to go to Texas and seek his fortune there. Lots of people are moving there to take advantage of land grants. Therefore, there's a great need for trained surveyors. He also plans to get his own land and start a farm, but he can't go it alone. He needs a good man to help him. When I went to town today, I transferred ownership of Jefferson to Will. He and Jefferson will be going to Texas together."

After worrying all day about the purpose of the meeting, now Jessie was doing all she could to stifle tears and hold back the sobs that were welling in her throat. Amos and Jefferson were too shocked to respond.

"Jessie, you and Amos both know I've never separated children from their parents and never will. But Jefferson is a grown man now — has been for some time. It's time he moved out from his mama and papa anyway." He looked at Jefferson. "Jefferson, I want Will to have the best man anybody could ask for. That's why I want you to go with him. With you two looking out for each other, I'll feel more comfortable for both of you." He turned to look at Jefferson's parents. "Amos, you and Jessie have raised a fine boy. You've taught him well and you should be proud of him. I'm proud of him and confident to send my son off into the wilderness with him."

Henry walked over to Jefferson, clasped his thick shoulder, and looked him in the eyes. "Take care of each other, Jefferson. I know you'll do well together."

Jefferson didn't know how to respond. Everything was happening so suddenly. He was thrilled at the thought of being part of the adventure that Henry had just described, but he was saddened at the thought of leaving his family. He cleared the lump in his throat and stammered, "Yes, sir. Thank you, sir. I'll do my best."

Henry started back toward his chair, then turned with an afterthought. "Oh yeah, I called the family together tonight to tell them about Will's plans. No one knows about you going with him yet, not even Will. Let's keep it that way until I tell them."

"Yes sir," they mumbled in unison as they turned to leave.

Jessie turned back before reaching the door, "Mister Bowman?"

"Yes?" he responded before sitting down.

"How long do I have my boy before he go away?"

"It probably won't be for a couple of weeks. There are things to prepare. Besides, I want to have a party for Will before he goes."

"I'll try to get in a partyin' mood, but it sho gonna be hard."

"I know it will, Jessie, but you'll do fine. You always have. I know you probably don't feel much like working or partying after what I've told you, but you've got dinner to serve in a little while. There will be time enough for fretting later."

After they left Henry in the parlor and returned to the kitchen, Amos said, "Now, y'all straighten' up an' act right. Y'all hear what Mister Bowman say. Don't let on about dis. Dey all learn soon enough."

Mary and Anna greeted the three sons and their wives as they arrived for dinner at six-thirty. Each was dressed in nice suits or gaily colored party dresses with wide skirts for Henry's dinner. Henry and Will soon joined them in conversation regarding children and crops. It wasn't long before Jessie announced that dinner was ready.

They assembled in the spacious dining room, gathering

around the table set with crystal, china, and silver. Everyone joined hands and Henry offered thanks for the food before them. The conversation during dinner was subdued except for the girls telling of the prank they pulled on Will from the apple tree.

After dessert was served, Henry explained why he had called the family together.

"I'm sure you all wondered why I called you all together tonight. It obviously isn't a holiday. There is going to be a change happening that I need to share with you" He hesitated as moment and looked at Will. It seems that my youngest son and your brother is more of an adventurer than I ever thought he would be. He wants to immigrate to Texas and help develop a new colony for new settlers and get his own land grant. I've decided to support Will's plan and give him my blessing, even though I do have some misgivings as to the safety of this venture. However, Will is a grown man, well educated, and capable of making his own decisions. That new country needs men like him."

Will was embarrassed as the family applauded, some patting his back, others reaching to shake his hand, all showing their approval of his mission.

Henry continued. "Will's goal, though admirable in concept, is not something he can do alone. A surveyor must have a helper, and a gentleman must have a servant to assist in his day-to- day needs. I have transferred ownership of Jefferson to Will. I have already talked to Jefferson, Amos and Jessie, and they are aware of this plan. I want Will to have a good man he can depend on.

"Also, due to many circumstances, Will hasn't yet become a full business partner in this plantation like the rest of you boys have, nor has he shared in the profits as you have. But he has earned his way and done his part through his years, growing up without cash payment. I want him to have one-thousand dollars in cash to take with him, and there's an account in his name at the Bank of New Orleans with an additional three thousand dollars. He has earned at least that much from his work over the years on the plantation." He turned to Will, handing him the envelope. "I hope this will get you started and give you a little nest egg to fall back on if times get hard."

Will was overwhelmed. He hadn't dreamed his father would be so generous. It took a few moments before he could speak. He cleared his throat several times, then rose and faced his father. "Thank you, sir, for your generosity. It was totally unexpected but will be put to good use, I assure you. As for the gift of Jefferson, thanks again. I couldn't have asked for a better traveling companion and assistant. I'll take good care of him." Will glanced around the table. "And to the rest of you, thanks for your support. Please keep me in your prayers. I think I'll need all the help I can get."

Again there was an ovation. Henry stood at the end of the table and raised his glass. "To Will . . . may you find the success you seek as you help open the new frontier of Texas!"

Will raised his glass, accepted the toast and thanked everyone around the table. His gaze shifted to Anna. She sat across the table from him, quietly looking into his happy face. Her sad eyes met his, and she lifted her glass and forced a smile as a tear spilled onto her cheek.

Later, after the dinner party, Will paid a visit to Jefferson at Amos and Jessie's cabin. Amos opened the door after Will's quiet knock.

"Why, Mister William, come in!"

Will stepped into the small cabin and saw Jefferson sitting at the rough table across the room. As their eyes met, their faces lit with wide grins of acknowledgment, acceptance, and friendship. Will strode across the cabin in a few steps as Jefferson stood. Will took Jefferson's hand and pumped it as they broke into explosive laughter.

"Going with me to Texas, huh?"

"That's what Mister Bowman said."

"Jeff, I couldn't hope for any better."

"Thank you, sir. I'll be proud to go with you and do my best."

"You always have."

Jessie couldn't stay quiet any longer. "Mister Will, I know what's done is done but I don't want my baby to go away. Or you neither. You been my baby, too."

Will chuckled as he turned to Jessie. "Why, you can't quite call either of us babies anymore. Just look at Jeff. Big and strong as an ox."

"I know dat. But he always be my baby. You too. I raised both of you."

Will gently wrapped his arms around Jessie and pulled her close in an embrace, then held her at arm's length. "I know you did, and I love you for it, but we have a chance to do something that really matters. Jessie, important things are happening in Texas. Someday that country will develop into something great, and we'll be a part of making it happen. Jeff and I are going to survey much of the new frontier and open it up for settlement, and some of those settlements may grow into towns, maybe even cities, some even as big as Richmond or bigger. Why, people will come from all over the world to settle, build and grow on the land your boys will survey."

Jessie was wide eyed. "My boys're gonna do all dat?"

"We sure are. And who knows, maybe even more — *lots* more!"

"Lawzee!" exclaimed Jessie.

Will chuckled and started for the door. "Jeff, tomorrow I'll make arrangements for you to start showing one of the other boys how to take care of the stock. You and I have some planning to do." He reached for the door, then turned back, lifted Jessie from the floor and spun her around, then kissed her on the cheek before setting her down. Once out the door, he set all the dogs to barking when he jumped as high as he could, threw his hands high in the air and yelled, "We're going to Texas! Yeehaa!"

Chapter 4

Jefferson worked for several days with fourteen year old Toby, a former field hand, teaching him the chores of a stable boy. He showed him how to take care of the stock and taught him the basic skills of smithing: how to use the bellows and furnace and how to work steel with hammer, tongs, and anvil. He was thorough in his training, pushing the boy to understand his new tasks. Jefferson had other important projects awaiting him.

Will spent several hours with Jefferson making and modifying a list of supplies and provisions. They concentrated on equipment they'd need to sustain two men, traveling cross-country on horseback, living and working outdoors.

He decided to limit his stock to two saddle horses and two pack horses. Will already owned two good saddle horses: Baron, a stately looking and well-behaved white gelding that his father had given him as a present when he'd graduated from the academy, and Buck, a lively buckskin gelding he that he couldn't bear to part with when his father gave him Baron. He bought two more from a neighbor to complete his livestock needs.

The morning after Will bought the additional horses, he and Jefferson left for Roanoke to outfit themselves. Jessie stepped onto the back porch to throw out a pan of dishwater as they rode from the barn lot and turned toward the main road.

"Y'all gonna be back for supper? Gonna have pork chops tonight."

"Fix up plenty, Jessie," Will answered. "I'm sure we'll be back by supper and I imagine we'll be hungry."

Henry watched the young men from the window of his parlor as they headed toward the main road. Will sat tall and straight in the saddle on his handsome white gelding, properly dressed as a Virginia gentleman in his neatly blocked, wide-brimmed hat and carefully pressed gray wool suit with his shiny dress boots. Jefferson rode slightly behind Will, leading the packhorses. Riding bareback on the buckskin, he bounced awkwardly until Will set the pace at a more comfortable gait. Wearing worn, high top work shoes and faded, patched overalls and a floppy, shapeless hat, Jefferson presented quite a contrast to his master as he led the two unburdened pack animals along the trail.

The sun was already below the pines when Mary called from a front window, “Papa! Jessie! Come here! Look at this!”

The caravan approaching the plantation house in the twilight was noticeably different from the one that had left in the morning sun.

Will had exchanged his dress clothes for more suitable traveling attire. He wore a lightweight blue denim coat over a dark shirt and work trousers stuffed into sturdy, knee-high black boots. He was sitting in a new saddle with rifle holsters on both sides, housing new weapons. A bedroll, a rain slicker and bulging saddlebags were tied to the back of his saddle. While Will looked more casual in his traveling outfit, a magnificent transition had occurred in Jefferson's appearance. He wore all new clothes, similar to Will's, but he had a bright red kerchief tied around his neck, arranged so he could cover his face as protection from trail dust. He wore knee-high boots like Will's and a new black, wide-brimmed felt hat. He sat tall and proud in Will's old saddle on the buckskin with a holstered rifle strapped to each side. The two packhorses followed, loaded with bulging bags of gear covered with canvas.

Will planned to start their trip on a Monday morning, so Henry sent invitations to all the neighbors and friends to attend a party in Will's honor the Saturday before they left. Henry thrilled Mary by asking her to take charge of planning the affair. She started planning immediately. Then she and Jessie got busy making a new dress.

Anna Thompson arrived on Friday to help Mary with the final details of the party and to spend Friday night with her. She and Mary wanted to dress for the party together and help each other with their hair.

The next evening, after a busy day of preparation, everything was in place for the party, and the guests started arriving. Jefferson and Toby met the carriages at the front yard gate and took them to the barn lot.

Henry and Will, dressed in their finest suits, greeted the family, neighbors and friends in the large main room, which had been converted into a ballroom. Most of the guests had arrived by seven when Mary and Anna made their entrance at the top of the wide staircase.

They were both beautiful in their splendid, long dresses with flowing, full skirts. Mary's face was framed by her blond hair, curled to shiny ringlets above her soft, cotton, pale-yellow dress.

Anna's pretty blue eyes were accented even more by the soft black curls surrounding her face and cascading onto her bare shoulders. She wore an elegant, light-blue cotton dress trimmed in white lace. It had a daring cut at the bodice revealing a hint of her developing womanhood. She was the picture of grace and confidence as she stood at the top of the staircase.

The lively conversation stopped abruptly, except for a few oohs and aahs as the two lovely young ladies descended to the ballroom floor. Henry and Will crossed the room to meet them at the bottom of the wide staircase; Mary took Henry's arm and Anna took Will's.

Will was as surprised as everyone else when he saw his sister and Anna at the top of the stairs. Until tonight, they had always been just his little sister and her playmate, someone to tease and chase around the yard. He'd never thought of them as attractive young women. Mary was pretty in her new yellow dress, but Anna . . . Will thought she had become a woman overnight. He was almost speechless when she reached for his arm and nestled close to him to circulate among the guests.

Anna was looking straight ahead with a faint smile spreading across her slightly reddened lips. “How are you this evening, Mister Bowman?"

"Why, uh . . . just fine, Anna. And how about you?"

"Oh, I'm fine, thank you. So you're about to head west to Texas?"

"Yes, day after tomorrow, as a matter of fact."

They continued their formal conversation, Anna wishing all the while she could tell Will how she felt about him, how she had always felt about him.

Their awkward conversation was interrupted by Anna's father, who wanted to take her to the next room to show her off to some friends. "Save me a dance later?" Will asked as she walked away. She turned back, smiled and gave a quick nod as her father led her toward his friends.

The little band struck up a lively tune and Henry started the dancing with Mary. A few other couples ventured out to dance. Then Mary took a turn on the floor with each of her four brothers.

Will quietly watched Anna all evening. Several times they exchanged glances and smiles but shyly turned away. Finally, Will noticed she wasn't occupied in conversation and took the opportunity to ask her to dance.

The band had just started a waltz. As he took her in his arms, he noticed how much taller he was than she. The top of her head came only to his chin. He also noticed how good she felt in his arms. Her hand was so soft as she held his, her waist so small. She seemed to glide with him so easily. It was as if they were one as their bodies moved to the music. They said little to each other as they danced. Will marveled about this woman-child. *How could she be such a child in my eyes one day, and such a beautiful young woman the next? If she had blossomed into such a woman before her fifteenth birthday, how much more intriguing will she be when she's eighteen or twenty?*

Anna felt she must be dreaming. William Bowman was actually dancing with her and making her feel so grown up. She dared not look at his face while they were dancing though dancing with him was so easy. It felt comfortable to be held by him. She wished he would hold her closer. She closed her eyes and hoped the music would never end.

After their dance ended she held Will's arm as they went to the punch bowl where he poured them both a cup of punch. She looked up at him. “We're going to miss you, Will.”

“I'm going to miss this place and all of you, too.” Will was trying not to single Anna out but realized he would miss her especially.

“Are there ways to get letters back and forth between here and Texas?”

“I guess I could get mail by way of Uncle John. I'd sure like to hear from home, if you'd like to write.”

“I would, if you don't mind. Mary and I might write some letters together.”

“Thanks. I'll look forward to them.” He was beginning to feel more comfortable talking to the new, grown-up Anna standing beside him.

“How long do you think it will take you to get there?”

“Should take about a month to six weeks, best I can figure.”

There was one other question burning inside Anna. She couldn't hold back any longer. “Will, do you think you'll ever . . . I mean . . . will you ever come back to Virginia?” *There,* she thought. *I've said it.* She looked at Will with hope in her heart, but tried not to show it too much in her eyes.

“I'm sure I will, Anna. Might be a while, though. Once I get started, I'll be staying busy, but I'll be back to visit. I just don't know when.”

Anna didn't need to know more. *He'll be coming back. That's all I need to hold on to. Then I'll be older. Then . . . .*

The party to honor Will inside the big house wasn't the only party going on at the Bowman estate that night. Jessie had doubled the quantities of all the food she prepared for the party and took half of it out the back door after dark. Jefferson and Amos had set up tables in the yard, beyond the glow of lights from the big house but still close enough to hear the music coming through the open windows and doors. All of Jefferson's friends were soon dancing and having a good time, even though it was a bittersweet farewell to one of their own. They would all miss him and some were a bit envious of the adventure he was undertaking. They all liked Mister Will and knew he would treat Jefferson well, but Jefferson's big smiling face would be sorely missed.

Both parties broke up around midnight. The carriages and wagons were brought around front as the guests started leaving. Will, Henry and Mary followed them to the wide verandah to bid farewell and thank them for coming. All the ladies hugged Will on the way out and the men shook his hand and wished him well.

The Thompsons were among the last to leave. Mrs. Thompson, like several of the women who had watched Will grow into manhood, choked back tears as she hugged him goodbye. Anna's mother and father were already down the steps when Anna stepped up to Will, quietly put her arms around him and buried her face in his chest. She held him tightly for a moment, then ran to join her parents at their carriage. As they pulled down the lane, she turned and called, “Stop by our place Monday when you leave.”

“I promise,” Will called back to her.

Anna was thankful her father had ordered the double-seated carriage before they left home that evening. She had the back seat to herself as she cried quietly into her handkerchief during the dark ride home while her parents talked about Texas.

There was little sleep for Will the Sunday night before he and Jefferson were to leave. The anticipation of their journey caused him to toss and tumble most of the night. He finally fell asleep but was awake again before the roosters as the sky turned pink. He got up and dressed in the clothes he had put out the night before.

When he got to the barn, he found that Jefferson had already loaded one packhorse and was working on the second.

"What're you doing out here so early?"

Jefferson grinned. "Didn't sleep much last night."

They worked in silence. There was too much on both of their minds for conversation. It wasn't long before they'd finished their packing and saddling and were ready for their last home-cooked meal for awhile.

Jessie was up early too, making sure her boys got a good breakfast before they started. When the two young men sat down at the kitchen table where Jessie took her meals, it looked as if she had spread every possible breakfast food she could think of across the table. There was ham, bacon, sausage, eggs, grits, pancakes, biscuits, gravy and coffee.

After their meal, goodbyes and embraces were repeated a final time. There were some tears, especially from Mary and Jessie. Then, eager to be on their way, the two young adventurers swung into their saddles and waved goodbye as they spurred toward the main road.

Down the road two miles, Anna watched through her bedroom window. She knew Will said he would stop by her home on his way out, but she was too nervous to simply wait. She had awakened and dressed before daylight, not knowing what time they would arrive. She wanted to be ready. *Just be calm and don't act like a fool,* she kept telling herself.

Finally she saw them in the distance riding west along the main road. She paced the floor as she waited, watching them beyond the yard and field as they rode toward the lane leading to the house. She went downstairs and waited inside the front door when she saw them turn onto the lane. It seemed an interminable time, but it was only a few minutes until she heard Will's familiar voice. "Hello, in the house."

Anna's mother and father joined her at the front of the house by way of the side porch from the dining room where they were having breakfast.

"Good morning, Will," Thompson said. "You're just in time for breakfast. Why don't you step down and come on in?"

"Thank you, sir, but we've already eaten. Just wanted to stop by and tell you all goodbye. We're headin' out this morning."

"Looks like you're packed to stay a spell. How long do you think it'll be before you get back to these parts?"

"Probably at least a couple of years, but I'll not be a stranger to letter writing."

Will tried not to be too obvious, looking at Anna as she stood between her mother and father on the porch, but he noticed she was just as pretty as she had been at the party.

"Won't you at least get down and have a cup of coffee?" Mrs. Thompson asked.

"No Ma'am, but thank you anyway. Jessie filled us up on everything before we left. Just didn't want to leave before we stopped by to say goodbye . . . Well, guess we'd better be making tracks."

Mister Thompson walked over to the riders and shook Will's hand. Will tipped his hat to Mrs. Thompson. He took it off as he addressed Anna. "Anna, you take care of yourself. I'll see if I can't get a letter off to you when we get to Texas."

Their eyes met for a final moment before he turned and gently spurred his horse to a walk across the yard toward the lane.

Anna hesitated a moment watching Will ride away. Then she ran down the steps. "Will, wait!" She ran across the yard and caught up with him in a few strides. Reaching up for his hand with both of hers, she gently put something in it and closed his fingers over his palm. She held his closed hand inside both of hers for a moment, searching his face as her eyes filled with tears. Then she slowly pulled her fingers away. "Will Bowman, you take good care of yourself." Then almost in a whisper, she said, "Please — please promise me you'll come back."

"I will. I'll come back." He lingered a moment, looking into her moist eyes, watching a tear spill onto her cheek, then spurred his horse into a trot. When he and Jefferson reached the road, they turned west.

Chapter 5

At the end of the first day on the road, after the chores were done and supper was finished, Will pulled the gold locket and chain from his pocket and rubbed it between his fingers. He didn't realize it then, but the little heart-shaped locket that Anna had placed in his hand would be the one thing that would bring him close to home no matter how far away he traveled. The feel of the locket between his fingers brought back thoughts of home, thoughts of his family, and thoughts of Anna. Not the face of the tearful Anna bidding him goodbye in her father's yard, but the beautiful Anna smiling at him as she stood at the top of the staircase in his father's home. Finally he put away the locket, pulled out his journal and began to write:

> First day on the road with Jefferson at the beginning of our travels, immigration, and business ventures in Texas. We are both quieter today than we will be on the trail in the future, but I am satisfied that Jefferson had as much on his mind today as I. A new life started for us today. May God be with us.
>
> WB

Days and nights fell into an easy routine along the well-traveled roads of western Virginia, eastern Tennessee and on toward the Mississippi River.

Will decided to take advantage of the long days in the saddle and evenings by the campfire to instruct Jefferson in the basics of surveying. He caught on quickly to the use of the instruments, but Will became frustrated by how little Jefferson could accomplish with no understanding of mathematics. He soon realized that an otherwise capable individual was limited in what he could accomplish without further education. He recognized that Jefferson would always be a great help dragging the measuring chain over terrain and holding the sighting rod, but he could contribute so much more and make the surveying enterprise much more efficient if he could understand maps, plats, legal descriptions, mathematics, and geometry. Will realized that he not only needed, but wanted more of Jefferson than the usual expectations of a personal slave. He also recognized that there was a struggle within himself regarding his attitude toward Jefferson as a person.

He and Jefferson were brought up at opposite poles in the eyes of Southern society, but he always felt differently about Jefferson than about other Negroes he had known. Perhaps it was because they spent so much time together as children. Maybe it was because Jessie had taken care of him and treated him as her own when he was a child. Although he knew it was his birthright and Southern responsibility to feel superior to Jefferson, he had never held that attitude. He'd always thought of Jefferson more as a trusted friend than a subordinate.

He also recognized Jefferson's differences from other slaves — some subtle, some not. Perhaps his close association with Will and his family had provided Jefferson with a more positive attitude and self-confidence than his peers. Always willing and eager to learn new things, Jefferson had intelligence and an aptitude for catching on quickly. With just a few sessions with Will's brother, he became a proficient blacksmith when he was only fourteen years old. He was mechanically inclined and could make a part for a wagon, carriage or piece of farming equipment just by observing its function, then fabricating it in his shop.

There were other characteristics that set him apart from other black workers. As a house servant and stable blacksmith, he resided at a social level above the ordinary field hands. The slaves as well as the whites had their own pecking order. One of the most obvious differences between Jefferson and the other plantation workers was his manner of speaking.

When they were children, Jefferson frequently pestered Will to help him learn to speak more like Will. Will saw no harm in playing school with his playmate and enjoyed seeing Jefferson progress. As with all his lessons, he responded well and learned to pronounce words more like the white master than most white sharecroppers in the area. Although the other slaves thought his speech peculiar for a Negro slave, it didn't set him apart from them because of his good nature.

In addition to surveying training, Will and Jefferson filled their days and nights along the Natchez Trace between the Tennessee and Mississippi rivers with endless conversation. One afternoon to pass time as they rode, Jefferson shared legends of his ancestor's home that had been passed from his grandfather to his father and then to him.

"Oh, they loved to hunt. They went after lions and water buffalo and even elephants, usually with nothing more than just long spears. No guns or anything like that. Why, they'd have some really big celebrations after a hunt, especially when a young man got his first large game. They had some special dances that were accompanied with music from drums and whistles. They really loved to have a good time." Jeff smiled at the thought.

He stared at the horse's mane as he thought of places and times far away. "And they weren't just hunters. They were real fighters when they had to be. I was told that my great-great grandfather was selected to be the tribal chief after showing bravery on the battlefield and leading his warriors to victory over a much larger army. He was chief for over forty years — for the rest of his life, and kept peace with the neighboring tribes most of those years. According to what my grandfather passed down, those people governed themselves in a tribal society with associations among the tribes to form nations. They were a proud people and governed themselves accordingly."

Will smiled. "That story reminds me of my own ancestors and how they came to be in Virginia. They came to America from England in search of a better life. But America was still under the rule of England, and their laws were harsh. The new settlers wanted to break away from English rule, so they declared their independence and then engaged in a war with England to secure it. You know, Jeff, my grandfather fought with General George Washington during that war. He died before I was born, but I remember my father retelling the stories of the campaigns that my grandfather had passed on to him: Valley Forge, Lexington, and others. Those men endured a lot of hardship during that war like hunger, cold, and limited supplies, but they persevered and won their independence. I guess when it gets right down to it, men are willing to endure great sacrifice to win their freedom."

There was a silence. Then Jefferson responded in a quiet voice, "I guess."

Will turned to look at Jefferson. When he saw the expressionless, down-turned stare, Will realized he'd been talking about men's sacrifices to win freedom to a man whose ancestors had been proud warriors and who had been stolen from their family and home, beaten into submission, and shipped to a distant land under conditions of brutality and abuse. Those who survived the voyage were sold into slavery, and they and future generations were denied the very freedoms he was discussing.

"I . . . uh. . . Jeff . . . Sometimes I forget."

"That's all right, Mister Will. Sometimes when I'm with you I almost forget too."

The two men were quiet the rest of the afternoon and evening as compared to the lively conversation earlier that day. Jefferson didn't want to disturb Will while he appeared to be in such deep thought.

They went about their chores that evening after setting up camp in a grove of trees next to a creek. While Jefferson cooked supper over the fire, Will headed toward the creek. He strolled quietly by himself, tossing pebbles into the slow-moving water, watching the ripples reflect twinkling glimmers of moonlight. He'd already made a decision regarding Jefferson's future. He was in the process of justifying it to himself.

After a time of thorough soul searching, Will returned to the campsite and took his writing materials from his saddlebags. He sat on the ground, and leaned back against a tree. Laying his journal across his legs as a desk, he started writing on a sheet of paper. In a few minutes he finished, folded the paper and put it in his pocket.

After a quiet supper with little conversation, they sat within the circle of firelight watching the glowing coals while Jeff poured another cup to finish the coffee.

Will idly poked a stick at the coals. "Jeff?"

"Yes, sir?"

"I've been thinking a lot about what we've got to do when we get to Texas."

"Yes, sir?"

"In order to be effective, we're both going to have to carry our own weight on our surveying jobs."

Jefferson was beginning to feel uneasy. "Yes, sir. You know I always work hard."

"I know that, but that's not what I'm talking about."

"Yes, sir." Jefferson was confused as to where the conversation was going.

"What I mean is . . . I need you to do more than just pull the chain and hold the rod for me while I take sightings and make all the calculations."

"Yes, sir. It's going take just a little more practice, and I'll understand those instruments."

"That's what I want to talk about — your training and your future"

"Yes, sir?"

"I want you to learn more than just the instruments — a lot more. You're too willing and intelligent to be limited in what you can do because of your lack of education. I need the help of someone who doesn't have those limitations. I need —"

"But, Mister Will, I can do it." A wave of panic flooded over Jefferson. "I . . . I can learn! I know I can!"

Will motioned with his hand. "Now calm down and wait a minute. Let me finish." He took a deep breath and reached for the paper in his pocket. "Jeff, I made out a paper here that says you're a free man."

Jefferson spilled hot coffee on his fingers as his body went slack. He ignored the pain but sat the coffee cup in the dirt as his hands began to tremble.

Will continued. "We're going into a new country that calls for a new and different way of life. A man doing the kind of business that we've got to do doesn't need a personal servant with limited capabilities. He needs a good man, well trained to do his job, working on a project in which he has a financial interest. These last few weeks on the road with you have confirmed to me who you really are and what you mean to me. Jeff, the truth is, I love you like a brother, and I can't hold you as a slave any more.

"I know you can learn anything you set your mind to. That includes reading, writing, arithmetic and geometry — all of it. With us working together in the evenings, within a few months you'll be reading everything you want and writing as well as your namesake. By law, a slave can't do that, but a free man can."

Will averted his gaze, looking into the fire for a moment. "I realize that as a free man you've got a right to go any place and do anything you want to do. But Jeff, I want you to know I hope you'll stay and work with me . . . help me survey. It's a lot of hard work but it could be profitable for both of us." Will hesitated for a moment, letting the impact of what he said soak in. Then he looked back up at Jefferson. "Well, what do you think?"

Jefferson made several halting attempts to respond, but the tightness in his throat and the tears that blurred his vision made it impossible. He wiped the tears away with his hand. Looking Will in the eyes, he said: "Oh, Mister Will, I —"

Will held up his hand. "Now wait a minute. I don't call my friend Mister Jefferson, so I don't expect him to call me Mister Will. All right?"

"I can't believe this!" Jefferson said, his voice still choked. "Mis — I mean, Will, I'll be the best surveyor you've ever seen."

They both broke into a mixture of laughter and tears as Will reached over to Jeff to grab and shake his hand, then pulled him into a back-slapping embrace.

Will unfolded the paper and gave it to Jefferson. "We'll have a more formal, official document drawn up when we get to Texas, but this proves your status as a free man."

Jeff looked in awe at the paper. "What does it say?"

Will began to read: "It says, 'May 24, 1829. This document is to affirm my intention and desire to release from bondage a Negro male known as Jefferson. Effective this day and forever hereafter this man, Jefferson, is a free man with all the rights, privileges, and responsibilities of any other free man. I hereby renounce my ownership of this man known as Jefferson. Signed, William H. Bowman, May 24, 1829.'"

Will handed the paper to Jefferson. Jefferson stared it intently. "Someday I want to read this to my mama and papa."

"Someday you will, but first, we've got a lot to do."

Chapter 6

Will wrote in his journal:

June 3, 1829

Today, Jefferson and I crossed the Sabine River into Texas. It's been a long and tiring trip since leaving Virginia, but we are healthy and fit with fresh air, sunshine and long hours in the saddle to toughen us.

The horses are doing well and appear to be healthy. I am blessed to have Jefferson with me.

Glad to be in Texas.

WB

Both Will and Jefferson felt alive with the anticipation of arriving in the first Texas settlement since crossing into their new home. They camped about five miles from Nacogdoches and bathed, shaved and dressed in clean clothes before breaking camp and riding into town. Jefferson's attire wasn't as splendid as Will's but he, like Will, was dressed in clean clothes and shined boots. They both wanted to make a good impression on the Mexican officials they expected to meet in town.

Nacogdoches was more of a town than Will expected. It had several streets laid out around a plaza, situated on a hill overlooking a green valley south of town. As they approached the town from the east, they found most of the homes on the outskirts were constructed of logs. When they got closer to the plaza, they saw several newer houses finished with milled lumber, looking as respectable as if they were sitting in downtown Richmond or Baltimore.

The green, white and red Mexican flag ruffling in the light breeze atop a flagpole outside one of the older buildings on the north side of the plaza pointed them to the government office.

"Close the door," came a strongly accented, deep voice from across the room as Will and Jefferson stepped inside the government building.

Will had trouble finding the owner of the voice at the far side of the dimly lit room after coming in from the brightness of the midday sun. It took several seconds for their eyes to adjust enough to see the figure behind the desk in the dark, windowless room.

"I am Sergeant Canales." The Mexican official was a round-faced, middle-aged man with a shock of unruly gray hair and a large, untrimmed, gray mustache. He was dressed in a worn and faded blue uniform jacket, open at the stiff, high collar. He was having his lunch. Canales didn't look up from his plate of beans and tortillas. He chewed with his mouth open and talked around his lunch. "What is your business?"

Will was glad to find a Mexican official who spoke reasonably good English. "Sir, my name is William Bowman. This is Jefferson. We're here at the invitation of Stephen Austin and John Bell with the intention of immigrating. We came to apply for citizenship and to exercise our trade of surveying."

Sergeant Canales watched the two men in front of him with flat, dark eyes while he slowly continued chewing his beans.

Will and Jeff stood in the middle of the room in silence, hats in hand, waiting for Canales to respond.

After a while Canales answered, speaking to his plate rather than his visitors. "You must see Señor Vargas."

Again they waited for further instruction, but none came. Realizing that Canales wasn't going to volunteer additional information, Will asked, "And when, sir, could we see Mister Vargas?"

"Come back later."

"You mean, later today?"

"Si, si. Now go away. You're interrupting my lunch." He waved them away with the back of his hand in a gesture of annoyance, as if shooing away a fly.

Will and Jefferson found themselves back in the dusty yard. As they untied the horses and started leading them across the plaza, Jefferson said, "Seems like we were talking to the wrong man."

Looking around for signs of an inn or hotel, Will said, "We'll find somebody who can tell us something about this Vargas." They stopped in front of a run-down log house around the southeast corner from the plaza that had a small sign nailed to a porch post: *FOOD.*

"Hello in the house," Will called through the open door. "Is anybody home?"

In a few moments, a heavy set, red-faced woman about sixty years old with wisps of gray hair escaping from a carelessly made bun appeared in the doorway wiping biscuit dough from her chapped hands with the bottom of her apron.

"Hello, Ma'am," Will removed his hat and presented an earnest smile. "Sign says food. Are you able to feed a couple of hungry travelers?"

The woman studied Will and Jefferson and pushed an errant strand of hair away from her face with the back of her hand. "Believe I can. "I got some venison, a few new 'taters and some early squash." The s sounds quietly slipped between her toothless gums and wrinkled, withered lips. "Fixin' up a batch of biscuits now. They'll be mighty good with some fresh butter wild plum preserves if you don't mind waitin' a bit."

"That sounds perfect, Ma'am," Will said. "We have plenty of time. If you don't mind, we'll just wait out here on the porch in the breeze."

'Could you stand a dipper of cool water while you wait?"

"Yes Ma'am," Will answered. "It's mighty hot and thirsty on the trail."

The woman disappeared from the doorway but soon

returned with a wooden bucket of water in one hand and a long-handled dipper and tin cup in the other. She sat the bucket down next to Will and handed Jefferson the cup.

"Here boy, you drink from this."

"Thank you, Ma'am," Jefferson smiled, taking the cup.

"Where 'bouts y'all coming from, Mister?"

"Virginia, Ma'am."

"Y'all comin' fer your land?"

"Yes, but we're also here to do some surveying. I understand there's a strong demand for surveying in these parts."

"Not so much right 'round here no more, but you'll find plenty to do toward the southwest in Austin's or Dewitt's grants or some of the others. I guess there's still fifteen or twenty grants that somebody or other is tryin' to fill."

"I guess you see a lot of folks coming through here looking for land."

"Jest 'bout ever' day in the late fall and on through the winter and early spring. There's a steady stream of 'em comin' through here. Sometimes three, four families a day. Kinda slows down a little in the summer, though. Gettin' nigh on too late to plant now. 'Course, this ain't the only place people come into the territory. They be coming in from all over. They come through the Arkansas, all along the Sabine and along the coast. Lots of folks been comin' in by boat, from what I hear. Jest come right up the rivers. Yep, there'll be plenty fer you to do if it's surveyin' yer after. Y'all 'scuse me now. I gotta check on them biscuits."

Will and Jefferson sat on the porch in the shade, enjoying the southern breeze and listening to the sounds from the kitchen as the cook hummed an old hymn and occasionally clattered pots and pans.

After a few minutes, she brought plates out to the porch for Will and Jefferson.

"Fresh coffee's a-makin'. I'll fetch it fer you in a minute. Be sure to save room fer some peach pie. It ain't hot. Made it yesterday, but it's purty good."

“Thanks, Ma’am,” Will said, taking his first bite.

When the woman returned with their coffee, Will said, “Ma’am, I've got to tell you, this is the best food we've had in weeks. I'm sorry, but I haven't introduced myself. I'm Will Bowman and this is Jefferson. I want to know the name of the best cook in Texas.”

The old woman rested her fists on her ample hips and gave out a throaty laugh exposing her toothless gums. “Don't know 'bout the best in Texas but best in these parts, anyway . . . Bessielu Styles. Most folks 'round here jest call me Aunt Bess.” She was still smiling at the compliment.

“Well, Aunt Bess, since I haven't tasted much Texas cooking, and no offense to Jeff here, but I can say it's the best we've had this side of Virginia. What do you think, Jeff?”

“Yes, sir. Mighty good, Ma’am.” Jefferson nodded and smiled his approval between bites.

Bess went back inside the cabin. This time she returned dragging a rocking chair in one hand and carrying her snuff jar in the other. She sat in the chair across the porch from her guests, loaded her lip with snuff and proceeded to keep the men company while they enjoyed their meal.

As Will buttered his second biscuit, he asked, “Aunt Bess, what's it like, living here in Nacogdoches?”

“Aw, guess it's purty quiet most the time, 'cept fer settlers coming through. Get a few Cherokees in here fer tradin' now and then and other travelers, both white and Meskin.”

“Tell me, do all the people coming through to claim their land go through the government office on the plaza over there?”

“They 'sposed to. Why?”

“We stopped in and talked to a fella named Canales. He just wasn't very helpful.”

Bess slowly turned her head and spat a string of brown juice into the dirt before answering. “That Canales.” She squinted her eyes with a look of contempt. “Watch out fer him. He's jest low-down mean. Don't like white folks. The Meskin government moved him up here 'bout a year ago to be Vargas' assistant. He don't like bein' here. Don't like the people around here. Jest don't like nothin' 'bout it.

"Vargas is all right, though, fer a Meskin. He's the one you need to talk to. Usually comes back to his office 'round four or so in the afternoon. You can prob'ly talk to him then. Speaks English purty good, too. That's more than you can say fer most of 'um."

"We'll just go back after four and see Mister Vargas," Will said between bites of his lunch.

"Call him Señor."

"Ma'am?"

"Señor. Means Mister. Señor Vargas means the same as Mister Vargas."

"Thanks, we'll remember that. Look here, Jefferson, We're already learning Spanish."

Will and Jefferson spent the rest of the afternoon visiting with Aunt Bess until they could meet with Señor Vargas. They found her to be a delightful character, if a bit rough around the edges.

Time passed quickly as the young travelers listened to the fascinating stories the old woman told about life in East Texas. As it neared four o'clock, they decided to make a second attempt to become Mexican citizens and got up to thank Aunt Bess and pay for their meal.

"Y'all ought'a jest come on back fer supper. I got some boiled chicken and I can throw some dumplin's in. I even got a little Kentucky mash fer later, if you're a mind."

"You drive a hard bargain, Aunt Bess," Will said. "Yes Ma'am, we'll look forward to it."

"Since it'll be so late after supper, y'all might as well plan on jest stayin' over here. You can spread out your rolls on the porch and put up your stock in the barn out back."

"Thanks, we'll take you up on your offer."

Will and Jefferson returned to the government building to

meet Señor Vargas. Once inside the anteroom, they again found Sergeant Canales. This time he had his feet propped up on his desk, drinking coffee.

"Hello again, Sergeant," Will said in a friendly voice. "Is Señor Vargas in now?"

"Si."

"May we see him?"

Canales sat there for a moment, staring at the two in front of him. He eventually got to his feet and went through the door at the back of the office, closing it behind him. In a few moments, he returned. Without looking at either of his visitors, he said, "Go in."

They went through the doorway, down a hallway and turned into Señor Vargas' office. His working area was as light and airy as Canales' was dark. There were open windows on both sides and at the rear of the room.

Señor Vargas was seated behind a heavy, highly carved wooden desk. Similarly carved furniture decorated the rest of the room. Vargas was a tall, slender man in his fifties with gray, brushed-back hair and a neatly trimmed beard and mustache. His dark, well-tailored suit completed the image of a man of power and influence.

Vargas greeted them with a slight bow, smiling as he stood behind his desk. "Good afternoon, gentlemen." His English held only a hint of a Mexican accent. "I am Rafael Vargas, Commissioner of the Northeastern Region of Coahuila and Texas, your representative of the Mexican government."

Will introduced himself and Jefferson as they shook hands and took seats across the desk from Vargas.

Señor Vargas started the interview. "Tell me, what is your business in Mexico?"

Will answered: "We're here at the invitation of Stephen Austin and John Bell for the purpose of immigration and to become Mexican citizens. We also want to obtain land for farming and raising livestock. I also have the credentials, training and experience to pursue my business of land surveying."

Although the interview was quite lengthy, Señor Vargas put them at ease with his official but friendly manner.

He was not only interested in Will's goals and intentions in becoming a Mexican citizen. He was also very interested in his background. He asked questions about his military experience, criminal history, family history, marital status, trades and work experience. He was also interested in Jefferson's status as a free man. Jefferson showed him his freedom paper, and Vargas seemed satisfied. Will showed him his letter from Stephen Austin and four letters of character verification from prominent landowners and neighbors in Virginia.

Vargas discussed, in some detail, the regulations and expectations of those seeking citizenship and went into some length explaining the laws of land allotments of the Mexican land grants. He also explained to Jefferson that as a free man, he would enjoy all the rights and privileges of other citizens of Mexico.

"Now, do you both understand everything I have told you and agree to the terms of citizenship that I have defined?"

"Yes sir," they said in unison.

"Then please stand and raise your right hands."

Will and Jefferson both stood and raised their hands.

Vargas continued. "Since I have determined that you meet the citizenship requirements of the Republic of Mexico, do you swear to assume the Catholic religion and promise your loyalty to the Holy Father and the laws of the Catholic Church?"

"I do," they answered.

"Do you furthermore swear your allegiance to the government of Mexico, to uphold and defend its constitution and laws, so help you God?"

"I do"

"I, Rafael Vargas, Commissioner of the Northeastern Region of Coahuila and Texas, Republic of Mexico, grant you citizenship in the Republic of Mexico. Congratulations, gentlemen, and welcome to Mexico." Vargas walked around his desk and again shook hands with both men.

"Thank you, sir. Is that all there is to it?" Will asked.

"All but the paperwork, and we'll get that completed now."

Vargas took several documents from a cabinet and returned to his desk.

He addressed Will. "All right, what is your full name?"

"William Henry Bowman."

Vargas wrote Will's name in artful script at the top of the document.

He looked at Jefferson. "And your name is . . . Jefferson?"

After a long hesitation, Jefferson said, "Jefferson's the only name I've ever had, sir."

Will interrupted, "Sir, if we could have just a moment?"

Vargas nodded and gestured for them to confer privately, if necessary.

"Jeff, sometimes slave owners give their slaves their family names. Sort of a tag of ownership, I guess. I'd be honored for you to carry the Bowman name as your last name, because you're like family to me, but I don't want you to feel like you have to. This is a special opportunity to do something for yourself. You have the freedom to select your own name, one that belongs just to you. You are your own man now, free to make your own decisions. You're doing something right now that few people ever have the chance to do for themselves."

Jefferson sat for a moment, his eyes downcast, thinking. Then he lifted his gaze to Vargas. A smile of satisfaction slowly spread across his broad, brown features. "Jefferson . . . Jefferson's my name. I want to keep Jefferson as my last name because I was told I was named after Thomas Jefferson, who was president of the United States of America when I was born. I was told that he was a very smart man. I believe he was a smart man because he was educated. Now that I'm free, I'm going to be educated, too. And Jeff — that's my first name. Jeff Jefferson!

I've had it all along. I just never put it together. Will, you've been calling me Jeff since we were little boys. I just never thought of it as a real name put together that way, but it is. Yes sir, that's it. Jeff Jefferson. Sounds pretty good, doesn't it?" He was smiling broadly at Vargas and Will and nodding affirmation to himself.

Vargas said Jeff's name out loud as he wrote it.

"So it is, Mister Jeff . . . Jefferson."

Vargas then signed both documents and turned them around to the two new citizens for their signatures.

"Now to make it official, I need your signatures on the documents." He handed the quill pen to Will. Will signed in the place indicated and passed the pen to Jeff. Jeff then proudly penned his signature for the first time in his life on a formal document. He said it out loud as he signed it: "Jeff . . . Jefferson."

"Nice signature, Mister Jefferson," Vargas said as he picked up the documents and handed them to Will and Jeff. "Your official documents of citizenship," Vargas said.

They both thanked Vargas as they received their papers.

"Señor Vargas, there's one other thing I'd like to ask of you before we leave," Will said.

"What's that?"

"You saw the freedom letter I gave Jeff. Well, that's just an old piece of paper that I scratched out a few lines on while we were on the trail. Would it be possible for you to make a more formal freedom document?"

Vargas thought a moment, then smiled. "I think I can do something for you. Yes, I'd be happy to. May I see the letter again, Mister Jefferson?"

Jeff pulled the letter from the pouch on his belt and handed it to Vargas. He made a few quick notes and gave it back.

"Come back tomorrow about ten o'clock. I'll have it ready for you."

"Señor Vargas, thank you very much. You've made us both very happy men today. We'll see you tomorrow morning," Will said as they turned to leave his office.

Later, at Aunt Bess' cabin, the new Texans celebrated their status after supper with their hostess. True to her promise, Bess brought a bottle of Kentucky sour mash whiskey to the porch, twisted out the cork and poured each of them a drink. Will sat back for a few moments, savoring the spirits. “Tell me, Aunt Bess, what's it really been like living here, you might say on the edge of civilization?”

Bess took another sip of whiskey and looked up at the stars for a moment before answering. “I can tell you, it ain't been real easy, but then I've had it a whole lot better than some folks that settled in remote areas early on.”

That night the two young men heard the most detailed account of life in Texas they had received so far. They learned of several instances of whole families being wiped out in Indian raids. In other cases, just the men were killed and the women and children were taken away to be used as slaves or tortured and used for the entertainment of the warriors and their women. Most settlers believed the only way to ever be safe from the Comanches was to kill them all. Bess believed the plan of the Mexican Government to create a buffer zone of Anglo settlers between the Indians and the Mexican population was slowly working, because for every settler that was killed or scared back across the Sabine, ten more took his place. Most of the early settlement was in a region not much wider than a hundred and fifty miles west of the Sabine and north of the Gulf of Mexico. The area around Austin's first colony was becoming well populated.

“Where I'd go, if I was young and a man, is up in Austin's new colony, located north of his original one. From what I hear, that part of the country is where the good cotton's goin' to be comin' from. Not that the rest of the country ain't doin' all right in cotton already. Matter of fact, the Austin grant alone produced 500 bales last year. But that black land farther north is where the real bounty's gonna come from one of these days. What I hear is that black land almost throws them cotton bolls right up at you when you go to pick it."

Will laughed. "That I've got to see. What do you think, Jeff? You know your cotton."

Jeff was grinning. "I just want to make sure we're there at picking time, so I can just walk through the fields with a bushel basket on my shoulder and catch all the cotton as it jumps off the bush."

Bess spent the next couple of hours discussing the advantages and disadvantages of living on the frontier. Finally, after downing the last of the whiskey in her glass, she got up from her chair, grabbed what was left of the whiskey and her snuff jar, and announced she was going to bed.

The next morning the men were awakened to the aroma of coffee brewing and bacon frying. After breakfast and settling up with their hostess, Will and Jeff completed saddling and packing the horses. When they finished, Jeff stepped up to Bess with a sincere smile and an outstretched hand.

"Thank you, Ma'am, for the good food and hospitality. We really appreciate it."

She hesitated a second, then shook his hand and returned his smile. "You're welcome. Glad you enjoyed it."

Then she shook Will's hand. "Good luck to you Mister Bowman. You and Jeff there will do right well with yer surveyin'."

The two young men timed their departure so they would be at Vargas' office shortly after ten. Once inside, they were again met by the dour Canales. This time it only took a moment before they entered Vargas' office.

"Good morning, gentlemen," Vargas said, obviously in a good humor. "Please, please, have a seat."

Will and Jeff seated themselves, curious to learn why Vargas was so pleased with himself.

"Yesterday, I didn't elaborate on my own attitude and the

Mexican government's position regarding slavery, but today I will. Personally I deplore the practice of holding human beings in bondage. I feel it is wrong and not what God intended. Fortunately, my government feels the same way. Two years ago a law was passed disallowing any further introduction of slaves into Texas.

"But today I'm dealing with a man who gave another man his freedom from slavery, not because he was forced to do so by law but because he knew it was the right thing to do for a life-long friend and someone he respected as a man — not a piece of property. God bless you, Mister Bowman, and congratulations, Mister Jefferson."

Both Will and Jeff were moved by the sincere empathy of Señor Vargas for the plight of slaves.

"Thank you, sir," they both responded.

"Now," Vargas smiled as he rubbed his hands together. "Let me show you what I've prepared." He pulled a large, fine, parchment paper from his desk.

Will noticed the day before that Vargas had very distinctive handwriting but never realized he would take such great pains to prepare Jeff's freedom document. The script was impeccable, with handsome flourishes decorating the text. It was a work of art.

Jeff was awestruck. He had learned just enough reading to understand some of the words, but the overall appearance of the document overwhelmed him. "Señor Vargas, it's beautiful! How can I ever thank you or pay you enough for this?"

Vargas hesitated, thoughtful for a moment, then answered. "You can thank me by continuing your education, then helping others like yourself. There are not many free colored people in Texas now, but there will be some day, and you need to be prepared to assist them by providing them with a good example and helping with their education if you can."

"This is so . . . so special." Jeff hesitated a moment, staring at the document. "I can make out some of the words, but not all of them. Would you read it?"

"Señor Jefferson, I'd be happy to. I wrote it in English rather than Spanish because I thought you might have to prove your status as a free man to Anglos more than to native Mexicans." Vargas began to read:

> "WHEREAS all who witness this document, take notice: The man known as Jeff Jefferson is a free man and is not held in bondage by any other man. Mister Jefferson has been granted his freedom by his former owner, William H. Bowman, a citizen of Mexico. Mister Jefferson's freedom was awarded in the year of our LORD 1829. Let all who witness this document know that Mister Jeff Jefferson is a free citizen of Mexico with all the rights, privileges, and responsibilities of all Mexican citizens.
>
> This document is executed on this the 9th day of July, 1829 by the office of Rafael Vargas, Commissioner of the Northeastern Region of Coahulia and Texas, Republic of Mexico."

There was silence for a few moments after Vargas finished reading the document. Jeff's eyes filled with tears as his gaze moved from the document to Vargas' face. He swallowed hard. "Thank you, sir. I really appreciate this."

"Well, I enjoyed doing it for you. Now all we need are signatures, and you'll be ready to go."

All three put their signatures at the bottom of the document. Vargas put his title, beside his name.

"Gentlemen, if there is ever anything I can do for you, please don't hesitate to ask. Perhaps I can be of some help."

"You've been very kind," Will said as they shook hands all around.

"Please send my regards to Señors Bell and Austin."

Back outside, the two new Mexican citizens mounted up and turned their horses southwest, heading farther into their new country.

Chapter 7

Three days and two river crossings later they were finally into their last day of travel. The road that split off the El Camino Real toward San Felipe had been well traveled by hundreds of families over the years seeking Austin's headquarters to claim their headright.

Will and Jeff enjoyed their morning's ride into San Felipe and arrived before midday. The town was much smaller and newer than Nacogdoches. A few of the buildings were made from milled lumber, but most were built of logs. At the center of town was a small, single-story building covered with unpainted wood siding. The sign over the door read *Austin Land Office.* Will counted eight places of business in the small town.

Will found his uncle's store across the street from Austin's land office, next to the fur and skins trader. The log building had a sign that read *Bell's General Merchandise* over the open door. Will looked inside the store as they reined up next to the hitching post. It looked unoccupied. Once inside they still didn't see anyone. Will called, "Hello? Anybody here?" They heard some rustling about and muttering in the back room. Will smiled and winked at Jeff as he recognized his uncle's voice.

"Hold on out there," the old man yelled. "Everybody's always in a hurry. I'll be there in a minute. Tad? Tad! Where are you, boy? Get in the store and see who's there."

Will and Jeff stood in the middle of the store looking around at the goods for sale and waiting for a greeting from someone.

"Yes, sir, Mister Bell," came a loud voice behind them. Will and Jeff were both startled by the child's voice coming through the door.

"Can I help you, sir?" the slender, Negro boy, about nine years old asked Will respectfully, then looked behind him at Jeff.

"I'd like to see Mister Bell, please."

"Yes sir." The boy walked around Will and Jeff, looking intently at Jeff, and disappeared into the back room.

Will and Jeff heard the boy call out to his master in a loud voice, almost a yell, "Mister Bell, they's a man out there. Say he wanna see you."

"Oh, all right. I guess this can wait." Bell walked through the back door into the shop, but looked at Will and Jeff with no recognition.

Will asked in a loud voice, "Is lunch about ready, Uncle John?"

John then saw the resemblance of his sister's face in the smiling, young man.

"William Bowman, is that you?" the old man asked as he walked toward Will, his arms outstretched.

"Yes, sir, it sure is. All the way from Virginia."

The old man threw his arms around him, then pushed him back to arm's length. "Here, let me look at you. My God, look at you, boy! What are you anyway, seven feet tall?"

"Not quite." Will chuckled. "Somewhere around six-two, I guess."

"Well, I knew you were grown up but I didn't know how much. Tell me about your trip. No, tell me about your family first. How's your papa, your brothers, and that cute baby sister of yours? No, wait, let me take care of this first." He glanced toward the back door. "Tad, come here."

"Yes sir?" the boy answered as he appeared from the door at the back of the shop.

"You run home and tell Libby we have a guest for lunch. You run now, all the way. Don't you fool around any on the way, you hear?"

"Yes sir." The boy started to run out of the store.

"Wait a minute, I'm not through."

"Yes sir?" The boy stopped, patiently awaiting further orders. "You tell her this is a special guest, and he looks hungry. Tell her we'll be home at about twelve-thirty. Tell her he's got a boy with him looks like he could use some feeding too."

Will and Jeff shared a smile over the excitement of the old man at having kinfolk arrive for a visit. Bell had known that Will was coming for several weeks, but he didn't know exactly when he would arrive.

Bell looked at Will again and grinned. "That girl ought to have us something good for lunch by the time we get there." He walked behind the counter in front of a wall lined with shelves of cotton yard goods, hats, and boots. "I've got something for you, if I can just remember where I put it." He looked under the counter. "Let's see." He pulled odds and ends from under the counter as he continued looking. "I knew you were coming because I already got some mail for you. You know the mail from the east can beat a man traveling cross-country even when the boat stops for awhile at New Orleans. Where is that letter? Oh yes, I remember. Here, this is for you." He pulled a letter off a shelf and handed it to Will. "Came about a week ago."

"Thanks." Will tucked the letter in his pocket and continued his visit. He spent the next half-hour or so bringing his uncle up to date on the health of his family and the number of his new nieces and nephews.

The old man shook his head. "Hard for me to imagine Mary as a young woman now. She was such a little girl the last time I saw her."

Will knew his Aunt Elizabeth had passed away four years earlier. His father had learned of her death from a letter he'd received at the time, but John seemed to be doing all right as a widower, Will thought, in spite of his partial loss of hearing.

Jeff enjoyed watching Will and his uncle visit and share stories of loved ones, but he realized for the first time since they'd left home that he felt a little homesick. The closeness of

Will's and John's family ties and their enjoyment of visiting with each other reminded him of his mama and papa.

Jeff was brought out of his reverie by Bell getting up from his straight-backed chair and announcing it was time for lunch.

Will and Jeff untied their horses as Bell locked the store, and they headed south toward the edge of town. Will and John continued their visit as they walked down the middle of the road while Jeff followed, leading the horses.

"I want you to know, I expect you to stay at my place whenever you're in San Felipe." John told Will. "If you decide to make this your headquarters, you'll be here quite a lot between your surveying jobs. I've got a big house here in town with nobody using it but me and my help. Sure would be nice to have some family around here again. Just about the time I got used to Elizabeth's being gone, Sarah married a lawyer that didn't take well to living way out here and he took her back to New Orleans. 'Course that left me here without family, but I do all right."

"How's Sarah doing?"

"Oh, she's fine. No children yet, but they're hoping." The old man shook his head. "I sure miss that girl, Will."

"I imagine you do, Uncle John. I've been a little homesick myself on this trip, but Jeff keeps me company."

John acknowledged Jeff as he turned back to look him over. Jeff smiled and nodded at the recognition.

"That boy's a stout one," John said.

"I'm lucky to have him with me. He's going to be a fine surveyor. And a great help."

"What do you mean a surveyor? Him?"

"He's a free man Uncle John, and a good friend."

Bell gave Jeff another glance over his shoulder.

They soon approached a single-story white house made of milled lumber. It was set back from the road a good distance, giving it a large front yard. It had a wide porch with columns extending across the front of the comfortable looking house.

"Here we are," Bell said, stepping into the shade of a thick-branched Spanish oak in the front yard. “You wait here with the horses,” he told Jeff. “I'll get Tad to show you around the barn, then you can take care of your stock. You can get your food in the kitchen.”

“Thank you sir, I appreciate it.” Jeff said respectfully, nodding to the old man.

“This is really a nice place,” Will said, admiring the large white house as they walked up the steps onto the porch. “We haven't seen many painted houses west of the Mississippi.”

“I tried to make life as comfortable as possible for Elizabeth and Sarah after spending the first couple of years in Texas in the old, rough cabin out on the farm. We couldn't get a house built like this then. In a few years, after more settlers came in, a couple of German brothers put in a saw mill down river a ways. I guess my place here was one of the first made of milled lumber in these parts. Took a while to get it finished, though. Had to wait almost six months to get doors, windows, paint and a bunch of hardware from the east.”

“It looks really comfortable. You've done well for yourself.”

“Oh, it’s too much for an old man and a couple of servants. I’ll tell you, I'm really glad to have some family here for a change.” Bell turned his wrinkled face toward Will and gave his arm a warm squeeze as he ushered him into the house. “Smells like we've got some lunch ready. Come on in. Let's see.”

Jeff waited under the shade of the tree for a few minutes until he saw the boy round the corner of the house.

“Mister Bell say for me to show you the barn.”

“Thanks, I'd be much obliged.”

“My name's Tad. What's yours?”

“I'm Jeff. Glad to know you, Tad,” Jeff extended his large hand toward the boy. They shook hands before leading the horses around the house toward the outbuildings.

“They call me Tad 'cause they say I looked like a tadpole when I was born.”

“Well, I wouldn't say you look like a tadpole now. You look like a fine young man to me.”

The youngster flashed Jeff a smile. “Y'all gonna stay here?”

“I guess we will when we're not out on survey jobs. I heard Mister Bell tell Will, that’s his nephew, he wanted us to stay here when we're in town.”

“Mister Will, is that his name? Mister Will?”

“I imagine Mister Will would be all right with him. Will Bowman. That's his name.”

“So, Mister Will . . . he a surveyor?”

“He sure is. Mister Austin sent him a letter and asked him to come to Texas and do surveying for him.”

“What you do for him?”

"I'm his assistant.”

“What's an assistant?"

“That's somebody who helps the surveyor. They do most everything the surveyor does. Will's teaching me how to do it. He's teaching me how to use the instruments.”

Jeff decided it might be better to hold off on revealing the details of the rest of his education until he knew these people a little better.

“Where you come from?” Tad asked as they led the horses under the loafing shed on the south side of the barn.

“All the way from Virginia.”

“That very far away?”

“Pretty far. Took us a long time to get here.”

Tad cocked his head, looking up at Jeff. “How come you talk so funny?”

Jeff chuckled. “What do you mean, I talk funny? You're the one who talks funny.”

“I don't talk funny neither. You talk like some of them white folks that come in the store.”

“All right, neither one of us talks funny. Help me unload these horses so we can go eat.”

They continued their conversation while they worked, with Tad asking one question after another as Jeff expected of a boy his age.

Jeff decided he really liked the curious youngster. He also learned a lot from Tad.

“It’s just me and my sister Libby that takes care of this place. She’s seventeen, and she does what both her and Mama used to do when Mister Bell’s whole family was here. My mama died of a fever when I was a little kid, and Papa died two years ago when a wagon he was working on fell on him. I guess they been with Mister Bell a long time, even before I was born. I help Mister Bell at the store, and I take care of the vegetable garden around there behind the house, and I take care of the livestock. Libby, she does all the cooking and cleaning mostly by herself. I help her out sometimes, though.

“Mister Bell, he got another place, a big ol’ farm, down south a ways along the river. He got a bunch of folks down there working the farm. He got a white man there named Farley. He the boss on the place. Master hired him last winter when the other man got married and started farming his own place. That Mister Farley, now he's a hard man," Tad said shaking his head and frowning. "He ain't nothin' like Mister Bell. Mister Bell, he’s a good man. He takes good care of his folks. But that Mister Farley, he just got a mean look about him. He looks at me awful mean when he come up here. I just stay outta his way. Glad I'm up here doing stuff for the master instead of down yonder on the farm.”

He explained that Bell built the house in town for the benefit of his wife before she got sick. “That lady just couldn't abide staying out in the country once the town started building up. Sure was a nice lady. She liked to have people around, and she and Miss Sarah even had parties here sometimes. Mister Bell only opened the store to give him a good reason to stay in town instead of going back and forth to the farm all the time.”

They soon finished tending the animals and headed toward

the back porch. Jeff smelled the home-cooked food before they even stepped onto the porch. As they got closer to the house, the aroma of good cooking brought a fleeting memory of his mama and the Bowman kitchen back in Virginia.

“Libby, this here's Jeff,” Tad announced to his sister while he held the door open for Jeff. “He's an assistant surveyor, and he come all the way from Virginia.” He looked at Jeff and grinned. “He talks funny, but I think he's gonna be all right."

“Glad to meet you, Libby.” Jeff smiled at the pretty girl in the plain, gray homemade dress covered with a long, white apron, and shook her hand. “Goodness gracious! This kitchen sure does smell good! Just like back home in my mama's kitchen. You can always tell a good cook by the way her kitchen smells. Sure hope you didn't go to any trouble for me.” He glanced at the plate on the kitchen table sitting next to the cloth covering several bowls on the table.

“Wasn't any trouble at all.” Libby said, smiling but a little embarrassed, not being used to compliments. “Had to fix dinner for Mister Bell and Mister Bowman anyway. I've got everything ready. You can wash up over there at the basin if you want to.” She motioned toward a pottery bowl and pitcher on a counter along the wall. “I don't know about you, but Tad gets awfully dirty between breakfast and lunch. Sometimes I think he just gets out and rolls in the dirt just to pester me. Tad, you let Jeff wash first.”

After washing and drying and Libby checking in the dining room to see if Will and his uncle needed anything else for their lunch, the three sat down at the small kitchen table.

Libby looked at her brother. “Tad, will you give thanks?”

Tad looked at the plate in front of him, then smiled. “Dear Lord, thank you for the food and 'specially for the fried squash, cause you and Libby know I like fried squash. And thank you for helpin' Jeff make his journey safe. Amen.”

“I appreciate that, Tad,” Jeff said, reaching for the platter of ham.

In between bites of food and answering a torrent of questions from Tad, Jeff noticed Libby's long lashes and sparkling, expressive eyes. Though she could hardly get a word into the conversation between Tad's questions, Jeff could tell she was enjoying the company and news of something other than events at the store.

Jeff would normally have been shy around a pretty girl close to his own age, but for some reason he immediately felt comfortable with Libby. *Maybe its because Tad and I have already started developing a friendship*, he thought.

Jeff had no experience with girls, as there were none close to his age on the Bowman place. He had seen young women working the fields as he passed on the road with Mister Henry or one of the sons on their way to town for supplies, but he had never gotten to know any of them. He really hadn't thought much about girls. He just always assumed that whenever Mister Henry wanted him to have a woman, he would see to it that he got one. As a slave, he didn't see much point in getting his emotions involved in something that he had no control over, so he just tried to put thoughts of women out of his mind.

He was a little relieved when Libby finally hushed Tad by telling him that Jeff was hardly getting a chance to eat his dinner with all his questions. Then she related how she and Tad took care of the Bell household.

"Seems like there's always things to do around here. I take care of the house, and Tad helps me a lot. I sew for Tad and myself, but Mister Bell likes to get his clothes ready made. I do a lot of canning during the summer. Tad really makes a good garden, and I preserve what we eat most of the winter. We have a milk cow that keep us in fresh milk. We get pork and beef from the farm whenever we need it and we keep chickens out back. Whenever there's heavy work to be done, Mister Bell will get Farley to bring one of the men from the farm to help do it."

Jeff recognized the pride she took in what she did.

"There are eight people at the farm that do the work there.

All of the people down there came to Texas with Mister Bell except the children that were born here. They are all good, hard working people. But I'm concerned about the new overseer."

"That's what Tad was telling me. You think he's mistreating the folks out there?"

"I don't know. Tad and I haven't been there since he came on the place. But you know the look a mean white man has?"

Jeff nodded. "I've never seen it in the Bowman family, but I've seen it in other white men."

"Well, he's got it. Scares me some when he's around. At least Mister Bell's with him when he's around here." She hesitated a moment, then lifted her eyes toward Jeff with an apologetic look. "Sorry to get off on unpleasant things. Why don't you tell me about the towns and people you saw along the way?"

Libby listened as she cleaned the dishes from the table and started heating wash water. Tad listened wide-eyed while Jeff told of far away places and adventures. Soon Bell called Libby from the dining room.

"Yes, sir?"

"Libby, I'm going to take Will down to meet Austin. He's got some business to attend. I want you and Tad to take Jeff and y'all go out there and see what you can do to fix up that extra cabin. You know, the one where we store that old bedstead and stuff. Jeff will need his own place to stay when they're in town. Just take the extra things that he won't need and put them in the barn somewhere. We'll be home before dark."

"Yes sir."

Jeff expected that he would meet Austin later and learn the Mexican ways of surveying from him with Will. For now, he would be setting up his new home away from the trail at the Bell place and getting better acquainted with two very interesting people.

Chapter 8

Bell told Will about some of Austin's accomplishments as they walked back to town. “I'll tell you Will, that feller is a born statesman. You know, he just took right up where his pap, old Moses, left off when he died. Stephen finished the agreements with the Mexican government to establish his colonies and has been building them up ever since. Because there wasn't any other law or soldiers around, they gave him complete military and civil control over his colonies. He's been strict with the kind of people he lets in. Can't say as much for some of the other impresarios, but Austin keeps a tight rein on his grant.”

Will had already formed an opinion that Austin must have been a man of strong determination and influence in order to mold this new country out of a wilderness. His uncle's description of Austin's accomplishments only confirmed his attitude.

As he and Bell approached Austin's headquarters, Will got a closer look at the exterior of the building than when they'd first arrived in town. It was a simple wooden structure built of unpainted, rough-sawed planks with a small covered porch at the front. The building looked like most of the others in the town, with nothing noteworthy to indicate that hundreds of people had their lifetime dreams of owning and farming their own land fulfilled by passing through the front door of the gray, weathered, shabby-looking building.

When his uncle led Will into the sparsely furnished front room, they found a small, pinched-featured man going over a stack of papers on his desk.

“Good. You're in,” the old man said to the young, clean-shaven man behind the desk. "I figured you'd be back by now from your lunch break. Stephen Austin, this here's the young surveyor I told you to write back in Virginia and get him on out here so you can finish filling up your grant. This is my nephew, William Bowman. Will, this is the man I've been telling you about, Stephen F. Austin."

"John, have you been telling tales about me again?" Austin laughed as he stood and walked around his desk to shake Will's hand.

While they were shaking hands, another man joined them from the back room.

"Mister Bowman," Austin said, gesturing toward the other man. "This is Sam Williams, my partner. We both take care of the paperwork here."

"Nice to meet you, Mister Williams," Will said, shaking Williams' hand.

"How many traveling in your party?" Austin asked.

"Just two of us, myself and my assistant, Jeff."

"Which way did you come?"

"Down the Natchez Trace and over through Nacogdoches. A couple of your friends said to send their regards from Nacogdoches."

"Yes, who was that?"

"Señor Vargas and Aunt Bess both send their best wishes."

"Well, I guess if you made it through the scrutiny of Vargas and Aunt Bess, you must be the kind of people we're looking for."

Bell interrupted. "I imagine you fellers have business to discuss, and I've gotta get back to the store. Will, come on by the store when you get done here."

"Yes sir," Will answered as the old man excused himself. Williams also excused himself to return to his work in the back room.

Austin returned to his chair and motioned for Will to sit in front of him. "So what do you think of Texas so far?"

"I haven't seen much of it yet, but from what I have seen, I'm really impressed."

“Mister Bowman, I'm going to ask you a very direct and personal question.”

“All right.”

“What I want to know is . . . why are you here? Why are you *really* here? Oh, I know I wrote you and asked you to come do some surveying, but you can do that anywhere. The way the states are expanding west, there'll always be plenty of surveying work. The conditions would be a lot safer and probably more comfortable back east. I'm just curious as to what your motivation is. Is it the land, or the opportunity to earn money surveying, or the adventure of dealing with the unknown? I just like to get to know the men I'll be working with so we can get the most out of our relationship.”

“I really appreciate your interest, Mister Austin. I don't mind telling you, I guess I'm here for a little of all of it. Like any other man, I'm here for the opportunity to own my own land. You know, I'll own more land at my age than my father owns after a lifetime of working to put his place together and expand it. As far as the money, of course I expect to earn some money. I've got to pay my expenses, but I've been wondering if there’s a way that part of my pay could be traded out in land. You see, my needs are simple now. There's just Jeff and me to be concerned about, and we don't need a lot now. But someday, I hope to have a family and that's ultimately why I'm here. If I can start off with the grant that I get now and add to it with my earnings, by the time I'm married and have a family, I should own a sizable place and be able to support them the way I'd like.”

“Looks like you've done a bit of thinking and planning for your future.”

“I guess there is a serious, careful side to me, but if the truth be known, I'm really excited about the adventure of being here too. I'm excited about the potential of how I can influence my future and perhaps be of some service to those around me in this new land.

“Just being here with all the other young families building

their homes and their lives here is exciting to me. I want to be a part of helping others fulfill their dreams of settling their own land and seeing it produce and themselves prosper. I want to see this country grow, and I want to grow with it. I want to help with my surveying or in whatever way I can to bring in families and give them the chance to own land. Sir, I believe this is a country where opportunity abounds, and success is only limited by the boundaries of one's imagination."

Will realized that Austin was staring at him intently as he finished his statement. He surprised himself by revealing so much of his private self to this man he had just met, but for some reason, he felt comfortable with Austin.

Austin rose from the chair behind his desk. "Mister Bowman, we're going to get along just fine. I really admire a young man with goals and ambition like yours. I believe your goals will fit in very well with what we're trying to do here, and yes, I'm sure we can work out a trade of extra land for surveying." He led Will across the room to a map pinned to the wall. "You'll soon learn that if there's one thing we're long on in Texas its land and one thing we're short on is cash. Are you interested in claiming your own place right away?"

"No, I was actually thinking that after I'd done some surveying, I'd be more familiar with the land and have a clearer idea of where I want to make my home."

"I agree. This territory is big, and the natural features differ so much from one area to another. It takes a while for a man to understand what's out there. Most men will never see it all. It's just too vast. Why, just look at this map here." Austin gestured toward the large pen and ink map on his wall.

"Mexican Texas stretches from the gulf coast at the Sabine north to the Red River, then west and north way up to around Santa Fe." Austin traced the boundaries on the map with his finger. "From there, the border goes south along the Rio Grande del Norte to the Gulf coast again. Millions and millions of acres. There's everything within these borders from swamps and pine thickets to grass covered savannas, to deserts and mountains. There's every kind of vegetation imaginable and anything in the world can grow here, if one selects the area with the right soil and climate. The greatest portion of this territory is uninhabited by white people. There are millions of buffalo, and thousands of wild horses, and cattle left by the Spanish. There are also dozens of tribes of savages scattered all over the plains. We have a flare-up with them occasionally. That's good farm and grass land out there. Some day, I'm sure, we'll push the Indians farther north and west and take that land too, but for the time being there's still a lot of country open for settlement where we're putting people in our newer grant, up along the Brazos River.

“As you can see, there have been quite a few grants issued by the government," Austin said, gesturing toward the map again. "Some impresarios have been successful in filling their grants, and others have not. Most have not, as a matter of fact. We've managed to do well with ours, though. We're now on our fourth contract with the government and so far have settled over 1200 families. It's a lot of work, but for the most part, I find it very satisfying.”

Austin continued to point out the different grants on the map and which were active and which were not. Then he focused on a map on an adjoining wall that showed the current grant they were settling. It covered almost the entire wall and showed, in great detail, the rivers, streams, creeks, and the topography of the land. The platted grants were noted by number along the rivers and streams.

“My partner Sam and I will work with you until you become familiar with the Mexican ways of land surveying and documentation. Will you be ready to start your training tomorrow?”

“Yes sir. Will it be all right with you if we include my assistant in the training?”

“It's fine with me, if you think he will comprehend the material.”

"I don't think that will be a problem. I've been teaching him some surveying basics along the way."

"So we'll see you again first thing in the morning?"

"Yes sir, first thing. And thanks again for giving me this opportunity."

"My pleasure, sir." Austin shook Will's hand to seal their working relationship.

Chapter 9

"Well, now," Jeff said, standing in the middle of the cabin and smiling at the results of the afternoon's work. "Isn't this a fine place? Why, I never had a place so nice back home. I just had a little corner of my mama and papa's cabin. Who would have ever thought?"

Jeff enjoyed the afternoon, working with Libby and Tad. It seemed the longer they were together, the more Libby's shyness melted away.

Once they'd moved out the items going to the barn, she went back to the big house and returned with a broom, a bucket of water and rags for cleaning the dusty furniture. She quickly went to work scrubbing the old chair, the little table and the simple rail bedstead while Jeff swept away the dead spiders and cobwebs along the walls and rafters. After they finished cleaning, they went to the corn crib in the barn and filled a mattress cover with corn husks.

"I guess it will be a little noisy 'til you get used to it," Libby said as they placed it on the bed.

"Oh, it won't be a bother. I bet it will be a lot more comfortable than sleeping on the ground. That's what I've gotten used to now."

"I'll tell you what I'll do," Libby said. "I'll make sure I keep all the down and small feathers when I fix a chicken or turkey. Before long, I'll have enough for a nice feather bed."

"You really would spoil me for sleeping on the ground then. That's the kind of bed I had back home. My mama fluffed it up every six months or so with fresh feathers while I was growing up. She said I kept outgrowing it."

Before they knew it, the afternoon was almost gone.

"I've got to get back to the house and get busy in the kitchen," Libby said. "Tad, why don't you run on back down to the store to see if there's anything Mister Bell needs you to do before he comes home? Jeff, I imagine you want to take care of your stock and bring your pack inside the cabin to make yourself more at home. You might want to spread your blankets out on the bed and maybe hang up some of your clothes. I'll have Tad bring the washtub out to your cabin before he goes to town, and I'll heat some water for a bath if you'd like."

Jeff grinned. "Libby, I don't think you have any idea just how wonderful a hot bath would feel to me after all those weeks on the road bathing in creeks and rivers. Yes, that would be great. Thank you."

After Libby left the cabin, Jeff sat on the edge of the bed for a moment, then stretched out to test its comfort and found it not as comfortable as the feather bed he had back home but much better than the ground. His thoughts drifted to Libby. *She seemed to really enjoy the afternoon, working with me,* he thought. They both seemed to be comfortable in each other's company. Libby was pleasant, satisfied with her place in life and comfortable in her role. Jeff also judged her to be an efficient housekeeper, from what he saw of the Bell home.

He pictured her as he closed his eyes for a moment. Petite, but filled out the way he thought a nice looking woman should be. He smiled as he remembered her figure, and his thoughts drifted to her face. Her features weren't as broad and thick as his. He wouldn't say she had delicate features, but she wasn't fleshy either. Her mouth was full of expression. She smiled easily and seemed ready to laugh at any moment. But her eyes were her most expressive feature. Jeff thought it would be impossible for her to tell a lie, because her eyes would give her away in a moment. *Yes,* he thought as he sat up on the bed and stood to finish his chores. *I think I'm going to like this place.*

Later that evening, after Will excused himself from conversation with his uncle, and Jeff finished supper with Libby and Tad, Jeff delivered Will's saddlebags and a pack of clothing and personal items to his room. He was also anxious to learn Will's first impression of Stephen Austin.

Will took the saddlebags and pulled Jeff into the small bedroom. "Jeff, I'm so excited about what we're getting into here. Mister Austin showed me his maps, plans and progress to date filling the grant. He's just scratched the surface. There's *so* much more to be done. Austin has a good arrangement with the government, and good people from back east are arriving in a steady stream to take advantage of the land grants. I think we're going to be busy."

Jeff grinned at Will's enthusiasm. "Sounds like your day went as well as mine." Jeff grasped Will's hand and pumped it vigorously. "I'm really going to like it here."

Finally alone in the bedroom, Will reached for the letter that his uncle had given him back at the store. He had put it in the inside pocket of his coat after first looking at the return address on the envelope. The neat script told him it was from Anna. He had carried this first letter from her with him all day. Several times during the day, he'd reached toward his breast pocket and touched it, but he had managed to put those thoughts aside while he was discussing business with Austin. Now he carefully opened the letter and began to read:

> Dear Will,
>
> I hope this letter finds you well at the end of your journey. I am writing it the day after you left. Papa had to take care of some business at Roanoke this morning, and I rode with him in the carriage. I asked him to stop by your place to get your uncle's address from your father. They are all fine but are missing you. Jessie looks a little listless, missing Jeff, but your father says she'll get over it. Mary said if I write to you to say hello for her and to tell you she loves you.

I hope you didn't think I was a baby, the way I cried when you left, but I just know how far away Texas is, and I know you'll be gone a long time.

Papa says he wants to send me to finishing school in Richmond next fall. I think that will be exciting. I'm going to see if he will talk to your father to ask if he will send Mary. I think it would be fun for us to be together.

I will close this letter now as it's getting late. I will send you the address of the school in Richmond, so you can write if you find time.

Will, please be careful in Texas.

Affectionately,
Anna

Chapter 10

By the end of a week of training, Will and Jeff had a good understanding of Austin's expectations regarding surveying and the settlement of new citizens.

Austin and Sam Williams had taken turns working with them on the details of grant laws, Mexican measurement methods, and the Austin Land Company's plan to fill the available area with settlers. The plan was to settle the grant from south to north along the Brazos River, then along the creeks and streams feeding the river. Settlers were encouraged to select their land as close to their neighbors as possible. New arrivals were reminded that the land they were moving into had been the home of Indians for hundreds of years. They were also advised that they were to provide their own militia and would need the support of neighbors for their safety.

Will and Jeff also understood that they would always be working on the outer edge of the frontier and would be especially exposed to possible encounters with Indians.

"We haven't had trouble in several months, but I advise you to stay on the alert," Austin warned. "Keep your weapons ready at all times, and don't let your horses stray away from camp at night. It might even be worthwhile to learn to sleep with one eye open, or take shifts sleeping. Comanches can steal your horses and your hair before you know what's happening. We've had some close calls, but I haven't lost a surveyor to Indians yet, and I'm not planning to start now because of a lack of preparation. I don't guess you brought a dog with you, did you?"

"No sir," Will answered.

"You need to have a dog. There's some folks just south of town whose bitch had a litter about three months ago. Last I heard, they hadn't got rid of all the pups yet. I want you to send Jeff down there to pick up a dog. I'll send a note with him. A good dog will give you warning if anything is approaching your camp. It might just be a possum trying to steal your bacon, or it could be a raiding party with horseflesh and murder on their mind. A good dog will let you know if you have company."

On the last day of their training, Will spent most of the afternoon copying a map detailing the area that he and Jeff would be surveying for the next several months.

He asked Jeff to go back to the house and get his horse, then follow Austin's directions to the farmer's place to pick up the dog. He hoped there would still be one left from the litter and gave Jeff some money to offer the farmer if he seemed reluctant to part with one.

When Jeff arrived at the house to saddle up for his trip, Libby met him in the yard. She appeared to be upset. He grew more concerned as he drew closer.

"What's wrong?" She was pacing back and forth in the yard, clenching and unclenching her fists. "What's wrong Libby?" he asked again, reaching for her arm.

She sighed deeply. "Oh, nothing really, I guess. I'm just a little scared, that's all."

"Why? What happened?"

"Oh, it's just me. Nothing really happened."

"Libby, something has you upset. I want to know what it is."

"Oh, Jeff, it was that Mister Farley. He just scares me."

"Farley? That overseer you told me about? He was here?"

"He left just a little while before you got here. I just had to get out here and get some fresh air."

"What did he want?"

"Nothing, really. He said he'd been to town to see Mister Bell and stopped by here on his way back to the farm. Said he wanted to stop by for a little visit and a cup of coffee. He did pick up some harness from the barn before he left. I guess that's what he came for.

"Anyway, I was in the parlor picking up and dusting and I

heard something in the kitchen. There he stood, right there in the middle of the kitchen. I guess I might have screamed a little and dropped my dust rag. I was just so startled to see him there.

"He laughed that he'd scared me so and said nobody was around to hear me scream. He said he knew there wasn't anybody else around since Mister Bell and Tad were in town. I don't know if he knows you and Mister Will are here or not. Oh Jeff, he just scared me, that's all. He just wanted a cup of coffee, and he talked a while. Then he left."

"He didn't touch you or hurt you or anything?"

"No. I'm just making more out of it than I should. I'm not used to people showing up all of a sudden inside the house like that."

"No, I don't think you're making too much of it. The man scared you. And he didn't have any business in the house. If Mister Bell told him to get some harness, that's all he needed to do, just get the harness and go. He didn't have any business bothering you. I think you ought to tell Mister Bell."

"Oh no, I can't do that!"

"Why not, for God's sake?"

"He's a white man, that's why! I'm not going to cause trouble for a white man. There's no telling what he might come back here and do to me or Tad. No sir. I'm not saying a thing. I know if I said something to Mister Bell about it, he wouldn't let it pass. He'd go out there and threaten to fire Farley. Then all of Mister Bell's folks would have to pay for it, including me and Tad."

Libby finally convinced Jeff she was right. There really wasn't anything she could do about it but keep her mouth shut.

Jeff wanted to stay with Libby until she calmed down, but he had to see about the dog before it got too late. Libby followed him into the barn and watched while he saddled Buck. As he tightened the cinch and belted it up under the stirrup, he said, "I wish I could stay awhile, at least till you get your wits back about you. I hate to leave you alone now."

"No, you go on. I'll be fine." She pushed a smile onto her face.

Jeff bent his head down to look her in the eyes and gently tilted her head back, lifting her chin with his finger. "You're sure you're all right?"

"Thanks for being here when I needed you," Libby said, meeting his gaze. "You need to be on your way. I'm fine now."

"I'll try to be back for supper," Jeff said as he mounted up and rode out of the barn.

Libby stood, framed by the large double doorway of the barn watching Jeff ride away. She suddenly realized that just his touch made everything right with her. She didn't fully understand this warm new feeling, but she enjoyed it.

Bell sent Tad home shortly after Jeff left to tell Libby that guests were invited for supper. "He said he knows he don't give you much time, but you can serve off that big ham in the smoke house. He said just make some biscuits and boil up some taters and open one of them jars of peas you put up last summer. He told` me to get you to fix up some of them fried peach pies, you know, the way you fixed them the last time Mister Austin was here."

"Is Mister Austin all that's coming besides Mister Will?"

"Naw, Mister Williams, he comin' along too."

"All right, I think I can handle that. Just the most important men in the whole grant for dinner on short notice. Go out to the smoke house and bring in that big ham. You know the biggest one, hanging on the far end of the rack. After you bring it in, you can go back to the cellar and bring back a jar of those peas and a jar of beets."

Libby set herself to preparing a special meal for Austin's guests. When Tad completed his chores of gathering food, she put him to work getting out the good china and silver. Before long she was well on her way to producing a steamy, savory meal for company.

As she worked, the incident with Farley weighed heavily on her mind. Usually she wasn't intimidated by or concerned with white men. She had lived all her life under Bell's roof and felt protected in her environment, especially before Mrs. Bell died and Sarah married. There was always someone home then, someone to talk to and keep her company. But now, most days she spent alone.

She wished she hadn't carried on the way she had in front of Jeff, but she just couldn't help herself. His appearing just when he did was a great relief after the scare Farley had given her. She didn't know how she would deal with Farley in the future. Although he hadn't touched her this time, the way he'd looked at her and the remarks he'd made left no doubt what was on his mind. Having absolutely no experience with men and with her mother dying before she was old enough to advise her on the subject, Libby really didn't know what to do. She just knew that she couldn't say anything to Mister Bell. She hoped she hadn't made a mistake by telling Jeff.

Somehow she knew she could trust Jeff. In the short time they had spent together, she had come to feel very comfortable with him. She enjoyed having dinner with him every night in the kitchen while the master and Mister Will were eating in the dining room. There was an air of excitement about him as he told of his studies during the day and his eagerness to get out on the job and explore more of Texas. Her thoughts of Jeff, visualizing his broad smile and wide arm-waving gestures as he described a story at the table, brought a smile back to her face as she worked in the kitchen.

"Lib? Lib . . . ? Are you listenin' to me?"

Libby realized Tad was standing behind her asking a question.

"I'm sorry, Tad, I was thinking about something. What did you say?"

"I said I was finished settin' the table. What else?"

"I think you've done it all. You've been a big help. Why

don't you go out and watch for Mister Bell, and when they get here, ask them if they want something to drink before supper."

When Tad stepped onto the front porch, he saw that Bell, Austin, Williams, and Will were approaching the yard. He held the door open for them as Bell ushered his guests into the sitting room. "Would you gentlemens like something to drink?"

"Good idea," Bell said, and looked at Austin. "I've got some pretty good whiskey if you want, or a cool glass of mint tea."

They all expressed a desire for the tea to slake their thirst on the hot summer evening.

Tad pulled a few sprigs of mint from beside the back porch steps while Libby prepared the tea. When he returned with the tray of tea glasses, the men were discussing plans for further populating the grant.

"There's three families camped outside of town now that are heading north with Will tomorrow," said Austin. "The way they've been coming in this year so far, we've been averaging about two, sometimes three families a week. There's already one surveying crew working the area up north and staying busy all the time. They only get a rest every couple of months when they come in for supplies."

Dinner was soon served. Afterward the men went to the porch chairs to enjoy the evening breeze and have glass of brandy and smoke as the conversation turned more toward the mechanics of surveying and the conditions Will should expect while living and working for months at a time in the open.

"I guess Jeff and I are well adjusted to living on the trail by now," Will said. "At least we won't have to be moving every day."

"That's true," agreed Austin. "But have you ever tented out in the middle of winter?"

"No sir, not yet, but we sure look forward to trying it out."

Their laughter was arrested by the sharp, high-pitched barking of a puppy coming from the road in front of the house.

"Well," said Will. "Looks like Jeff found us a watchdog.

Let's see what he got."

Jeff was just turning into the yard when the dog registered his alarm at the men laughing. Will grabbed Jeff's horse's bridle when he approached the cluster of men now standing in the yard. Jeff swung down with the dog under his arm and sat the brindle-colored, short-haired, mixed-breed male pup on the ground.

"What do you think of him, Jeff?" Will asked.

"I believe we've got us the best watchdog in Texas. We spooked a couple of cottontails along the trail and he kicked up a ruckus both times. Then you heard him as I came on the place. He's loud enough for sure."

"Looks like he'll do just fine," Will said.

Tad heard the dog bark and came running from the rear of the house.

"Tad, would you like to look after him while Jeff takes care of his horse?" Will asked.

"Yes sir!" Tad answered, grinning. He took the thin rope tied around the dog's neck and led him toward the barn with Jeff.

Jeff hurried through his barn chores. He was more interested in checking on Libby to make sure she was all right than he was in giving Buck the care he usually gave him.

Jeff was glad Bell had company tonight even though it meant extra work. *Libby needs to be busy to set her mind straight,* he thought.

He was amused watching Tad play with the dog. For someone who normally was so full of conversation, Tad was completely ignoring him. Once in the barn, he got on the ground with the dog, letting it climb all over him and lick him in the face. Jeff thought, *What a lonely life Tad must have, not having anyone his own age to play with and spending most of his time in the store with Mister Bell.* Jeff finished in the barn as soon as he could and headed for the house. "Tad, keep the dog outside," Jeff said, stepping onto the back porch. "He can't come in."

"What's his name?" Tad asked, looking up at Jeff.

"I guess he doesn't have one yet. Why don't you see if you

can think of a good one for him?"

"Thanks, Jeff." Tad's grin widened, surprised and pleased that he was given the honor of choosing the dog's name.

Libby left the dishes she was washing in the pan when she heard Jeff's voice. "That's a cute dog," she said, holding the door open for Jeff. "Thanks for letting Tad play with him awhile."

"I'm more concerned about you right now. How are you?"

"Oh, I'm all right. Don't worry yourself about it any more. I've kept your supper warm for you. Here, let me fix your plate." She was quiet while she dished out portions onto the plate as Jeff washed his hands. In a few moments, she asked, "How far north will you and Mister Bowman be working?"

"Quite a ways, I guess. Out beyond where anybody's living now."

She put his plate before him as he sat down at the table. She took the chair next to him to keep him company while he ate. "How long do you think you'll be gone?"

"Don't really know for sure. We'll be meeting new folks all the time coming out for their land, but we'll need to come back to town sooner or later for supplies."

Her brow wrinkled with concern. "Aren't there still a lot of Indians out there?"

"No," he lied. "From what I hear, most of the troublesome Indians are far off to the northwest. There's nothing to worry about where we'll be."

"I can't help but worry."

Jeff watched her as he ate, but she wouldn't return his gaze. She sat, fidgeting with her fingers and staring at the tablecloth.

She shifted her gaze to his, and her eyes were now filled with more than just worry. "It's not just the Indians." The edginess of emotion in her day was starting to overflow. "Jeff, there's danger all around you out there. Everything from rattlesnakes to bears. There's buffalo stampedes, drowning in rivers, and riding accidents. There's just plain sickness. Don't you tell me not to worry, Jeff Jefferson.

“I stay here by myself everyday, working for the master, taking care of this place with nobody to talk to but Tad. Then here you come, in all your big, good-looking glory and give me a little company and treat me nice and stay just long enough for me to really get used to having you around. Then off you go, just like that!” She snapped her fingers. “And for who knows how long? I don't know if I'll ever even see you again! No sir-ree, don't you tell me not to worry!”

Libby was breathless. She hadn't really known, until now, how she felt toward Jeff. The words had just tumbled out, and once she got started, she couldn't stop. She sat at the table trying to hold back the tears that wouldn't stay inside.

Jeff watched her trying to control herself. Slowly, he slid his big hand across the table and placed it over both of hers, gently stroking her soft skin with his fingers. “Thank you,” he said quietly. “Is it all right with you if I worry about you, too?”

She lifted her tear-filled eyes and nodded. They sat there for a long moment, sharing a feeling of unspoken understanding. Finally Libby cleared her throat, pulled her hands free and got up from the table. “I'd better get back to these dishes or I'll never get finished tonight," she said as she went to pour fresh hot water into the pan. "You go on and finish your supper, and we'll see how Tad's doing naming the dog.”

On the front porch, the men were finishing their brandy and cigars and Will was getting last-minute surveying instructions.

Austin reached for his hat. “It's getting late. Guess we'd better let you turn in. You and Jeff have a big day tomorrow.” He turned to Will’s uncle. “John thanks for the hospitality. You tell Libby her dinner was excellent, as usual. Someday, I'd like to steal her away from you.”

“Never gonna happen, Stephen. My dear wife taught that girl how to cook. It's almost as if she never stopped cooking for me.”

“I guess I can understand that. She sure knows her business.”

"Thanks. I'll pass it on."

Although Will had enjoyed the company and conversation during the evening, he was glad when the guests left, as he had so much he wanted to do before bedtime. He bade his uncle good night and excused himself to his room as soon as Austin and Williams left. His studies and other activities had kept him so busy during the week that he had not yet answered the letter from Anna.

He reached for his writing materials next to his journal and his fingers brushed the golden locket in his saddlebags. He placed the locket next to the paper and quill pen on the desk and sat down to write.

Dear Anna,

I was pleased to find your letter waiting for me when Jeff and I arrived in San Felipe. Uncle John was holding it for me. Yes, we've finished our journey and are ready to start our surveying business. We are eager to see more of Texas, as what we have seen to date has been beautiful. I am even more convinced that I made the right decision in establishing my home here.

I was glad to hear that you will be going away to finishing school in the fall. I know you will enjoy it. I hope this letter reaches you before you leave. Tell my father that I said he should send Mary with you to school, as she could use some finishing.

Jeff and I will be leaving in the morning so I won't be able to post any mail while we are working in the field, but I will write again as soon as I can.

I must close this now, as I still have packing to do.

Affectionately,

Will

P.S. I just want to let you know that your little locket has given me comfort many times when I've needed it. My fingers cross it at least once a day as I reach for my journal. Thank you for giving me something I can touch that reminds me of you. Please write again soon,

WB

Jeff helped Libby finish cleaning the kitchen. After she asked Bell whether he needed her anymore for the evening, they turned off the lamp in the kitchen and went looking for Tad.

They didn't find him around the back porch, so they assumed he had gone on to Libby's cabin. The full moon and stars in the cloudless sky lit the well-worn path between the cabins and the big house. The flower garden that Mrs. Bell had started and Libby and Tad now maintained was in full bloom and the sweet scent of roses wafted in the light breeze. As they slowly walked along the path toward Jeff's cabin, Libby slipped her hand into Jeff's. "I'm sorry for the way I talked to you earlier," she said.

"What are you sorry for? You didn't say anything wrong."

"Sometimes my mouth just says things before my mind thinks about what I'm saying."

"Did you mean what you said?"

"Yes."

"So there's nothing to be sorry for."

Soon they were at Jeff's cabin door. They stood in awkward silence for a moment, still holding hands. Libby started to turn away. "I'll send Tad back over here with the dog."

Jeff grasped her hand tighter and gently pulled her close to him. He slid his large arms under hers and around her small waist. Her hands caressed his muscular arms as they moved upward toward his shoulders. They quietly held each other in a gentle caress until their lips came together in a kiss. After a few moments Jeff just held her close.

She buried her head in his thick chest. "Jeff, please be careful out there," she whispered.

"You be careful here," he said quietly.

Finally he pulled away. Still holding her by the arms, he said, "You go on over to your place. There's something I want to bring over in a minute." They shared another quick kiss. Then Libby left and headed toward the glow of lamp light from the window of her cabin.

Libby found Tad, as she expected, still wrestling with the dog. "How's the dog naming coming along?"

"I got one I like, but I'll have to see if Jeff likes it too. Where is he, anyway?"

"He'll be over here directly." As she sat down, the pup came over to her, wagging his tail and dancing in circles.

She knelt, petting and talking to the puppy.

Jeff knocked softly on the door, and teased Tad as he stepped inside. "I wondered if you'd stolen my dog."

"No, I just had him over here trying to see what name fit him best."

"What did you come up with?"

Tad turned toward the dog, slapped his knees and called, 'Come here, Jake."

The puppy spun away from Libby and raced back to Tad.

"Seems like he goes by Jake," Tad said.

"Then Jake it is," Jeff said, laughing. "Thanks, Tad, I don't think I would have come up with such a natural name." Jeff walked over to the rough table next to the fireplace. "Please come over here and sit down a minute, there's something I want to show both of you." All three sat around the table.

Jeff turned up the lamp wick and unrolled the document he

was carrying. Placing the sugar bowl at the top of it and a coffee tin at the bottom to weigh it down, he quietly admired the document. "What you're looking at is very important to me," he said after a few moments.

"It was made special for me by Señor Vargas in Nacogdoches. I want to leave it here with you while I'm gone."

Tad and Libby studied the document but didn't understand its meaning.

"It's mighty fancy looking, Jeff. What is it?" Tad asked.

Jeff smiled as he stared at the document. "It's my freedom paper."

"Your what?" Libby asked, her attention now riveted on Jeff rather than the paper.

Jeff hesitated a moment, then nodded slightly and smiled before answering. "Will gave me my freedom on the trail from Virginia, and he gave me a paper to prove it. He said his conscience wouldn't allow him to keep me as a slave any more. I always carry that paper in my satchel here." Jeff patted the leather case attached to his belt. "But he wanted me to have formal papers drawn up by the government of Mexico when we became citizens, so Señor Vargas did this for me."

Libby looked at him in astonishment. "But . . . if you're free, you can go anywhere and do anything you want!"

"I guess that's right."

"So you don't have to go off into the wilderness tomorrow!"

"That's right, too, but I'm going. I'm going because it's my job. I'm going because my friend needs me, and I'm going because I've got a stake in this country too. I'm a free man, a citizen of Mexico, and, yes, I've got a right to live my life any way I want. And that's what I'm doing, living my life the way I want. I want to help Will and men like Mister Austin build this country into something to be proud of — something I'll be proud of because I'll be part of it. I can do those things because I'm free.

"My freedom might not mean much to most white men

today, but someday it will. Someday, there will be more people who think like Will. Someday, Libby, someday, Tad, we'll *all* be free. I believe it, and I've got faith that it will happen. It won't happen this year or next year, or maybe even twenty years from now, but sooner or later it will come.

"You know, this freedom paper looks nice, and I'm mighty proud of it, but I really won't be free, not really, totally free, till all my brothers and sisters are free too.

"Now, why am I telling you all of this? Well, I'm telling you, Tad, because your sister has some notion that some misfortune might overcome me and I might not come back. I just want to tell you both that I'll be back. I know my destiny. I must learn all I can. I've been getting an education. Will's been teaching me to read and write and a lot of other things. Some day, I want to help others. That's where it all begins. That's where freedom starts, with learning. I want to help you learn, too. I've still got a lot to learn myself, but I will, and when I do, I want to teach others what I've learned.

"Tad, there's a lot of white men who wouldn't like to hear this kind of talk — in fact, some wouldn't tolerate it — so you can't talk to anybody but Libby and me about it. *Any* of it. You understand?"

"Yes sir," Tad answered quietly, still in awe of what he had just heard.

"Now let me read this to you, so you'll know what it says."

Jeff had been practicing reading the document, so he felt comfortable reading it out loud. He read it slowly and deliberately, making sure he didn't stumble on any of the words. When he finished, he sat there staring at the document. Then he felt Libby's hand reach for his and squeeze it. He looked up to find her eyes rimmed with tears.

"That's beautiful, Jeff. I'm so proud of you! We'll be honored to keep it for you. I feel better about you going now. We won't worry about you quite so much. But I want to worry about you some, all right?"

Chapter 11

The next morning, shortly after daylight, Will and Jeff were in the barn finishing their packing and waiting for Mister Bell. Will wanted to walk to town with his uncle and replenish his supplies at the store before heading out to pick up the new settlers. He was securing his saddlebags when Bell arrived. Bell motioned toward Jeff and Libby talking at the back of the barn. “Looks like Libby's kind of taken a shine to Jeff back there.”

“That's good,” Will said, “if you don't have any objections.”

“No, I don't have any objections. It will be good for her to look forward to a little company from time to time. I reckon the only time she ever sees much of her own kind these days have been the few times I've taken her and Tad out to the farm with me.”

Will turned toward Jeff. “Jeff, looks like I'm ready. How about you?”

“Be right with you.”

“We'll be back in a couple of months or so,” Jeff told Libby as he started leading his horse toward the front of the barn. He grinned. “Just don't forget how to cook while we're gone.”

“Oh, I won't. I'll make something really special when you come back.”

As they led their horses out of the yard, Jeff turned, smiled, and winked at Libby, then waved goodbye, leaving her standing alone under the large oak tree.

Tad was playing with the dog in the yard and fell in next to Jeff as they reached the road. “Don't you need somebody to come along to look after Jake?”

Jeff smiled, “I imagine Jake will be looking after us soon enough. Besides, who'd help take care of the store and look after your sister if you were gone? You know how much Mister Bell and Libby depend on you.”

"Yeah, I guess you're right." Tad understood his responsibility but still longed to take part in Jeff's adventure.

Will was concerned about his uncle. He noticed that Bell looked tired as they walked toward town. Will knew Bell prided himself on his independence and wouldn't complain if he was feeling bad, but Will decided to ask about his health. "Uncle John, are you all right? You getting enough rest?"

"Oh, I'm fine, Son. Just a little tired, I guess. I've been concerned about the farm. Just gotta spend more time out there. Thought I smelled whiskey on the overseer's breath the last time he was in town. Then he was here again yesterday, and I know I smelled it on him then. He'd been over at Babcock's saloon. Now, don't get me wrong, I got no problem with a man having a drink now and then, but it concerns me if he's taking care of my place and my people while he's drunk. He wasn't drunk yesterday. I asked him about it. Said he just stopped in for a couple of drinks while I was away from the store, back at the house for lunch. Said he was just waiting to see me. I think I'd better keep a closer eye on him, that's all. Me and Tad might take the buggy down to the farm this afternoon, just to see how things are going. It's been about three weeks since I've been down there anyway. It's about time I checked up on things."

After the short walk to town, it took Will, Jeff and Tad less than an hour to fill the list of supplies and re-distribute the loads on the pack horses. Bell and Tad were standing outside the store watching Will help Jeff tie the canvas over the second pack horse when Stephen Austin strode across the street from his land office.

"Looks like you boys are about ready to go," he said as he approached the small caravan.

"Yes sir, we'd like to make some headway today after we pick up the settlers."

"They should be ready when you get there. I sent my man out last night to tell them you'd be on your way this morning. Do you feel comfortable about finding your rendezvous up north?"

"Yes sir, the finishing touches I did on the map yesterday should see us through."

"You should run into Jacobson's camp a few days up river," Austin said. "We'll continue to send people to that location till you get word back that you're moving farther north."

"You just keep sending them to us, and we'll see that they get settled in," Will said, swinging into his saddle. He extended his hand to shake with Austin, then reached over and shook his uncle's hand. "John, you take care of yourself, now."

"Oh, don't worry 'bout me. I'll be fine."

Jeff removed his hat and extended his hand to Stephen Austin. "Thank you, sir, for the training. We'll do you a good job." He turned and shook Bell's hand as well. "And thank you, sir, for your hospitality. I really appreciate it."

"You're welcome, Jeff. You know you've got your place there whenever you come back to town too."

"Well, Tad," Jeff said, squatting next to the boy holding the puppy. "You'd better say goodbye to Jake. I sure appreciate you finding a name for him."

Tad swallowed hard and slowly handed the dog over to Jeff. "I guess he'll be all growed up next time I see him." Tad was trying hard not to let his lip quiver as he spoke.

"You take care," Jeff said as he hugged the boy and swallowed a lump in his own throat. "You take care of your sister too. She needs you to help her out."

"Yes sir."

Jeff stood and shoved his hand into his pants pocket. He came out with a pocket knife that Will had given him. It was one of several that Will had bought as gifts when they shopped in Natchez on their way to Texas. Jeff had decided if anybody needed a gift right now, it was Tad.

"Here, Tad, this might help in doing some of your chores. Watch out now, it's sharp."

"Thanks," Tad said, forcing a smile as he examined the

knife and wiped a tear from his face with the cuff of his shirt.

Jeff turned back to his horse, swung into the saddle, placed his hat back on his head, and cradled the dog on his saddle between himself and the horn. He grinned broadly at Will. “Let’s go survey some land!”

They found the group of settlers camped under a grove of hackberry trees a couple of miles north of town. The three families, eager to be on their way, already had their horses hitched to the three wagons strung out in a line along the side of the trail. A tall, slender man with a full growth of blond, curly whiskers approached them as they rode up to the wagons. “Howdy. You must be the fellers Mister Austin sent to fetch us up to our land.”

“Guess that's us, then,” Will said, dismounting. He introduced himself and Jeff.

“I'm Tom Bigelow,” the bearded fellow said as he shook Will's hand. “This here's my brother, Charles.” He motioned to a younger version of himself with darker hair and a full, drooping mustache. “Over yonder, that's Oliver Cartwright.” He pointed toward the heavy set, red-haired man tightening the harness on the last team in the wagon line. Cartwright smiled and waved from where he was working. “We kept you some coffee going. Come on over fer a cup. You need to meet the womenfolk.”

Soon, Will and Jeff were introduced to the entire Bigelow and Cartwright clan. Will determined that Cartwright's wife was Tom and Charles' sister. The resemblance was too strong to miss. She was a small blond woman of about thirty but looked older than her years after the long, exhausting trip, bouncing cross-country in a worn-out wagon and taking care of her family along the way. The two Bigelow women had much the same look about them as the Cartwright woman: tired-looking but eager to be on their way to find their new home. Altogether, there were ten children, ranging in age from Tom's boy, Roger, who looked to be about thirteen, to Charles and Ella's baby girl, Sallyanne.

It took Will and Jeff's horses a while to adjust to the much slower pace of the wagon train from the gait they were used to. Moving at the rate of the heavy, loaded wagons, Will estimated they would do well to travel twelve miles a day.

The trail north loosely followed the west bank of the Brazos River, beyond the riverbank timbers. It was well-traveled at this point and in good condition. Hundreds of wagons had already covered this trail over the last several years. It could almost be called a road.

After the first day, the road deteriorated with each passing mile. By the morning of the third day out of San Felipe, it was nothing more than slight impressions in the tall prairie grass where a few wagons had passed before. They came upon the surveyor's camp that afternoon.

Jacobson's camp consisted of what remained of several cook fires spaced fifty paces or so apart in a semicircle around a filthy canvas spread across a rope strung between two trees and staked out to form a makeshift tent. The camp was in a grove of scrub oaks next to a creek. Wagon tracks indicated that previous settlers had occupied the spaces next to the scattered mounds of ashes, so the Bigelows and Cartwrights positioned their wagons accordingly.

The camp was abandoned, except for the dirty canvas. Will assumed the Jacobson surveying party was in the field at work and would return later in the evening.

"Folks," Will said, walking toward the wagons after he tied Baron to a tree. "Might as well make yourself at home. We won't be able to determine what's available until I update my map from what Jacobson's done. He should be in later. Then we'll check out the property tomorrow. There's going to be plenty of work after that. You might want to take advantage of whatever rest you can get."

"You reckon we can be on our own places by tomorrow night?" Tom Bigelow asked as he started unhitching his team.

"Don't know for sure but I'd say it's possible. I don't imagine

Jacobson would be camping too far from the work."

"I reckon one more night won't hurt us, long as we been on the road already," Bigelow said, loosening the harness on one of his big bay geldings.

Will soon realized that his comment about getting some rest had fallen on deaf ears throughout the camp. It seemed there never was time for rest for these people. While the men were taking care of the horses, everyone else went about their normal chores setting up camp. The women took advantage of a couple of extra hours of daylight to wash out a few items of clothes in the creek.

After Jeff got his and Will's tent set up some distance from Jacobson's shelter, he asked some of the children to look after Jake. He then took his rifle and headed out west of camp along the creek to find supper.

Jacobson and his helper, a Mexican boy about fifteen years old, returned to camp a little before dark. It appeared to Will that Jacobson had given up on personal hygiene some seasons earlier. He was wearing greasy buckskin britches and a threadbare, homespun shirt. He was shod in worn moccasins and his floppy, sweat-stained hat wouldn't hold water due to the holes where creases used to be. Most of his face was hidden behind an unruly scruff of dark whiskers that wrapped around his neck to blend with the same unruly hair falling down his back. He had a stench about him that would turn a weaker man's stomach, but Will found, after going over his maps, that he was a knowledgeable surveyor.

While the Mexican boy went about setting up Jacobson's camp, Jacobson informed Will and Jeff about the area they'd be working. Will and Jeff stretched out their maps on the ground next to Jacobson's tent and brought Will's map up to date with the locations of the latest settler's names and their boundaries. He also noted the reference points Jacobson used on each claim and where he should start on the next claim.

"Were goin' right up the west side of the river fer now,"

Jacobson said. "Most folks want to be on the river. Just keep on puttin' 'em on the west side all the way to the north end of the grant. Then we'll come back south and start workin' both sides of the creeks and streams leadin' to the Brazos from the west. Hell, there's enough waterways in this grant to keep us busy fer a long time just puttin' folks on property with runnin' water. You got a long way to go up the Brazos 'fore ya get to the end of the grant.

"Mister Austin's got surveyin' teams workin' the east side of the Brazos and along the Colorado, too. There's folks comin' in all over the grant, but it'll take years to fill up this country."

Jacobson rolled up his maps. "I tell you, Bowman, I'm glad to see you fellers show up. I ain't seen the old lady in about four months. It's 'bout time I let her know I'm still alive."

"Tell me," Will asked. "What about the Indians?"

"What about 'em?"

"You seen any?"

"Aw, ever' once in a while we'll see signs of a few braves wanderin' through these parts on a huntin' party, but they usually don't cause much trouble. Kiowas and Wichitas, mostly. Ain't had a shootin' fight with 'em in almost six months now. Ain't seen no Comanches where I been workin,' but then we're gettin' farther into their territory. They usually run more to the west and north. You and your boy there stay close to them weapons, and you'll do all right."

Will liked Jacobson in spite of his unwashed ways, but he was glad that he and Jeff had chosen a spot upwind from Jacobson's camp to pitch their tent. That night, after supper, Will and Jeff settled down with their writing materials. Jeff, as usual, continued his studies, but Will wanted to send a letter out with Jacobson the next day and have him post it at San Felipe. He had no idea when he would have an opportunity to send mail again.

Will felt Anna's locket when he reached for his writing gear in his saddlebags. He sat, leaning against a tree, preparing to write by the firelight, rubbing the locket between his fingers and thinking of people and places far away.

Dear Anna,

I will send this to the address you gave me for your school. You should be a student in good standing by the time this reaches you. I hope you enjoy your studies. I can't imagine why your father would want to send you to school to learn to be a lady. I think you have always been a lady, but if you enjoy your studies, I'm happy for you.

Jeff and I are now camped on the west bank of the Brazos River in the middle of the Austin and Williams grant in Texas. We have three families with us whose land will be the first we survey.

I get such a feeling of gratification from being a part of what's going on here. I've never before seen such a sense of pride and hope as I see in these families. With every family I meet along the way, my belief is stronger that this country will be something truly great some day. I can see it in their faces, in the way they work, and in the tireless devotion and commitment of their leaders. I feel honored to be a part of it.

Anna, I think of you often and try to remember that it has only been a few months since I left home. So much has happened in my life, and so much distance separates me from those I care for.

I will be back in San Felipe in a couple of months and look forward to receiving a letter from you upon my return.

Tomorrow I start the work that I have so long prepared for. Please keep me in your prayers.

Affectionately,

Will

Chapter 12

The next morning, after getting a clear understanding from Jacobson of the exact location of the reference point for beginning the next survey, Will, Jeff, the two Bigelow brothers and Cartwright took off on horseback toward the river. The plan was for the settlers to scout the land while Will and Jeff started measuring the river frontage and marking off the water boundaries of the first parcel of land.

It took almost an hour to reach the reference point Jacobson had staked along the bank of the Brazos. A pile of round river rocks marked the last property line he had completed.

"Boys, here's where we begin," Will said, bringing Baron to a halt. "Jeff and I will start running the chain right down there." He pointed to the edge of the water. "You can start looking over the landscape if you like. There should be another pile of rocks due west to indicate the back corner. It will take us a while to get to the next reference point, so you boys take your time and enjoy the countryside. We'll meet up with you somewhere up river."

The Bigelows and Cartwright didn't waste any time with goodbyes. Will was amused at the excitement and anticipation on their faces. After agreeing to meet upstream, they took off in search of good home site locations and a better understanding of what their new land had to offer.

Will expected that they wouldn't have trouble finding suitable building sites. He assumed that most of the land in the area would be much the same as he had already seen: woods extending about a half-mile from the river, then scattered trees to open country beyond. The wooded area would have natural clearings scattered about that would be ideal for cabins and other out-buildings. Some of the clearings would even be large enough to support a vegetable garden and orchard.

"Well, Mister Surveyor, are you ready to get started?" Will

asked as he watched Jeff pull the chain from its sack.

"Yep, ready as I'll ever be."

Will and Jeff started to work, doing the job they had traveled half a continent to do. They were finally Texas surveyors.

Late that afternoon, they were almost finished with their second measure of river frontage when they heard riders splashing toward them from up stream. The excitement the young settlers left with in the morning had multiplied upon their return.

"This place is wonderful!" Tom Bigelow shouted when he got within earshot. "This here's the most beautiful country I ever seen in my whole life!" All three riders were laughing and shouting like children on Christmas morning.

"This is jest like the Garden of Eden," Charles Bigelow said as they drew up even with the surveyors. "Why, we ran acrost wild plums and grapes and turkeys galore and deer and — How many deer did we see, Tom?"

"Must'a been at least fifteen or twenty."

"An' fish," Charles continued. "There's a big ole fishin' hole back up yonder. That water's so clear you can jest see them big ole cats an' perch a-swimmin' round, waitin' fer you to take 'em out. There's land fer plantin' an' fer grazin'! My Lord, I never seen such good, rich dirt. I can't hardly wait to sink a plow in it."

"So you think you made the right decision coming out here then?" Will teased.

"You bet we did." Cartwright answered. "You ain't never gonna get me off this place."

"Did you find spots for your cabins?"

"Lordy, we found so many, we're jest gonna let the women decide on that," Tom said. "We're jest gonna load up everybody and bring 'em on over here in the mornin' an' turn 'em loose. Here you boys been workin' all day an' we been playin'." Tom swung down from his saddle. "You jest tell us what to do an' we'll help you finish up right quick, an' we'll all ride back to camp together."

Tom and Charles took the chain while Cartwright handled all the horses. Will and Jeff could hardly keep up with the Bigelows as they moved the chain along the riverbank. Will had to ask them to slow down so he could make accurate sightings and mark the bends along the river. Jeff marveled at the energy excited men could generate.

It didn't take long before they completed the survey line they were working on, got it logged on the map, and piled a stack of rocks at the reference point.

"Did you decide who gets which piece of land?" Will asked while he and Jeff stowed the instruments.

Tom answered. "I'm goin' on the north end, Sister and Oliver will be in the middle, an' Charles an' his brood on the south end. Thought we'd all work together on the cabins, startin' with Charles'. Should go a lot easier and faster, all of us workin' together that way."

The sun had already set, and it was almost dark before they rode back into camp. The women were tending a stew simmering in a big kettle on the fire. Young Roger had provided the meat with several jackrabbits he'd brought back to camp after a short walk along the creek. The pup was already napping, full from the scraps Roger pitched him while he dressed the rabbits.

The women could tell by the expressions on their men's faces that they were thrilled with what they had seen and could hardly wait to tell of it.

Will and Jeff chose a spot to have their supper in the outer ring of fire light, aside from the family members. Somehow it seemed more proper for them to just watch and listen as the young families shared their dreams by the fire. After the men finished eating, the younger children found their father's laps. The campfires snapped and crackled as they shared stories of what it would be like in their new homes.

Cartwright's normally rosy cheeks were even more flushed as he and the others told the women and children what they could expect. "An' whenever we want to, we'll jest cut us some long poles and dig up some big ole worms and go down to that fishin' hole an' bring us home a mess o' fish like you ain't never seen. Then when we get tired of fishin', we'll jest go swimmin' right there in the river to cool off. Now, won't that be nice?"

Little Mattie looked up at her father from his lap. "I bet I catch one this big, Papa." She stretched her arms as wide as they would go.

"I bet you will too, Honey," Oliver said, stroking her hair. He looked at his wife, sitting next to him with her feet curled under her dress. "You ain't forgot how to bake pies since we been on the road have you, Mama?"

"No, I don't think so, why?"

"Cause I'm gonna cover you up in pecans this fall from all them pecan trees growin' down along the river. We'll have pecan pies all year long, an' plum preserves from all them wild plum trees we seen scattered around. We run across at least a half-dozen big ole blackberry patches. Oh, I can jest taste a blackberry cobbler! We even seen a bunch of grapevines growing back down there too. They was one spot where they was jest a growin' all over the place." He looked at Tom. "Tom, you 'member when your pappy showed us how to make mustang wine when we was kids? You 'member that?"

"Yeah, I think I do." Tom chuckled, then added, "I think I also remember a couple kids sneaking a sip or two till they got caught and got their hides tanned over it."

Tom's wife, Rose, poked him in the ribs, stifling a grin as she scolded him with her eyes for telling stories of his childhood indiscretions in front of the children. The older children giggled at the vision of their fathers getting into trouble when they were growing up.

Tom quickly changed the subject: "You know, even if we ever had a bad year with the crops, there's always gonna be meat for the table. There's deer all over the place, an' rabbits, squirrels, an' turkeys. We even seen a couple of foxes. Scared up some quail and doves too. We seen all kind of tracks in the river mud. Some of 'em looked like some purty good sized cats. We even seen some droppin's out on the prairie, looked like it might'a been buffalo, or maybe wild cow. Don't know what it was from for sure, but it's big, whatever it was. Looked like there might be some wild horses around these parts, too. We seen some fresh horse tracks up on the northern end of what'll be our place. Looked like they was laid down where we crossed 'em jest a little earlier today. Wasn't many, though, maybe three or four. Looked like they was a headin' fer the water. I wouldn't mind catching me some of them wild horses one of these days."

"You were talkin' bout failed crops. I can't imagine us ever havin' a failed crop," Charles offered. "When we was out on the grass land, we got down and scratched up a few different places. I want you to know, we can grow *anything* in this dirt. Why, I'd go so far to say that by this time next year, we'll have corn growin' taller than a horse's ear and sorghum so thick a man can't walk through it an' cotton so heavy with bolls it'll look like it's snowed in September. I'm of a mind to even put in some wheat someday."

"I'll tell you what I want to do," Rose Bigelow said. "I want to find us a clearing for the cabin that will be big enough to have the kind of garden and orchard that I've always wanted. You remember, Tom, Papa gave us that big sack of peach seeds he'd been saving. I can't wait to get those in the ground. There's enough seeds for all of us. I want a big garden too. I'll take care of it, Tom, after you plow it and help me plant. I already know what I want to put in next spring. I want sweet potatoes, squash, okra, onions, tomatoes, and beans — lots of beans — and turnips, beets, and watermelons. But we're going to have to put a rail fence all around it to keep the deer out."

Rose paused to look at her family in the fading firelight and found that most of the children had nodded off to sleep in their father's arms or had curled up next to their parents, pillowing their heads on their mother or father's laps. "My goodness, I've put these children to sleep, going on about my garden. Come on, lets get these kids to bed, and we'll pick a garden spot tomorrow."

The men continued their conversation as the women put the foodstuffs away to protect them from the night-prowling animals.

Will had spread his maps next to the fire to go over the sightings he'd made earlier in the day to double-check the accuracy of the water-edge property lines, but he couldn't keep his mind on his work. Something was bothering him. Something Tom said earlier in his description of their findings during the day just didn't seem right, but Will didn't want to alarm the others without more to go on.

Jeff had been reading the surveying book while Will was at his maps but had given it up to the dying firelight. Will rolled up the maps and put them in their bag. The camp grew quiet as the settlers drifted off to their pallets.

Jeff yawned as he sat on a log in the dark next to their tent to take off his boots.

"Don't take your boots off yet," Will said quietly, looking at the wagons. Jeff straightened, questioning with his eyes.

Will continued, "I've been concerned about something ever since Tom mentioned those horse tracks. Maybe I'm wrong. I hope I am, but I don't think wild horses would be this close to where folks are settling and they sure wouldn't be traveling in numbers of three or four. They'd be traveling in a much larger herd. I didn't want to say anything to scare the women and children, but those may have been Indian pony tracks they saw today."

Jeff was suddenly wide-awake. "You think so?"

"I don't know, but Tom said they were fresh. If it was Indians, they know we're here. They'd have smelled the fire. I won't sleep a wink all night unless I at least take a look around."

"Which way do you want me to go?" Jeff was reaching for his long rifle next to his blanket.

Will looked toward the sky, gauging the light that was cast by the cloud-covered half moon. “All right, here's what we'll do. If they’re out there, they'll be after the horses. If there's only three or four of them they won’t attack us because they don't have us out-numbered. If they're after the horses, they'll be coming in across the grass toward where we have them hobbled.” He nodded toward the grassland, northwest of the grove where they had their camp.

“Take all the firepower you can carry. You go south and I'll go north, then circle around. See that clump of trees way out there?” Will nodded to a point about two hundred yards beyond where the horses were hobbled. “We'll meet there and work our way back toward camp across the grassland. Just walk out of camp like you're answering the call of nature and then stay low and in the shadows. If you see anything move, don't hesitate to shoot and raise a ruckus. That will at least alarm the others.”

They quickly drew their second rifle from their saddle holsters and strung their powder horns over their shoulders. They both checked to insure that the leather pouch, with a supply of ball and patches, was still secured to their belts. Then they separated to head out of camp.

The pup started complaining with a high-pitched whine about being left alone and tied to a tree. Jeff returned to briefly pet and reassure him. Within seconds, the dog was once again silent and Jeff quietly walked out of camp, south toward the creek.

Jeff picked his way through the dark shadows of the brush along the creek. He didn't have to feel his heart racing to know how tense he was. Every muscle was strung tight. Every nerve was poised to see, hear, or smell . . . to sense something — anything.

He tried to calm himself so he wouldn't react to natural sounds of the night. He heard the hushed rustling of the leaves in the light breeze. A bird softly settled himself in his roost. He avoided the area under the trees to keep from crushing the dry leaves. Treading along the edge of the grassland, he crouched low in the almost waist-high grass, scanning the tall grass between himself and the grove of trees.

The sky was dotted with thin clouds that blew across the half moon, lighting and shading the veiled landscape as Jeff silently made his round-about way toward the trees. He could see the horses to his right and the trees ahead until the moon went behind a cloud. Then details became hazy. Every minute or so he stopped. Holding his breath and crouching statue-like in the weeds, he listened for alien noises and watched the grass gently undulate as the soft night winds blew through it. Seeing nothing to cause alarm, he quickly and quietly moved on.

After what seemed like an eternity, he found himself approaching the thicket. He circled wide and came in from the back. His lungs were ready to burst from holding his breath, then trying to control his breathing as he eased into the edge of the thicket. Watching his foot placement to avoid breaking twigs or crushing leaves, he moved from bush to bush and tree to tree, easing toward the front of the thicket, stopping and listening every few seconds. He raised his left foot and was about to place it down again carefully in front of the other when the alarm went out.

Jake's excited, high-pitched yelping echoed across the stillness of the night like a bugle.

An owl hooted. Jeff's thoughts raced. *Not from a tree! From the ground! Too low! That's not an owl!*

He dropped the rifle in his left hand and cocked the hammer on the one in his right as an explosion erupted to his left and fire flew from Will's rifle muzzle.

The horse screamed as it went down. Pandemonium broke out immediately in front of Jeff. Terrified horses were rearing and screaming from the flash of fire and smoke. A dark figure scrambled onto the back of one and broke from the timber.

"Indians!" Will and Jeff both yelled as the rider charged away from the trees, leading two other horses. Jeff raced to the edge of the thicket to get a bead on the rider and saw three other men spring from the grass, halfway between him and the hobbled horses, running toward the rider. The rider bent low against his galloping horse's neck, reducing Jeff's target area.

Jeff shifted his aim to one of the running men, lead him just a hair and pulled the trigger. The man went down, clutching his leg an instant after Jeff fired. Jeff realized as he pulled his handgun from his belt that Will was at his side leveling his rifle for a shot. Will's second shot missed, but by then they heard shots from the camp.

The crossfire was more than the Indians wanted. None of them got off an arrow. The two runners lifted the wounded man behind the rider. The others scrambled onto their ponies and galloped southwest toward the thicket along the creek, each leaning into his horse's mane, becoming part of his mount.

Jeff got off a departing shot with his handgun but missed as the Indians raced into the brush extending along the creek.

Jeff ran back into the thicket and past the writhing horse to retrieve the rifle he'd dropped in the grass. He noticed a large, spreading stain along the horse's upper leg in the moonlight. It was clear, even in the shadows of the thicket, that the lead ball from Will's rifle had shattered the horse's shoulder. It took him a few moments to find his rifle in the weeds. He walked back to the horse and put his last load into the horse's head.

Something light colored on the ground next to the dead horse caught Jeff's attention. Reaching to pick it up, he realized it was a fourteen-foot long lance with a long, sharp, filed-metal tip on the business end. The light colors he had noticed on the ground were eagle feathers attached for decoration. The young Indian who had been holding the horses had dropped it in his panic to flee. Jeff imagined the disgrace he would face by his brethren, not only for allowing a horse to be lost and their mission scrubbed but also for losing his own weapon in his fright.

Will was reloading as Jeff met him on the edge of the

thicket. They both continued reloading as they called out to the Bigelows and the Cartwrights and told them it appeared to be all over. The dog was still barking and the children crying, their mothers trying to comfort them, terrified themselves by the attack.

When they walked into camp, Jeff immediately went to Jake to praise him for sounding the alarm. The pup met him with his tail wagging, dancing around in his excitement.

"How did you know they were out there, and why didn't you let us know?" Tom Bigelow demanded, bare-chested and just now pulling his suspenders over his shoulders. "Good God man, they could have killed us all!"

"We didn't know they were out there," Will said. "I just had a strange feeling all evening. I didn't want to frighten your wives and children on a hunch."

Oliver Cartwright stepped between the still-angry Tom Bigelow and Will. "Take it easy, Tom. These two fellers just saved our lives. What hunch was that, Will?"

Will explained his guess about the source of the tracks they had seen earlier in the day.

"We should'a seen that ourselves," Bigelow said, shaking his head. He then shifted his rifle to his left hand and extended his hand to Will. "Thanks, Bowman. You, too, Jeff," he said as he shook hands with them both. "Sorry about taking my feelings out on you just then. I guess I was so caught up in the ruckus I wasn't thinkin' straight. I reckon Indians was the last things on our minds when we was looking over our land today. But I guarantee you, we' ain't never gonna make that mistake again."

"Look, Tom," Will said. "We're all new to this. We're all going to make our share of mistakes. I should have let you all in on my concerns, but everybody was having such a good time earlier; I didn't want to cause any undue alarm. But it just kept gnawing at me."

"Well, I'm glad it did, and thanks again. You know, you two could have got yourselves killed out there."

"I guess so, but I believe they were as surprised to see us as we were them. I think they were trying real hard just to get the horses and avoid any trouble. In fact, I think the one holding their horses was trying to call the others off when the dog started barking. If he hadn't hooted like an owl when he did, Jeff and I both might have walked right up to him before we saw him, it was so dark in that thicket. I didn't really see what I was shooting at. I just pointed at the sound and fired."

Charles Bigelow put a log on the fire and started poking at the coals with a stick. "I don't think anybody's very sleepy any more. Y'all want some fresh coffee?"

Oliver Cartwright started walking toward his wagon. "Go ahead an' fix some, if you want to, but I know three or four fellers that could use somethin' a long shot stronger than coffee about now."

"I'll take some coffee," Jeff said, then lowered his voice as he looked toward the wagons. "Me and ole Jake will take the first watch. I imagine they're long gone by now, but it won't hurt to keep an eye out just in case, will it, Boy." Jeff scooped the dog into his arms to give him some more well-deserved attention.

Cartwright returned to the now brightly lit fire after retrieving his jug and reassuring his family all was well. The Bigelow brothers also returned to their wagons to help their wives comfort the children and try to get them settled back down. Before long the camp had once again grown quiet, and the men drifted back to the fire.

Jeff took his coffee and the dog and moved into the shadows, away from the fire. He sat next to a tree and gently petted and talked to the dog in his low, calming voice. He scanned the moonlit prairie, two freshly loaded muskets at his side and his hand-gun in his belt. He spent his watch wondering how much bloodshed would occur in Texas as the new settlers continued to push the red man from the home he'd lived and hunted in for centuries.

Chapter 13

Will expected that another group of settlers would be arriving soon, and he wanted to be caught up with the surveying projects at hand before he had settlers stacking up.

The next few days both Will and Jeff got a good taste of what real back-woods surveying was like in the middle of a Texas summer. It didn't take long to work their way from the river into the thicket. As the day got longer and the brush got thicker, they lost the advantage of the cooling breeze that had made their work tolerable along the river and found chiggers and ticks along with the sweltering heat in the brush and high grass.

They realized that in order to get true dimensional accuracy along a property line, Jeff frequently had to drag the chain through the brush. They found the progress painstakingly slow through the thickets. Sometimes they stopped long enough to clear a trail of sorts through the thicket with axes or long bladed knives. Other times they just pushed their way through.

As they got closer to closing the loop on the first property survey at the river, Jeff's anticipation increased with each step. He was confident in his surveying skills, but they were approaching the true test of a surveyor's ability. He had already calculated what the exact distance should be from their last corner marker to the marker they'd placed along the river three days earlier. If he'd selected the last marker location correctly, and if his directional calculations were right along the line they were working on, they should break out of the brush right at the original river marker and his distance calculations should agree with their actual measurement.

Jeff felt the cool river breeze before he saw or heard the river. Soon he stepped out from the brush and dragged the chain down the slope toward the river.

"Do you see it?" Will called, still in the shade of the trees.

"It's here! Right where it's supposed to be!" Jeff's wide grin reflected his feeling of accomplishment.

"Hang on to the chain when you get to the marker. I'll be right there." Will came out of the woods to gauge their success. He approached Jeff and took the chain from him to note the distance to the marker.

"Well?" Jeff was anxious for Will to finish his verification calculations.

"Mister Surveyor, looks like you just finished your first perfect surveying job. Congratulations!"

"All *right*!" Jeff pumped Will's hand, laughing a big throaty laugh. "All right. Whew! I'm glad that one's over." Jeff removed this hat to wipe the sweat from his head. "I imagine they'll get easier from here on out."

"We're not finished yet," Will said. "There's one more thing to do. Let's get the horses and stow the gear."

"If we're not through, why are we going to stow the gear?"

"You'll see. Come on, we've got to go find those settlers. I imagine they're down river a ways at one of those clearings we saw back off the river the other day. We'll just run on down there and let them know we're done with Charles' place. If you want to, we'll camp with them tonight."

Jeff grinned. "Sounds good to me. I do enjoy those ladies' cooking."

They finished stowing the gear and turned their horses down river. It was late afternoon when they came upon their friends working in a clearing. The location for their cabin was on a bluff, overlooking the river to the east and the countryside beyond it.

"Howdy!" Charles Bigelow called when he saw them approaching. His hands were full of harness reins as he walked behind his team pulling a log to what Will had determined was their building site. Several other logs already had been felled, trimmed, and brought to the site.

"Looks like you've found a perfect location for your home,"

Will said. "Just look at the view!" He faced east, scanning the countryside beyond the bluff and river to the valley on the other side.

"You're going to get a good summer breeze here too. It sure feels good now."

"We didn't look no more when we found this place. Did you fellers get done with the surveyin' here?"

"Just a little while ago," Will answered. "We wanted to come down and see what spot you had taken for your cabin. From the looks of it, I don't think you could have done any better."

"I know the missus likes it." Charles unfastened the chain from around the log. "She was still pretty upset over that Indian scrape when we took off yesterday mornin' lookin' for our cabin site. But you know, soon as she saw this place, it was like she almost forgot all about it."

"I know she'll be even happier when you get your cabin up," Jeff said.

"Got a lot of work in front of us, but we'll have a roof over our heads before long with all of us workin' together. I got one more log to drag back that the boys are finishin' trimmin' up now. Then we're gonna quit fer the day. Come along with me and say hello. You boys are gonna have supper with us and stay here tonight, ain't ya?"

Will chuckled. "We could be persuaded."

Will and Jeff greeted and complimented the men on their work as they finished trimming the log they had just felled. They all headed back to the cabin site with Charles' team dragging the last log of the day. They had established a comfortable campsite under some live oaks in what would be the back yard of the cabin.

The women were working on supper, which included several fried squirrels that Roger Bigelow had bagged earlier in the day. It looked like the teenager had been given the assignment of providing meat for the three families while the men labored on the home-building chores.

While Jeff and the other men were taking care of the horses for the night, Will pulled a clean piece of paper from his saddlebags and sat down next to the working maps he had updated earlier. At the top of the page, he neatly wrote:

> Land Grant
>
> Issued to Charles Bigelow and family, consisting of one labor and one league of land which amounts to 4,605 acres of land. This parcel of land is situated on the west bank of the Brazos River as indicated below. Title to be registered in San Felipe, Texas by the Austin and Williams Land Company.

Will then carefully drew a map of the property lines, indicating the distance between and the exact locations as they related to the latitude and longitude of the reference points. Below the map, he again carefully printed

> Survey completed and ownership celebration performed August 19, 1829.
>
> William H. Bowman and Jeff Jefferson, Surveyors

By the time Will finished the map; Jeff had tended to the animals for the evening and was returning to the camp.

"Come here a minute, Jeff," Will called. Jeff and the pup came over and sat next to Will. "This is our unfinished business." Will penned his signature at the bottom of the page and then handed it to Jeff.

A smile spread across Jeff's face as he slowly read the document. "They'll be proud of this." He dipped the quill pen in the ink bottle and carefully signed his name and handed the paper and pen back to Will.

"We'll take care of this after supper," Will said before he blew the ink dry and put the paper back in his folder.

After supper and clean up, there were still a few minutes of twilight left at the end of the long summer day. The families were beginning to relax around the campfire when Will spoke. "Charles, even though you've taken possession of your property and started building your home, there are still some things that need to be done before we can make your ownership official."

A worry wrinkle formed on Charles' brow. "What's that?"

"We can't do it here. We have to all get up and go over there by the bluff to do it." Will got to his feet and motioned for everyone to follow. "All right, everybody up. Come on, everybody — men, women, and kids — everybody." They all got up to follow him across the clearing to the bluff overlooking the panoramic view of the river and the tree-tops beyond. Each was looking toward the others and at Jeff, wondering whether this normally serious young surveyor had taken leave of his senses.

When he arrived at a spot about thirty feet from the edge of the bluff, Will stopped and took a deep breath, enjoying the evening breeze as it blew through his hair while he waited for everyone to gather around him.

"All right, I want you to form a circle around me, husbands and wives together and their children next to them." They all started moving around him forming a circle, each beginning to share a smile as they joined hands.

"Now what we are going to do is something that's very special that Mister Austin requires of all his settlers. It's a tradition that we call the ownership celebration. He even writes it in your title that you've done this to seal the ownership of your land.

"First I want to give this to you, Charles. It needs to be read out loud." He handed the crisp paper that he'd completed before supper to Charles Bigelow.

Bigelow stood for a moment looking at the paper. When he recognized what it was, his throat tightened and his vision blurred for a moment. Then he cleared his throat and took a deep breath. “It's a map. It's a map of our property lines.” He looked up at his wife and smiled before looking back at the paper. “It says we've got four thousand, six hundred and five acres. Says that the title will be registered in San Felipe by Mister Austin and it's dated and signed by Will and Jeff.” He continued to look at the paper in silence for a moment, then his brother started clapping his hands. Everyone joined in the clapping and shouting congratulations to the new land owners.

When the clapping died down, Will, still standing in the center of the circle, said, “You and me and the people before you and the people that will come after you, all come to Texas for the same reasons. We come to make a new life in a new country.” Will moved slowly in a tight circle so everyone could see his face. “This land you're standing on is the richest land in the world. It will provide well for you if you take care of it. It's the most valuable possession that most of us will ever own, but you won't pay for it with gold and silver. The gold and silver is small, but the toil, blisters and sweat is great. You all came here knowing there would be hardship, and there's already been some danger. There may be more. Your strength might be tested in many ways, but your reward in owning a piece of this country will far outweigh anything else.”

Will looked at the children holding hands in the circle around him and squatted down to meet their level. “For you children, I want you to understand that your mothers and fathers have taken a huge risk moving you so far away from your old homes. There were special reasons they did this for you. They did it so all of you can have a better life as you grow up, and later, when you become mommies and daddies yourselves.”

Will stood again and addressed the adults. “There's hard work ahead for everybody, but there will also be tremendous satisfaction. This land will always be here for you, and for your children and your children's children. You are just the beginning. This is your land. Manage it well and the rewards will be returned to you and yours for generations to come."

Will hesitated for a moment, and smiled at those surrounding him as he continued. "Now, everybody squat down. Come on, just squat down right where you are in the circle just like me." Still clasping hands, everybody started squatting down with some giggling from the children. "Now I want everybody to get two big handfuls of grass and dirt. Just grab as much in each hand as you can." Will was pulling grass and scratching handfuls of dirt along with the others.

Little Mattie lost her balance as she was squatting and fell over to the giggles of the other children. Her father helped her back into the squatting position without her losing any of the grass and dirt in her chubby little hands.

"Now when I count to three, I want everybody to jump up as high as they can and throw the grass and dirt in the air and yell and hoot and holler and make as much noise as you can. Then I want all the mamas and papas and children to hug each other and the men to shake hands. Everybody understand? All right, is everybody ready? Here goes my count: one . . . two . . . three!"

Jeff led the group by hurling his body as high as he could into the air, kicking his legs as he yelled and laughed and threw the bits of grass and dirt high over his head.

The echo of the rites of ownership spread across the valley as the twilight breeze caught the handfuls of grass and the dirt rained back to the earth.

Suddenly the hardship and uncertainty of weeks of travel across country and the wearying work of starting a home on the frontier was forgotten as the entire group was caught up in the celebration. There was an emotional release with the yelling and laughing and jumping up and down, but the real significance of the celebration for the new owners was the confirmation that finally, they were standing on land that would be theirs forever.

Chapter 14

Will and Jeff's work schedule fell into a routine over the next several weeks. They continued to camp where they worked for three or four days, then joined the family whose grant they had completed for a meal. The arrival of new settlers kept them busy, and they had little time to do more than the surveying jobs at hand. By late September they had moved a good distance up the river and the work seemed to get easier in the thickets as the weather started cooling off. After such a hot August, they were enjoying sleeping inside their tent under covers as the night air cooled.

Jacobson and his helper returned in early October with a group of five families. "Looks like we're gonna be kept busy fer awhile," he said the morning he caught up with Will and Jeff. They were stacking stones on a corner marker along the river. "Brought in a bunch of folks with me, and Austin says there will be plenty more comin' soon as harvest is over back east."

Jacobson was a little cleaner looking and smelling than when they had seen him last. He'd had a haircut and a shave, although he now had what appeared to be about an eight day beard. It looked as if someone had attempted to scrub the grease off of his buckskin outfit.

Will said, "We should make good progress with both teams working now. If we can get a little ahead, Jeff and I would like to head back to San Felipe in a few weeks for some rest."

They hadn't intended to stay in the field as long as they had. Their original plan had been to stay two months or so, but they had already been out for over four months. They were both ready for a break from their work and a return to the comforts of civilization. Before daylight one crisp November morning, they left Jacobson with only three families to get settled and headed back to San Felipe. With their horses in good health and well-rested from several months of near idleness, they made good time on the trail south.

They reached San Felipe shortly after dark on their second day on the trail. Because of the hour, all the shops and stores were closed except for the saloon, so they rode directly through town to the Bell home.

The lamp glowed through the front windows as they approached the house. They could see Uncle John through the window, reading by the fire. Jeff imagined Libby would be finishing up in the kitchen after supper.

“Hello in the house!" Will called. “Anybody home?”

Jake, footsore from the long walk, also announced his presence with several deep-throated barks. He had been untethered and allowed to run free for months, but he preferred to stay close to Jeff most of the time. He now ran past the riders to the house, sniffing along the edge of the porch.

They saw John through a window, startled by the noise in the midst of his reading. He pushed himself from his chair, took a moment for his stiff joints to allow him to become erect, and started for the door. Before he got across the room, the door was flung wide by Libby who heard Will’s call and the barking from the kitchen. She stood at the door for a moment, speechless, looking up at Jeff on his mount.

Jeff grinned. “Well, aren't you going to say hello?”

“Oh Jeff! You're back!” She ran across the porch and met him as he slid off his saddle. She grabbed him by his hands and held him out away from her in order to see him better. "And all in one piece, too.”

By then Bell and Tad were on the porch.

“Why, look who's here!” Bell said. “We been looking for you two for a month or better now. You didn't have any trouble did you?”

“No sir,” Will said, “just mighty busy. Jacobson brought a bunch of folks with him when he came back last month. Then they just kept coming in. We didn't meet anybody on the road heading north as we were coming back toward San Felipe, so maybe he can handle it by himself for awhile.”

“What are you doing standing out here in the cold?” Bell said. “Get on in here by the fire, Will, and let them boys take care of the stock.”

Will looked up and down at Tad before handing him his reins. “My gosh, looks like you've grown some since we left.”

“Yes sir, a mite, I guess.”

Will smiled at Libby, who was still holding Jeff's hand. “And it looks like someone made your day.”

“Yes he did. Thanks for bringing him home.”

“It was time for both of us to get out of the woods for a while.”

“Libby, get these men something to eat,” Bell said. “I bet they're starving. Will, get on in the house. It's cold out here.”

“Yes sir.” Will chuckled, following his uncle into the house.

“Tad, go get your coat and I'll meet you around back,” Jeff said as he squeezed Libby's hand with one of his and took Baron's reins from Tad with the other.

Tad picked up a stick from the ground and threw it toward the corner of the house, then took off running after Jake as the dog went after the stick.

“I really missed you, Libby,” Jeff said as they slowly followed Tad toward the corner of the house.

“I missed you, too.” They had reached the corner of the house, out of sight from the front windows and before they turned into Tad's view. Jeff pulled Libby close and just held her for a moment. She lifted her face to meet his in an eager kiss. Jeff could feel her tremble beneath the thin fabric of her dress. As their lips parted, she said, “I was all right for the first couple of months, but the longer you were gone, the more I worried.”

“I told you before we left, I'd be fine. Now here I am, safe and sound."

As they continued their walk toward the rear of the house, Jeff realized Libby was shivering.

"Here," he said when they reached the back door. "You have no business out here in the cold in just that dress. You get on back inside. Tad and I will be back in a little while." He gave her another quick kiss before she went inside.

Tad was coming out of the kitchen door as she entered.

"I tole ya he'd be all growed up next time I seen him," Tad said, reaching to grab at Jake's ears as they walked toward the barn. "Shore is turnin' out to be a bigun, ain't he?"

"I guess he is. I know he can't ride on my saddle with me like he did when we rode out of here. He sure is a good dog. Even brings in supper sometimes."

"Really?" Tad gave Jeff a questioning look as if Jeff might be stretching the truth a little about his dog.

"Really. He's brought in rabbits several times when all he'd done is just break their neck. He brought them right into camp and laid them at my feet with hardly any more damage than a little slobber. Of course there were a few times he brought in varmints that weren't fit for the pot, but that wasn't his fault. He just doesn't distinguish one animal from the other. He thinks if he can bring it down, we ought to eat it. He's a good hunting dog, but he's an even better watch dog."

By then they reached the barn. After Jeff found and lit a lantern, Tad began unsaddling Baron while Jeff started on the pack horses.

"Did he bring an Indian back to the camp for supper too, with nothing but slobber on him?" Tad laughed.

"No, but he did scare up a few who were trying to steal the horses one night."

"He did?" Tad suddenly forgot about jokes and immediately become serious. "What happened?"

Jeff left out a few details of his Indian story and told it as if Jake had just scared the Indians away with his barking. "Oh, yes,

I almost forgot." Jeff walked to the far side of one of the pack horses and untied the long, colorful lance he had been saving. "Somebody told me this was Kiowa. One of them dropped it trying to steal the horses when ole Jake flushed them out. I understand they don't attack the settlers too often, but they're born to steal. Here," he said, and handed it to Tad. "I've been saving it for you."

"Gosh, thanks, Jeff!" Tad rubbed his hands over the shaft and fingered the metal point and the feathers.

"Thanks a lot!"

When they returned to the house, Jeff gave Jake instructions to stay by the back door before they went inside.

Libby was working with her back to the door, preparing two plates with leftovers when Jeff and Tad opened the door, allowing the cold wind to blow in with them.

"Lookey here what Jeff gave me!" Tad said, dragging the colorful lance through the door.

Libby's breath caught in her throat when she turned from the counter to see the weapon in Tad's hand. Now that she was in the light, Jeff saw the swelling and discoloration on her left cheek.

"Where did you get that?" Libby asked, shocked, pointing at the lance.

"That's not important, Libby. What I want to know is how you got *that*?" Jeff approached Libby for a closer look at her face. Outside, in the dark, he hadn't seen the bruises and swelling. Now, in the light, he could see what she had hoped to hide from him. He gently put his hands on either side of her face and tilted her cheek so he could see her injury better.

She averted her gaze as he looked at her cheek. "I fell. It's nothing." She pulled away from Jeff and went back to work fixing Jeff's and Will's plates. "I just tripped and fell down the back steps the other day. It'll be all right."

They were interrupted when Bell came in the kitchen to ask if Will's supper was ready.

"Yes sir, I'll bring it right out." Libby grabbed the plate of food and retrieved silverware and a napkin from drawers in a cabinet. "Tad, bring a glass and that pitcher of milk."

After delivering Will's supper with an apology for the leftovers and a promise of a proper supper the next night, Libby returned to the kitchen where Jeff was finishing washing his hands in the basin.

Jeff had taken off his coat exposing his worn shirt and trousers with the many rips and tears he had accumulated over the months when he stretched the chain through mesquite brush and other thorny thickets. He'd attempted to make repairs himself with the needle and thread his mama put in his kit before he left Virginia. He soon realized he was much better at almost anything than dealing with a needle and thread with his large hands.

"Goodness gracious!" Libby said. "Did you get in a fight with a bobcat?"

"Kinda looks like it, doesn't it?" Jeff grinned as he looked down at his tattered clothes. "More like a bunch of scuffles with mesquite brush and other thickets out there. I'm afraid I'm not too good with a needle and thread."

"You shouldn't have to be. I'll take care of those later."

"I don't think there's much left to patch. I just thought I'd buy some new from Mister Bell. But enough about me. Tell me about you. Are you all right?"

Libby knew exactly what Jeff was asking, and she knew she had to make herself sound convincing. As much as she had prayed for the day when Jeff would return, she dreaded the fact that she would have to lie to him.

"I'm fine Jeff; everything's all right."

Jeff couldn't ask all the questions he wanted to with Tad sitting across the table, but he was concerned about her swollen and bruised cheek. "When did you fall?"

"It must have been about four days ago."

"You should'a seen her then," Tad offered. "The whole side

of her face was all swoled up. It's a lot better now."

Libby sat Jeff's plate in front of him and seated herself at the table next to him. "I told you I'm fine, now let's talk about you. Tell me what all you've been doing." She smiled, looking into his eyes as he cut into the roast beef she had placed in front of him. "Don't leave out a thing."

John Bell stared across the table at the hungry young man with a week's growth of beard on his chin and his light brown hair hanging well below his frayed collar as he ate his supper. Will's clothes were only in slightly better shape than Jeff's. "Looks like you two earned your pay out there."

Will smiled between bites of biscuit and potatoes. "I am afraid my papa wouldn't claim me if he saw me now. I imagine I must be a mess."

"No different from most men around here. You run across any Indians up north?"

"Oh, a handful tried to run the horses off one night, right after we got up to where the surveying started but we haven't seen any since. Jacobson said the lance they dropped in their getaway indicated that they were Kiowa."

"That's good. If they was Comanches, they would'a got them horses and maybe that long hair of yours too. Boy, it concerns me, you being that far north and all. You're getting into Comanche country."

"We learned a few things this trip, and we had the help of old Jake out there. I think he's just a natural Indian dog. He's the one that spooked them that night. He won't even sleep in the tent with us. He likes to be outside, just kind of keeping an eye on things."

John noticed that Will had cleaned his plate and was finishing the milk in his glass. "How about some more?"

"Oh, no sir, that was plenty. My, that girl can cook!"

"That's just leftovers. Wait 'til tomorrow night. You'll think you'd died and gone to heaven. I'll have her fix one of her pies. I guess you'll probably want a bath. Let me get Libby to start heating up some water. Oh, by the way, you got some mail while you were gone. I went ahead and brought it home. It's on the dresser in your room." He turned toward the kitchen. "Libby!" he called in a louder than normal voice. "Put some water on to heat; Will's going to take a bath."

Libby's and Tad's visit with Jeff was cut short as Tad and Jeff shared the chore of bringing in several buckets full of water from the well behind the house. Tad brought the bathtub from where it hung on a nail on the back porch and put it in the middle of Will's bedroom while Libby heated water in two big pots over the fire. Jeff took the table scraps and some of the leftover beef out to feed Jake, then went out to the barn to bring in Will's saddlebags, some clean underwear and his dress suit, which was the only decent outfit Will had left to wear.

Then Jeff continued telling Libby about his life in the wilderness, living in a tent and working through the summer heat and into the late fall while she cleaned the kitchen. Between trips helping Tad carry buckets of hot water to Will's room for his bath, he described the positive attitude and hard-working nature of the settlers, who work from daylight to dark to provide a home for their families as soon as possible after locating their land.

Libby was beginning to overcome her nervousness at seeing Jeff again as she pressed the wrinkles out of Will's suit with the heavy pressing iron that she heated with hot coals. Jeff's deep voice soothed and comforted her while she worked. He recounted his days of living, working, hunting, and sleeping in the wild country. She wondered whether he thought of her the many lonely nights that she'd lain awake in her bed thinking of him. There was so much she wanted to share with him. She wanted to tell him about her fears; about the nights she wished he was with her to wrap his big arms around her and make the fear go away. But they were fears she couldn't share with anyone.

Never before had she been afraid of anything while working

for Mister Bell until Farley came along. She didn't know whether she hated him or feared him more. He had stayed away for a good while after Bell and Tad went out to the farm right after Jeff and Will headed north, but recently he had been back twice. Both times had been in the afternoon, after he had been drinking in town. The first time was like the initial encounter. He walked into the kitchen just wanting coffee. Libby was uncomfortable when he stared at her and made several suggestive remarks, but was relieved when he left before Bell got home. The last time he came, just four days earlier, he started grabbing at her. As she tried to push him away, he hit her with his fist and knocked her to the floor. Her fighting must have had a sobering effect on him. He left her lying on the floor trying to push away from him. Her last memory of the incident was him standing over her, swaying and pointing at her as he screamed, "I'll be back. You'll give me what I'm after!"

She had already decided that whatever happened with Farley she would handle it herself. She knew that if she told Bell, even if Bell fired him, somehow Farley would do something vengeful. She also knew she couldn't tell Jeff. Though she had known him only for a short while before he left, she knew that inside that hulk of a man was a gentle and tender heart. She also knew that his gentleness would be overcome by his outrage at what another man had done to her if he knew. Jeff, with all his strength, would break Farley like a match. And like every other slave, she knew what would happen if a black man attacked a white man. No, she couldn't tell Jeff. This was her problem. She would have to handle it in whatever way she could.

Will felt better after his bath and shave than he had in months. Several times while he was soaking in his bath in between Tad and Jeff's deliveries of hot water he had glanced at the dressing table where the letter was waiting to be read. He picked up the envelope before he got undressed for his bath and held it for a moment — then put it back in place. He wanted to wait until he was clean and relaxed to read it.

Now that Tad had finished emptying the tub and removed it from the room, Will was alone with his letter. He picked it up from the dressing table and took it to the bed. After turning up the lamp, he crawled under the covers, opened the envelope and started to read.

> My Dear Will,
>
> I am so excited! I just got your letter. Thank you for writing to me. I know that you are away from where you can get this mail, but I just wanted to write you anyway. I know I won't hear from you for awhile, but it won't keep me from thinking about you. Please don't think of me as a silly girl for telling you what I feel. I'm old enough to know my feelings.
>
> The next time you write to me, tell me exactly what you do when you survey the land. I want to imagine that I see you as you go about your work.
>
> I hope it's not cold where you are. Mary told me you sleep in a tent. I hope you can stay warm.
>
> We are going home for Christmas. Papa has already hired a driver to take us home. I'll be glad to see the family again. I wish you could be there too. I hope you can at least spend the holiday with your uncle.
>
> I've got to finish this now. It's getting late, but I wanted you to know how much I look forward to hearing from you and knowing that you are safe and well.
>
> Thinking of you daily,
>
> Anna

Will reached over and blew out the lamp, then lay there in the clean, soft, warm bed and thought of Anna. *If she wants mail from me, she should be pleasantly surprised when she receives her next packet of mail from Texas.*

There were many nights that Jeff read by the fire while Will wrote letters, knowing they would have to wait awhile before they could be mailed. He wrote to everyone in his family and some friends from the academy, but most of the letters were written to Anna. He wondered whether she had been thinking of him at the same times he was thinking of and writing to her. He finally ran out of writing paper, but still continued to put his thoughts in his journal. He hoped that if he posted the letters with a package tomorrow, they would arrive before Christmas.

Will's eyes closed to the soundest sleep he had enjoyed in months, the letter still in his hand.

Chapter 15

"It's sure going to feel good to get all that off my neck and shoulders," Will told Libby as she started trimming his long hair. Libby had cut her master's hair for years, though most of it had thinned so that now she usually just trimmed a little around his ears and at the back of his neck. She also cut her brother's hair when she could get him to sit still long enough.

Will had his haircut first, before Jeff. Afterwards, he dressed in his freshly pressed suit and the boots that Tad had shined and headed to town with his uncle and Tad.

Before he stepped off the porch with Will, Bell said, "Libby, I want you to plan a nice welcome home dinner for Will tonight."

"I'll throw in some of your favorites too," Libby answered, smiling, already planning her menu.

After the other men and Tad left the house, Jeff sat in the straight-backed chair Libby brought out to the porch from the kitchen for the haircuts. He had a towel draped over his broad shoulders and Jake at his feet. The cool morning air was warming into what would become a warm late-November day. He enjoyed the feel of Libby's fingers and comb running through his hair, gauging the length for each cut of her scissors. He daydreamed, thinking about his and Libby's reunion and their goodnight kiss the night before. She quietly hummed as she cut his hair.

He decided to let the concern that he had about Farley pass. Libby didn't want to talk about it, and he wanted to keep his time with her pleasant instead of bringing up troublesome matters. Jeff thought Bell's visit to the farm had put a stop to Farley's drinking in town and his visits to the Bell home. He hoped so anyway. He wasn't going to spoil Libby's mood or happiness by mentioning it again.

Jeff was dressed in his best clothes, which weren't as ragged as those he wore the night before. He gave his other shirt and trousers to Libby to use as rags around the house.

“What are you and Mister Will planning to do while you're here?”

“I imagine we'll do some work for Mister Austin. We've got to bring his maps up to date with what we've done up north, and Will wants to learn more about registering the titles and some of the other paperwork that goes along with the people getting their land. We might be able to help Mister Bell some at the store too, and maybe do a little fishing and hunting.”

“How long do you think you can stay before you have to go back north?”

“Will says we'll stay till after the New Year. By then the new folks should be stacking up on us again. Besides, we've still got to decide on our own places.”

“You mean Mister Will hasn't found his own place yet?”

“No, nor me either. We've been too busy settling other people in to think much about our own property.”

“Wait a minute.” Libby stopped cutting Jeff's hair and moved around to look directly at him. “You mean you're getting land, just like a white man?”

“That's right.” Jeff smiled up at Libby. “That's what Señor Vargas told me and Will when he gave me my freedom papers. He said I've got the same rights as any other man. That means I get the same share of land as other men. All I've got to do is decide which piece I want for myself and pay Mister Austin a fee of thirty dollars. Will said Mister Austin will even take that out in trade for work. Then I pay the government $87.50. I don't even have to pay the government their money for four years.

“Naturally I'm not going to choose my land until Will gets ready to choose his. Then I'll have my place next to his. The best part about it is, the law says I don't have to do anything with it for six years if I don't want to. Then I've got to start working it to keep it. In the meantime, I can keep surveying and earn more money. That way, I'll be able to earn the money to do whatever I want when I do take up the land." Jeff's face broke into a bright smile as he watched Libby's expression turn to awe.

As she stood, listening to him explain the rights of new Texas settlers, her jaw got more slack with every benefit he mentioned. She slowly sat on the other chair that Bell brought to the porch to sit on while she finished Will's haircut.

"I never imagined one of us would ever own his own land, much less be free to do with it whatever he wanted. Jeff, I'm so happy for you. It makes me so proud to know you. You can read and write, and you know how to do something more important than hoe cotton."

"Don't you put down chopping cotton. That's an honorable thing to do, especially if it's your own cotton you're chopping. One of these days, that's exactly what I'll be doing. I'll be working my own land. This surveying won't last forever. When it plays out, we'll have our land. That land will always be there, and it will always be ours. That's what we all came for. It will just be up to its owner to make something out of it. Will and I plan to do just that."

"I'm going to start adding Mister Will to my prayers every night when I ask the Lord to watch over you. He's such a good man to have done what he has for you."

"Libby, I guess I'd do anything for that man. He's already shown me he'll do anything for me. He's given me so much already. I'll never be able to repay him for what he's done for me."

"Maybe someday you'll find a way."

Will found Austin and Williams in their office as he had hoped and visited with them awhile, bringing them up to date regarding the activities up north. He didn't bring his maps or other documentation with him, as he had planned to spend the next several days working in the land office with Austin, making the maps current and filing the settler's papers.

"Looks like living in the wild agrees with you, Bowman," Austin said.

"Guess I just thrive on fresh air and plenty of room to move around. Besides, Jeff's gotten to be a pretty good cook. I will admit, though, we do enjoy a meal every now and then cooked by some of the ladies who are settling in. But you know what we enjoy most?"

"What's that?"

"When the surveying is done on each plot, we hold the ownership celebration with each family. Somehow it's always turned into a nice little party. It's a really good way for the new people to celebrate the completion of a long journey and the ownership of their new land, but it also allows Jeff and me to celebrate our completion of another job."

Will and Austin firmed their agreement on how Austin would credit Will for part of his wages in extra land allotment. Then they settled the remainder in cash. Will traded a third of his fee for extra land. The remainder he took in cash so he could pay Jefferson his split and keep a little for himself.

Will left the land office and headed across the street to his uncle's store.

"Come on in, Will," the old man called over a customer's shoulder, his loud voice startling the woman he was assisting. "Go on and look around."

Will spent the next few minutes wandering around the store, inspecting his uncle's merchandise. This was the first time he really had an opportunity to spend much time browsing in the store. The last time he and Jeff were in town, they had been so busy working with Austin, they hadn't had time to visit with Bell in his store except the day they picked up a few supplies before heading north.

Will found the store surprisingly well stocked. There was a section set aside for saddles, harnesses, and other leather goods. Tools of all description were scattered about the store. Some leaned in a corner. Others sat propped along the walls and hung from the ceiling. He also had a handful of guns, kegs of powder and pounds of lead for melting down into rifle balls. He also had a display of knives along part of one wall. Several shelves housed ready-made shoes, boots and clothes for men, women and children. There were bolts of cotton and wool for those who didn't spin and weave their own. In another section he stored his staple goods. Sacks of sugar, salt, coffee, corn meal, wheat flour and rice were neatly stacked on the floor. Tins of other edible goods crowded the shelves. Tobacco goods of all kinds were available. Bunches of raw leaves were hanging from the ceiling. Cigars and blended pipe tobacco was arranged behind the counter. Jugs of whiskey and rum was available as well.

In a case next to the cash drawer counter, Will found some items that he least expected to see in such a remote part of Texas. Under the glass in the display, he found several finely decorated carved bone, ivory, and cast-pewter items that looked out of place in the littered general store. The items in this case appeared to have been imported from around the world. There were bone-handled razors from England and ivory-handled scissors from Italy. There were also several pewter cups and comb and mirror sets from elsewhere in Europe. He was also surprised to see some brightly colored silk fans from the orient.

After a few minutes the customer Bell was dealing with made her purchase and left. John joined Will at the display case.

"Pretty fancy stuff for an old country store, huh? A feller came in here two or three months ago with these things. He'd bought them off a merchant ship at New Orleans. I get all kinds of stuff in here from time to time. Even got a piano in here last year. Sold it to one of the big planters who has his place down south of here a ways."

"Looks to me like you have just about anything anybody would want," Will said.

"I do all right, I guess. Just getting too old to mess with all of this, though. I set this place up just to keep myself busy when my wife talked me into moving to town. Now between running the store full time and still trying to keep the farm going, it's about to get me down. I did all right with the farm ‘til my last foreman left me. Seems like I've got to keep a close eye on the one I've got out there now, just to keep him on the job. I’ve caught him drinking several times.” Bell looked at the floor and shook his head, then looked back at Will. “I just don't trust him. I'd run him off if I could find someone else to take over. Nobody's interested in looking after somebody else's place when they can get their own as easy as they can. As long as I run out there every couple of weeks or so and take the supplies myself and try to see that there's no whiskey on the place, he does all right, I guess.

Well anyway, enough of that. I shouldn't be burdening you with all that. Did you find what you want to send home to that pretty sister of yours?”

“I guess I've found everything right here in this case that I want to send home.”

“Didn't you tell me you had a bunch of mail to send home too?”

“Yes sir. I've got a good sized bundle here in my pocket.”

“We'd better get it all packaged up then if it's to leave on that barge this afternoon.” Bell went off looking for a wooden box in which to pack Will's gifts and packages.

Will selected one of the comb and mirror sets for Anna, a silk fan for Mary and a fancy, bone-handled razor for his father. While he was packaging his gifts individually, Jeff entered the store to do his own shopping. After investigating the entire store as Will had done earlier, he settled on a small pair of scissors for this mother and a razor similar to the one Will had selected for his father. It was apparent that Jeff’s and Will's tastes for gifts were similar when he selected another of the comb and mirror sets for Libby. He also chose a shiny red spinning top for Tad while Tad was in the back room. As they completed packaging each of their gifts, Bell produced a small but stout wooden box from the back of the store. After Will wrote "Do not open ‘til

Christmas" on all the packages, the goods were placed inside with all the letters that Will had written, and the box was prepared for shipping.

Once the letters and Christmas gifts were packed and ready for pick up, Will and Jeff turned to the men's ready-made section of the store to outfit themselves. They both selected two pairs of pants and two shirts. They also bought blankets for the cold nights that would come in January when they headed back to their surveying.

With his shopping completed, Jeff returned to the house to help Libby with her chores. She was glad for the help but enjoyed Jeff's company even more than his assistance. The work wasn't much like work at all with Jeff giving her a hand when she needed it and her shooing him out of the way when she didn't. Most of all, she enjoyed how he made her laugh. She hadn't realized how long it had been since she'd heard herself laugh.

She kneaded a batch of wheat dough while Jeff watched from the table. “You haven't told me much about your studies,” she said. “How's that going? Is Mister Will still working with you?”

“Not every day like he used to, but I don't need that much help anymore. I guess I can read about as well as most people now. I've read all the books we brought with us, and I go back to Will's bible almost every day and read some of it. I try to memorize words and meanings from the dictionary several times a week. When Will works with me now, it's usually with math. I really enjoy some of the problems he gives me. It's sort of like solving puzzles. I can use all the surveying instruments almost as good as he can. The last several jobs we did, he let me do all the instrument work. He just checked my calculations to make sure I was right. I really like that part. I was right most every time. The few times I was off a little, we figured out why right then and there, and I learned not to make that mistake again.”

Libby stopped working to look Jeff in the eyes.

“Oh Jeff, just think — less than a year ago you were a stable slave and a blacksmith. Now you’re an educated man. Why, there's places back in the states where it's against the law for a slave to even have a pen and paper. Violations like that would draw a whipping for sure.”

“I know,” Jeff said. “There are some people who think like that here, too. That's why I don't make much of what I can do. Most white folks that we've run into don't even know I'm a free man, but I do and Will does. That's what matters. He treats me like a man and a friend.

“If I ever do get into a situation where Will's not around and I have to prove my freedom, I can. That's why I always carry this case with my freedom letter and my little journal with writing materials right here on my belt. I can always prove my status.”

For the next couple of weeks Will and Jeff worked long hours at the land office with Austin and Williams bringing their maps up to date and preparing title information that Austin then translated into Spanish. The influx of new settlers had caused a buildup of land title paperwork that needed to be completed and then filed with the government.

One afternoon Austin approached Will and Jeff shortly after he returned from lunch. “You two have really made a difference since you’ve been helping Williams and me get caught up on the paperwork. We’ve almost got the backlog taken care of now. Why don’t you give yourselves a break and take off the rest of the day and tomorrow and do what you intended to do when you came back to town — get some rest.”

“I guess a fellow can’t turn down an offer like that,” Will said looking up from his work. “Jeff, what do you say we take him up on it?”

Jeff looked at Austin. “You sure you can make do all right?”

“We’ll do fine. You boys go on home. You deserve some time to yourselves.”

Will and Jeff left the land office and walked across the street to Bell's store to let John know they were going home early. As soon as Jeff followed Will into the store they could tell something had the old man stirred up.

"What's the matter?" Will asked.

"Oh, it's that Farley! I should have run him off the last time I warned him about this. I just talked to the saloon keeper down the street. Said Farley's been there all morning. Left a little while ago, roaring drunk."

"How long has he been gone?" Jeff demanded, trying not to scream the words as a flood of panic rushed over him.

"I don't know, maybe a half-hour or better, I guess. Why?"

"Come on, Will!" Jeff spun around and ran for the door. As he reached the door, he looked back to find Will and Bell still standing where he had left them, shocked by his behavior and the fearful expression on his face. "Will, I don't have time to explain! Come on! *Now!*"

By the time Will made it out the door, Jeff was already beyond the stores, running as fast as he could toward the Bell home. He covered the quarter-mile between the store and the house in just a few minutes. He saw the sorrel with the worn saddle tied to the tree as he approached the house. He raced to the back of the house and through the back door. "Libby! Libby!" he shouted as he rushed through each room of the house.

Will was approaching the house as Jeff ran out the back door and sprinted toward Libby's cabin.

Outside the cabin door Jeff heard a muffled scream. He threw the door open and found Libby sprawled across her bed, trying to fight off a dirty, fat man three times her size.

The lifelong knowledge of what happens to a black man who attacks a white man fled Jeff's mind when he saw the terror and pain on Libby's face. The man was holding what was left of the top of her dress in one fist and hitting her in the face with his other. Jeff's rage erupted in a scream as he lunged at the man. Farley turned away from Libby just as Jeff grabbed his shirt collar and spun him around, then knocked him to the floor with a blow to his jaw. Jeff fell on top of him, pinning him to the floor, raining one blow after the other into the man's face with his huge, rock-hard fists.

The scene became clear to Will when he saw the horse tied to the tree and Jeff running from the house toward the cabin calling Libby's name. Jeff was pummeling the man when Will raced through the door. “Jeff, stop! Stop it! You hear me? You're going to kill him!” Will pulled Jeff off the bloody lump on the floor. Jeff looked at Farley’s face, then at his own fists, stifling a cry as he slowly realized how close he had come to beating a man to death. He pushed himself away from Farley and turned to Libby.

She sat on the bed, trying to hold her dress together, crying. Blood and tears were flowing together down her face. “Oh Jeff! I thought he was going to kill me!”

He knelt and gently folded his arms around her. Tenderly, he stroked her hair as she buried her head in his shoulder and sobbed. “You're all right now. Nobody's going hurt you anymore. You'll be fine. It’s gonna be all right, Libby.” He took his kerchief from around his neck. Cradling her face in both of his hands, one of them bleeding at the knuckles, he started wiping away the blood and tears to see how badly she was hurt. After determining that she had a cut on her eyebrow, another on her lip, and a couple of scrapes and bruises on her cheeks that were starting to swell, he again held her close to comfort her.

Will pulled the unconscious Farley across the floor, away from Jeff and Libby, thinking Farley probably had passed out as much from his drinking as from the beating. Jake, who had been scratching and whining at the cabin door, was now by Jeff's side whimpering in his confusion.

“Jeff?” Will said quietly from across the room. “I'm taking him on out of here. Come give me a hand when you can leave her.”

Jeff nodded his understanding and continued whispering in

Libby's ear and stroking her hair.

Will dragged Farley into the yard, then returned to the cabin. “Come on, Jake; they need to be alone.” The dog followed Will from the cabin and started sniffing at Farley as Will closed the door. When Jake hiked his leg over Farley, Will just turned his back.

Bell and Tad rounded the corner by the back porch as Will turned back to Farley.

“That’s about what I figured!” Bell said when he got close to Will and recognized the figure on the ground. “She didn't fall and hit her head on the steps awhile back either, did she?”

“Probably not," Will said.

“That bastard!” Bell said flatly. “Libby — how is she?”

“She's pretty shaken up. A few cuts and bruises, but I think he was too drunk for anything else. Jeff's in there with her now.”

Bell reached down and lifted the man's face out of the dirt by his hair. “Good Lord! Who did this?” He grimaced at the bloody mess that used to be the fat man's face.

“I’m pretty sure he fell down,” Will said.

The magnitude of the afternoon’s events suddenly hit Tad, who had been quietly taking it all in. He started crying and begging to see his sister. Bell knelt on one knee and put his arm around the scared boy’s shoulder. “She's all right, Boy,” Bell said calmly. “Jeff's with her now. He's taking care of her. She'll be all right. You'll see.”

Bell was still calming Tad with his back to the cabin door when Jeff emerged from the cabin. He stood there for a moment, watching the old man comfort a member of the only family he’d had for the last several years.

“Tad, she'll be all right,” Jeff said quietly. “She just needs to rest for a while. I'm sure she'd like to see you if you want to go in for a few minutes. Just don't stay long, okay?”

Tad nodded, then quietly opened the door and stepped into the cabin, closing the door behind him.

Will looked at his uncle and nodded toward the still

unconscious figure on the ground. “What should we do with this?"

“If things had been just a little different, I’d have the bastard dancing at the end of a rope.” Bell said scornfully. “I guess under the circumstances the most we can do is just run him out of the territory.

“Will, try to sober him up. When you get him to where he can sit a horse and understand what a man is saying to him, let me know. I've got a thing or two to say, and I want to make sure he understands every word.”

Bell turned without another word and went into the house. Will and Jeff dragged Farley across the yard and propped him against the rock wall of the water well. Jeff drew a bucketful of water and threw the contents in Farley's face. There was a little reaction but Farley didn't regain his senses. After four more buckets-full in the chilly December afternoon, Farley was completely drenched and his shivering brought him around. When Will was convinced that Farley knew who and where he was, he asked Jeff to go get his uncle.

Bell returned to the yard and stood before the shivering man cowering next to the well. “All right, you sorry bastard, can you hear me?” It was the coldest voice Will had ever heard. Farley nodded without looking up.

“You better hear every word I say and hear it good, because your life depends on it.” Bell said. He hesitated a moment, then continued. “That little girl you half-killed in there is like family to me. My wife pulled her out of her mama's womb. I've taken care of her all her life and I expect her to take care of me the rest of mine. I ought to just turn these boys loose on you and let them finish what they started, but I'm too disgusted with you to ask them to dirty their hands on you any more. I'm going to let somebody else hang you or blow your head off because you won't last much longer in a decent man's world.

“Listen close to what I have to say. I want you to understand that you are to get your sorry ass out of Texas as fast as that horse will take you. If you ride that horse to the ground, then you'd better pray your shoe leather holds out. You're not to stop till you cross the Sabine River.

"You know I'm not without influence throughout Texas. I'm tellin' you, the word goes out on you tonight. You damn well better hope you stay ahead of it. You're not welcome anywhere in Texas. I hope you never make me wish I'd killed you tonight, because I promise you Mister, if I *ever* see your sorry face again as long as I live, I'll kill you. You're not to go back to my place and get your things. You just forfeited whatever you've got there. Now, do you understand everything I've said?"

Farley peered through the bloody slits of his rapidly swelling eyes at the men standing over him and nodded again, still shivering.

"All right, I'm glad we understand each other. Now you get on that horse, ride out to that road there, turn north, ride as hard as you can till you get to the Nacogdoches road, then go east. Now *get*!"

Farley scrambled to his feet, climbed on his horse and within seconds was gone.

Chapter 16

Jeff was up by daylight, making coffee before anyone else was moving about. Bell had told Libby the night before to stay in her cabin and rest a day or two. Jeff offered to see that everybody got fed and take care of the house until she started feeling better.

Tad came in the back door with an armload of kindling and started the fire in the sitting room to take the morning chill off the house.

"How's she doing this morning?" Jeff asked as Tad sat down in the kitchen chair for a couple of minutes before he went to get a bigger log for the fire.

"She was asleep when I left, but I think she was awake most all night."

"We'll let her sleep awhile; then I'll take her a tray out later."

Jeff had started the bacon in the frying pan when he heard Bell coughing. Soon Bell and Will were both in the sitting room, putting their boots on by the fire.

"Will?" Bell said, scratching the white stubble on his neck. "Do you think you and Tad could look after the store for a couple of days? Tad knows all the prices and most of the customers. He can almost run the place by himself. You'd just have to handle the money and make change."

"You know I will. Why? Where are you going?"

"I just thought if it was all right with you, I'd see if Jeff would ride out to the farm with me and help me take care of a little business down there."

"Sure. I imagine Jeff would be happy to give you a hand. We weren't planning to head back up north 'til after the first of the year anyway."

Soon Jeff announced that breakfast was ready. They all

gathered in the kitchen where Bell had his breakfast every morning with Libby and Tad. He had given up eating by himself after his wife died.

While they were eating, Bell asked Jeff to go along with him to the farm and instructed Tad on how to help Will understand the merchandise. “Just finish stacking the new shipment of flour and sugar closer to the front door. We don't want the ladies to forget the sugar for whatever Christmas baking they'll be doing.”

Will eased Jeff's mind. “I’ll send Tad home for lunch to check on Libby while you’re gone.”

Will and Tad went out to hitch up the team while Jeff hurried into the kitchen to scramble eggs for Libby. He put two strips of bacon on the plate with the eggs and poured a cup of coffee, then put it all on a tray.

“Here, let me take that.” Bell picked up the tray up from the table. “I want to see how she's feeling this morning. You can see her before we leave.”

Jeff opened the door for Bell and watched him head for the cabin, then hurried to clean the breakfast dishes.

Later, with the chores finished and while Bell packed a few things to stay a couple of days away from home, Jeff tapped on Libby's cabin door, then opened it to let himself in. “Libby, you awake?”

“I'm awake. I tried to eat but I’m not hungry.”

Jeff came across the room and knelt beside the bed. He could see why she couldn't eat. She had a terrible swelling along her jaw and her lip was swollen to twice its normal size. He took her hand in his.

She looked into his eyes as tears started welling in hers. “Jeff, I didn't thank you last night. I think he would have killed me if you hadn't got here when you did.”

“I'm just sorry we didn't get here sooner. You're all right now. That's all that matters. You won't have to ever worry about anything like this happening again. Farley's probably already ridden his horse to the ground and is still running as fast as his legs can carry him.

"I'll tell you Lib, that Mister Bell sure surprised me last night. Little old man that he is, he's tough as a boot. I don't think I've ever seen one man as scared of another as Farley was of Mister Bell. And I don't believe I've ever seen a white man as angry as that little man was last night."

Libby tried to laugh at the vision but winced at the pain of her swollen lip.

"Anyway, I just wanted to let you know that I'm going to be gone for a couple of days with Mister Bell. He said he wants me to help him take care of some business out on the farm but we'll be back in a day or two. Will and Tad will keep a close watch on you. Jake will be around here too. You'll be fine with a little rest."

Jeff gently kissed her on the forehead. He stood beside the bed a moment, holding her hand, looking into her eyes before he left.

When he closed the cabin door, he saw that Will and Bell were waiting for him in the wagon. Tad was sitting at the rear of the wagon bed, dangling his legs off the end, grinning at him as he raced across the yard and jumped onto the tail-gate, next to Tad.

They went by the store first to pick up a few items to take to the people on the farm. They loaded a couple of sacks of wheat flour, some sugar, salt and some coffee into the wagon. Bell selected some candy for the children and several bolts of new cotton fabric and thread that he recently received. After a few last minute instructions to Will and Tad, Bell slapped the reins against the horses and turned the wagon south.

It was about a three-hour ride from San Felipe along the Brazos to the Bell farm. Old John was quiet in his own thoughts for the first part of the trip. After a while he spoke. "Well, Boy, what do you think of Texas so far?"

"I think it's the most beautiful place on earth, Mister Bell. I really like it."

"From the looks of you and Will when you first came back from your surveying, it looked to me like you two had seen some of its roughest country."

"Not really, sir. It's just that in the kind of work we do, we can't stand back and enjoy the beauty; we get right in with all of it. Working that close to God's wonders, a man has to take the thorns with the roses. When you see a country as close up as we have, you really get to know it. And when you work with people as close as we have with some of the settlers, you get to know them well too."

"You know, Jeff, Will thinks a lot of you and your capabilities. I'd like to ask you a question."

"What's that, sir?"

"Do you think you are a good judge of people?"

Jeff hesitated a moment before he spoke. "I try to find some good in folks 'til I'm proven wrong. But I guess I've seen a few that I've had my doubts about from the beginning, and they always proved me right."

"The reason I'm asking is that I want you to get to know the men out on my place. I've been around them all for years, but I only know them from my point of view. I guess you'd know better than anybody else that a master doesn't always know his people as they really are. He sees them as they are when they're around him. They might be somebody completely different when he's out of sight.

"There's three men out there. I think they are all good people. They all work hard and don't ask for much. I try to take as good care of them as I can. They and the women and their kids run the place pretty much by themselves. God knows they weren't getting much help or direction from Farley. I just hope he hasn't ruined any of 'em. I've never had any trouble from any of 'em. They've had no reason to give me any. I've never struck any of 'em — ever. All of 'em except the kids have been with me since long before we came to Texas. They've helped make me a decent living, and I owe them good treatment for that. I'm just sorry I didn't run old Farley off long before I did.

“Jeff, what I want you to do is just work with them a day or two and get to know them. I want to honestly know how they feel about the farm and their loyalty to me. I want to know if they still consider Kado their leader. He always seemed to be the spokesman for them. I hope you wouldn't feel that you would be spying on them by doing this. I'm not ready to tell you my reasons for asking you to do this, but I'll have to ask you to trust me. I will tell you that what I'm considering is for their benefit and whatever you tell me won't hurt any of them. Will you do that for me?”

Jeff sat for a moment, quietly thinking before he answered.

“Mister Bell, last night I saw how you comforted that little boy who was crying for his sister, and I saw how concerned you were for Libby. I'll do whatever you ask. I've already seen how you treat your people. They don't have any call to be afraid of you, and I have every reason in the world to trust you. Yes sir, I'll help you.”

Bell had developed an interest in this large black man that spoke more like an educated white man than any slave he had ever known. As they rode southward along the rutted trail, he continued to ask Jeff questions. “I guess you're quite a curiosity around here, Jeff. I don't reckon I've ever known another free black man. How did that come about anyway?”

“I'll have to admit, sir, it was the biggest surprise in my life. I had accepted the fact that I was Mister Will's personal servant. I was given to him by Mister Henry back home. Then on the way down here, he told me he needed a surveying partner more than he needed a servant. He gave me my freedom papers, and he's been teaching me ever since.”

“What are you going to do with this freedom now that you've got it and Will has taught you how to be a surveyor? Are you going to strike out on your own? You know there's plenty of surveying work all over the grants. I hear they’re working their way pretty far up the Colorado in DeWitt's grant."

"Oh, no. I'm going to stay with Will. You see, we're a team. We work together. I imagine I'll always work with him in one way or the other. We'll both settle on our own places one of these days, but I expect I'll be around doing what I can for him as long as he'll let me."

"Well, he's lucky to have you as a friend, Jeff."

"Thank you, sir."

Bell, now genuinely impressed by the earnestness of this young man, continued to ask him about his work background and how his education was developing.

Jeff, although a little embarrassed to have the conversation focused on him, continued to answer Bell's questions during the rest of the trip.

As they pulled up a rise toward a cluster of log buildings on a ridge above the river, a small group of people came out from the houses and barn and gathered at the front of the larger cabin. By the time the wagon reached the main house and Bell set the brake, all of his workers were giving them a warm welcome.

Seeing this group of dark, smiling faces gave Jeff the comfortable feeling of being among his people. This gathering made him think of home.

He remembered the many times he and his papa had met Mister Henry and the rest of the Bowmans as they pulled up under the apple tree in front of the big white house back in Virginia.

Standing in front were three men whom Bell introduced as Kado, Robert, and Willis. Behind them were two women and four children ranging in ages from about two to twelve. Of the men, Kado was the oldest and, as Jeff learned later, was Robert's father. When introduced, Kado, a small, stringy man of about fifty-five with a row of wrinkles winding their way along his cheeks above a ragged beard, shifted his hat to his left hand to shake hands with Jeff.

"Jeff's been working up north with my nephew doing some

surveying," Bell said. "They came back to visit for awhile. I brought him down here a day or two to give y'all a hand chopping some wood. I need to take a load back to town. We're about out at the house, and I need to lay in a store before January."

"Mister Bell, we ain't seen Boss Farley for two, maybe three days now," Kado said as he pulled Bell's satchel from the wagon bed. "I'm feared he might'a done fell offen his horse or somethin'."

A small smile creased Bell's face. "We saw him in town yesterday. He took a sudden interest in going back east. He won't be back."

Jeff searched Kado's rugged face for any hint of a reaction to Bell's news. There was little except for a faint smile under his curly gray whiskers.

After unloading the wagon and passing out candy to the children and the bolts of cloth to the women, Jeff set out with the men toward a grove of scrub oak. Several trees had been felled and left to dry before cutting them and splitting them into firewood. The men worked together the rest of the afternoon; Jeff and Kado worked as a team on the long, cross-cut saw and Robert and Willis shared the splitting and loading.

Jeff's companions were glad to have the extra help. Kado found that he just had to hang on to the long saw most of the time, while the much larger and stronger Jeff seemed to revel in good, hard labor, pushing the saw back and forth through the logs. Jeff enjoyed being among new friends and stretching some long-unused muscles.

There was an openness among the men and they talked freely with each other. Kado, Robert, and Willis were eager to hear of events outside their plantation, and Jeff was interested to know of their successes in farming.

"We had a good harvest this year," Kado said. "Brought in 'bout fifty-five bushels of corn to the acre, best as I can reckon. Done good on cotton, too. 'Bout the time we was done with the corn, the cotton was ready. Mister Bell said we got 'bout thirty-five hundred pounds to the acre. We jest finished up pickin' a little while ago. Still got the fields to clean up though."

"How was it working for Mister Farley?" Jeff asked.

Kado let go of his end of the saw and stretched his back before answering. "Shoot, dat ole boss didn't do much of nothin' round here. Don't know what the Master paid him for what he done, but I couldn't see that he done much of nothin'. Me an' the boys planned out the work, an' we jest done it. The women and kids joined us in the fields most ever' day but ole Farley jest kind'a laid around at the cabin most the time.

"He took a belt to Robert, over there." He nodded toward the taller of the two men splitting logs. "Done that a few days after he got here, I reckon just to show us all who's boss. Claimed he sassed him. After that, he jest left us alone to do our work.

"We purty much took care of the whole last season on our own. 'Course none of us would ever say nothin' to the master about what Farley was doin, 'cause we seen what he done to Robert. He acted like a big ole rooster when the master was around, claiming he'd done dis an' dat, an' the other, but we knowed who really done it.

"We all sho hated to see the master an' missus move off to town to the new place. Why, when my woman was sick, before she passed, I seen the master ride all night to fetch the doctor back to try to make her well. The missus, she cried like it was her own sister when my woman passed. My Eller been takin' care of the missus for a long time before she got sick and died. I jest hope that whoever the master brings in to be the next boss treats us all right. We all works hard.

"We seen what a bad boss done to a man a couple o' years back." Kado said. "Me and Robert was gatherin' pecans down in a thicket by the river, 'bout two winters ago, I reckon it was. All of a sudden we heared somebody callin' to us from the brush. We found this feller hidin' in there. Looked like he was 'bout starved to death. Weren't hardly more than a bag of bones, with a few rags hangin' off him. Said he'd been running for nigh on to a month. He told us he'd run off from a plantation in Louisiana an' was headin' on down south to central Mexico. He said he could get away from the slavers if he got that far. Well, we fed him for two or three days an' gave him some clothes and a blanket. This was winter time when we found him and all he had was the clothes on his back and they was bout to fall apart from all the running in the brush and walkin' creeks. He didn't talk like us and we had a little trouble understandin' him, but he told us he'd been off the boat from Africa ten years and was sold four times. Each time he was sold, the whuppin's got worse. Anyway when he put on the clothes we give him, we seen his back. I tell you, Jeff, I don't never want to see a sight like that again. His back looked like somebody done been whuppin' the hide offen him regular for a long time. He had so many big ole raised scars on his back, I didn't even try to count 'em. The day he left out headin' south, he tried to get us to go with him, but none of us would go."

"Why not?"

"No reason to. This is our home. Master never has laid a strap or a belt on any of us. I 'magine if he knew about the time Farley took the belt to Robert, he would a give ol' Farley a thrashing he wouldn't ever forget fer it. We works hard, an' raise or grow most of what we need here, and he brings in the rest. We raise hogs and cattle and chickens besides the crops. Ever' time he comes down here, he brings a load of whatever we need an' takes home a load of butter, milk, eggs and meat for the house and the store. Just look at us: We eat good, we're healthy, and we don't wear no rags. We takes care of him, and he takes care of us."

The men finished their work, and before dark had a full load of firewood by the time they returned to the house.

Bell had spent his afternoon visiting with the women and children while they prepared two freshly butchered hogs the men had killed, gutted, and scalded that morning. While one of the women worked with a sharp knife and hatchet, separating the parts and trimming off the fat, the other tended the fires under the two big, black kettles where she was rendering the lard and frying cracklings from the thinly cut strips of skin. The women were finishing with the hogs about the time the men returned with the load of firewood.

After dinner, Bell settled into the cabin that he, his wife, and daughter had shared when they first came to Texas. Jeff went to the cabin that Kado shared with Robert and his family. At bedtime, they made Jeff a pallet on the floor. He enjoyed a comfortable sleep after an afternoon of invigorating and exhausting labor.

The next morning, Bell requested that a couple of horses be saddled and invited Jeff to join him for a ride to see the fields. While they rode through the dried corn and spent cotton stalks, he said, “Jeff, I'm going to ask you a question straight out. I value your judgment, and I believe you will give me an honest answer.”

“I'll try, sir.”

“You've spent a few hours working with my men here. Hopefully you know them from a point of view that I can't have. Do you think I could leave one of them in charge of this place and let one of my own people be the boss rather than trying to hire a new overseer?” Bell reined-in his horse and looked at Jeff while he waited for an answer.

Jeff sat for a moment looking at his horse's mane, feeling honored that such an important decision could weigh on his recommendation. He raised his gaze to meet Bell’s. “Yes, sir I do. The men wouldn't tell you this because of their fear of Farley, but I think that you suspected it already. They ran this plantation this whole last season without much direction at all from Farley. They said he was asleep or drunk most of the time he was on the place. It didn't take much to see that Kado is the natural leader here. They all respond to whatever he asks without complaint. They respect his age, experience, and natural instincts. As far as their loyalty to you, they will all do whatever you ask. They know what they have here with you, and they know how much better off they are than many. They appreciate the value that you place on them. No one would ever leave you of his own accord."

"Thank you, Jeff," Bell said, and extended his hand. "I appreciate your honesty. It makes me feel much better about my decision."

After lunch, Bell was ready to return home. He passed word that he wanted to see everybody at the wagon as soon as it was loaded.

The area immediately behind and under the seat of the wagon was loaded with milk, butter, eggs, two hams, and several slabs of bacon wrapped in burlap. Two large burlap bags of pecans that had been gathered along the river and three bags of peanuts from the garden were loaded on top of the firewood. Lastly, three sacks of sweet potatoes were squeezed in next to the tail gate, and twelve large pumpkins were balanced among the load.

Once the loading was done, Bell climbed onto the wagon bench and looked at his group of workers. "Most of you come to see me off whenever I leave anyway, but I wanted you all here today to hear what I have to say. I just want to let you know that I'm not going to hire another overseer to run this place. I'm putting Kado in charge of everything that goes on here. I trust him, and I feel that all of you respect him and are willing to take direction from him. We'll be going into another planting season soon, and there's a lot of work to be done to get ready for it. You've all done a fine job taking care of the animals and crops, and I'm proud of you.

"I expect you to give Kado the same support as you would me. I'll be back in three or four weeks and we'll do more planning for the next season. Oh yes, Kado?" Bell looked directly at the man. "The boss and his family live in the big house. You and your family can move in whenever you want to. I can't afford to be gone from the store much with the town growing like it is, so I'll only be coming in the mornings and going home in the afternoon. I won't be needing a place to sleep any more."

Kado stood proudly next to the wagon with his hat in his hand, looking up at his master. "Thank you, sir, for believin' in us. These folks have always worked hard for you an' nothin's gonna change now."

The small knot of people gathered around Kado, pumping his hand and hugging him. They were still hugging each other as the wagon pulled away.

Jeff and Bell rode in the heavily loaded wagon for some time before either one spoke. Jeff finally broke the silence. “That was a fine thing you did back there, sir.”

"Well, somebody needed to be put in charge, and Kado can do it. I'm just not going to worry about this place anymore."

“I don't think you'll need to. You'll probably get the best results you've ever had. They'll do whatever they can to prove that you made the right decision.”

The rest of the ride home was enlivened by Bell’s humorous accounts of life on the farm with his wife and daughter before his daughter married and moved away and his wife got sick and needed to be closer to the doctor.

By late afternoon they pulled into San Felipe and went directly to the store to unload the goods he expected to sell. Tad saw them as they pulled up in front. Both he and Will joined them in the street to help unload.

“How's the new store keeper?” Bell asked Will, grinning as he carefully climbed down from the wagon.

“I think Tad and I did fine,” Will answered. “Might even have made you a little profit. We had quite a few customers, didn't we, Tad?”

“Yes sir.”

Bell gave directions as to what was to go inside the store and what was to go home, and they all pitched in unloading.

When Jeff and Tad went back to the wagon by themselves to carry in more pumpkins, Jeff asked, “How's Libby?"

“She seems to be all right. She was up fixin' breakfast this morning. She rested all day yesterday but said she had too much to do to lay around today, so she got up and went to work. Her face ain't quite so fat neither.”

Soon they finished unloading the goods for the store. Since it was almost closing time, they locked the store and went home together in the wagon, with Tad and Jeff riding on top of the load of wood.

Arriving at the house, they all went in through the back door and found Libby preparing their supper in the kitchen.

“How you doing, Girl?” Bell asked, walking directly to Libby to examine her face.

“I'm better, sir. Thank you.” She tried to smile.

She shifted her gaze to Jeff, who was relieved to see her looking much better than he'd last seen her.

Bell and Will went to the sitting room to rest and talk before supper, and Tad went back outside to take care of his evening chores and play with the dog.

After Jeff helped put the butter, milk, and eggs away, he moved toward Libby, who was still working at the stove.

“I missed you.” He slid his arm around her waist, gently pressing a kiss on her neck.

Libby leaned against him, enjoying the feel of his strong arm around her and the closeness of him against her back. “I missed you, too. Now, shoo!" She turned around with a stern but playful look and pushed Jeff away. “I've got to finish supper, and I can't do it unless you sit in that chair, way over there.” She pointed with the spoon she had been holding toward the chair at the table.

“All right.” Jeff chuckled, holding his hands up in mock defense as he backed away from her toward the chair.

"Now tell me everything you did while you were gone and how everybody is doing out there."

Jeff gave her a full account of what happened at the farm and related his respect for Bell and his decision to give Kado the opportunity to manage the plantation.

After supper, Will and Bell went to their bedrooms early, and Jeff helped Libby finish in the kitchen. When the work was done, Libby walked with Jeff to his cabin, stopping outside the door in the cool night air to say goodnight. She leaned her head into his chest as he held her. "Jeff, how soon do you have to go back up north?"

"Probably a few days after Christmas. Maybe we'll wait 'til after the New Year. Why?"

"I just enjoy you being here with me, that's all."

"Lib, there's something you're going to have to understand." He placed his hands on her shoulders and looked directly into her face. "You're beginning to mean a lot to me — a *whole* lot. I'll always want to be with you, but I've got a job to do. The kind of work I do is going to take me away from you. I'll be gone two to three months at a time. But that doesn't mean I won't be thinking about you. I'll be thinking about you every day. Then the time we're together will be really special to us. I'm earning money now. It's a good feeling. Every time Will and I finish a job, I've earned more. If a man has land and money, he can build a future."

"What kind of future do you want?"

Jeff pulled her close and held her tightly for a moment. After a long hesitation he said: "I'll tell you all about that some other time. It's getting late, and you need to get out of this night air." He kissed her lightly on the cheek and watched her walk to her cabin where she turned and waved before going inside.

Chapter 17

During the next several days as Christmas approached, Will divided his time between helping his uncle at the store and assisting Austin in the land office.

Jeff spent the few days before Christmas helping with chores at the Bell house so he and Libby could have more time to themselves. One day, after the morning work was done, they took a walk by the river. On the way back to the house, Jeff cut several small branches from a cedar tree. When they returned to the house, he and Libby decorated the sitting and dining rooms with the greenery and some red ribbon that Mister Bell's daughter had left when she moved away. They also made some garlands and draped them around the front door. Libby told Jeff the Bell home had never looked so colorful and smelled so fresh.

Jeff got up before daylight on Christmas Eve morning to go hunting for the Christmas turkey. He wanted to provide meat for the table, but he also wanted time to himself to think. By early afternoon he returned with a huge tom turkey.

Libby laughed when Jeff presented it at the back door. "I don't know if I have a pan big enough for that thing!"

"I would have been back hours ago if I knew you wanted a smaller one. I passed up several scrawny looking hens while I was looking for 'ole Tom, here. Anyway, he won't look so big when he's naked."

Libby helped Jeff dress the turkey on the back porch, and then started making the dressing.

Late that afternoon, Jeff went to town with something on his mind — something he wanted to get resolved before another day went by. He had wanted to talk to Bell for several days, but the time never seemed right to approach him about such an important matter. He finally decided he would just have to seize the opportunity and deliver his message.

Jeff opened the door to find several people in the store with both Tad and Will helping Bell with the customers. Jeff tried to stay out of the way as much as he could, but it seemed that wherever he was, he was in somebody's way. Finally he went back out to the street and paced back and forth, rehearsing what he would say to Bell.

When the customers started thinning out toward closing time, Jeff went back inside to ask a favor of Will.

Will addressed his uncle after talking with Jeff. “Uncle John, Libby sent word with Jeff that she needed some sage for the dressing. Looks like we're about finished here. If it's all right with you, Tad and I will go ahead and take it on home to her. Besides, Jeff's here. He can help you lock up and walk on back with you.”

The old man gave Will a dismissing wave as he continued to count the day's receipts. A few minutes later, Bell closed the shop and rattled the door after locking it. Then he and Jeff turned south and started walking along the road in the early evening darkness.

After a deep breath, Jeff said, “Mister Bell, I asked Will and Tad to go home ahead of us so I could have a word with you in private.”

Bell glanced at Jeff. “Well, what is it?”

Jeff hesitated a moment, then said, “Sir, I want to marry Libby.”

Bell stopped in the middle of the road.

“What do you mean, marry Libby? Why, she's only a child!”

“Sir, she's eighteen now, and I'm over twenty three. We're both old enough. Mister Bell, I love her, and I think she feels the same toward me.”

“Do you know that?”

“No, sir. I haven't talked to her about it yet. I wanted to talk to you first.”

“I appreciate that, but—”

“Sir, please hear me out on this. I know how much she means to you, and I know you would really have a hard time managing without her, but nothing would change for awhile. I'll be spending most of my time in the field with Will. She could continue doing everything for you that she always has.” Jeff took another big breath. “Then when I get enough money saved, I want to buy her freedom.

“Sir, Will and I will probably be surveying for a few more years, and the way we live has no place for a woman. But I've found the woman I love, and when I do settle my own place, I want to have her with me."

“I think she's happy the way things are now,” Bell said.

“Sir, she's dedicated to you. I think she loves me. There's a difference.”

“Don't get impudent with me,” Bell said, cutting his eyes toward Jeff.

“I'm sorry, sir, I didn't mean any disrespect. It's just that I want to see her happy. I want her to have something to look forward to. I want to have something to look forward to myself. I believe she wants me, too. I just don't have the right to ask her without your approval. Just tell me how much she's worth to you sir. I'll pay you for her freedom.”

Bell was silent for a moment while they walked in the dark. Finally he said, “It took a lot of guts for you to say all that, didn't it?”

“You don't know how I've been wanting to talk to you for the last few days, but I just couldn't work up the courage until today. If I wasn't a free man, I would have asked Will to talk to you for me, but I'm my own man now, and I have to do things for myself.” He stopped walking and looked at Bell. “Sir, I've never asked for much or really ever expected much in my life. I just got lucky when I was given to Will. But now I'm asking for one of the most important things in my life. I'm asking you to let a woman love me.”

“Jeff, you're a good man. You're honest and hard working

man. Even though it rubs a little crosswise to the culture I've spent all my life living, I guess I'm glad you're a free man. You're ambitious and you're making something of yourself." He sucked air through his teeth and let out a sigh. "I just don't know. Let me think on it a bit. That's fair, isn't it?"

"Yes sir, that's fair. Thank you for listening to me and taking some time to think about it. Thank you very much."

By mid-mid-morning on Christmas day, the aromas coming from the kitchen had caused Bell and Will to visit the kitchen more than once to sample the pecan bars, pumpkin pie and turkey dressing Libby was preparing.

Later that morning, Bell slipped out of the house and went to town, returning in less than an hour with a package under his arm.

Jeff and Tad rearranged the greenery in the dining room and fashioned a colorful centerpiece on the dining room table the way Jeff had seen his mama do in the Bowman house back in Virginia.

Shortly before noon, Tad brought out two settings of the good china and silver they used when Bell had guests for dinner. As he was arranging them on either end of the table for Will and Bell, Bell walked in to the dining room. "Go ahead and set three more places at the table."

"Yes sir. You having company?"

"No, I want you, Libby, and Jeff to join us in here for dinner."

Tad looked at Bell and raised his eyebrows. He and Libby had never eaten in the dining room. Bell ate in the kitchen with them all the time when he didn't have company, but this was strange, he thought. Tad went back to the kitchen to get more of the fine china and silver.

"Mister Bell told me to fix you and me and Jeff places at the dining table," he told Libby as he gathered the silver and dishes. "We ain't never done that before."

Libby was too busy with the finishing touches of the special dinner to be too concerned about the seating arrangements, but she did agree with Tad that it would be odd to eat in the dining room with the master and Mister Will.

Before the food was placed on the table, everyone who had gifts brought them to the dining room and placed the wrapped packages next to the recipient's plates. There was a least one present beside each plate. Tad had four.

Finally, Libby and Jeff brought the turkey and the other dishes into the dining room and everybody gathered around the table. After Bell said an abbreviated blessing, they all sat down. Bell and Will were at opposite ends of the table, Tad was on one side and Libby and Jeff were sitting together on the other.

"Merry Christmas, everybody," Bell said. "All right, what are you waiting for? Open your presents."

Everybody started tearing into their gifts. Jeff and Will both found the same thing inside their packages—a beautiful set of soft, yellow buckskin shirt and pants.

"I hope they fit," Libby said. Mister Bell got me the leather, and I sewed it up." She smiled. "Thought I never would get them finished with Jeff around the house as much as he was. Jeff, I used the old clothes you gave me for rags as a pattern, and Mister Will, I just made yours a little smaller than his."

"Oh, I'm sure they'll fit fine," Will said, feeling the softness of the leather and admiring her skill as a seamstress. "Libby, they're beautiful. Thank you."

Jeff realized she must have stayed up late every night to do all the stitching. "These will hold up better than any store-bought clothes for what we've got to do, won't they Will? Thanks Libby. I guess all of you keep a pretty good secret."

"Libby asked me to get that leather the morning after you got back in town," Bell said.

Tad opened his largest package first. It was a leather vest that Libby had stitched together from some pieces that were left over from the men's clothes. He also got the spinning top from

Jeff and shiny half-dollars from Will and Bell.

Bell opened his package with the razor from Will at the same time Libby opened her package that held her comb and mirror from Jeff.

"Oh, thank you, Jeff! They're beautiful!" she said.

"A pretty girl needs to see what she looks like from time to time," he said

Jeff had one more gift to open. It was a large knife with fourteen inch long blade and a bone handle from Will.

"Thanks, Will. This will do perfectly for thinning out some of the brush we have to crawl through."

"All right, let's get to the eating before everything gets cold," Bell said.

Conversation flowed throughout the dinner, with everyone feeling comfortable eating together at the dining table for the first time. The feast was leisurely, but took much less time to eat than it did to prepare. Soon they all had desert and were finishing their coffee.

"There's something else I want to say on this special day," Bell said, getting everybody's attention. "Libby, I asked you and Tad and Jeff to come join Will and me for a reason other than having dinner together, which I will say I enjoyed very much. Now, you all know I don't beat around the bush when I have something to say, so I'll just come right out with it.

"Libby, last night Jeff told me that he loves you and wants to marry you. Now, what I want to know is, do you love him?"

Libby's mouth flew open as she raised her hands to her face in shock and happiness. She looked at Jeff, who had an embarrassed grin on his face, then back at Bell. Her breath caught in her throat as she tried to answer. Finally she managed to get out a quiet, "Yes, sir." Then she looked back at Jeff for his response. He still had the same grin on his face.

"Last night he also told me that he wanted to buy your freedom. All this freedom stuff for colored people is contrary to the way I was raised and lived my whole life, but if the Mexican government has its way, things might go in that direction someday anyhow. In the meantime, the plain truth is Libby — I need you.

"I don't need to tell anybody here that I'm an old man. And Libby can tell you all because she knows — sometime I'm a sick old man. That girl right there has been a lot of comfort to me, and I'm going to need her even more when it gets closer to my time. But Jeff says that he don't plan to settle onto his own place and take her away from me for awhile yet. Maybe several years. Maybe I'll last that long and maybe I won't. Only the Lord knows that. Well, here's what I propose: If you two want to get married, well, go on and step over the broom, but I want her to live here as long as I'm alive. You won't have your own place for a while anyway. This is her and Tad's home. Save your money, Jeff. They'll both get their freedom when I'm gone. You can be with her whenever you're in town, and then start your own place when I'm gone. Is that a fair arrangement?"

Jeff turned to look at Libby, who seemed stunned by what was going on around her. "What do you think?" he asked quietly, cupping his large hand over hers.

Libby stared straight ahead for a moment, then looked at Jeff, her eyes flooding with tears. She couldn't make the words come out, so she quietly nodded. Then she couldn't hold back any longer. She threw her arms around Jeff's neck and buried her face in his chest. "Oh Jeff! She sobbed.

"Now, come on, Libby," Bell said. "This is supposed to be a happy time. I never could understand women. Always crying when they're supposed to be happy. Here, maybe this'll cheer you up."

Bell reached beside his chair for another package he had secreted there earlier. It was the item he had brought from town that morning. "Here," he said, handing the package to Libby. "See if this will change your tune."

Libby quickly wiped the tears away with the hem of her apron. Accepting the package, she thanked the old man with her expressive eyes.

"Well, go on," Bell said, grinning. "Open it up."

Libby carefully opened the package to find a pretty, light-blue cotton dress with white lace at the shoulders, bodice, and hem.

"I'm afraid I didn't have time to get you a white one, but maybe that will do for a wedding," Bell said, smiling.

"It's beautiful, sir," Libby said in a small, quivering voice. "Thank you."

Libby sat for a moment, clutching Jeff's hand with one of hers and holding the dress to her breast with the other. Then she turned to Bell. "Mister Bell, you know I haven't had my mama and papa for a long time. Since they've been gone, you've been like both a mama and papa to me. They'd be mighty happy if they could see what happened here today. Do you think . . . just this once . . . it would be all right if I gave you a hug?"

Bell looked at her, a smile adding to the creases across his face, "I guess on Christmas day the old man could handle a little hug, come here."

Chapter 18

Bell gave Libby two days off from her housework and loaned Jeff his wagon, so that Jeff, Libby, and Tad could celebrate the wedding with their friends at the Bell plantation.

By midday on the day after Christmas, they pulled up to the cabins at the Bell plantation. One of the children spread word of an approaching wagon and all the people spilled out of the cabins to meet it.

“What y'all doin' back so soon? And whar's Mister Bell?” Kado asked as Jeff jumped off the wagon to go around and help Libby down.

“He didn't come with us this time. No reason to. This is a social visit. Libby hasn't been down to visit with you all in a while, so we thought we'd all just leave Mister Bell to take care of things himself and come down here and just sit a spell and visit. Thought we might even have a party.”

Libby had to turn away from Kado because she was having trouble keeping a straight face and didn't want to spoil Jeff's fun.

“You ain't makin' no sense at all, Boy. We ain't got no time for parties,” Kado said, sounding concerned. “We got work to do. Now what have you done with the master?”

“We haven't done anything with him,” Jeff said, still maintaining his serious tone. “In fact, he told us to tell you to make *sure* we have a party tonight.”

“I swear, dat man must’a took leave of his senses.”

Libby and Tad couldn't contain themselves anymore and burst out laughing. Tad broke the news by shouting, “Mister Bell gonna let Libby step over the broom with Jeff! He sent us all down here to do it!”

“Well, I'll be!” Kado laughed. “Is dat the truth, Girl?”

“I reckon it's so.” Libby smiled at the whole group. "Mister

Bell agreed to it yesterday, so here we are."

"Well, come on then, Girl," Robert's wife, Emily said as she stepped between Libby and Jeff and took Libby by the arm. "If you gonna step over da broom, we gonna have us a real party. We got some work to do." Libby headed off toward the cabin with the other women, casting a backward look toward Jeff. The women were all chattering and laughing at the same time as they disappeared into the nearest cabin.

Kado and the other men started helping Jeff unload the wagon. "If we gonna have you two steppin' over da broom, I guess dat *do* call for a party," he said. "Looks like we got a little work to do ourselves."

That afternoon the women stayed inside the cabin where they baked a cake and prepared several other dishes at the corner hearth. The men dug a large fire pit behind the cabins and filled it with oak and hickory logs, then set it afire to burn down to a thick bed of coals. They warmed themselves beside the fire most of the afternoon and swapped stories while they tasted berry wine that Kado had managed to keep hidden from Farley.

By mid-afternoon when the fire burned down to a large bank of glowing embers, they skewered a huge cut of beef to roast. Several tables were brought outside and lined up in a row. By dark everything was ready for the party.

Kado produced a fresh cache of wine when the women joined the men and children outside. They gathered close to the fire in the late December evening and watched the juices bubble on the meat and splatter in the fire, enticed by the dancing flame and a plume of aromatic smoke.

When the beef was charred on the outside and just right on the inside, they took it off the spit and laid it on one of the tables with the other food the women had spent the afternoon preparing. They all sat down to a feast worthy of celebrating a wedding.

Jeff wanted music for dancing similar to what he had heard

at Will's brothers' weddings back in Virginia, but they made do without instruments or musicians. They all sang the several songs they knew. Then Robert led a few songs with made-up verses about the new bride and groom:

"Big ole Jeff, he happy and gay,
He an' Libby gonna fly away.
Gonna fly away as bride an' groom
Gonna fly real high jumpin' over da broom."

Hey dilly, dilly day,
Hey dilly, dilly doom,
Hey dilly, dilly day,
Gonna fly real high jumpin' over da broom.

Libby be a woman now,
Growed up purty an' fine.
Jeff jest swept her off her feet,
An' say dat woman's mine.

Hey dilly, dilly day,
Hey dilly, dilly dine,
Hey, dilly, dilly day,
He say dat woman's mine."

When it was Kado's turn to compose new verses and lead the singing, Robert started tapping out the rhythm with spoons pounded against anything that produced a sound. Soon, several of the others produced makeshift rhythm instruments from pots and pans and thick glass bottles and were gleefully banging away to the rhythm set by the singer.

Libby and Jeff were the most colorful merrymakers. She had changed into her new blue dress and Jeff was wearing his new yellow buckskins.

The evening was filled with eating and laughter, with each

taking turns teasing Libby and Jeff about their wedding night. Finally Jeff asked Libby to join him in dancing as the rest sang and played their makeshift instruments.

Jeff gently held her hand and placed his other along her back and set the speed of the rhythm being tapped out on wooden bowls and pots and pans by the makeshift band. Slowly they danced in a large circle around the dim outer glow of the fire. Jeff's gaze never left Libby's face as they moved at a slightly faster rate with each circuit.

Before Libby and Jeff finished their first turn around the fire pit, Willis and Robert added fresh logs to the fire, and Kado brought a broom from the house and placed it on the ground next to the fire. The tempo of the rhythm increased while the flames leaped and the air grew hot. They danced faster and closer to the broom, circling ever faster until they were almost a blur. Then, when they could go no faster, their bodies wet from the heat of the roaring flames and the exertion of the dancing, they jumped over the broom to deafening shouts and noise-making all around them.

Libby was picked up by the revelers and paraded in a snake dance as Jeff looked on, laughing at her expression. When they deposited her back on the ground next to Jeff, the men picked him up and carried him on their shoulders around the cabins. Finally they brought him back to Libby, who was beginning to worry about the safety of her new husband on the shoulders of men who had spent much of the afternoon and evening drinking berry wine.

Soon it was time for Jeff and Libby to make their way to the cabin that had been prepared for them. Jeff thanked his new friends for such a fine party and shook hands all around, and Libby hugged everybody. Once again, at the door of the cabin, they turned and thanked everybody, then slowly closed the door.

With the door closed behind them, the chivaree started in earnest outside the cabin, lasting noisily and long into the night.

A party of a different sort began inside the cabin. The heat that fanned from the bonfire was only a prelude to the passion that was released between the two bodies aglow with love and desire for each other. Jeff pulled Libby into a tight embrace and felt her heart beat a rhythm faster and stronger than on any homemade drum outside.

That night marked the beginning of Jeff's and Libby's awakening to real love. They forged an emotional bond that would grow and nurture them for a lifetime.

By early afternoon the next day, Jeff and Tad had the wagon hitched. After saying goodbye with promises to return when they could, Libby, Jeff, and Tad were heading back to San Felipe. The short wedding trip would soon be over. Jeff and Libby both knew there would be little time to spend together before Jeff left to go back to his surveying, but they enjoyed what time they had together for the next several days.

Chapter 19

Early on New Year's Day, Jeff and Will were again packed and ready to return to surveying. This time it was a tearful goodbye. Jeff hated to leave Libby again only days after their wedding and was already looking forward to their next reunion. Understanding that Jeff was working now to prepare for their future helped ease their parting. Someday, they would have the rest of their lives together.

Will and Jeff rode out from the Bell house into the January morning chill, leading their pack horses. Jake darted back and forth, sniffing the trail in front of them.

The seasoned Texas frontiersmen in their buckskins, riding into the north wind, presented a distinctly different image than when they'd left Virginia, or even when they'd arrived in San Felipe the first time.

Will thought back to the trip they made cross-country to Texas as he pushed Baron into a canter. It seemed like such a long time ago, but it had been less than a year. He and Jeff were excited about their adventure at the time. They couldn't know of the changes that would affect them as they changed the land.

They were no longer the young adventurer and slave who left Virginia. They were now two men with a mission. Their meeting and working with Stephen Austin and others who shared his vision had given them both a greater perspective of the magnitude of what they were doing.

Jeff's meeting, loving, and marrying Libby had strengthened his focus and ambition to improve himself and the lives of those he loved. Will could see that he was achieving the goal that he had defined to his father before he left his boyhood home; he had indeed become a part of building something great.

These two young men couldn't know on that frosty morning of the first day of 1830 just how much more their world would change.

Settlers continued pouring into Texas for the well-publicized land ownership opportunities at the beginning of the new decade. Word spread through the United States and Europe of the land opportunities in Texas. For a while the influx of new settlers created more than enough work for Will and Jeff, Austin and Williams and others like them.

However, during the same period, other forces were at work to stem the flow of immigration from America. There had been a change of heart toward the Anglos by Mexican officials. Many in the government believed the Texans were nothing more than shrewd and unruly slave-holders. Some senior government officials believed that they must take serious action to stop the American immigration and American influence, or Mexico would lose Texas forever.

On April 6, 1830 a decree was issued that prohibited Anglo-Americans from settling in the Republic. The new law also suspended many of the impresario contracts. Another article in the law planned for establishing military posts, occupied by convict-soldiers. It furthermore strictly prohibited any further introduction of slaves.

This was a calamity to scores of businessmen such as Bell and Austin who had invested a fortune in time, money and labor toward developing their dream of Texas colonization. However, Austin and DeWitt, another land contractor with a large grant south of Austin's, managed to skirt the law through an interpretation that enabled them to complete their quota of families for their grants. Although American immigration slowed considerably in 1830 for most of Texas, it continued in the Austin grant for another year and a half.

At first the political climate had little effect on Will and Jeff while they were in the field working with the new settlers. But with each trip back to San Felipe, they found that the farmers, businessmen and land dealers were increasingly frustrated by the interference of the government in their affairs.

It was during a visit to San Felipe in November of 1831 that Will and Jeff learned that their future and way of life would soon be changing. As usual, when they arrived in town, Will stopped in to visit with his uncle and pick up his mail that had collected while he was working.

"Mister Bell, look who's here," Tad called toward the back of the store. "Mister Will done come home." He turned back to Will. "Where's Jeff?"

"Oh, I imagine he's giving your sister a big hug about now." Will looked the boy up and down. "My gosh, you must have grown a half a foot since I saw you last!"

"Yes sir, I reckon. Libby says she can't hardly keep me in britches no more."

"Well, I can see why. All you are is arms and legs." Will laughed as he put his arm around the boy's shoulder.

"Welcome back," the old man said, shuffling out from the back of the store. Bell had taken to using a walking cane most of the time due to stiffness and pain in his knees. "Been looking for you for two or three weeks now, ever since Austin told me the new settlers had about petered out."

"I'll have to admit things have slowed a bit, but Jeff and I went ahead and took advantage of the opportunity to stake off our own places."

"So you finally got around to your own places, did you?"

"Yes sir. I believe we've found about the best land in Texas. It's way up the Brazos, beyond everybody else. Got a bunch of good cross-creeks running through it. Good water all over the place with plenty of timber and the richest farm land you ever saw. Most of it is covered in prairie grass that would feed thousands of cows. Who knows, one of these days I might even try my hand at raising a little livestock.

"When I first started surveying here, I made arrangements with Austin to take part of my wages in trade for land. He credited me for so much land every time we came back into town, and I'm going to collect on it this time. I want you to know that as soon as we get the papers filed, your nephew will own almost ten thousand acres of the best land in the world. It's on a point where the river takes a turn toward the west. We're going to call it Virginia Point. Jeff has his place next to mine. There's also some other folks from Virginia down river from us. There's still plenty of spots on both sides of the river for more settlers when they come. I keep hoping some of the family might come on out here someday. Oh, speaking of family, do I have any mail?"

Bell grinned. "Yep, but not so much from family. One letter from your sister and one from your paw. You got two or three from that little gal back home though. Looks like she thinks right smart of you."

"She's a pretty special young lady to me too."

Bell retrieved the letters and handed them to Will.

"Thanks." Will tucked the mail into a buckskin pouch slung over his shoulder. "You look like you're holding your own these days."

"Aw, just slowed down a little. Can't do as much walking as I used to. Tad has to harness the carriage for me every morning now. Can't even walk from here to the house any more, but I guess I'm doing all right. I'm just so damn mad I could spit about what the government's doing now, though."

"Why? What's going on now?"

"Just last week there was another troop of them convict soldiers come through here, going out to set up a garrison on the Trinity River. From what I hear they got 'em scattered all over south of here and more going in to the north and east. Biggest bunch of cut-throat looking characters I ever saw. Nothing more than a gang of thieves and criminals, if you ask me. Sure hate to see our good people bothered by their kind. That's the third troop come through here in the last few months, heading east and north. We just don't need or want their kind in these parts."

"I don't imagine we can stop the government from sending them up here," Will said, hoping to calm his uncle. "And we *could* use some more help keeping the Indians out of the settlements."

"That last bunch of tramps didn't look like they'd even follow orders, much less join in an organized fight. I think they just sent 'em up here to aggravate us. And that's not all of it. We're also damn mad about the way they're collecting taxes along the coast." The old man's anger built as he told of more problems with the Mexicans.

"Why, they've set up custom houses along the coast and aren't letting any shippers get in or out without paying them off. The shippers have to pass their costs onto the farmers and businessmen like me trying to get their goods to market. I'll tell you this: We're all mad as hell over the way we're being treated by the government these days."

Will watched the color rise in his uncle's face. "Just calm down, Uncle John. No need for you to get all worked up over it. I need to visit with Austin anyway. Might as well get caught up on all the news while I'm there. You just take it easy and don't worry about this mess. I'll see you later at the house."

Will found Austin at his cluttered desk in the front room of the Austin Land Company.

"Well, look whose back in town!" Austin said as Will came through the door. "Guess you finally ran out of people to survey for."

"Yes sir, ran out of new settlers, so Jeff and I did a little surveying for ourselves."

"So you want to cash in your reserves?"

Will nodded. "Yes sir. I've got all the paperwork for our places and the others out in my saddlebags. I thought we'd get started on that tomorrow, if it's all right with you. Right now, I'm more interested in hearing about what's going with the government. Uncle John mentioned something about problems with customs collections down along the coast. What's going on?"

“I'll tell you, Will, it's about all I can do to keep things calm around here, much less all over Texas, but I try the best I can. Seems about all I'm doing these days is writing letters to try to keep the citizens off the government officials and the officials off the citizens. Your uncle is about ready to ride off to Saltillo himself with guns a-blazing. I believe the old coot would too, if he was able. I *know* he would if he was twenty years younger.

“We're used to governing ourselves. We've managed quite nicely for the last ten years, but we’re seeing that privilege go farther and farther out of reach. I'm beginning to understand that the only way that I can really work toward the unity of our country and maintain the peace is to go to Saltillo or maybe even Mexico City myself and talk with the politicians down there face to face.

“I guess if anyone should be bitter about the turn of events, I should. My livelihood was practically destroyed when they stopped the immigration from the United States, but I still believe we can make a change.”

“I hope you're right,” Will said. “I'm not too happy about this myself. I'm going to spend the rest of my life here. Someday I hope to have a family here. In fact, Jeff and I are going to start putting up our cabins as soon as we get back up north. With surveying dropping off the way it has, it looks like we might get a chance to put in a crop next year. That's the plan anyway.

“I have to admit, though, that I feel guilty just going on with my life with things in such a turmoil the way they are. Is there anything I can do to help you with what you're trying to accomplish?”

Austin sat quietly for a moment, thinking over Will's offer before he answered. “Yes, there is. We need level-headed men like you here in the grants, talking to your neighbors, convincing them that political negotiations will rule in the end. The people up your way along the Brazos know you and trust you. They'll follow your lead. Keep them calm and assure them that I'm working every day for their rights as citizens.”

"Thanks for your confidence. You know I'd go with you to help you or my country in any way I can, but if you feel I could be of more service in these parts, I'll stay and do what I can."

"I appreciate that. If you really want to help, just keep talking to your neighbors and keep them calm.

"You need to know there's an active war party in the colonies that would just as soon see us jump right in and start a fight to win our independence or have us become a part of the United States. But there are also a lot of us loyal Mexicans who believe we can work things out. That's why I must go to Saltillo; I've got to try to get back some of the rights and privileges we had in the Constitution of 1824."

"Well sir, I know I speak for most of my neighbors in telling you that we appreciate what you're doing. If anybody can do any good there, you can."

"Thanks, I appreciate that. I guess I'll be leaving in the next day or two. How long will you be in town before heading back?"

"Oh, not more than a couple of weeks if we can get the hardware and tools that we'll need for our cabins."

Will reached for his hat and started to leave, but instead leaned forward in his chair with another question for Austin. "I need to know one more thing before I go. You're probably my uncle's best friend. I need your honest opinion on something."

"I'll give it if I can."

"I just left him a little while ago. He doesn't look well. Looks to me like he's going down hill. He tells me he's fine, but I don't believe him. You see him every day. What do you think?"

Austin stared at his battered desk top for a moment before answering. "He's a tough old bird. He won't admit to anything. He sure won't like me telling you this, but he had a blackout spell a couple of weeks ago at the store. Tad had to run get the doctor. He got to feeling better after a while and told the doctor it was just a little indigestion. Doc Crew thought otherwise.

"He wouldn't want you asking around about him, or me talking about him, so you keep what I told you under your hat.

He's not going to slow down anymore than he has to or change his ways as long as he's able to get about. He's got Libby and Tad, and they take care of him very well. The last thing he would want is you or anybody else worrying over him. Just go on letting him do what he's able, and he'll be happy."

Will arrived at the Bell house to find Jeff and Libby both in the kitchen. Libby was at the counter preparing dinner and Jeff was sitting at the table with a smile on his face like none Will had seen since the day Bell told him he could marry Libby.

"Hello, Lib," Will said as he walked across the floor to give her a hug. He looked at Jeff. "You look mighty pleased with yourself."

"Isn't she about the prettiest thing you ever saw?" Jeff said, still beaming at Libby.

"Well, yeah," Will said, as he eyed the embarrassed Libby. "I'll admit she's a fine-looking woman."

"You two cut that out," Libby said as she wriggled away from Will. "How do you expect a girl to get her work done with all that kind of talk going on around here? And Jeff Jefferson, you behave!"

"Oh, I'm behaving." Jeff chuckled. "I'm just enjoying watching you."

Libby, still embarrassed by Jeff's talk in front of Will quickly turned her back to both of them and returned to her work, shaking her head.

"You still haven't told me why you have that big grin on your face." Will sat in the chair beside Jeff. "I can understand you being happy to see Libby after a few months of being away, but you're grinning like a possum eating briars."

Jeff started laughing. "Will, my friend, you'd be grinning too if your wife just told you that you were going to be a papa."

"You *are*?" Will almost shouted as he jumped up to hug Libby again. "Are you really?" The question was unnecessary. He could read the answer in her face. She nodded timidly as he embraced her and held her close for a moment.

Jeff joined Libby and Will and wrapped his large arms around both of them.

"I'm so happy for both of you," Will said, looking first at Libby, then Jeff.

"We're happy too," Jeff said. "And we want to thank you for making this all possible."

"What's that?"

"If it wasn't for you, why I'd never be in Texas and I'd never have met my Libby."

"You can thank my papa for that. He's the one that gave you to me. So he made it possible."

"In that case, if it's all right with you and Mister Henry, we want to name the baby William Henry Jefferson if it's a boy."

"I'm sure it would be all right with papa, and it's definitely all right with me. Thank you. And what if it's a girl?"

"Libby gets to name it if it's a girl. We haven't even talked about that yet."

"Now if this isn't something! Here you are with a wife and a baby on the way and I'm still single. For some reason I always thought I'd be first between the two of us to start a family."

Jeff looked at Will with a knowing smile. "Your time's coming. You know we promised to go back to Virginia one of these days. Maybe that time will be sooner than you think."

"Maybe," Will said, a smile creeping across his face.

Later that evening, after dinner and a short visit with his uncle, Will retired to his room to read his long-awaited mail. He read the letter from his father first. It was filled with news of the plantation and their recent harvest.

Mary's letter held newsy information about the family and a party that she had attended at a neighbor's home. She also told of her recent visit with Anna for several days and how she was disappointed that Anna didn't seem to have any interest in attending the party with her. She also reported the birth of a nephew and how the rest of the children had grown.

Will raced through Mary's letter, telling himself he would

read it again after he finished reading Anna's letters.

Anna . . . . He tore into her first letter. He had come to really look forward to her letters each time he and Jeff returned to town. Her letters were lengthy and her conversational tone made him almost feel she was in the same room talking to him.

During the months she was away at finishing school she'd shared her feelings about being away from her home and family. Later, as she got more used to living away from home, she kept him informed about the pranks that the girls played on each other.

Later, after she and Mary completed their education and returned home, she shared the details of her projects with him. She wrote of the quilting and other sewing projects she had taken on. She even sent him two fine shirts that she made.

Anna loved the out of doors and wrote of the work she and her mother did in their flower gardens. She also loved to ride and told him of her solitary rides across the countryside.

She asked Will questions about Texas and expressed a keen interest in his surroundings as he worked. She wanted to know about the people who moved into the new country and how the women were adjusting to life on the frontier.

It seemed to Will that the progression of their writing over the months had taken a natural path. They were both very open, and after a while their affection for each other began to show in their letters. For the last year, Anna's letters opened with *My dearest Will* and closed with *Love, Anna.*

As Will finished reading the letters, he sat on the edge of the bed and thought of all the possibility in his life. He knew he had a strong affection for Anna. He felt that they had come to know each other very well through their writing. Although they had been apart, he'd seen her mature in her interests and in the way she expressed herself.

The two and a half years of separation had been a time of growth and maturity for both of them. Will had a much stronger understanding of his loyalties, commitments and values. He recognized that he lived in a time and place in which, if he applied himself and worked hard enough, he could do and be anything he wanted.

He had long since stopped thinking of Anna as a child. He'd seen the beginnings of her maturity before he left Virginia, and had noticed that her attitudes toward life had taken on more meaning and purpose. He also knew she shared his sense of adventure from the questions she asked about Texas.

As he sat on the edge of the bed that night, holding her letters in his hand, he realized that neither of them had expressed their feelings toward the other openly, but he knew how they each felt. He also knew that it was time to start making firm plans about his future.

While Anna's words were still fresh in his mind, he got out his writing materials to compose another letter to her.

> My Dearest Anna,
>
> Jeff and I just arrived back in town after three months surveying the Austin grant. This has been the most rewarding trip of all because I finally selected my own future home site. The place I've selected is situated on the Brazos River and includes several miles of river frontage and has other streams and creeks within its boundaries. The game is plentiful, and the land is suitable for farming, raising livestock, or both with vast areas of rolling plains with live oak trees and scattered cedars dotting the landscape.
>
> I will build a cabin along a tree line next to a stream that flows into the Brazos from the west. I will build it with the intent that it would be a temporary home for a few years while I develop my land. I have selected a much more suitable spot, not far from the cabin site, which would be the location of a much larger and finer home.
>
> Anna, I told you that some day I would return to

Virginia. I will keep that promise. I have made plans to return for a visit next fall. Now that immigration has stopped for a while, Jeff and I will have the time and opportunity to build our homes and start our farms. Before I return to Virginia, I want to have my cabin completed and my first crop in. I will then feel that I will have accomplished the first of my goals in Texas.

I've got great news. Jeff and Libby are going to have a baby and said they want to name it after me if it's a boy. They are both healthy and very happy.

Love, Will

Chapter 20

Now with a firm plan in place and a timetable to work toward, there was little rest during their short visit in San Felipe. After inquiring around town, Will and Jeff managed to find two sturdy long-bed wagons for sale and became acquainted with a German settler across the river that raised mules. Due to the reduction in their surveying activities and with the purchase of the wagons, they decided they had little need for their pack animals. After considerable horse trading with the contrary German, they made a deal to trade their pack horses for two teams of mules. Then, with the harness they'd purchased from Bell, they had the means for hauling their building supplies and for whatever other tasks they'd encounter as farmers.

They took both wagons south along the river, beyond the Bell plantation, to the saw mill the Mueller brothers established a few years earlier. The wagons were loaded with milled lumber for dozens of uses, from constructing doors to making furniture. They also loaded some ready-made windows.

The only tool they had brought with them from Virginia was a double-bladed ax, so they had a lengthy list of tools and hardware to purchase. Within ten days, they were outfitted and ready to head back to Virginia Point and start their new venture.

Jeff told Libby they should complete both cabins by early February and would return for a load of farm gear in time to start breaking the land for spring planting.

Once again the two young men, now homesteaders and farmers, headed north, loaded with building materials for their new homes. This time Jake rode on the wagon seat, cushioning his head on Jeff's leg, while the two saddle horses trailed behind.

Will and Jeff enjoyed the change of pace, working in the

cool winter air while they watched their homes take shape. They built Jeff's place first so he could make the trip back for the farming tools and a short visit with Libby while Will stayed behind to finish the work on his own place.

They made good progress through most of the winter. There were only two days in December when it was too cold and icy to work. In early January, they got the roof finished on Jeff's cabin, closing it in from the weather. They completed the roofing just in time to beat a blue norther that brought ice and snow and kept them inside for three days. They found they had done a good job with the fireplace and chimney as it didn't smoke inside the cabin and did well reflecting the heat back into the room.

Faster progress was made with Will's cabin than with Jeff's as they learned to avoid the errors they'd had to correct on Jeff's cabin. By early February they had the roof on Will's cabin and it was time for Jeff to return for the farming equipment.

"Do you realize this is the first time in almost three years that we won't be together?" Will said as he stood beside the wagon while Jeff readied it to return to San Felipe.

"I was thinking about that the other day." Jeff answered. "It doesn't seem like three years, does it?"

"No, but lot's happened in that time, with all the surveying and working with settlers and the problems with the government. Be sure to stop by the land office and see whether Mister Austin is back from Saltillo. Be sure and get a run down from either him or Mister Williams on the latest news with the government."

Jeff lifted his right foot high onto the spoke of the front wheel and pulled himself onto the wagon seat. He waved as he rolled away from the cabin while Will held Jake to keep him from following. Will squatted, rubbing the dog's neck, and watched the wagon move into the distance. He then turned his interest to the cabin.

Nice piece of work, he thought as he admired their work on the cabin. He walked around it, looking for places that might need more mud in the cracks between the logs and didn't find any. He examined the chimney and realized that they had, indeed, done a good job on the entire structure. He was proud of their accomplishment, but he also realized this was just a temporary home. Someday it would become a barn or smoke house. Someday he would have a fine house built with milled lumber and finished siding up there on the rise, looking out over the prairie.

Will thought of his future home as he walked up the gentle grade of the hill, crested with large live oak trees. He leaned back against one of the trees, resting his foot on the base of the trunk, visualizing the home he would build someday. *A large two-story house,* he thought, *with a big front porches all around the house with columns. It would be painted white with plenty of large windows where you could see for miles from the upstairs bedrooms. A place for children and laughter. Someday . . . .*

Will took advantage of the break between finishing the cabins and starting the plowing. He also spent several days fulfilling the promise he had made to Austin to visit his neighbors and keep them advised of the news of the tariff situations and Austin's efforts to obtain concessions to the new immigration laws and other changes. As expected, his neighbors had concerns regarding the changes in policy, especially those who had relatives planning to join them in Texas. But Will's optimism in Austin's ongoing effort to return policy to the agreements of the 1824 constitution had a calming effect on those who were inclined to take a more aggressive role in forcing change. Upon returning to his cabin after four days of visiting, he felt a sense of accomplishment in maintaining a wait-and-see attitude among his neighbors.

For the next several days, while he awaited Jeff's return, Will set about constructing furniture. His plan was to build a long, roomy bed that would accommodate his height. Then he planned to use more of the milled lumber to construct a table, chairs and a cupboard. If he had enough left, he wanted to assemble a wardrobe for keeping extra clothes and blankets.

Although he chose to live on the frontier, he wanted a few comforts in his life. He knew the day would soon come when his journeys to civilized and comfortable places like San Felipe would be few and far between. He also realized it would take time to build all the furniture he wanted in a craftsman-like manner and expected that much of his furniture building would have to be done after planting, during the summer. At least he had a few days to get started before Jeff returned. He wanted to have the cabin completely furnished before he left for Virginia in the fall.

Jeff came home as scheduled with a load of farm tools and seed. Will was smoothing the wood on the bed frame with a draw plane in front of the cabin when Jeff pulled up.

“Were you able to get everything on the list?” Will asked, putting the plane down.

“Everything but some of the vegetable seeds that we wanted, so I substituted a few.”

After Jeff brought Will up to date on his uncle’s health, which was continuing to get worse, and on Libby, who continued to get bigger, and Tad, who was still getting taller, they unloaded the wagon. Will inspected each piece as they unloaded.

“Looks like we got everything we need to put a crop in. You going to be ready to start breaking ground tomorrow?”

“The sooner, the better. The baby is due sometime in late April. I promised Libby I'd be back in early April to be with her when the baby comes.”

“If we plant by the signs of the moon like Papa taught me, we should be finished by the first of April,” Will said. “With both of us working together, I imagine we'll have all the corn we can harvest and cotton we can pick by ourselves in the ground by then.”

The next morning they started their farming business. They worked Will's place first, then duplicated their efforts on the edge of the prairie close to Jeff's cabin. With good cooperation from the weather and long, hard days behind the plows they completed their planting by late March.

Will could tell by Jeff's insistence on being behind the plow at the break of dawn and working with only a short break at midday and then again until the sun was completely down every day that he was eager to get back to Libby.

They were drinking their coffee after supper the day they finished planting when Will said, “Why don't you take ole Buck and head back into San Felipe first thing in the morning? That way you can look after both Libby and Uncle John while I finish up a few chores around here. I'll go ahead and get the vegetable garden in, then I'll come on in for a visit myself. After the baby comes and everything's all right there, we'll ride back out here together.”

“I hate to leave you again with work to be done. I should be helping you.”

“No, I imagine Libby needs you more than you're needed here.”

Jeff rode out at first light the next day.

Will got busy, and in three days he used all the vegetable seed that Jeff had brought. With the garden seeds in the ground behind both cabins, he made plans to head for San Felipe before the weeds started showing too badly.

After dropping off the mules at the nearest neighbor's place, he headed south for what he expected would be his last visit before harvest.

Will arrived in town two days later in the early afternoon and was surprised to find his uncle's store closed and the door locked. He knew something was wrong. He hurriedly walked across the street to the land office to learn of his uncle's condition from Austin. He found Sam Williams working at Austin's desk.

“Hello, Will. I'm sure glad to see you,” Williams said with a pained look.

“How's my uncle, Sam?” Will sank into the chair across the desk from Williams. He could tell by the expression on

William's face that the news wouldn't be good.

“Not well at all, I'm afraid.” Sam hesitated for a moment. “He's dying, Will. The doc stopped by here early this morning after spending most of the night with him and told Stephen that John had been asking for him. He’s out there now.”

Just then they heard a galloping horse stopping outside. Looking out the window, Williams said, “There's Jeff.”

Will met Jeff at the door.

“I'm glad to find you here,” Jeff said, catching his breath. “I saw Baron across the street. I didn't know how far I'd have to ride to find you. It's your uncle. You'd better come now.”

They both ran out to their horses and in minutes were at the Bell home.

Will went inside through the kitchen door while Jeff took care of the horses.

He found Libby and Tad sitting at the kitchen table.

“Oh Will!" Libby said as she rose from her chair. “He's so sick!”

“I know, Lib, I know.” He held Libby close for a moment.

“Mister Austin's in there with him now, but you go on in. He's been waiting for you.”

Will quietly entered his uncle's bedroom and found Austin sitting in a straight-backed chair beside the bed. He rose as Will entered and offered him the chair. Will sat and gently took the old man's wrinkled hand in his.

“Uncle John, it's Will.”

The old man looked small and frail in the bed. His eyelids fluttered slightly, and then slowly opened. “Will?” The voice was so weak. Will leaned forward to hear him. “I didn't think I'd ever see you in this life again. Son, I think I'm going to die today.”

“You're doing fine, Uncle John. Don't tire yourself out by talking so much.”

“Libby and the boy, take care of 'em. They’ve been good to me.” His voice was so weak; Will had to lower his head close to the bed to hear.

Will interrupted, seeing the old man was out of breath. “You know I will. Jeff will take good care of them too, but I'll always be there for all of them if they need me. I'll always see that they’re taken care of. You don't worry about that.”

“Will?”

“Yes sir?”

“Tell my baby, Sarah . . . I love her”

“Yes sir, I will. I'll tell her personally when I see her.”

“Son?”

“Yes sir?”

“You're strong, good man. Help Austin . . . . Help Texas.”

“Yes sir, I will. You need your rest now. You just take it easy awhile.”

Two days later, Will, Jeff, Libby, Tad, Sam Williams and all the people from the Bell plantation gathered in the yard of the Bell home after returning from the grave yard. They moved closer to the front porch as Austin stepped onto the porch and asked for their attention. “I asked you all to come on back to the house because there's some things I need to tell you.”

“Mister Bell came to visit Sam and me about a month ago. He was sick then and knew he didn't have long to live. He wanted to revise his will. He asked me to take care of his affairs after his death, and Sam was a witness to his testimony. I'm not going to read the entire document. Will and Jeff can read it themselves later if they want to, but I'll tell you how Mister Bell wanted his property distributed.

“The first property he mentioned is his store. He wanted the store and contents sold and the proceeds of the sale, along with any cash and savings he had at the time of his death, to be sent to his daughter in New Orleans. Next, his home, where we are now. He wanted Libby and Tad to stay here until Jeff finished their place at Virginia Point and the baby was born. He instructed me to sell it then, with half the proceeds to go to Libby and Tad and the other half to his nephew, Will. Next there is the Bell plantation. He asked that the property be divided equally and that the title and deed be given to the people who have worked it for him for years.

"I guess you all understand that slaves can't hold property. He understood that too. He instructed Sam and me to draw up papers that gave you all your freedom upon his death. You are all now free citizens of Mexico and property owners.

You may wonder why he didn't just give everything to his daughter. He loves his daughter very much, but she and her husband live in a different world. They will never come back to Texas. Her husband is wealthy in his own right and Mister Bell has seen to his daughter's financial comfort in the past. He felt that he owed his success to all of you and wanted to see you rewarded for your loyalty.

"He and I talked a lot about slavery over the last several months. He saw for himself what the opportunity of freedom did for Mister Jefferson. He came to believe he owed you all the same opportunity.

If any of you have questions about your rights and privileges as free citizens, please talk with me or Will Bowman or Jeff Jefferson. I've got the paperwork with me which I will give to all of you to prove your status. I'd like to ask Will and Jeff to do the surveying of your places as soon as practical. You will get title to your property then. You should go ahead and complete this year's crop and share equally in the profits. Are there any questions?"

Austin looked out at the faces before him. The women were quietly crying and the men were stunned. They were still too saddened by the loss of their master and too overwhelmed with his generosity for celebration.

Will had the difficult task that evening of composing a letter to his cousin, Sarah, in New Orleans, advising her of the loss of her father and the details of his will. He told her of her father's love for her and his mention of her in his last words. He included a copy of the will in the envelope and promised to visit with her in the fall on his way back to Virginia.

Will, Tad and Jeff spent the next few days going through and sorting Bell's personal effects from both the store and home, which were packaged and sent to New Orleans.

After making sure Libby would be all right without them for a few days, they collected the surveying instruments that Will had stored in Bell's barn until he finished his cabin and headed to the Bell plantation to divide it up for Kado and the others.

They returned four days later to find Libby still in good condition and Tad looking after her. Libby still wasn't showing any indications of having her baby anytime soon. Will and Jeff agreed that it would be several weeks before she would be able to travel after the birth, so they planned for Will to return to Virginia Point and take Tad along to help with the work until Libby could travel.

The next morning, Jeff helped Tad saddle Buck. He strapped the sacks of food Libby had prepared behind the saddle. After Tad assured Libby he would work hard and do what Will told him, they were on their way.

They arrived to find their cabins undisturbed and the crops doing well but with enough weeds to keep them busy for awhile.

Tad and Will developed an effective routine of chopping weeds first on one farm till they had them under control, then rotating to the other place and weeding there.

There were a few good rains through April and May and by the first of June the cotton was producing what looked like a potentially good yield. The corn was already over waist high and developing lots of ears. They were taking good care of the vegetable garden and had dug some new potatoes and harvested a few beans and squash.

Every evening, Will worked on his furniture. By mid-June, he had completed his bed, the table and two chairs.

He and Tad were working on chair seats late one afternoon under the shade tree next to Jeff's cabin when they heard harness chains rattling. Looking up, they saw a wagon approaching along the trail between the corn and the timberline.

"It's them!" Tad shouted as he jumped up and ran toward the wagon. "Come on, Mister Will! It's them! They're finally here!"

Will stood and watched the barefoot boy race across the grassland toward the approaching wagon with Jake close on his heels. Jeff stopped the team long enough for Tad to scramble onto the bench with them. Both he and Libby waved their arms wildly at Will from the distance when they stopped for Tad. Soon they pulled up in front of the cabin.

"If you two aren't a sight for sore eyes, I don't know what is!" Will said with a big smile as Jeff set the brake and jumped from the wagon.

"Good to see you too." Jeff reached over to shake hands. He then took the baby from Libby's arms. Holding the baby out for Will to take, he said, "Mister William Henry Bowman, I'd like you to meet Mister William Henry Jefferson."

"I don't know if I know how to hold a baby," Will said, awkwardly taking the sleeping infant in his arms.

"He won't break," Libby said as Jeff helped her down from the wagon. "If he can handle this bumpy ride, he can handle anything."

"He's beautiful," Will said. "Thank you for naming him after me."

"We call him Billy," Jeff said, smiling at the baby, then at Will.

"Oh Jeff, this is a *wonderful* cabin!" Libby ran to the door to look inside. "It's much nicer than you described! Just look how big it is! Why it's twice as big as my old place! Look, it's even got a window!"

"Hey, this is just a start, Girl. You'll really see big when I add the breezeway and second cabin to it. A young man as big as Tad needs to have his own place to sleep. Then who knows what we'll do when little Billy gets big enough to want to sleep by himself. We might have buildings all over the place by then." He turned to grin at Will. "Speaking of big, Will, what have you been doing with that corn?'

"Just watching it grow. That's all. I told you we could grow anything here. Come on, let's unload the wagon. I think Tad and I have enough leftovers from supper to feed you when we get done."

After settling in the few pieces of furniture that Libby brought in the wagon and eating supper, they all went back outside to enjoy the cool late evening breeze. Libby spread a pallet on the ground for little Billy and sat down next to him and Jeff. The sun had just gone down beyond the cornfield, spreading its orange glow across the golden corn tassels. They watched the colors of the evening change as the western sky shaded through its majestic palate.

"Jeff," Libby said as she hugged his arm. "It's so beautiful here. I love it."

"Hey, we almost forgot something," Will said as he got to his feet. "Come on." He grabbed Libby by the hand. "Everybody up. There's something we've got to do before it gets too dark."

Jeff started grinning as Will led them all out to a big open area on a rise between the cabin and the cornfield.

"All right, everybody join hands in a big circle . . . ."

The four figures silhouetted against the sky looked as if they were involved in a pagan ritual as Will quietly explained the purpose of the Texas ownership celebration. Then their voices rang out in unison, echoing across the countryside as they squatted, then sprang into the air, flinging dirt and grasses high over their heads. Jeff flew higher than the rest, kicking his feet in the air as he jumped for the sheer joy and thankfulness of having his family all together and healthy on his own land.

Chapter 21

The chores of summer farm life kept everyone busy as the corn and cotton matured. Libby seemed to take the hard work in stride as she and the baby settled comfortably into frontier life. She frequently spent part of her day in the fields working with the men, leaving the baby on a pallet to coo in the shade of one of the large oaks next to the field.

Will and Jeff agreed to share in the labor and profit of their communal farming venture for the first year and see how that worked out. They felt they could accomplish more together than separately. During the summer they took time out from their work in the fields to construct two out buildings behind Jeff's cabin. One would serve as a corn crib and the other a smoke house. They also put up a corral with a lean-to on the north side to protect the horses and mules from the winter weather.

They spent several days digging a root cellar where they would store sweet potatoes that they'd dig throughout the summer. The cellar would also provide protection from storms if necessary.

By mid-mid-September, the cotton was coming into full maturity and was ready to pick. Jeff soon learned that Aunt Bess' story of cotton jumping off the bush wasn't quite true. The yield was as good as they had hoped, but the picking was a slow, tiring, back-aching job. Libby sewed long, spacious cotton sacks for everyone to use, picking the cotton. There was a mini celebration when each sack was emptied into a wagon. Will and Jeff made and attached tall side boards to the wagons and packed the cotton tightly every time a sack was dumped.

When they'd filled the first two wagons with as much as they could carry, Will and Tad left for San Felipe. Jeff and Libby stayed behind to continue picking and loading the wagon that Austin had given them from Mister Bell's estate.

The interval while Will and Tad were gone went slowly for Jeff and Libby, as they labored in the fields, but at least the weather had turned cooler, and the baby was not quite as fussy as he had been in the middle of the summer heat.

Will was impressed with the help he was getting from Tad. He worked as hard as any grown man and didn't complain about his tasks. He handled his team well and guided them over stream crossings without incident.

They made much better time on their return trip and pulled alongside Jeff's wagon near the cotton field on the afternoon of the eighth day, as expected.

Will could tell that Jeff and Libby had worked hard while he and Tad were away. They had the third wagon loaded and a huge mound of cotton was piled up on large sheets spread on the ground.

Picking continued without delay until they got the second wagon loaded and packed down. By then the corn had fully dried on the stalks. While they still had one empty wagon, they moved from the cotton to the cornfields and harvested the corn, filling the crib to capacity.

Then they moved back to the last of the cotton, stripping the fields completely and loading the last wagon.

"I thought we'd be picking cotton till doomsday," Tad said, standing at the end of a row of dried and stripped cotton stalks, wiping the sweat from his brow.

"It looks like it might be worth it," Will said. "If the last two loads are any indication of what we'll get from all of it, we'll do all right."

That evening, they sat in Jeff's yard on their cotton sacks after supper, admiring the three loaded wagons parked in a row ready to go to market, and talked of their success and plans for things to come.

"Sure, it's hard work," Jeff said. "I've worked hard all my life. But this is different. This time I'm working for something for my family. Just look around. This is ours. We built it. We'll work hard for everything good we have."

Jeff reached over and took the baby from Libby and held him out at arm's length. "Some day, little man, you'll have it even better than me. You know why? Because you'll have a good education. That's something nobody can take away. You too, Tad. Just as soon as Will and I get back from Virginia, you're starting on your lessons. You and Libby both. I'll bring back books we can all enjoy. We'll be the best read family in all of Texas."

Will had been listening to Jeff, but he was thinking of something more pressing.

"When will you all be ready to head back to town?" he asked. "I really would like to get that cotton moving while the weather's still holding."

"We can be ready by midday tomorrow," Jeff answered. "At least we can get a half-day on the road."

Libby knew that this trip to San Felipe would be the beginning of the journey back to Virginia for Will and Jeff. She had tried to prepare herself once again for the long separation from Jeff, but was dreading it.

"How long do you think you'll be gone?" She asked Will.

"Once we take care of our business in San Felipe and drop you, Tad, and Billy off to stay with the folks at the old Bell farm, we should be able to make the coast in another two or three days on horseback. We may have to wait a while to catch a ship going to New Orleans. After a couple of days visiting my cousin and her husband there, we'll be off to Richmond. From there, we'll probably hire a carriage to take us on home. I imagine we'll be gone at least two full months, maybe a little longer. We have to be back in time for planting."

"The boys and I will miss you, but I know you both need to see your folks. Three and a half years is a long time."

Will said as he rose from the ground and headed toward his horse. "I'll get up early and stop over at a couple of the neighbors to let them know we'll be away and ask them to look after our places while we're gone. See you about noon tomorrow."

On October 21, 1832, Will, Jeff, Libby, Tad, and little Billy once again loaded themselves and their traveling gear into the wagons and headed south. Libby and the boys would be making an extended visit with old friends and Will and Jeff were on a journey of a different type — back to family and Anna.

Chapter 22

The trip back south to San Felipe was filled with both anticipation and dread. They all shared the anticipation of the sale of their first crop and a realization that their labor was, indeed, worthwhile. Will and Jeff also shared the anticipation of starting on the first leg of their long journey back to Virginia. But Jeff and Libby shared the dread of another long separation.

It seemed to Libby that even though she and Jeff had been married for some time, they had really just started their life together. From the moment she'd first seen the small cabin with Tad running out to meet them, she'd loved Virginia Point. Setting up her own home and being with Jeff was like paradise to her. She didn't mind the hard work and the demands of a baby. She loved her man. She loved her new home, and she loved her new life. Now she was going to have to put it all on hold. She was willing to do it for Jeff. She knew he wanted to see his parents again. She knew that he wanted them to see what he had become; that all their prayers for him, and more, had been answered. Their son was a free, educated man. Their son owned his own land with a wonderful home. And their son had his own son, born into freedom.

After several days of slow travel in the heavy, tightly packed wagons, they rolled into town late in the afternoon, just in time to transact their business with the cotton buyer and get their wagons unloaded before he locked up for the day.

After they made their sale and split the proceeds, Will went to visit Austin while Jeff and Tad helped the workers unload the wagons.

I hoped I'd still find you here," Will said as he found Austin working over papers in the fading light.

"Was that you who rolled in with those cotton wagons a little while ago?" Austin asked.

"Yes sir. Those three wagons made a total of five loads."

"So how did you do?"

"Much better than I expected on our first crop. We still have at least two or three loads of corn back at the place, more than we'll need for ourselves, but it will have to wait till later to sell. Jeff and I are going to head back to Virginia for a little visit."

"I guess you picked as good a time as any to take off for a spell with your crop in and all. Won't be much to do for a while."

"Seems like there's always plenty to do around my place," Will said.

"I was hoping you'd drop by sometime soon," Austin said. "I've got something for you and Libby." Austin unlocked the drawer to his desk. "We sold Mister Bell's house a couple of weeks ago. A fella that had his place a few miles west of town bought it. I think I got a fair price. Here's an envelope for you and one for Libby." Austin handed the envelopes to Will. "I hope you're both satisfied with it."

"I'm sure whatever you got is fair."

"I've also been in correspondence with Mister Bell's daughter in New Orleans," Austin said. "She's in full agreement with the terms of the will and I've already shipped everything she asked for. She asked about you in her letters and said she's looking forward to your visit."

"Jeff and I want to get some miles behind us, but we dread the long trip. We're going by ship this time. Should cut a lot of time off the travel. Anyway, I can't stay but just a minute, but I wanted to know what's happening with Santa Anna. Is he president yet?"

"You *have* been away for awhile, haven't you? Yes, he and his Liberalists are in power now. It just so happened that he was struggling for power with the central government at the same time we were having a few little rebellions ourselves here in Texas. Some of our boys from around here were trying to run those convict soldiers out of Texas. It seems that Santa Anna's reform movement down south fell in line with some of the things we were trying to do here, so we were able to convince him we're loyal to his cause.

"The times are right with a new popular president in power for us to present our position for modifying the laws affecting Texas. Some of the grant contractors like myself and others from around the settlements have made plans to have a series of conventions to prepare our proposals for Santa Anna. I think we all want the same things. We basically want the agreements of the Constitution of 1824 reinstated. We want the immigration laws changed and some relaxation of the stiff tariff laws. There's also a strong push for us have our own state government here in Texas. I imagine before it's over with, I'll have to make a trip to Mexico City and talk to Santa Anna face to face."

"I wish I could be here to take part in the conventions, but we probably won't be back 'til February. I'll sure make a point of stopping by here as soon as I get back to see if there's anything I can do to give you a hand."

"Probably the best thing you can do while you're gone is promote Texas. I feel confident we'll win our right to re-establish immigration one of these days."

"I'll be sure to do that. But if we don't make tracks, we won't be able to promote anything. We'll see you in February. Thanks for selling the house. I'll see that Libby gets her share."

As Will was walking toward the cotton broker's building, Jeff, Libby and Tad pulled the three empty wagons onto the street from behind the building.

"Looks like we all got through with our business at about the same time," Will said. He followed Jeff to the wagon Libby was driving. After Jeff climbed up the wheel and sat next to Libby, Will pulled the envelope out of his pouch.

"This is yours, Libby." Will handed her the envelope. "Mister Austin sold Uncle John's house. This is yours and Tad's share."

Libby took the envelope. She felt its thickness, but didn't open it.

“Well, go ahead” Jeff said. “Open it up.”

Libby carefully opened the envelope and looked inside. Her breath caught when she saw the contents. “Here, Jeff, you take it.” Her hands were trembling as she handed the envelope to Jeff. He looked inside and let out a low whistle as he thumbed through the currency.

“If the only way we can have money is because the master died, then I don't want it,” she said, tears starting to well in her eyes.

“He didn't want you to look at it that way,” Will said, gently taking her hand. “This is his gift to you and Tad, just like your freedom. You and Tad were all he had during the last years of his life. You took care of him and made him comfortable. This is his way of thanking you. He may never have thanked you for all the things you did for him when he was alive, but this is his way now. You take it and do whatever you want with it. You can buy hogs, or cattle, or whatever you want. It's yours to enjoy. That's what he wanted. Do you understand?”

Libby nodded slowly, grieving anew for her master.

“Thanks, Will,” Jeff said, putting his arm around Libby and giving her a hug. “Now, if we're going to make the plantation before bedtime, we'd better get rolling.”

Chapter 23

Daybreak the next morning found Will and Jeff saddling Baron and Buck for their ride to the coast. Libby had never asked Jeff to stay with her and not go with Will, but it was all she could do that morning to conceal her fears. It would help to be with friends to pass the time while he was gone, but she would still worry about his safety and miss him every day.

Jeff hugged her and kissed her on the cheek. He took the baby from Tad. He gently kissed him on the head. “Don't you grow up before I get back,” he said. Handing him back to Libby, he reached for Tad and hugged him tightly. “You look after your sister and that baby and do what Kado tells you.”

Will mounted up while Jeff said his goodbyes, then Jeff swung into his saddle.

“We'll be back before you know it,” Will said as he reached down and squeezed Libby's hand. “Tad, hold Jake so he doesn't try to follow us.”

They turned their horses south and, after walking a few steps, spurred into a comfortable canter.

They followed the trail south that paralleled the Brazos to Brazoria. There they found the man Austin said could be trusted with their horses. After making arrangements with him to take care of their mounts and saddles while they were gone, they caught a cotton barge ferrying its load into the bay and to the sailing ship waiting there.

They found the ship’s captain to be a pleasant enough heavy-set Scot named McGinnis. He quoted what they considered reasonable passenger rates to New Orleans.

“I don't make my money off passengers anyway,” McGinnis said in his Scottish brogue, pushing his cap to the back of his head. “There's enough to be made in Texas cotton. If you don't mind eatin' what the crew eats and sleepin' in hammocks or on the deck, you're welcome to sail with us. You were lucky to catch that barge when you did. That's the last of our load. We'll be settin' sail soon as it's loaded an' secured. Is New Orleans your final stop, or are you goin' on up river from there?"

"Actually, we're only going to stay in New Orleans a couple of days, then sail on around to Richmond."

"Well, sir, we've got a layover scheduled at New Orleans, then we were goin' to make port in Savannah, then Norfolk and Baltimore before we sail back across the big water. You're welcome to go on to Norfolk with us if you're a mind. Then you can catch a barge up the river to Richmond. I'll tell you up front, you could travel a lot more comfortable on some other vessels, but we make good time and won't gouge you on the fare."

"Captain, Jeff and I aren't used to a lot of comfort. What we're most interested in now is time."

"Well then, you just see how it goes between here and New Orleans. Looks like we'll be havin' good weather and a favorable wind. You can decide about the rest of the way when we get there."

McGinnis was right. They made even better time than he had forecasted. Once they got into the coastal waters, they caught a good wind and anchored at New Orleans a half-day ahead of schedule. Both Will and Jeff were impressed with Captain McGinnis' ability on the sea. By the time they arrived at New Orleans, they'd booked passage all the way to Norfolk.

Will had a brief but enjoyable visit with his cousin and her husband, and in two days they were again underway, heading southeast to skirt the coast of Florida.

Jeff became acquainted with several of the sailors and particularly enjoyed the company of the captain's servant and cook, Elijah. He learned that Elijah had been with the captain for fourteen years and had traveled over most of the civilized world and some places that weren't so civilized. Jeff also passed his time with books he'd bought in Brazoria before they boarded the ship. To keep a record of their travels he'd also bought a small journal, a bottle of ink and a writing quill that would fit in the pouch on his belt. During the trip, he developed the habit of documenting his thoughts from time to time, further honing his writing skills.

Will became friendly with the captain as the days went by. With his surveying experience, he easily learned to assist in taking navigational sightings with the captain's sextant. McGinnis also taught him how to control the helm and allowed him to take a partial watch occasionally. McGinnis enjoyed Will's company and frequently invited him to dinner. He seldom had the opportunity to spend time with a man of Will's ability and background. Each found the other an interesting conversationalist. McGinnis told Will stories of the sea, and Will shared tales of the Texas frontier.

They made reasonably good time around the tip of Florida and up the Atlantic coastline. They experienced only two small storms off the coast of Florida during their trip, enjoying fair weather and favorable winds the rest of the way.

A couple of weeks after they'd left Texas, they anchored at Norfolk. Will and Jeff bid the captain and crew farewell and found passage on an empty cotton barge, heading up river for another load of cotton to bring back to port.

Since Jeff hadn't gone ashore in New Orleans, he had never seen a city the size of Richmond. As they walked away from their ship, he tried to take in all the activity along the docks. The waterfront area was bustling with dark-skinned men loading and unloading barges and small boats with foremen barking orders. The swarm of people on the crowded streets was almost more than he could absorb at one time.

They drew a considerable amount of attention themselves. Two men, one black and one white wearing worn buckskins and moccasins weren't everyday sights on the streets of Richmond. Will had long since worn out the only suit he'd taken west and hadn't had time to shop in New Orleans.

"So Jeff, what do you think of Richmond?" Will asked as

they walked down the street toward a hotel.

"Looks like a mighty fine place, but I'm afraid it's way too big for me."

"Me too. Too many buildings and people. Looks like they're all in a hurry to get somewhere." They stepped aside as a wagon rattled along beside them.

"Here's a hotel down here," Will nodded down the street. "Let's see if they've got a place to put us up." Will suspected a town the size of Richmond would have a hotel with accommodations for traveler's servants. He at least hoped Jeff wouldn't have to sleep in a stable.

Will was able to get a room for himself and made arrangements with the clerk for Jeff to stay with the servants at the hotel.

"It's still pretty early," Will said as they finished registering at the desk. "Why don't we get cleaned up a little, and I'll meet you in front of the hotel. We need to do a little shopping."

"What kind of shopping?" Jeff asked.

"You don't want Jessie and Amos to see us looking like this, do you?"

Jeff looked down at his faded and stained buckskins and worn moccasins as a smile spread across his face. "I never thought about how we're dressed. We just look like every body else back home. Don't much fit in around here, though." Jeff noticed the hotel clerk looking over his spectacles at them. "I'll meet you out front in a half-hour."

It was still early afternoon when they met again outside the hotel, clean as a sponge bath and dirty clothes would allow.

"Well, Mister Jefferson," Will said, "let's see if we can find some clothes suitable for successful Texas planters." Will grinned and slapped Jeff on the back as they headed up the street.

They looked through two stores before they found one that had ready made suits wide enough to fit Jeff's shoulders and long enough to fit Will's arms. The small, balding shopkeeper was eager to wait on Will, but ignored Jeff. Jeff had asked several questions of the shopkeeper and received only an icy stare. He finally started finding his own sizes without the help of the store owner. While Jeff looked at suits along a rack at the front of the store, Will pulled the little man to the rear of the store and into a fitting room.

"Sir, you may not like the color of Mister Jefferson's skin, but I imagine you'll like the color of his money. If he's treated properly, he could be willing to spend some of it here — perhaps quite a lot of it."

"But sir, you don't understand," the shopkeeper whispered as he squirmed under Will's glare. "The finest men in Richmond shop here."

"No, it's you who doesn't understand," Will said as he poked his finger in the man's chest. "We're talking about a total purchase by Mister Jefferson of at least two good suits, maybe more, two expensive hats, a pair of shoes and a pair of boots, at least six shirts and six sets of underwear. I believe that makes Mister Jefferson over there one of the finest men in Richmond. Now do you understand?"

The shopkeeper swallowed the lump in his throat, nodded and smiled. "Sorry for any misunderstanding. I understand perfectly." He quickly walked to the front door, flipped his closed sign toward the outside, locked the door, pulled down the shade and turned to Jeff. "Now, Mister Jefferson," he said with a wide smile and bowed slightly while rubbing his hands together. "How may I be of service to you?"

Will and Jeff had more fun that afternoon than they'd had since they were kids. They realized later they must have looked like school girls, trying on dozens of hats, shirts, shoes, dress coats and pants. They spent most of the afternoon in the shop and left the harried but well-paid shopkeeper to deliver their goods to the hotel.

That evening in his room after a comfortable, hot bath, Will again tried on his new clothes and looked at his image in the oval shaped mirror hanging on the wall over the wash stand. He'd worn nothing but buckskin for so long that the touch of finely woven, professionally made and nicely pressed clothes was a welcome sensation. After satisfying his vanity in the mirror with each set of clothes, he carefully folded and put away everything except what he would wear the next day.

While he arranged the things in his bag, his fingers ran across the familiar shape of the gold locket that Anna had given him. He removed it from the bag and rubbed it between his fingers as he had done hundreds of times over the last two and a half years. He realized he'd worn the surface smooth. As he held it in his fingers, he again thought of Anna. They had become so close in their letters. He felt he knew her perhaps better than anyone else in the world. Now, closer to home, he realized just how much he missed her and how much her letters had meant to him. They'd never really expressed their love for each other in their letters, but there was no doubt in Will's mind how he felt about Anna as he went to bed that night in Richmond.

Will and Jeff still had more shopping to do the next morning. They both wanted to take gifts to family and friends at the plantation. They agreed to meet in the hotel lobby at nine.

Jeff was up early and dressed in his fine new clothes. He was wearing his new dark brown suit, a fresh white shirt and cravat. A fashionably tall hat and shiny new shoes completed his outfit. He also wore a big, bright smile as he greeted Will in the hotel lobby.

"Good morning!" Jeff said as Will stepped off the stairway landing. Will's jaw dropped as he saw his friend dressed in the fine suit of clothes.

"Oh my goodness!" Will said as he saw Jeff and descended the final few steps. "I wish Libby could see you now. You look great."

"You look mighty nice yourself." Jeff said. "Been a while

since I've seen you dress like that." Will was also dressed in one of his nice, new suits.

They each already had their breakfast, so they went on another shopping spree. After visiting several stores, they returned to the hotel loaded with gaily wrapped packages. Leaving Jeff at the hotel, Will said, "Why don't you start getting your things packed while I see what kind of a deal we can get on a carriage to take us home. I've also got one other bit of shipping to do. I'll bring lunch and meet you here shortly after noon."

Will did have more shopping on his mind. He was looking for something very special.

About half past noon, Will pulled up in front of the hotel in a light weight, open carriage. The carriage was outfitted with leather upholstery and had room for packages and luggage behind the rear seat. A well-conditioned, stout-looking bay gelding pulled the fine-looking rig.

Will promised a boy on the street a dollar to watch the rig while he took a bag of sandwiches and bottled beer into the hotel. He found Jeff in the lobby waiting for him. He motioned for Jeff to follow him up the stairs to his room. They ate the quick lunch, and Jeff helped Will bring his packages to the street.

"Nice rig," Jeff said as he and Will stood on the street looking at the carriage.

"I had a choice between a buckboard, a long-bed wagon and this. I just figured nothing was too good for a couple of well-dressed, successful Texas planters like us. Besides, the rental price was right. What do you think?"

"Will Bowman, I like your style." Jeff laughed as he put his and Wills packages and traveling bags behind the seat, and stepped into the carriage. "Now, let's go home!"

Will paid the boy that was looking after the rig, put the carriage in motion and headed west.

Chapter 24

Anna Thompson had kept all of Will's letters tied in two bundles in a cherry-wood box on the table next to her bed. Hardly a day went by that she didn't re-read at least one of them. She felt that she knew Libby, Tad, Stephen Austin and Will's neighbors as well as she knew her own family and neighbors. She grieved with Will when his letter told of the loss of his uncle and was joyous when she read of the birth of Jeff and Libby's baby. She shared his concerns at the turn of events with the Mexican government but, like Will, she remained confident that through Austin's efforts and a few others like him, a peaceful solution would prevail.

Anna was actually a bit embarrassed that she was more knowledgeable of Mexican politics than she was of American. She had attempted to engage her father in discussions of Mexican politics a few times at the dinner table, but he had told her those matters weren't things that should concern a young lady and had changed the subject to matters closer to home.

The last two letters from Will told of his plans to return to Virginia after his harvest. She had no idea when he would arrive, but if Texas harvest times were similar to Virginia's, and allowing time for travel, she expected he would be home sometime in late November or early December,

She took a keener interest in the harvest of her father's crops that year than she ever had in the past. She frequently rode out to watch the progress of the workers as they picked cotton and loaded the wagons. She tried to visualize Will and Jeff working in their fields as she watched the dark-skinned men and women pick cotton from her father's plantation.

Anna spent the late summer and fall sewing for herself. She wanted to look her best when Will arrived. She made several new dresses and bonnets and put them away to wear later.

The harvest was over. Her father sent the last load of cotton to market two weeks ago. She had been expecting Will to arrive any day, but she'd been expecting that, or hoping anyway, for weeks.

One morning, Mister Thompson announced that he needed to go to Roanoke for supplies and asked if Anna and her mother wanted to keep him company. He reminded them that Christmas was just around the corner, and if they were going to do their usual holiday cooking and baking, they might want to join him.

Anna debated the wisdom of leaving home at such a critical time, but she needed several things to finish some sewing and had some special gifts in mind that she wanted to buy. She and her mother decided to go. Shortly after breakfast, Anna climbed into the back seat of the carriage dressed in a new dark-blue dress and a matching bonnet with a wool cape wrapped around her to ward off the early winter chill. With a sense of holiday excitement, they left in their carriage, heading east toward Roanoke.

That morning, after two days on the road, before leaving their hotel in Roanoke and heading west, Will had dressed in his new dark gray suit and light gray hat with a fresh white shirt and cravat and black shoes. Jeff dressed in his black suit with a white shirt and cravat and then brushed his new black hat clean and shined his shoes. They felt as good as they looked when they stepped into the carriage, which the livery man had freshly wiped clean of dust. They both looked forward to the three-hour ride to the plantation as they rolled out of Roanoke.

They were in familiar country now. Will enjoyed watching the countryside pass by as Jeff maintained a good, effortless pace with the stout bay. Will had traveled this road dozens of times when he was growing up. On several occasions they passed workers and planters in the fields and waved as they passed, momentarily stopping the progress of work as the workers were unaccustomed to seeing such finely outfitted travelers along their road.

There were several small creeks and streams to cross. Most of them were spanned by wooden bridges. As they approached a bridge near the halfway point between Roanoke and his father's plantation, Will noticed another carriage approaching them from the other side of the stream.

“Let’s pull over here and let them pass,” Will said. “Looks like a couple of ladies and a man coming toward us. Shouldn't make them wait on us.”

Jeff pulled off the roadway and waited for the approaching carriage to pass over the bridge.

Anna had been daydreaming as they rode, enjoying the crispness of the late fall air but thankful for the warming sunshine.

“Fancy looking rig up ahead,” her father said as they approached the bridge. “Looks like they've pulled over to let us by. Must be traveling through. Don't recall seeing that rig around here before. We'll go ahead and move across so we don't hold them up.”

Anna's attention was drawn to the carriage waiting on the other side. As they approached the bridge, she saw the two men in the carriage. Recognition flooded over her as they reached the half-way point of the bridge.

"Will!” she screamed with full realization of who waited on the other side of the bridge. “Papa! Mama! That's Will!” She wildly waved her arms. “Will! Oh, Papa, hurry!"

Will knew it was Anna before she called his name. Their eyes met at the same time. She yanked off her bonnet as she called his name so he could better see her face.

“It's Anna, Jeff! Look, it's Anna!” Will handed the reins to Jeff and stepped from his seat and waited beside the carriage as the Thompson's carriage wheeled noisily across the bridge. He saw the lovely Anna in the back seat waving her bonnet wildly, her dark hair blowing in the wind as her father pressed his team faster across the bridge.

Thompson pulled to a stop as he drew alongside Will's and Jeff's carriage. Will reached for Anna as she scrambled out of the carriage and into his arms. “Oh Will!” She threw her arms around him. “You're finally here!”

“In the flesh.” Will laughed as he recovered from the shock of meeting the Thompsons on the road and Anna's excited greeting. He reached up to shake Thompson's hand, and leaned over to hug Mrs. Thompson as she reached both arms toward him.

“My, you look good — both of you,” Thompson said, acknowledging Jeff. “Hello Jefferson.”

“Morning, Mister Thompson.” Jeff removed his hat. “Miz Thompson, Miss Anna. Glad to see you all again.”

“We're glad to see both of you,” Mrs. Thompson said, smiling. “I know Anna's been looking for you for weeks. Looks like Texas agrees with you.”

“Thank you, Ma’am,” Will answered. “Must be all that fresh air and hard work.

After her initial hug, Anna settled on just holding Will's hand while he visited with her parents. They continued their conversation for a few minutes, the Thompsons asking about life in Texas and Will asking about their health and the recent harvest.

Finally Anna said, “Papa, I want to ride back to the Bowman place with Will and Jeff. I'd like to visit with him and Mary today if that's all right. Mama, you know what I need in town. Would you pick it up for me?” Mrs. Thompson turned briefly toward her husband. Her bonnet hid the facial gestures she made to him and the small nod of her head, but her encouragement worked.

“I guess that would be all right," Thompson said, smiling at Will. “Shall we pick you up on our way back?”

“I'll bring her home tonight, if that would be all right,” Will said.

“That would be fine,” Mrs. Thompson said. “Come visit

with us, Will, when you have time, and tell us all about Texas."

"I will, Ma'am. You can count on it." Will squeezed Anna's hand.

After rearranging packages, Will and Anna rode in the back seat as Jeff drove and enjoyed the excited conversation behind him. It was as if Anna wanted to learn everything that had happened in three and a half years within the time it took to finish the ride home. Anna immediately felt at ease with Will. She had been afraid that their first meeting upon his return might be awkward and uneasy, but she quickly remembered how easy it was to be with him. She felt like they had been best friends for years, now reunited after a long separation. They chatted the rest of the way to the plantation, oblivious to everything around them.

Soon they were interrupted by Jeff. "Will, Miss Anna, look where we are." He was pulling off the road onto the lane to the Bowman plantation house. "There it is, just up ahead."

"Come on, Jeff," Will said, sitting forward in his seat. "Put a little spark in that bay. Let's let them know we're here." Jeff put the whip to the horse, bringing him to a fast trot as Will stood in the carriage, holding Jeff's shoulder with one hand and taking off his hat with the other. When they got within a hundred yards of the house, he started yelling and waving his hat.

"Hey, y'all we're home! Papa! Mary! Jessie! Amos! We're home!" Jeff and Anna joined in the yelling, caught up in the excitement of the homecoming.

The racket from the yard produced the desired results. First Mary burst through the front door. Then Jessie flew around to the front from the side porch. Henry followed Mary, and Amos came running from the barn. It took a few seconds for Jeff to stop the excited animal and apply the carriage brake. He and Will scrambled out of the carriage. Everyone was laughing and talking and hugging all at once.

"Lordy mercy! Let me look at you!" Jessie said when some of the commotion quieted. "You don't look nothin' like the boys that left out of here. Why, I thought you was Andy Jackson hisself come rolling up here a-lookin' like dis. My goodness, you both such *handsome* young men!"

"Thank you, Jessie," Will said. "Maybe there have been a few changes. Reckon Jeff will tell you all about it later. Now, you and Amos go visit with Jeff. You've got a lot of catching up to do."

"Come on in the house," Henry said. "You still haven't told us where you found this pretty thing here." Will followed his father into the house with one arm around Mary's waist and the other around Anna's.

Jessie found that Will, Jeff and Anna hadn't had lunch and she immediately put together a snack. "Now y'all save up plenty of room for supper," Jessie said as she served the meal in the dining room. "We gonna have us a welcome home dinner tonight."

Will, Henry, Mary and Anna spent the rest of the afternoon visiting in the living room. Will described the work he and Jeff did for the settlers, and told some of his favorite stories about living in the old tent with Jeff and their dog Jake. He described the settlers and told of their hard work and dreams of building a future for their families there. He recounted the success of their first crop and his hopes of expanding his planting acreage next year.

Before they knew it, the afternoon had passed and Jessie was calling them to dinner. True to her promise, she had prepared a big dinner for Will consisting of all his favorites. During dinner Henry and Mary caught Will up on the events in their lives. Henry declared, much to the embarrassment of Mary, that she was being courted by half the young men in the county, but none had proposed.

"Why, I wouldn't marry any of those silly 'ole boys," Mary said, cutting her meat. "But the right one may come along one of these days and just sweep me off my feet. Sometimes, though, I wish I was more like Anna and just didn't waste my time with the boys around here."

Anna smiled quietly as her cheeks slightly flushed.

Changing the subject, Henry suggested, "Mary and I have talked about having a party while you're here. How long can you stay, Son?"

"No longer than a month, I'm afraid. We've got to get back in time to get the ground ready for planting."

"This is the party season anyway," Mary said. "Papa, can I go ahead and plan one for Will?"

"If it's all right with Will, it's all right with me."

"Sounds fine to me," Will said.

"Then a party it is!" said Mary excitedly. "Two weeks from Saturday. I'll start putting things in motion tomorrow."

After dinner, Will asked that the carriage be brought around. Anna said her goodbyes and promised to help Mary plan the party.

Once away from the house and shaded by darkness, Anna moved close to Will on the carriage seat, and slid her arm under his.

"I'm so glad you're home," she said, squeezing his arm.

"Me too." Will looked up at the stars in the clear, moonless night. He studied the glitter of the skies for a few moments with only the sounds of the horse's hooves on the hard packed road breaking the silence.

"You know, Anna, I spent a lot of nights under those stars, just looking up at them. Some nights were so hot, all I could do was sweat and listen to the mosquitoes. Others were so cold, I just huddled in my blankets, shivering and waiting for dawn. All kinds of nights. A whole lot of good nights, but some not so comfortable. Even a few scary ones. Sometimes I couldn't see the stars for the rain or snow clouds, but I knew they were there, just like I knew you'd be here when I came home. I want you to know that every one of those nights I had a little piece of home to comfort me." Will reached into his pocket and pulled out the locket and chain that Anna had given him so long ago.

“Remember this?” He handed Anna the locket.

Anna saw a twinkle of starlight reflecting off the locket and felt its shape. “It's my locket.”

“Now rub it between your fingers. What do you feel?”

“It's so smooth!” She smiled, feeling the surface of the little gold heart.

“I guess there wasn't a night that went by that I didn't hold that little locket between my fingers and think of you. I'm afraid I rubbed most of the engraving off. You can barely see the little roses that used to be on it. Thank you for giving me something that brought me close to you when I was so far away.”

“Thank you for thinking of me," She hesitated a moment, then continued. “I had some long nights too, but I didn't have anything of yours until you sent me that comb and mirror. Some nights I would lie in bed and try to see you in my mind. Sometimes I'd see you riding that big white horse. You were always so tall and handsome in the saddle. Sometimes I would see you surveying in the buckskin outfit that Libby made for you. I pictured you standing up straight, sighting through your instruments, confident of your ability. Sometimes I just saw you sitting on the top of a hill with the wind in your face, looking off into the distance, your features set with a look of determination, dreaming your dreams.”

“Sounds like we've been spending our nights doing some of the same things,” Will said.

Suddenly, he realized they were at the turnoff to the Thompson estate. After he turned into the lane leading to the house, he stopped the carriage and turned to Anna.

“Thank you for waiting for me,” he said as he embraced her. Their lips slowly came together for their first long-awaited kiss.

Ever since Jeff first got his freedom, he’d asked Will not to mention it in his letters back to Virginia. That was the one thing he wanted the pleasure of someday being able to personally tell his mama and papa. Jessie and Amos had been told of Jeff's taking a wife and that they had a grandbaby, but they knew little else of Jeff's personal business.

Jeff spent all afternoon in the kitchen with Jessie and Amos, watching his mother work as he told them all about Libby and the baby. Jessie was so happy and excited to have her son home, she was asking one question after the other: "Is Libby a good cook? Is she a good house keeper? Does she know how to sew well? Is she pretty? Did she have an easy birth? Is the baby healthy? Is she a good mother? Does she take good care of you?"

Jessie stood at the counter making a pie crust while Jeff answered her questions.

"Well, I tell you dis," Jessie said, shaking a flour-coated finger at Jeff. "If she as good as you say she is, din boy, you better treat her and my grandbaby good. You treat a woman good an' take good care of her, she make you a happy man yo whole life."

"I am a happy man, Mama. I'm the happiest man I know, except maybe Will today, when he first saw Miss Anna."

After they finished serving supper, Jeff washed the dishes and Amos dried while Jessie put things away. After awhile, Jessie stopped what she was doing and just stood across the room watching Jeff and his father work, listening to Amos talk about a wagon repair job he and Toby had been working on. Jessie was so proud of her fine, strong son, standing there in his handsome new suit of clothes. She sat at the table, and rested her chin on her fist, admiring Jeff.

"Dat Mister Will sho is good to you, Honey, buyin' you a fine suit of clothes and all so you'd look nice when you come to see yo mama an' papa."

Jeff turned to see his mother smiling at him so contentedly.

"Mama," he said, drying his hands, then spreading the cloth out across the counter. "You don't really know just how good Will has been to me. Come on over here and sit down, Papa." Jeff pulled a chair out for Amos, and sat down between his parents. "I've got some more things to tell you.

"I bought these clothes myself with my own money. There's another new suit in my bag, and new shirts and new boots. I've got gifts for both of you and Miss Mary and Mister Henry. There are also things I bought to take home for Libby and the baby. I paid for my passage here on a sailing ship, and I paid all my expenses along the way. Everything was bought and paid for with my own money that I earned by working for it." Jeff paused a moment, looking first at Jessie, then Amos to gauge their reaction. They both sat expressionless.

"Mama, Papa . . . I'm a free man. Will gave me my freedom before we got to Texas."

Jeff hesitated a moment to give his parents time to comprehend the words he had just spoken. He smiled as he said, "Mister Will gave me my freedom because he respects me as a man. He didn't need a slave. What he needed was another good surveyor, a partner trained to share the work. He's helped me become educated, and he's taught me to be a surveyor. I can read and write as well as any man. Better than many. I know mathematics and geometry. I earn my own pay, same as Will and any other man doing the same work, and I pay my own way. I'm a citizen of Mexico, and I own my own land. Mama, I own over forty-five hundred acres of good, rich Texas land. I have my own home, just like the one we built for Will, and I'll be adding on to it next year. I've got corn in the crib from this year's crop, and I've already sold my cotton. I have a beautiful wife who loves me who has her freedom too, and we have a fine, healthy son who will never belong to anyone but himself.

"Mama, Papa, I'm a Texas planter with much more land than most land owners around these parts. I believe I must be the luckiest and happiest man who ever walked this earth. Yes Mama, Mister Will has been mighty good to me. He set me free and let me realize my dreams."

Jeff looked at Jessie, then Amos. They both had tears streaming down their faces.

"Oh, Lord, thank you," Jessie prayed as she leaned over to embrace Jeff. He pulled her close with one arm, then reached over and pulled Amos into their embrace.

"I just wish I could have you two there with me. That would make everything perfect." His tears fell onto his mother's head kerchief as he embraced his parents.

Will took full advantage of the time he had with his family and friends. He visited with his brothers and got re-acquainted with their families. He spent a several mornings visiting with some of the neighbors he had known all his life. It seemed that wherever he went, there was a meal or a slice of cake or pie to be eaten. But he reserved a special amount of time to be with Anna.

The second evening he was home, she invited him for dinner with her family. He enjoyed the dinner and the conversation with Mister Thompson. Thompson was interested in the agriculture and politics in Texas, and Will gave him a glowing account of both.

"Oh, there have been a few problems, mainly because of the culture differences between us and the native Mexicans," Will said. "You know how independent most Americans are. But Stephen Austin and some others are working hard to have Texas established as a Mexican state with our own state government. We'd like to have more local input to the laws that govern us. We have some conventions set for next spring to establish petitions, which will be presented to President Santa Anna. We'll be asking for liberalization of some of the immigration and tariff laws.

"Yes sir, I feel confident with my decision to move to Texas. There are a lot of good people there. My neighbors are some of the finest people I know. We've named our community Virginia Point because several of the families along the river are from Virginia. Everyone is willing to help his neighbor. We need that kind of support out there."

The conversation continued through dinner, with most of the discussion centered around life in Texas. Eventually Anna's parents excused themselves, leaving Anna and Will time for themselves.

Anna had grown into everything Will knew she would. He had known her most of her life, but she was no longer a little girl or an awkward teenager. She was a grown woman; a much more confident version of the beautiful, dark-haired teenager he had last seen before leaving for Texas. She was independent, intelligent, and strong in her attitudes. She was capable of participating and holding her own in any discussion on politics, agriculture or most any other subject that was brought about, Anna was a competent woman with a mind of her own. She also understood what it took to manage a household and an estate.

Even though her family had servants, her mother insisted that she learn to cook and take care of the other household responsibilities. Also, with no brothers, her father had trained her in the business of the plantation.

Will liked the confidence Anna exhibited. He appreciated her interest and involvement in conversations in which most women would show little concern. He felt comfortable with the way she looked at him, with no shyness in her gaze and with genuine interest, as he talked about the people of Texas.

They spent the remainder of the evening in the parlor, with Anna telling of her experiences at finishing school and Will sharing tales of Texas that Uncle John had told him as well as some of his own.

"Will," Anna said as she walked him to his horse, "why don't you ride over tomorrow? I'll have my horse ready and we'll take a ride. Looks like the weather will be nice. I'll pack a lunch, and you can see some of the countryside you haven't seen for a while."

"It just happens that I have absolutely nothing else planned." Will laughed. "How about ten o'clock?"

"I'll be ready."

Will pulled her to him in a gentle embrace that seemed as comfortable for both of them as if they had been together like this for years. They held each other for a moment and Will kissed her tenderly.

"I could really get used to this," he whispered in her ear.

"I hope so," Anna answered, pressing her cheek to his chest.

They held each other close for a few moments, then Anna slid her arms from around Will's shoulders, down his arms and finally held herself at arm's length, holding his strong hands.

"Ten in the morning?"

"I'll be here."

"Come hungry."

Will loped his father's black mare home, smiling at his good fortune in having his reunion with Anna be what he had hoped. She was the same warm, wonderful person he had grown to love in her letters. He looked forward to the next day together—alone.

Chapter 25

"It did turn out to be a pretty day," Will said as they walked their horses through the winter grass. "I'm surprised that we haven't had any snow yet."

"Maybe we'll have a white Christmas. Does it snow much in Texas?"

"Not much. The winters are usually comfortable, but every once in a while, we get what we call a blue norther that blows in and drops the temperature like a rock. The nights get cold sometimes, but it usually doesn't last more than a few days. A man can work most every day of the year."

As they approached the edge of the creek that flowed into the river, Will said, "Hey, look, there's our old swimming hole. Jeff and I used to go swimming here when we were kids. Why, there's even a piece of the old rope swing left." He pointed to the rotten strand of rope dangling from a knot wrapped around a fat limb of a large tree arcing over the water.

"I know. Mary and I came here sometimes too."

Will swung off his horse and walked around to help Anna dismount. He grinned mischievously. "You didn't come around while we were swimming without our clothes did you?"

"Maybe we did, maybe we didn't," Anna teased. "Are you getting hungry?"

"You told me to come hungry. I always do what I'm told."

They found a flat spot under the tree and spread a cover over the ground. Will untied the basket from Anna's horse and brought it over. He opened the lid and looked inside. "Goodness! Anna, there's just the two of us!"

She had packed several sandwiches made of ham and biscuits, several small jars of vegetables and fruit and half an apple pie. She had also included a bottle of wine from her father's ample supply in their cellar.

They enjoyed their lunch, recounting stories of their childhood. Anna laughed, recalling one of the favorite tricks she and Mary had played on Will when they were children. “Do you remember the time Mary and I went into your room while you were sleeping and stole your pants?”

“How could I ever forget that one?” Will laughed as he remembered. “You sewed the legs of the pants up before you returned them, then stood outside the door and yelled that the barn was on fire.”

“We were afraid to open the door to see what was going on when you tried to get into your pants, but we could sure imagine what was happening from all the banging around we heard from the other side of the door.” Anna chuckled.

“But I always managed to get back at you some way, didn't I?” Will asked. "Remember the time my brothers came in from a hunting trip late one night while you were staying over at our house?”

“Oh don't remind me of that!”

“They killed a bear. I wrapped up in the bear skin, head and all, and crawled into your room making noises like a bear.”

“Will Bowman, that wasn't funny! You almost scared us out of our wits!”

“You didn't play any tricks on me for awhile after that, did you?”

“Well, we might have slowed down a little.”

After they’d finished eating, Anna put away the food. “Come on, let’s take a walk.” She got to her feet and grabbed Will's hands. Will slid his arm around her waist as they slowly walked toward the creek and along the water’s edge. Anna watched the autumn leaves fall from the almost barren trees and tumble into the water and slowly float away.

“After you left for Texas, I worried that's what you were doing,” Anna said, looking at the dry leaves gently flowing downstream with the current.

“What's that?” Will asked, stopping and turning her to face

him.

"I was afraid you were just going to float away to Texas, never to be seen again. You almost broke my heart when you left."

"But I promised to come back, and I did, didn't I?"

"Yes, and I hung onto that promise every day you were gone."

Will took her hand, and they walked to a large, smooth rock and sat down. They sat quietly for a few moments, watching the water flow past some half-submerged rocks. Then Will look into Anna's eyes.

"Anna, I've made a life for myself in Texas. It can be a good life, but something very important is missing. He hesitated a moment and smiled at her. "You're what's missing in my life.

"I've done everything there with the goal of someday having a family to share it with. I've thought about you every day since I left Virginia. I can now admit that everything I did there, I did with you in mind. I was building a place for *us*. I knew I didn't have a right to tell you these things until I had myself established with a way to make a decent living and a home, but I have those things now.

"Anna, I love you. I thought I loved you as our relationship grew through our letters. Now, since I've been home, I have no doubts. I know I love you and need you to be with me. Please say you'll marry me and come back to Texas with me."

"Oh Will! You don't know how long I've dreamed of you saying those beautiful words to me! Yes! Yes, my darling!" Anna laughed, throwing her arms around Will's neck. "I'll marry you and go anywhere in this big, wide world with you."

Later, as they rode back to the Thompson plantation with the sunset in their faces, they were already making plans.

"I want you to know, the little cabin is just a temporary place," Will said. I've got a spot picked out on a hill, a short walk from the cabin, where we'll build a real house in a few years. It's a perfect spot for a big, two-story house with huge live oak trees scattered around shading the property. It looks out over the prairie. Anna, I believe it's the most beautiful spot on earth — or will be when you get there."

"Papa, Mama, we're back!" Anna called as they entered the large front room of the Thompson house. Mister and Mrs. Thompson came into the room from the back of the house.

"How was your lunch?" Mrs. Thompson asked Will as she entered the room.

"It was really good. That girl knows how to pack a picnic basket."

"Have a seat, Will," Thompson said. "How about something to drink?"

"Yes sir, thank you. I'll have whatever you're having."

"I was going to have a little shot of whiskey. Is that what you want?"

"Yes sir, if you don't mind."

"I'll go put on a pot of tea while you pour your drinks," Mrs. Thompson said, heading for the kitchen. "Anna, do you want a cup?"

"Yes ma'am, thank you." Anna sat on the settee next to Will.

"Anna loves to ride," Thompson said, handing Will his drink. "Never could get her to ride a side saddle like a proper lady, though."

"Oh, Daddy, those things are silly, and dangerous to boot."

"She just hikes up her skirts a bit," Thompson said, "and jumps up in a regular saddle and rides that pony like the wind."

"I know. She wanted to race me on the way back, but I was afraid she'd show me up on my papa's mare. If I had ole Baron here I'd give her a run for her money."

Mrs. Thompson returned, handed Anna her tea and sat in a chair next to her husband.

"So how was your ride?" Mrs. Thompson asked.

"Just fine, ma'am. Nice weather for a ride."

There was an awkward silence for a moment, then Will set his glass on a table, cleared his throat and said, "I'm glad you're both here this afternoon. There's something important I need to talk to you about." Anna looked at Will and noticed tiny beads of perspiration had popped out on his forehead.

"I've known Anna all her life, and we've been writing to each other all the time I've been in Texas. Well, the fact is, ma'am, sir . . . we love each other and want to get married." He hurried on without allowing them to respond. "I want you to know, this isn't a sudden decision for either of us. Even though I've been home only a few days, I think we both knew what we wanted long before I got home. I bought a ring in Richmond, hoping that she would accept my offer and you would approve." Will reached in his jacket pocket and pulled out a little gold band.

"Sir, I've worked hard to be able to obtain what I have to offer Anna. I own almost six thousand acres of prime Texas land and a home to make her comfortable, with plans to build a larger one in the next few years. I've already got one crop of cotton off my land and corn still in the crib that's waiting to go to market. I've got money in the bank and a promise of credit if I need it. I have everything I need to make a home, except the woman I love. I want to ask you to allow Anna to marry me. I promise I'll do everything I can to make her happy."

Will looked at the smiling Anna, then at her mother and father, awaiting their reply.

"I can't say his comes as a tremendous surprise to us," Mister Thompson said. "We've known how Anna feels about you for a long time. We've seen the way she acted when she got a letter from you. It was like she was walking on clouds for days after she received one. She even read parts of them to us, when you described things in Texas. Whenever we went to town, she picked up any publication she could find that had anything in it about Texas.

"When you left, her mother and I honestly didn't know whether you would ever come back here or not. We even tried to encourage Anna to go out and meet young men and have fun like your sister, but she had no interest. Yes, we've known how she has felt about you. We've also tried to prepare ourselves for this day when you would come and want to take our little girl away. I don't know if we are prepared for it yet." Thompson hesitated a moment as he tried to gain control of his voice.

In a few moments he continued, "Texas is so far away. It's not like she would be going to the next county. She would be all the way across the continent in a foreign country. How could we ever see her, or our grand babies that far away? And what about the Indians? You live out on the frontier. There are still wild Indians out there. Can you protect her from them? Then there's the Mexican government. From what I understand, they never have been too stable. What if the government changes and turns against you?"

"Sir, I appreciate your concerns," Will answered. "Those issues concern me too. As far as the distance, yes, it is far away, but I came back. We can both come back for a visit every few years, or you can visit us. We can even meet in New Orleans or someplace else that would be closer for both of us.

"And yes, there are still Indians in the territory that sometimes make trouble, but we haven't been bothered in quite some time now. The neighbors have formed a militia, and we look out for each other. Jeff's place isn't far away, and there are other neighbors in the area. As soon as immigration starts back again, there will be people all around us. I've also got plenty of fire power and know how to use it. Sir, I wouldn't take the woman I love anywhere that I didn't consider safe.

"You're right, too, that the Mexican government has been unstable, and we've had a few problems with it, but the new president, Santa Anna, appears to be in favor of some of the liberties we've asked for, and we expect some positive changes as early as next year."

Will took a deep breath. “Sir, I believe in Texas, and I believe in the people of Texas. They're all hard working people like me. They just want to provide a good home for their families. We're no different than those on any frontier of the United States for the past fifty years. We just want to build a future for our families.”

Thompson looked at Anna, who was clutching Will's hand in both of hers. “Is this what you want? Is this what you really want?”

Anna responded earnestly, “Yes, Papa, more than anything in the world.” She glanced between her father and Will.

Thompson looked at his wife. With tear-rimmed eyes, she nodded. He looked back at Will. “If you two are sure this is what you really want and promise to love each other and promise that we’ll visit from time to time, then you have our blessing.”

“Oh. thank you Papa, Mama!” Anna rushed over to hug both her parents. “We'll visit! You'll see!”

Chapter 26

"Oh, Anna, I'm so happy for you!" Mary said. "I can't believe it! Here he's only been home a few days, and already you're planning to marry!" Mary was almost as excited to learn the news as Anna was to tell it. Anna made Mary promise not to tell anyone of the marriage plans until they could announce it at the party.

"Now remember," Anna said in hushed tones. "It's got to be a surprise for everybody. I even swore my mama and papa to secrecy. I wanted you to know so you can help me plan the wedding. Everything's happening so fast! I'm going to need all the help I can get."

"Oh, my goodness!" Mary said, shaking her head. "A big party and a wedding all in the same month! Come on, Girl, we've got work to do."

The pace around both the Bowman and the Thompson plantations picked up in the days preceding the party. Everyone in the Bowman household was preparing for Will's welcome home party, while Anna and her mother were preparing for a celebration of another kind at their home.

Will stayed out of the way as Mary and Jessie readied things for his party. Since the party would be a week before Christmas, Mary had the entire house decorated with greenery and red ribbons. Amos and Jeff even made wreaths from cedar boughs to hang on each of the tall, white columns at the front of the house. They also laced the greenery along the stair railing and tied it with red ribbon.

By the afternoon of the party, the whole house smelled of cedar and the cinnamon from Jessie's baking. Everything was ready for the guests.

Mary invited everyone from the surrounding area. Shortly after dark, people started arriving. Will took the carriage to pick up Anna and her parents and returned to the Bowman home after most of the guests had arrived.

Unlike the last party that Will and Anna had attended, she stayed by his side as friends and neighbors visited with Will, asking questions about Texas and complimenting Anna on her gown and her beauty and Will on his rugged, outdoor good looks in his handsome suit.

Mary was pleased, as everyone seemed to be enjoying themselves sampling the holiday dishes that Jessie had laid out on the long table. The men were also enjoying Henry's whiskey.

Will noticed the musicians readying their instruments to start playing. He excused himself from the small group of people where he and Anna were visiting, and walked over to the band and had a quiet word with the leader. Then he made his way back to Anna and led her to the wide staircase. He left her to stand by her father while he ascended a couple of steps to a point above everyone so he could be seen and heard.

"May I have your attention please?" He waited for the room to quiet. "I have a few words I'd like to express to all you friends, neighbors and family that came out on such a chilly evening to welcome me home. Thank you so much. It's really great to be home and to visit with all of you.

"But as much as I love my family and looked forward to visiting with them and all of you here, there's another very special reason that brought me over fifteen hundred miles back to the people I love. It was for the love of a beautiful woman, and she has agreed to marry me! Miss Anna Thompson." Will's wide smile reflected his happiness. He reached out and took Anna's hand as she stepped up to stand beside him. The crowd applauded and some shouted their surprise and approval as Will and Anna beamed their joy across the room.

"We decided to announce our engagement at this party, because it seemed like the best way to get our wedding invitation out to everyone at the same time. The Thompsons asked me to make sure everyone got a personal invitation to the wedding, so now you've got it. We'd be honored to have you all celebrate our wedding with us. We'll be married on the morning of New Year’s Day at the Thompson home. We'll be leaving to make our home in Texas after the ceremony, so we'd like to see you all there again before we go.

“There are a couple of other things I'd like to say before we go on with the party. First, I want to thank Anna for making me the happiest man in the world by agreeing to be my wife, and I want to thank Mister and Mrs. Thompson for their blessing. I also want to promise them again, right here in front of all of you, we will come back to visit.

“I also want to thank my father and all my family for their support in my decision to make my home in Texas. My life will be complete by having the woman I love with me in the land that I love. The only thing that would make it better is if all of you would come join us there. There's room for everybody. Thank you all very much.”

Will kissed Anna on the cheek. Then they stepped down among their applauding friends as the band started playing a waltz. Will took Anna in his arms as an opening was made for them in the middle of the floor. Dancing to the music, smiling into each others’ eyes, they were oblivious to everyone and everything around them. For a few moments, only they alone existed, with the music a distant hum. Their senses knew only each other as they shared their love with their eyes.

The Thompsons soon joined them on the floor, followed by Henry and Mary. Soon all the guests were dancing, filling the room with a whirl of color and music.

“What a wonderful party!” Mrs. Thompson said later on the way home in Will's carriage. “The house was so pretty and everything was done up so nice! I just hope we can do as well with the wedding.”

“Oh, Mama, stop worrying about it.” Anna said. “We've got plenty of time. It's a full two weeks off. I've already given Clara and the others their instructions on the food and the house decorations. I'm about half-finished with my dress and Will and I have made a list of what we'll take with us and what we'll ship separately. Mama, it will be a wonderful wedding! Will's bringing Mary and Jeff over tomorrow morning. Mary's going to help me with my dress, and Will and Jeff will crate the things we'll be shipping. So see? You don't have anything to fret about."

"No . . . Nothing except how much your Papa and I will miss you after you leave," Mrs. Thompson said, raising her handkerchief to her eyes.

"Oh, Mama, we'll do the crying then. There's plenty to laugh about now. Let's enjoy the time we do have together."

The next two weeks went by faster than any of them could have imagined. Jeff spent most of his time with Jessie and Amos. Will split his time between the Bowman and Thompson plantations, and Anna kept herself more than busy preparing for the wedding.

Christmas came and went, with Henry and Mary inviting the Thompsons to their home for the holiday dinner with the entire Bowman family. Although it was a festive holiday with all the Christmas trimmings Jessie was famous for, it was still a bittersweet reunion. Everyone was proud of Will's accomplishments in Texas and were happy for him and Anna, but they were still saddened to again prepare for Will's departure and Anna's leaving home. Anna had spent so much time at the Bowman home during her growing up years; it was as if she was one of the family already.

Finally the morning of the wedding arrived. Mary spent the night with Anna as she had done so many times when she was a child. Exhausted as they both were from the stress of Anna's leaving and the preparations for the wedding, they still stayed up half the night. They laughed, remembering the childish pranks, most of them against Will Bowman, and cried as they realized Anna's life would be forever changed. Anna needed the time with Mary to say goodbye to her life as it was and look forward to the new life she would embrace as a frontier wife.

Chapter 27

The guests started arriving at the Thompson home by mid-morning. Soon everyone was seated in the large front room, which had been arranged for the wedding. Will had asked permission for Jeff to attend the wedding. He sat in the back of the room in his fine suit, smiling and nodding at the other guests, who were startled to find him there.

When it appeared to the preacher that everyone was present and seated, he motioned for Will to step forward and join him at the bottom of the stairs. Anna then came into view at the top of the wide staircase in her glorious, white satin dress with beaded lace trim. She was the most beautiful sight Will had ever seen. Their eyes met as she stopped at the top of the stairs. Will strode up the stairs to escort her down. When he reached her side, he slid his hand under her arm to walk with her to her father, never taking his eyes from her radiant face. She met her father at the bottom of the staircase and they took their positions beside Will in front of the preacher.

"Dearly beloved," the preacher began. Much of the ceremony seemed a surreal blur to Will and Anna. Suddenly the preacher said, "I now pronounce you husband and wife. Will, you may kiss your bride."

Will took Anna in a gentle embrace and kissed her lightly, feeling embarrassed to be kissing her in front of everyone, even though she was his wife.

They turned to face the crowd and everyone broke into applause, with some of Will's brothers shouting their congratulations. Everyone crowded around, pumping Will's hand and telling Anna what a beautiful bride she was.

Anna's mother was still crying, and her father shed a tear or two himself, so Mary took charge of the reception, directing everyone to the food and drink. Anna and Will mixed with the guests to receive everyone's well wishes. When it appeared to Mary that most of the family and guests were engaged in conversation with each other and enjoying the food, she escorted Anna back upstairs to change clothes for the trip.

Will continued receiving back slaps and congratulations while he tried to get a bite of food himself, finally hungry after having been too nervous for breakfast.

Jeff had seen that all of his, Will's, and Anna's bags were loaded and secured in the carriage before the wedding started. The only things left to load were the few items Anna had with her upstairs. He kept an eye on the top of the stairs. As soon as he saw Mary come from Anna's room, he went up to get the rest of Anna's things to secure in the carriage. He gathered an armload of bags. "Is that everything, Miss Anna?"

"I guess it is, Jeff. We should be loading up pretty soon if we intend to make Roanoke before dark."

Jeff started to take the bags downstairs, but stopped and turned back toward Anna. "You sure are a beautiful bride, Miss Anna. You know, Texas is a mighty pretty place but it's going to brighten up even more with you there."

"Thank you, Jeff." Anna touched Jeff's arm. "I'm so glad you were here for the wedding. It meant so much to us to have you here." When Jeff left, Anna closed the door behind him and turned to Mary. "I'm not going to cry now, but I'm going to miss you so much." She threw her arms around Mary's neck and held her tightly. Her vow not to cry didn't hold as the tears again started to flow. "You're just going to have to fall in love with an adventurer and come to Texas yourself."

"Don't you be too surprised if I do just that," Mary said, pushing Anna to arms' length and smiling. "If I can find one, I will."

"Oh Mary, I don't want to cry anymore, especially in front of Will. He might think I'm sorry I married him."

"He won't think any such thing. Now you get on downstairs and go to Texas with your husband."

Chapter 28

Goodbyes were shared at the Thompson home with the Bowman family and the Thompsons and all of their friends and neighbors, then again at the Bowman plantation so Jeff could hug his mother and father before once again riding away to Texas.

Jessie watched through a veil of tears as Jeff pulled the carriage away from the Bowman home. She waved with her handkerchief as Amos put his arm around her and pulled her close. Jeff, Will and Anna all waved and shouted their goodbyes as the bay moved into a comfortable trot, pulling the carriage away from the plantation house and the two slaves standing in the yard.

"Oh, I hate to see dem boys go off again, leavin' so soon." Jessie said, leaning her head on Amos' shoulder. "Seems like dey jest got here yesterday."

Amos pulled Jessie to face him and smiled. "Mama, 'member when dey left out of here da first time?"

Jessie didn't answer as she wiped away the tears and watched the carriage fade into the distance.

Amos answered for her. "Dey was boys leaving home den, with stars in their eyes an' 'venture in their heart. What you see rollin' down dat trail ain't boys leavin' home, Mama—Dey's men *goin'* home. Dey hopes and dreams is all in Texas. Dat's where Jefferson belong now. He got a reason an' purpose for bein' there. Just look at dat big, handsome man all dressed up in dat fine suit, a-drivin' dat fancy rig. You think he be doin' dat if he stay here? He doin' dat cause he free, Mama. We ain't never gonna see the day we be free, but our Jefferson is. I gonna miss him as much as you, but I'm happy he goin' home. He goin' home to a better life. He done foun' his promise land."

Will was glad he and Jeff had stayed in the finest hotel in Roanoke on their way from Richmond to visit their families, because he now knew what to expect on his return trip.

Jeff pulled the carriage up in front of the hotel and stepped around to help Anna out of the carriage. He then moved aside as Will stepped from the carriage next to Anna. "Mister and Mrs. Bowman, your hotel," Jeff said, then smiled and bowed gesturing widely with his arm toward the tall front doors of the hotel entrance. "You two go ahead and register and look over your room. I'll see that your bags get delivered."

Will and Anna went inside the three-storied, red-brick building and soon were alone in their room. Once the door closed after their bags were delivered, Anna came to her husband and slid her arms around his broad shoulders. He leaned over to kiss her and encircled her waist with his arms. He then lifted her off her feet and spun her around as she screamed with joy.

"We're married!" Will said excitedly as he slowed to a stop. "You're finally mine, and we're on our way home. I hope you'll learn to love Texas as much as I have."

"My Darling, if that's where you are, I know I'll love it." Their lips met again in an electrifying way that neither of them had known.

All the years and miles that for so long had been between them melted away like soft wax under a candle flame as they finally came together as man and wife.

The next day Jeff trotted the bay toward Richmond while Anna and Will dozed in the back seat of the carriage, making up for some of the sleep they'd lost the night before.

Once in Richmond, they returned the carriage and horse to the livery and caught a barge down to Norfolk the same afternoon. Will was eager to find a ship with comfortable quarters so he and Anna could enjoy their journey. They had to wait a week before they could book passage on a ship large enough to have what he considered adequate accommodations for Anna. He knew she would have to endure the lack of comforts soon enough, once they got to Texas.

The Carolina, out of Charleston, suited Will very well. She was a fairly new sailing ship with a refined southern captain and what appeared to be an experienced crew, used to carrying passengers all along the Atlantic coast and as far south as New Orleans.

On a chilly January morning they set sail, with Anna and Will settled into their small but comfortable cabin and Jeff bunking with the crew.

The journey provided a wonderful time for Anna and Will to enjoy each other that few newly married couples experience. Without the demands of a schedule during the days at sea, they made love and made plans for their life together. They enjoyed strolling on deck in the cool, crisp sea breeze when they wanted fresh air and sunshine. On several occasions, they were surprised by a playful group of dolphins darting in and out of the waves near the bow of the ship as it sliced through the water. They also enjoyed watching the stars on the beautifully clear nights. Will had studied astronomy as part of his surveying training at the academy and enjoyed pointing out the different celestial groupings to Anna. Several nights they spent hours just waiting for and counting shooting stars. The weather cooperated most of the time and they passed through only one mild storm when they sailed into gulf waters. With good wind in their sails, they arrived in New Orleans on schedule.

Since New Orleans was the final destination and turn around point for *The Carolina*, they had to find another ship for the last leg of their journey at sea.

After inquiring at the docks, Will learned that a stern wheeler called *The Lively* would be sailing to the mouth of the Brazos in two days. Although the accommodations weren't as spacious as on *The Carolina*, he and Anna would at least have their privacy, and their trip wouldn't be delayed too long.

Their two-day stay in a comfortable hotel allowed time for

Will to introduce his new bride to his cousin and for shopping trips at the last point of refinement before entering Texas. They were soon again on their way, closer, but still far from home.

By early February, they arrived at Brazoria. Will learned that the crates he and Jeff had packaged and shipped before they left Virginia had already arrived and had been shipped overland in a freight wagon to San Felipe.

They visited the man who had looked after Baron and Buck while they were gone and found them both to be in good condition, if not a little fatter than when they left them. Will offered to hire a buggy for Anna to travel the rest of the way to San Felipe, but she preferred to ride horseback instead. They managed to make a good purchase on a sorrel mare and a saddle for Anna and struck out on the last leg of their journey home.

After two days on the road to San Felipe and camping overnight along the way, the three riders finally saw the cabins at the Bell plantation. “Look, Will! Anna, there it is!” Jeff shouted. “My Libby's up there.” Jeff spurred Buck into a full gallop to close the distance between him and his family. As soon as he got within shouting distance he started yelling, “Libby! Tad! We're back! Hey, we're here!”

By the time he reined up at the cabins, the women were spilling out of the cabins and the men were coming in from the fields. Jake was barking and dancing excitedly around the horses. Libby scooped up the baby to carry him outside to see his father. Jeff was off his horse and had Libby in his arms before the horse had come to a complete stop.

“Oh, Jeff, I thought you'd never get home! It seems like you've been gone a year!”

Jeff held her tightly. “Baby, I won't ever leave you again if I can keep from it.” He hugged Tad, scooped up Billy and shook hands all around with the others as Will helped Anna dismount.

“Oh, excuse my manners,” Jeff said, embarrassed in his excitement when he noticed Anna standing, waiting to be introduced.

“Everybody,” Jeff removed his hat and stepped back beside Anna, who was holding Will's hand. “May I present Mrs. Anna Bowman, Will's new bride, direct from Virginia and a brand new Texan.”

“Welcome to Texas, Miz Anna,” Libby said, as she approached Anna with her hand extended to shake hands.

Anna took her hand and pulled her into an embrace. “It's just Anna, and I feel like I've known you for years from everything Jeff has told me. I'm so glad we are going to be neighbors.”

Will was shaking hands with Kado, Tad and the others while Anna and Libby were getting acquainted. He then turned to Libby. “I think I've been missing you and Tad and little Billy here almost as much as Jeff has.”

“Thank you for seeing that he got home safe.”

“Oh, it was Jeff who looked after us. You haven't forgotten how to cook while we've been gone, have you?”

“No, in fact I've been practicing on some new things. We were just starting supper when you pulled up. Y'all come on in where it's warm. I'll bet you're hungry.”

Libby, Jeff and the others made Anna and Will feel at home through dinner and visiting afterward. Jeff told of their experiences on the sailing ships and his shopping in Richmond. He gave Libby, Tad and little Billy their gifts.

Libby insisted that Will and Anna take the bedroom she had been using for the night, and she fixed a soft pallet for herself, Jeff and the baby on the floor in the main room. After visiting late into the night and getting re-acquainted, they finally drifted off to their beds.

The cabin started coming to life shortly after daylight to the smell of coffee brewing and bacon frying.

“Well, it's about time!” Libby teased Jeff as he came into the kitchen rubbing sleep from his eyes. “I thought you were just going to just lie around all day, and I never would get started for home. Tad and Kado are already harnessing the teams. We'll be ready to leave right after breakfast."

"I think you're as excited about getting back home as I am, aren't you?" Jeff pulled Libby close for a kiss.

"Yes, but we won't get anywhere today if you keep that up. Now you go on and give them a hand. I'll let you know when breakfast is ready."

After a hearty breakfast and some quick packing, Libby, Jeff, and the baby were all loaded into one wagon. Tad was in control of the second wagon, and Will and Anna were in the third with the saddle horses trailing along behind each wagon. Jake was running from one wagon to the other, barking and nipping at the horses feet, eager to get the caravan rolling.

"Kado, thanks for everything," Jeff said, shaking the old man's hand. "I really appreciate what you've done."

"Glad we could help. Y'all take care and come see us when you can. Libby, don't you let that boy grow up before we see him again."

"Oh, we won't," Libby called as Jeff slapped the team into motion with the reins. "We'll come visit after harvest."

The small group of former slaves stood in a tight knot, waving as they watched the three wagons slowly roll down the lane toward the road that would take them home.

Chapter 29

Several hours later they arrived in San Felipe and parked the wagon in front of the Austin land office.

"Well, here it is," Will said to Anna as he set the brake on the wagon. "I couldn't pass through town without introducing you to Mister Austin. He's the one responsible for me being here in the first place."

Will helped Anna from the wagon. As they stepped onto the wooden porch, they overheard part of a heated discussion coming from inside the building.

"I'm telling you, Williams, we can't let them get away with it! They just gonna let him sit there and rot! We've got to do more than just talk! We've got to take some action!"

"Now calm down, Buck. It's not the time for your kind of action. I'm as upset as you are about Stephen, but there are other ways of handling it — more diplomatic ways."

Will recognized Williams' voice, but he didn't recognize the voice of the other man. Finding a break in the conversation on the other side of the door, he tapped lightly.

"Come in!" Williams called. Will recognized a tone of relief at the interruption of the conversation inside the land office.

Will pushed the door open, and found Sam Williams sitting at Austin's desk. A tall young man with a stubborn, hard-set look to his jaw was pacing the floor.

"Hello, Bowman." Williams rose from his chair as he saw Anna being ushered into the office. "Welcome back. And who is the lovely lady you brought with you?"

"Sam Williams, I'd like you to meet my wife, Anna, formerly of Virginia."

Williams walked around the corner of the desk to take Anna's hand. "Welcome to Texas, Mrs. Bowman. What a lovely addition you make here. May I present Mister William Travis.

Travis, here, is an attorney and an advocate of state's and people's rights."

Travis' stern look softened into a smile with the introduction to Will and Anna. "My pleasure, Ma'am, Mister Bowman." He shook Will's hand and nodded to Anna. "Welcome to Texas, Mrs. Bowman. I hope you find it to your liking."

"Thank you, sir. I'm delighted by what I've seen so far."

Will asked, "Is Austin in?"

"No. As a matter of fact, that's what Travis and I were discussing before you arrived. You knew that he went to Mexico City to deliver petitions requesting immigration law changes and several states' rights revisions?"

Will nodded. "Yes, I knew that was the plan."

"Well, the long story short is that he said some things in anger to some officials there, and now they have him under arrest for treason. We've just learned of this turn of events, and Travis and I have been discussing what might be the most appropriate action to take from here."

"If you gentlemen will excuse me, I have a little shopping to do before we leave town," Anna said as she gracefully exited from what appeared to her as a serious conversation that might be inhibited by her presence. "Nice to have met you, gentlemen."

Will held the door open for her. "Anna, please ask Jeff to pick up the crates at the freight office. I'll meet you at the wagon in a few minutes."

After Anna's departure, Williams again addressed Travis. "Will, here, is a surveyor and a farmer with his place up north along the Brazos. He's always had a keen interest in our politics, and I'd like to get his opinion on this issue."

"Of course," Travis said. He looked at Will. "Perhaps you can make some sense of it. Since you've been out of the country, I assume you're not aware of the latest news from the capital."

"No, I'm not."

Travis brought Will up to date, explaining that Austin had gone to Mexico City with several requests from the people of

Texas and with the express purpose of meeting personally with President Santa Anna. When he arrived, Santa Anna was away and Vice President Farias was acting president.

He was able to meet with Farias and was accepted cordially, but a series of delays kept putting off any decisions. Austin, impatient with the delays, told Farias that unless the government remedied the evils that threatened Texas with ruin, the people of Texas would organize a state government without Mexico City's approval.

Farias considered Austin's communication a threat, and the two men quarreled. Austin, still angry, wrote a letter to the local leaders in San Antonio recommending that they start developing a plan to organize a state government without Mexico City's approval.

Later Austin and Farias reconciled and Austin eventually met with Santa Anna. The president did not approve Texas' separation from the state of Coahuila but did agree to almost every other request. He agreed to lessen the restrictions on immigration, to improve the mail service and modify the tariff. He also agreed to recommend that the state government offer trial by jury.

Austin left the city on December 10, but he was stopped in Saltillo because his letter to the leaders in San Antonio had been intercepted by government officials in Saltillo. The letter found its way back to Vice President Farias just after Austin left Mexico City. Austin was then arrested and taken back to Mexico City. He's being held in the Prison of the Inquisition.

Travis concluded his explanation with, "So you see that although he has won some concessions for Texas, we may never see him alive again."

Will released his breath in a long sigh. "Have we sent anybody to lobby on his behalf in Mexico City yet?"

"No," answered Williams. "Travis brought me the news just today, so the story hasn't yet circulated. We've gotta find someone with good negotiating skills to go to the capital and try to lobby for his release."

"I'll do it." Travis said. "I'm a lawyer. I'll make them listen to me."

Williams cut his gaze to Travis. "Like you did down at Anahuac last year trying to improve the tariff situation? As I recall you got yourself thrown in jail over that. Buck, I appreciate your concern and your passion, but what we need is very careful and patient diplomacy, not passion. We may very well need your passion at another time in another way. Besides, you already have a negative reputation with Santa Anna. He considers you and a couple of others hotheads, responsible for the uprising over tariffs. Thanks for offering, anyway."

Will asked, "What if we sent petitions out all over Texas and then had several patient but influential lawyers take them to Mexico City on behalf of the people of Texas? Petitions worked on the state's rights concessions we were asking for. I can contact everyone to the north. Sam, you can send someone east, and Travis, maybe you could collect signatures to the south. In the meantime, Sam, you can be recruiting the right people to take our message to Santa Anna."

"It's worth a try," Williams said, catching Will's enthusiasm. "What do you think, Buck?"

"You've got my support. I know several men who will help me spread the word and get signatures. Let's do it!"

They composed the letter that each of them would use to collect signatures of citizens to support the release of Stephen Austin. Will and Travis agreed to meet back in San Felipe in two weeks with their petitions. By then, Williams would have someone ready to carry their cause to Mexico City.

As Will stepped into the street, he realized that he had just agreed to take on a responsibility that would separate him from his new bride. He had brought her over fifteen hundred miles away from her home and family to this new place, and now he'd be leaving her to take care of political matters.

Not finding anyone around the wagons, Will headed across

the street to the general store that used to be owned by his uncle. Before he made it all the way across the street, Anna, Libby, Jeff and Tad carrying the baby came out of the store. Each of them had their arms full of supplies.

"Did you leave any merchandise inside?" Will teased.

"Not much," Anna said, as Will took her load.

After they had the supplies stowed in the wagons, Will asked his companions to gather around. "There's some news about Mister Austin I need to share with you."

After he told the story of Austin's plight and his commitment to gather petition signatures, he looked for Anna's reaction. "Well, what do you think?" he asked.

"I would have been ashamed of you if you hadn't offered to help, Will Bowman. That man's your friend. You've got to do whatever you can to help. You don't need to think of me as a frail little Southern Belle. We're in Texas now. I'm a Texan too. I knew what I was getting into when I married you. Don't you ever shirk your duty to your country on my account. This is my country now, and whatever you do for this country, you do for me. I can drive a team as well as the next person. You've got a saddle horse back there that's just itching for a hard ride. You could be out there collecting signatures but instead, here you are, worrying about my welfare. Libby can ride with me to keep me company. I've had you all to myself for a whole month but I've just met her, and we've got some catching up to do. You go on. You've got work to do. We'll meet you up the trail tonight at our camp."

A grin grew on Will's face as he saw that Jeff was trying to stifle a smile while he raised his eyebrows and rolled his eyes before he turned away to climb into his wagon.

Will saddled Baron hurriedly while the women positioned themselves on the bench of the second wagon. Will swung into the saddle and walked Baron alongside Anna's wagon. When he was parallel with Anna, he reached over and slid his arm around her neck and pulled her toward him to plant a kiss on her cheek.

"Thanks," he said, then spurred into a lope ahead of the wagons. Taking off his hat, he waved and called out to Jeff, "Meet you up at Rough Creek crossing tonight."

The three mostly empty wagons rolled along at a good pace, with Jeff in the lead, picking the spots for creek crossings and finding rest stops and camp sites. The women and baby were in the middle wagon, chatting the day away. Tad was in the last wagon, sometimes nodding away sleep as the sun warmed his skin.

Will managed to find their campsite every evening after spending the day spreading the news of Austin's imprisonment and gathering signatures on the petition for his release. He also enjoyed renewing old friendships with people he hadn't seen in awhile and catching up on the news of their families. At every farm, he was invited to eat or spend the night. He had to turn down most of the invitations, but was happy to share a noonday meal with several of his friends.

On the afternoon of the last day on the trail, Will had visited with all the settlers on the west side of the river and joined the wagons for the remainder of the ride. About an hour before sunset they topped a rise and saw Jeff's and Libby's cabin. Will and Anna heard Jeff's and Libby's shouts of joy from the lead wagon when they saw their cabin waiting for them. Picking up the pace, Jeff whipped the horses into a trot along the trail between the cornfield and the creek. As they pulled up in front of the cabin, Jeff jumped out and raced around, checking everything.

"Just the way we left it!" he shouted. "Not even an ear of corn disturbed in the corn crib."

"Why don't y'all get down and come on in?" Libby asked Will and Anna.

"We're as eager to see our place as you were to see yours," Will said. "I'll bring Anna back over here in two or three days when I head back south gathering signatures on the other side of the river. We'll see you then."

Chapter 30

Will turned the wagon back onto the trail to their farm. He could tell that Anna was getting more excited as they got closer to home. She already had a idea of what the cabin looked like because she knew that Will's and Jeff's cabins had been built alike.

Before long, they saw the cabin in the distance. They started yelling and hooting with the pure joy of being home. Almost before Will pulled the wagon to a stop, Anna was scrambling down to explore her new home.

“This is just perfect!” She exclaimed. Will pushed the cabin door open and ushered her inside to see the work that he had done finishing the inside and making furniture. “With everything you've done and the things we shipped, this is going to be a really comfortable home. Thank you, Will.”

“What are you thanking me for?”

“For marrying me and bringing me here.” She slipped her arms around Will's shoulders and kissed him long and tenderly.

Anna and Will spent the next two days intermittently organizing the cabin with the house wares and other items that they’d shipped from Virginia and exploring the countryside. Late in the afternoon of the third day after their arrival, after almost a full day of riding over the property, they returned to the small hill above the cabin — the future site of the home Will intended to build.

“But I'm happy with our cabin,” Anna said as she and Will walked over the proposed building location.

“It will serve our purpose for awhile, but sooner or later, we're going to need more room. One of these days, I hope to have a whole house full of little Bowmans running all over this place.

“It may be sooner than later.” Anna smiled as she stopped and looked Will in the eyes. “I think we might already have one on the way."

Will's jaw dropped. "Are you sure?" he asked, grabbing her by the shoulders.

"Well, no . . . not sure. Not yet anyway. Give me another month, and we'll be sure then. But I think so."

"A baby!" Will's excitement almost overcame him. "I can't believe it! A baby already!" Suddenly his expression changed to a look of worry. "How stupid of me. Here I've had you riding all over the countryside all day. A woman in your condition shouldn't be riding horses."

"I'm just fine, Will. I should be able to do anything I've always done, for awhile anyway. You don't worry about me. I'll take care of myself."

"But still, I want you to take it easy. I'll take you over to Jeff's and Libby's tomorrow morning. I want you to stay with them while I collect signatures on the east side of the river on my way back to San Felipe. I shouldn't be gone more than four or five days. Then, when I get back, it will be time to start getting the ground ready for planting. You'll find out then what life is really like for a Texas farmer's wife."

Will completed his mission without incident and returned to the farm to establish a routine of long, hard days in the early spring sunshine, walking miles behind the strong mule, controlling the turning plow. The weather had been ideal through the spring, with most of the rain holding off until the seeds were in the ground.

The hot days of summer passed into fall and, once again, harvest time.

The Bowmans and Jeffersons again shared their farming tasks and harvest time found them all working together in the fields picking cotton. Anna was heavy with her baby but insisted on doing whatever she could to help. She saw to it that everyone had enough cool water and cared for Billy while Libby worked. She brought a large midday meal every day to the rise overlooking the cotton fields. She enjoyed the shade under the large live oak trees and the view of what they had started calling "the new home place."

Anna had just spread out lunch on the ground under a tree and was about to call everyone in from the fields when Jake, who had been a constant companion to little Billy, started growling a low, throaty growl. Anna glanced at the dog to see what had attracted his attention. Suddenly he sprang to his feet, looking toward the edge of the clearing to the east, barking with such a frenzy but never leaving the baby's side. Anna spun to look in the direction that had Jake's attention.

No more than eighty yards away were two mounted Indians in black and red face paint and feathers. They were staring at her. Anna froze as chills ran up her back. The Indians sat on their horses, watching her for endless seconds. Then one of them moved forward a few steps, shook his lance in the air in a threatening gesture and screamed a piercing yelping noise. They then spun their mounts and rode into the cover of the thicket.

Anna stood for a moment trying to catch her breath, then realized the baby was crying, frightened by the sudden barking and yelling of the Indians.

Just as she picked him up to comfort him, Will and Jeff raced up the hill after retrieving their rifles from the wagon. Will could tell at a distance from the lack of color in Anna's face and by her expression that something was wrong.

"What was all that noise?" Will shouted, approaching the top of the rise.

At first all Anna could do was to point in the direction where the Indians had disappeared into the brush. Then in a shaky voice, she said, "Indians."

"How many? Where did they go?" Will asked excitedly, looking in the direction she had pointed.

"Two. Back in the trees." Anna grabbed Will's arm to steady herself as Jeff took the screaming baby from her.

Will saw how unsteady Anna was on her feet and helped her to the ground.

"Are you all right? Did they hurt you?"

"No. They just scared us. They just stood there looking . . . so evil looking." Anna shuddered as an uncontrollable shivering overcame her. Her shock gave way to silent tears as she saw Libby rushing up the hill, breathless and scared from the sounds of her baby's fearful crying.

"Let's go after 'em!" Tad said, checking the load on the rifle Jeff had given him.

Jeff glanced at Will for his response.

Will looked in the direction the Indians had taken, then back at Anna on the ground, breathing hard, releasing the surge of her stress.

"No . . . If they were after us or the stock, they'd have already done something. I think they just wanted us to know they're still here. They just wanted us to see them. They're gone now. It wouldn't serve any purpose to go after them. Let 'em go. They already have a good start on us anyway. Besides, I'm not leaving Anna."

Will sat down next to Anna and cradled her in his arms. Libby had started calming Billy. Soon Anna regained her composure and was apologizing for acting so childish.

"You weren't a bit childish — you were scared," Libby said. "I'm sure you did a lot better than I would have. I probably would have fainted dead away if I'd been in your shoes."

"I guess it was wishful thinking to believe that a few settlers moving in would have pushed those Indians further west," Will said. "Jeff and I have had only one other run-in with them all the time we've been here. We've occasionally seen signs of them traveling through, but they've never shown themselves like this. I guess we'll just have to be more on the alert. Jeff, what do you say we forego picking this afternoon and introduce the ladies to the fine art of shooting?"

That afternoon the women got another view of living beyond the edge of civilization — through the sights of a Tennessee, muzzle loading, flint lock rifle.

The cotton harvest continued until they had their first two wagons full. Then Jeff and Tad took them to San Felipe.

Anna was too far along with her pregnancy to travel, so Will and Libby stayed behind to continue the picking and look after Anna and Billy. They made good progress while Jeff and Tad were gone. By the time they returned, the third wagon was loaded and a substantial mound of cotton lay beside it.

Jeff and Tad had a surprise for Will, Libby and Anna when they returned. They didn't come alone. Four wagons returned from San Felipe instead of the two that left. Kado and Robert came back with them to help finish the picking and hauling.

"Look who we found roaming around in San Felipe with nothing to do after they got their cotton in," Jeff said as he swung down from his wagon.

"Glad to have you." Will greeted the two as each climbed down. "We'll use all the help we can get. I believe Jeff and I may have been a little ambitious with our planting this year. Between the extra acres we planted and the good yield, we've got more than we can handle. It might have taken us till after Christmas to finish picking and get everything to market."

That evening, Anna went into labor. Libby stayed with her and tried to comfort her as much as she could, and when the time came, she served as midwife.

The men were gathered around a fire in the front yard, comforting Will while his wife struggled through childbirth. Finally, in the early hours of the morning they heard the cries of a newborn baby from inside the cabin.

Will stood when he heard the cries and headed for the door. "We've got a baby, Jeff! We've got a baby!"

"Hold on a little while longer," Jeff said. "They don't need you in there yet. Libby will let you know when you can go in. Having babies is women's business. Waiting is men's business. Just sit down and take it easy. You'll get to see them soon enough."

Soon Libby opened the door and stepped out into the cool air, smiling. "Go on in and see your baby, Will."

Once inside, he found Anna looking beautiful but tired. A bundle with a shock of dark hair was cradled in her arms.

"Say hello to your daughter." Anna pulled the soft blanket away from the baby's face.

"A little girl? We've got a little girl? Anna, she's so beautiful! Just like you." Will kissed his wife on the forehead. "Thank you for giving me such a beautiful little girl."

"What are you going to name her?" Anna asked.

"I've been thinking about that all evening. Boy's names, girl's names — so many to choose from. But I think I have one that fits this little lady."

"What's that?"

"How about Texanna . . . Texanna Bowman? The Tex part because she's our first baby born in Texas and the Anna part from her beautiful mother."

"I like it, Will. She'll like it too — Texanna it is."

Chapter 31

The Bowman and Jefferson cotton crop of 1834 was a success. The weather, the yield and the market all came together to result in a good, profitable year, even after paying Robert and Kado for their labor picking and hauling.

They struck a deal for the next season for Robert and Kado to come back at both planting and harvesting time and to bring their families with them. The extra paid labor would allow for slightly less profit per acre, but could produce considerably more acreage in cultivation.

Will and Anna enjoyed the idleness of the winter months between harvest and planting, taking care of and playing with the baby and improving their home. Will built a smoke house with Jeff's help and constructed a shelter for the stock to protect them from the north wind.

He also spent time visiting with the neighbors and sharing news of the time. He learned that Stephen Austin was still in prison, even though the citizens of Texas had sent two of their most respected lawyers to Mexico City to plead his case. It seemed that they continued to be put off because no one could agree in whose jurisdiction his case should fall.

The instability of the national government didn't help Austin's case. The leadership switched back and forth between Santa Anna and his vice president several times as the power-driven Santa Anna was frequently away from the capital, quelling small rebellions within central Mexico and increasing his stature within the government with each victory. In time, he became the supreme ruler and dictator of Mexico.

There was a fear developing in Texas that with Santa Anna's increasing power, he could overturn the constitution at any moment and run roughshod over the entire nation, including Texas.

By early spring, 1835, there was a small but vocal and powerful war party of American settlers in Texas, which included Jim Bowie and William Travis. They warned that the only way for Texans to maintain their property and human rights was to keep it by force.

All of this turmoil seemed far away to Will and Jeff and their families in the northern settlements along the Brazos as they planned their largest-yet cotton crop.

Kado and his family arrived as promised after they completed an early planting on the old Bell place. With all the extra help, Will and Jeff were able to break twice as much new ground as they had in previous years. By summer they had as much land in cotton as many of the large planters with slave labor.

With the cotton planted, Will and Tad took a trip to San Felipe in late June for supplies. As they arrived in town, it looked strangely different. People milled about in the street, talking in tight knots.

Finding Sam Williams in one of the groups, Will stopped to see what was happening. As he approached the group of men, he heard Williams talking, “I'll tell you fellas, I don't know if it was the right thing to do or not, but maybe now we’ll get their attention.”

A whiskered man responded, “You bet we'll get their attention. We'll be looking down the barrel of a cannon before we know it. General Cos ain't going to sit idly by while we steal his letters from his courier and send a bunch of hotheads with a cannon off to Anahuac to attack his customs garrison there. He's Santa Anna's brother-in-law. You think he'll stand still for that? Not for long, I'd say.”

“What's going on, Sam?" Will asked when the man with the whiskers finished his speech. “Just got into town. Looks like a pretty big ruckus.”

“Aw, Will, it's just more trouble with the government. They've set up custom houses along the coast again, but they aren't consistent from one office to the next on how they collect the customs. Some are collecting tonnage duties only, while others are insisting on collecting payment on all duties. There's been a scuffle down at Anahuac, and one man got shot. A couple of others are in jail. It's about like what happened back in '32, but this time General Cos has reinforcements on the way from south of the Rio Grande. We know that, because this morning some boys here in town stopped a Mexican courier and read his mail. He was on his way to Anahuac to inform the soldiers that reinforcements are on the way. A group of the war party got together and agreed to send a bunch of zealots down there with a cannon and run the garrison off before the reinforcements get there. William Travis left, leading those hotspurs just a little while ago. Who knows where we go from here."

"I just hope it doesn't lead to war," Will said, shaking his head.

"So do I, Will . . . So do I." Williams patted Will on the shoulder and headed back into the land office.

Will and Tad went on to the general store and filled the list of supplies Anna and Libby had given them. Heading north again, they stopped several times along the way to share the news with their neighbors.

Back in Virginia Point, working in the fields through the summer and into harvest once again, Will managed to put political troubles aside to concentrate on matters closer at hand. His family and crop were his top priority. Anna was in love with him and her home, Texanna was healthy and growing, and the cotton was bountiful.

Kado and his crew once again showed up as promised for picking, this time bringing four wagons. Picking time, as always, was the busiest time of the year. The women stayed busy keeping the large group fed three times a day.

By late October, the cotton had been harvested, and the picking crew returned home. Once again, the Bowman and Jefferson plantations had been profitable. But the success of the season was dampened by news from the south.

Bad news accompanied every empty cotton wagon returning from San Felipe. Travis and his men had accomplished their goal of driving the Mexican garrison out of Anahuac, but the greater result was the inflammation of Anglo-Mexican relations. General Cos would not let this and other transgressions pass. He demanded that colonial officials arrest several leaders of the war party and turn them over to him for military trial. It was, of course, unthinkable for people who believed in a trial by a jury of their peers to turn their neighbors over to the mercies of a military tribunal.

There had been several meetings of delegates from the different districts in Texas to discuss the rapidly disintegrating relations between the colonists and central Mexico. By late fall it appeared that the entire territory was swinging more toward the goals of the war party than a negotiated peace.

Stephen Austin, home at last from his imprisonment, attended the Central Committee meeting at the new Texas government headquarters located down river from San Felipe at the town of Washington-on-the-Brazos. News arrived at the meeting that General Cos was on a march to San Antonio with reinforcements. The news dashed all hopes of negotiating a peace agreement, so Austin was appointed chairman of the Central Committee of Safety of San Felipe by general consent and became, in effect, the leader of the revolution. Acknowledging majority rule, the Central Committee declared, “War is our only recourse. There is no other remedy. We must defend our rights, ourselves, and our country by force of arms.”

While Will, Jeff, and most other Texas farmers were bringing in their crops, war had started to the southwest, around San Antonio and Gonzales. It wouldn't, however, take long until all of Texas was embroiled in the conflict.

One morning in late November, the quiet around the Bowman home was shattered by the hoofbeats of a dozen or so riders reining up in front of the cabin. Outside, Will found the

Bigelow brothers, Cartwright and several others in their buckskins and homespun, well armed and supplied.

Will greeted the men, surprised at the large group of men so obviously prepared for a long journey. “Hello, boys. Step on down and rest awhile. Looks like you've been riding hard.”

“We would if we had time, but we gotta head back south,” Tom Bigelow said. “We got a war on our hands, Will. Mister Austin's done issued a call to arms and I been passin' the word and gatherin' men all the way from San Felipe. We'll be pickin’ up more men along the way to San Antone. Riders are out all over the country collectin' men. Some are goin' to Gonzales, some to Goliad. We even got Sam Houston formin’ an army down around Goliad. Me and the boys here are goin' over to San Antone and teach them Meskins a lesson or two.

“Austin gave me this here letter and asked me to give it to you personal.” Bigelow handed the letter to Will. “He told me not to let you go with us. Said he had something else for you to do. He said it's all in the letter. You tell Jeff we didn't forget him. We just knew somebody needed to stay around and look after your families as far out north as y'all are and all. We better be makin' tracks. We got us a war to fight.”

“Good luck to you, boys. I guess I'll see you down the road somewhere.” Will stood and watched as the men rode out of the yard.

The riders spurred back down the trail, kicking up a cloud of dust behind them.

Anna stood at the doorway watching Will's back as he looked at the envelope. He walked a few feet away from the porch and leaned against a live oak tree, then slowly opened the envelope. Anna left him alone to read the letter. Will stood for the longest time, head bent, reading and re-reading the letter.

Finally Anna joined him in the yard and put her arm around his waist. “Are you going to tell me what it says?”

Will lifted his gaze from the letter and took a deep breath. He silently took her hand and led her across the yard toward the familiar hilltop. They walked quietly up the rise to the new home place and sat on the ground under one of the large live oaks before he answered her. He sat for a moment, staring at the paper. Then he opened it and started to read.

> November 25, 1835
> San Felipe
> Dear Will,
>
> You are aware by now of the plight that our country is in with its struggle with Mexico. As you know, for years I have been the most loyal supporter of the Mexican government, but after the endless months of solitude in Mexican prisons and in light of recent events in Texas, I can no longer tolerate the despotism that is befalling our country. We are now at war with our former government. In order for Texas and Texans to survive, we must protect and defend our homes and families from the evil of this devil, Santa Anna.
>
> I have no doubt that Santa Anna will bring the full force of his army, toughened from months of civil wars in central Mexico, to Texas in the spring to attempt to quell our revolt. We must be prepared.
>
> We have now created our government, and General Sam Houston has been selected as Commander of the Texas Army. He and others are recruiting and training our army now. But there is so much more that we need.
>
> I am leaving Texas today to travel to Washington in the United States to seek support for our cause. As much as we need dollars and arms to support our struggle, we need men even more. We need men with an adventurous spirit

and righteous hearts, willing to fight for the freedom of man.

Will, I am authorized to commission you with the rank of Captain in the Texas Army to seek out the kind of men we need to win this war. Go to Arkansas, Missouri and Tennessee. Bring back men who know how to handle a weapon. Bring men who not only want to win freedom for their brothers, but who want to immigrate to our new nation. Each man who comes to fight will not only help us win the war but will win land for himself in the country he has helped set free.

I am asking this of you because I know you are capable of the leadership required by such a task. I remember a young man telling me once that he wanted to be a part of making this country great. Sir, in order for this country to continue to develop into the vision of greatness that you and I share, it must survive. I am asking you to help make that happen. First, we'll make it survive. Then we'll continue our quest to make it great. We need the men you will bring back with you to make it happen.

You and your men shall report to General Houston upon your return.

May God be with you.

Stephen Austin

Anna knew and accepted both her and Will's responsibility. “All right, Captain Bowman, when are you leaving?” She was still dry-eyed and trying desperately to remain so.

“I guess the sooner I get started, the sooner I'll get back.”

“Come on." Anna stood, taking Will's hand. “I'll help you pack.”

Will, Anna and Texanna pulled up in front of Jeff's and Libby's cabin with Baron and Anna's mare trailing behind the wagon. After Will explained the turn of events, Jeff walked with Will to Baron and away from the women to give him a pouch of lead balls and an extra measure of powder.

When they were alone, Will said, "I know you'll be able to take care of anything that comes along, but we may be facing some difficult times. Jeff, If it looks like you may be having to deal with anything bigger than you can handle by yourself, either from the Comanches or the Mexicans, don't hang around. Get out of here fast and go east."

Jeff clasped Will's hand. "Friend, we'll be just fine."

"Jeff, if anything should happen to me —"

"Hey, hush about that kind of stuff. We got too much work around here for anything to happen to anybody. Anyway, we aren't rich enough yet." Jeff slapped Will on the back and let out his big, throaty laugh as the women came out to see Will off.

Will shook hands with Tad, now almost a man. He reached down, picked up Billy and gave him a hug.

"My God," Will said as he sat Billy back on his feet. "I hope these babies don't grow as much as Tad has while I'm gone."

He took Texanna from her mother and hugged her tightly against his cheek for a moment. He kissed her on the head as he reached for Anna. Holding the baby between them, he embraced Anna and kissed her. "I'll try not to be away too long," he said, handing the baby back to Anna. He took Baron's reins from Tad and swung into the saddle. "I hope to be back by planting time. I love you."

"Will . . ." The sunlight caught the faint glimmer of the golden chain spilling from Anna's hand as she once again placed the little locket in Will's hand, then pressed his fingers closed. "I love you too." She stepped away from the horse. "Now, you go, Captain Bowman. You've got a job to do."

Will looked at the golden locket in his hand, then back at

Anna, smiling up at him, doing everything she could to hold back the flood of tears. He swallowed hard, then spurred Baron into a lope along the trail beside the creek and headed south.

Chapter 32

Will watched the gray clouds thicken and pulled his coat collar as high as possible to block his ears from the cold wind. He hoped the fair weather they had enjoyed for several days would hold for awhile, but he finally resigned himself to the fact that he'd be traveling cross-country, on horseback, during the coldest part of the year.

He crossed the Brazos at the first low water point he came to and took off east instead of following the trail toward San Felipe. He felt he could cut at least a day's travel by taking a more direct route toward Nacogdoches.

By late afternoon, the light rain had turned to sleet. It bounced off Will's hat and slicker but froze on Baron's mane and parts of his thick, winter coat. Before dark, he approached a thicket that looked as if it might provide some protection from the storm. He found a campsite under some low-hanging cedar limbs. After seeing to Baron's comfort and safety, he built a small fire and made a pot of coffee.

Later, after eating a little jerky and cornbread that Anna had packed for him, Will sat warming his hands with his coffee cup, huddling next to his fire. Cold and wet, he missed his family and wished he had the old tent he and Jeff had used on so many nights like this while they were surveying. Jeff had suggested he take the tent before he left home, but Will wanted to travel light and not be bothered with a pack animal to transport the bulky tent.

He thought of the Bigelows and the others in the same storm in a different part of Texas. Those were men getting ready to lay their lives on the line for their country. *If they're weathering this storm, so can I.*

That thought carried Will through many cold, damp nights and gave him the dedication to persevere through icy river crossings and snow storms as he traveled farther north and east.

Will presented his message all along his journey. At every village, town and city, he talked on street corners, contacted newspaper editors to help put his story out, and stopped to visit with farmers along the way. He talked to all kinds of people, especially seeking out backwoods people; farmers, hunters and trappers — people who understood the frontier way of life.

Word of his mission preceded him. People in the larger towns sought him out on several occasions to learn more about Texas and offer their assistance with supplies and small amounts of money. By the time he had criss-crossed several American states, newspaper accounts of the struggle in Texas had brought the war closer to people in America.

His first-hand description of life and opportunity in a free Texas resulted in a sizable following of men either leaving right away for Texas or promising to meet him at specific points on his return trip. Even Davy Crockett, the former congressman from Tennessee and legendary bear hunter, after learning of the plight of the Texans, gathered several of his friends and struck out to the southwest.

In mid February, the Kentucky newspapers received word that Santa Anna's army was marching toward San Antonio. Will determined that he must end his recruiting and deliver his volunteers to General Houston.

Will had no idea how many stout-hearted riflemen he had influenced to go to Texas in small groups ahead of him, scores or perhaps hundreds, but by the time he arrived in Natchez, he had gathered a following of sixty-three men traveling to Texas with him.

Two weeks later, as the company of volunteers continued their journey to Texas, Will had no way of knowing, since news traveled slowly, that Texas had been dealt its first devastating blow of the war. He was unaware that many of his friends and neighbors had recently fallen at the Alamo in San Antonio. Jim Bowie, William Travis and Davy Crockett, whom he had recently met and sent to Texas, gave their lives fighting Santa Anna. Over one hundred and eighty good men died trying to win freedom for Texas.

Santa Anna had assembled over six thousand battle-hardened troops at San Antonio with the intent of striking down the rebellious Texans. Even as tremendously outnumbered as they were, the valiant defenders held their positions for twelve days, waiting for reinforcements that never came. Houston was in east Texas at the time, developing truce agreements with the Cherokees to keep them from joining the Mexican forces against Texas. By the time Houston heard of the fall of the Alamo, he had secured treaties with the Indians and was returning to Washington-on the-Brazos. The other Texas garrisons were too burdened with poor and indecisive leadership to respond in time to help defend the Alamo.

Chapter 33

The peacefulness of a rainy afternoon at Virginia point was shattered when Jeff, his family and Anna got the news of the Alamo and the panic that followed. Anna and Libby were sewing and Jeff and Tad were reading when they heard a lone rider approaching the cabin at a hard gallop.

"Hello in the house!" the breathless rider shouted as he neared the cabin.

Jeff opened the door and stepped onto the porch to see a rain-and mud-soaked rider on a worn-out, heaving mare.

"Where's your master?" The stranger asked, catching his breath from the hard ride.

"I own this property," Jeff said as he straightened himself to his full height. "My name is Jefferson. What can I do for you, sir?"

"General Houston sent me to spread the word. Everybody's gotta get out, and get out fast. That devil Santa Anna killed all our boys at San Antonio. Murdered every last one of them. Almost two hundred from what I been told. Now him and his cut throats, all six thousand of 'em, is spreadin' out and marchin' across Texas, burnin' an' lootin' an' killin' everything and everybody in their path. You best load up an' get gone as soon as you can. I don't know how far they are behind me. Maybe just a few hours, but prob'ly no more'n a day or two. You and yours best skedaddle toward the Sabine as fast as you can."

Anna, Libby and Tad stepped onto the porch beside Jeff.

"Ma'am," the young man tipped his hat when he saw Anna. Anna could see that the rider was not much more than a boy, not yet twenty. He wore a hollow-eyed look bordering on terror, as if Satan himself were chasing him.

"Ma'am, if you heard what I told him, you'll see that everybody moves out right away. There's no time to waste. Tell me, how many more farms farther north?"

"Just mine and my husband's place. We're the last one, and my husband is away recruiting soldiers."

"I hope he gets back soon and brings a bunch of men. We're gonna need all we can get."

"Mister, I can tell you're tired. Can't we give you something to eat or drink?" Anna asked.

"I could sure use a drink of water, and I'd gladly take something I can eat on the way, if I could get it fast. I've still got a lot of folks to warn. I'm supposed to cross the river and warn the people on the other side as I go back south to meet back up with the army. I could sure use a good fresh horse, if you could spare one." The young man had a pitiful, pleading look on his face. "I'm about to drive this poor mare into the ground."

"Tad, go catch my mare to give this man," Anna said.

"I'll go hitch up a wagon with the mules," Jeff called behind him as he dashed off the porch into the rain.

"Pick the best wagon," Anna said. "We need one that will stand up to some punishment." She turned back to the rider. "Mister, get on down and take your saddle and bridle off and turn that animal loose. I'll get you some water. We'll have you something to eat in a minute. Libby, pack up some baked sweet potatoes and jerky for this man, and I'll start getting things for us to take."

In a few minutes, Tad returned to the cabin riding the mare bareback with a rope halter. Within moments the young rider had drunk his fill of water and was saddled with a sack of food tied to his saddle horn.

"Thanks, Ma'am, I really appreciate all your help," the young rider said. "What's, your name? I'll tell the general where I got the horse."

"Anna Bowman. My husband is Captain William Bowman. I want to tell him about you. I'm sure he'll want to thank you for riding all the way out here to warn us. What's your name?"

"John Hayes, Ma'am. My friends call me Jack."

“Well, Jack, thank you for passing the word.”

Jeff pulled the wagon up to the front of the cabin as Hayes mounted the fresh mare.

“Thanks to you and your wife for the provisions,” Hayes said, settling into the saddle. “I saw a low water crossing downstream about four miles, but it looked like the water's rising fast with the rain. You'd better hurry if you’re gonna make it before it gets too high to cross.”

“We'll do that. Thanks,” Jeff called as Hayes spurred the mare into a gallop toward the river.

“All right, we need a plan,” Anna said as Jeff and Tad joined her and Libby on the porch. “Tad, Jeff is going to need his saddle horse; go get Buck and saddle him up. Jeff, don't you still have that old tent I've heard Will talk about?”

“Yes, it's out in the shed.”

“We'll need it.”

Jeff took off running toward the shed behind the cabin as Anna and Libby started gathering clothes, bedding and food. Jeff returned with the tent and placed it at the tailgate of the wagon, leaving room for the other goods to be placed behind the seat. Then he went inside to retrieve all his firearms and his bags of powder, patch and ball. Within minutes they were packed with only the barest necessities to sustain them on a trip into the unknown. They had no idea how long they would be gone, how far they would go or whether they would ever see their homes again. Once they were packed, Jeff spread the tent canvas over the food, clothes and bedding, paying particular attention to keeping his powder dry. He then pulled the canvas up over Libby and Billy in the bed of the wagon, then up over Anna and Texanna on the seat with Tad. Tad was driving.

The intensity of the rain had increased to a constant, soaking downpour.

Before they pulled away from the cabin, Jeff rode to the front of the wagon and looked under the canvas at Anna. “Is there anything you need to get from your place before we go?”

Anna, holding the baby in her arms looked straight-ahead, hesitated a moment, then quietly said, “Everything worth saving is right here with us. Let's go.”

Jeff dismounted and lifted the soggy, shivering Jake into the wagon under the canvas, explaining to the others that they would be moving too fast for him to keep up if he had to run alongside.

Tad put the team into a fast trot as they rolled through the mud toward the crossing. They knew if they couldn't get across at the first low water crossing, it would be another ten miles or so before they would have the next opportunity to cross the Brazos.

They arrived at the crossing to find a wagon attempting to cross and three more waiting their turn. All the wagons were filled with wet, cold and terrified women and children.

What was normally a low-water crossing with only five or six inches of gently flowing water passing over a smooth limestone bottom had turned into a series of small, but growing rapids with the rain.

Jeff rode to the wagon in the middle of the river to find a woman with four drenched children trying to control their wild-eyed team. The horses were rearing in the harness, trying to break loose as the water splashed around their bellies. The woman looked as angry as she was scared. She and her older children were screaming and whipping the horses to urge them across the river.

Jeff rode into the water alongside the horse on the right side and jumped from Buck's back onto the back of the frightened animal. Holding onto Buck's reins with one hand, he spurred and coaxed the team across the rising river to the other side. He then repeated the process until all the wagons were safely across the river.

They camped for the night with the rest of the refugees on a rise across the river as darkness set in. Anna, Libby and the babies managed to get some sleep in the tent, while Jeff and Tad sat up most of the night under the wagon, utilizing whatever protection it afforded.

They traveled in a generally eastward direction, cross country, looking to connect with the old King's Road. They were able to cross the Navasota River in much the same fashion as they did the Brazos, but many people were required to wade the river and help push the wagons through the mud. They came upon the King’s Road about six miles west of the Trinity River and found that the constant stream of families had grown to thousands moving east toward the Sabine. They had no way of knowing how many families had gone before them or how many were still behind. Jeff found only a few men along the road, but most of them were too old or too sick to be of any help pushing the wagons through the mire that the road had become. Most of the wagons avoided the deep ruts already in the road and traveled alongside it, widening the muddy mess to a quarter of a mile in some places. The downpour continued.

They’d been on the road and in the rain four days when they approached the Trinity River. They all understood that the only way to cross the Trinity, due to its rising depth and increasing width, would be by way of the ferry at the King's Road crossing, if it still existed.

As they approached the river, they saw a line of wagons almost a mile long, waiting to cross on the ferry. Jeff slowly rode ahead of his family to view the progress at the crossing.

Never in his life had he seen so much misery. Many people were sick from exposure, lying in sodden blankets and quilts in their wagons. As he moved from wagon to wagon, he found people in all states of physical exhaustion and emotional distress. He passed several wagons where mothers were begging for food for their children. In some cases, he learned that people had left their homes in such a panic that they’d left meat hanging in their smokehouses, believing the Mexicans were breathing down their necks. Not everyone traveled with wagons and teams of horses or mules. He found several people crossing the country on foot, with only the clothes on their backs. Before he got to the head of the line, he helped dig a grave for a child who'd died along the way. The little boy had been sick before his family fled, and he didn't have the strength to withstand the elements.

After filling the grave, Jeff left the grieving mother and her three remaining children and rode into the woods. Once he had ridden far enough into the thicket so he couldn't be seen, he slid off his horse, sat on a log and cried. He cried for all the mothers and babies who were enduring the devastation of war. He cried for those who would never see their homes again, and he cried for those who would never again see their husbands and fathers.

He sat with his head in his hands, sobbing. After several minutes, he realized that he was one of the very few healthy men in the entire throng of refugees. He realized he could make a difference to those suffering along the trail. He got up, wiped the tears from his face and went hunting. Within an hour, he had bagged two deer. He quickly field dressed the animals and returned to distribute the meat along the line with the families where it appeared to be most needed.

Tad, Anna, Libby and the children moved their wagon along the line, waiting for their turn on the ferry. They sat up all night, slowly inching their way to the water's edge, and just before daylight they were able to cross.

Eager to be moving again, they kept rolling eastward all day, ignoring their fatigue, pushing themselves and their animals toward safety in United States, beyond the Sabine.

There were still several rivers to cross but none as wide as the Trinity at flood stage. The crossings were made with Libby, Tad, and Jeff pushing on the wheels while Anna whipped the animals across.

The mud slowed them even more than the rivers. When they got into the deep east Texas woods, the forest came right up to the edge of the road, leaving the travelers no choice but to wade through the heavily traveled muck. The rain had stopped, but now the mud was their primary enemy. Much of the time everyone was outside the wagon, pushing at the wheels to extract them from the deep bogs.

They found the town of Nacogdoches deserted when they arrived. They continued rolling on through town, unwilling to stop with the Sabine so close. Finally, late in the afternoon they approached the Sabine. With no rain for the last two days, the river was passable without too much trouble. Once on the east side of the river, Jeff started looking for a place to camp. It appeared that a temporary town of filthy refugees had the same notion. Hundreds of people were camped along the east bank as far as the eye could see. Many appeared to be in a daze from their ordeal along the trail. Some were just lying in the mud, exhausted.

Jeff led his wagon upriver beyond most of the refugees. He knew the water would be fresher there. Eventually finding a spot beyond the other campers, he stopped and set up the tent.

Chapter 34

Will first learned of the fate of the Alamo and the Great Runaway Scrape, as the Texas exodus had become known, when he encountered the first refugees just after he and his men swam their horses across the Red River. The first group of wagons he met heading east from Texas was led by an elderly man named Osborne, driving a wagon carrying his family and followed by two more wagons loaded with slaves. Osborne related to Will the events of the Alamo as he had heard them and the account of the Mexican army burning and looting its way through Texas as it marched eastward.

Will took the news of the Alamo hard. The last he had seen of the Bigelow brothers and Oliver Cartwright was when they were on their way to San Antonio to defend the Alamo. Osborne also confirmed the loss of Travis, Bowie, and Crockett, all men whom Will knew and respected.

Some of Will's men scoffed at the idea that Santa Anna's army was spreading across Texas like a plague of locusts destroying everything in sight, but they all spurred westward a bit harder.

Soon the riders were met with a steady stream of refugees along the road. The closer they got to the Sabine, the larger the numbers became. Will started asking everyone they passed whether they had seen anything of Jeff's family and Anna and the baby, but everyone had been too concerned with their own miseries to pay much attention to anyone else.

It was already dark by the time Will and his men topped the rise that looked down on the banks of the Sabine. As they rode toward the river, Will was awestruck by the number of campfires and shabby campsites scattered along the river's edge. It looked as if a thousand fireflies had lit along the muddy edge of the crooked finger of water.

Will dispatched several of his men to spread through the campsites and help him look for his family. He sent the remainder of his troop to cross the river and make camp on the other side.

Will rode slowly from one campfire to the next calling for Anna, Jeff and Libby and getting no response. He continued his search northward, picking his way between wagons and pallets strewn between the fires, giving descriptions of his family.

Finally a frail, bedraggled woman reached for his leg as he rode past her wagon. "Mister, did I hear you say you were looking for a colored family traveling with a white woman and her baby?"

"Yes Ma'am, have you seen them?"

"That may have been the man that helped me bury my boy," she said in a sorrowful voice. "I thought I saw him with some other folks way on upstream when I was gathering firewood today. I never did thank him. Mister, please thank him for helping me, would you?"

"Sure Ma'am, I'll thank him for you."

"Thank him for the venison, too. I guess I forgot my manners," the woman called out weakly.

"Yes Ma'am, I'll tell him."

Will continued riding north, carefully picking his way among the wagons and people. He knew he would soon find Jeff and Anna and the others. The actions of the man the woman described were those Jeff would have taken under the circumstances. He continued quietly calling their names as he rode along the muddy river bank.

After awhile the campfires became more spread out and farther apart as he rode upstream from the crossing. He called more loudly as he ventured toward the more distant fires.

Suddenly Will's calling was interrupted by a warmly familiar and welcome sound. Jake was barking wildly and bounding across the ground to meet him. Within seconds the dog was dancing at Baron's feet, joyously wagging his tail. He heard

Jeff and Anna calling at the same time "Will! Will, over here!"

Will followed the sounds of their voices and jumped off Baron as he slid to a stop. He took Anna into his arms as she called his name over and over. "Oh Will, I've missed you so much!" She kissed him eagerly.

"I've been worried about you," Will said, still clutching her tightly. "Are you all right? Where's Texanna?"

"She's right here," Anna said, taking the baby from Libby and handing her to Will.

Will took the baby and held her tightly for a moment, kissing her on the cheek. He then reached over with his other arm and squeezed Jeff around the shoulders. "Thanks, partner. I appreciate everything you've done."

"No thanks needed. We just did everything together."

""Glad to see you, Lib." Will hugged Libby with his free arm while he still held Texanna. "Let me see that big boy there." Libby handed him Billy, and he exclaimed how much both of the babies had grown. "Thanks, Tad. I'm sure you played a big part in getting everybody here safely."

"Aw, I just drove a little."

"Now that I've found you, I have to leave for a little while. I've got to go make sure my men are settled in for the night. I'll be back soon. Don't go away, we've got some catching up to do."

As Will rode into the darkness, he felt an enormous weight being lifted from his shoulders. The cabin and everything at Virginia Point didn't matter now that he knew his family and Jeff's were safe.

Within an hour he was back at Jeff's campsite after making sure his men had eaten and had a comfortable and safe place to camp for the night.

When he returned, Libby had modified the sleeping arrangements. She was on the pallet under the wagon with Jeff and Tad had his bed in the wagon. Will, Anna and the children had the tent.

The next morning Will was up before everyone else and had

coffee brewing on the fire. He nudged Jeff on the shoulder, gesturing for Jeff to come with him. In a few moments they had walked away from the campsite to the river bank with their cups of coffee and were quietly arguing.

"Look, Will, they're out of Texas. They're safe now. I've only partially done my duty for my family. Now that they're out of danger, I've got to fight for them. Will, I probably know more than most men fighting that war what freedom's really all about. "I've tasted it, and I'm not about to give it up. I'm going with you to fight. That's all there is to it. Tad can handle the team as well as I can. He drove it all the way from Virginia Point in worse conditions than you've ever seen. I have no doubt that he can do anything that either one of us could do. They aren't that far from the Red River. They can sell the wagon and team there and catch a boat on down to New Orleans to your cousin's place."

"What's Libby going to say about you going with me?"

"We've already talked about it. I was going to leave to go back to join up with General Houston this morning, anyway, if you hadn't shown up."

Will nudged Jeff and grinned. "You never cease to amaze me."

"How many men do you have with you?"

"Sixty-four, including you."

"I imagine if we had a meeting this morning right here on these camp grounds, we could drum up some more men," Jeff said. "I suspect there may be a few more here just like me, ready to go and take back their homes and property now that they have their families out of Texas."

Will nodded. "We'll just have a little meeting after breakfast then."

During breakfast, Will and Jeff shared their plan with Anna, Libby, and Tad. Anna and Libby were prepared to go on to New Orleans to stay until the Texas army ran the Mexicans back across the Rio Grande.

Tad however, was not happy with the plan. "I don't see why

I can't go with you and fight. I can handle a gun as good as the next man. Jeff's seen to that. And I'm plenty old enough. I'm almost sixteen. I can carry my own weight. You already said you need more men. You're even going to have a meeting in a little while to try to talk some more into going with you. I don't understand why I can't go."

Libby looked at Jeff for an answer.

Jeff got to his feet and motioned for Tad to follow. "Tad, come on over here. Let's take a walk. I want to talk to you in private." Once they were out of ear shot of the others, Jeff put his arm around Tad's shoulders as they walked. "Brother, everything you said is true. I have no doubt you can handle yourself in a fight. I'm sure you'd do very well, maybe even be a hero. But I still can't let you go."

"But —"

"Now wait a minute. The reason I can't let you go is because I'm going. Tad, thing is, this is war, and . . . uh . . . I may not come back. If you went too and got shot down next to me, who'd look after Libby and Billy? Who would educate Billy the way I have you? Tad, Libby's a strong woman. Someday she'll be going back to that little house at Virginia Point. If I don't come back to be with her, she needs you to help run the place. Hell, boy, if it's a fight you want, I imagine we'll be up to our ears in Indians some day. We've just been lucky so far. You'll get your chance, but now is not your time. There's still a lot that you need to do between here and New Orleans. The area between the Sabine and the Red rivers is called the badlands for a reason. It's because of the outlaws that work through here. Those women and babies need your protection. I know you can shoot and I know you can fight. Both Will and I really need you to keep our families safe. Do you understand?"

"Yeah, I guess so," Tad said, reluctantly accepting his new role.

"Come on then, let's go finish breakfast; we've got a lot to do."

As soon as they finished with breakfast, Will and Jeff saddled up and rode from one end of the camp to the other calling all men to a meeting at the crossing. Soon they had a group of about eighty men of all ages and conditions gathered next to the crossing.

Will stepped onto a stump to deliver his message. “Men, you’re all here for the same reason. You and your families have been driven from your homes by the murdering Santa Anna. You, like me, have lost friends and maybe even kinfolk at the Alamo. We all came to Texas for the same reasons: to build our homes, farm our land and raise our children. Well, I'll tell you, I'm taking my place back. I'm not going to let that little dictator run me off. Now that my family is safe, I'm going back to fight. I have sixty-four good men riding with me. All but one of these men aren't even from Texas. They’re freedom loving men from Kentucky, Tennessee, Mississippi, Arkansas and Louisiana who are willing to fight for the freedom of Texas and Texans. There they are, just across the river. They're going to join General Houston and take revenge for their lost freedom-loving brothers who fell at the Alamo. Who among you will go with us to fight for your homes, your families, and your freedom?

“We are the Bowman Volunteers. Join us in an hour if you love freedom. You need at least one firearm in good working condition and a good horse, as we will be traveling hard and fast. Thank you, gentlemen, and God bless you.”

Will and Jeff returned to their camp to say goodbye to their families.

The farewell was brief but sweet. Both Anna and Libby understood that their men had a more urgent mission than ushering them to New Orleans. They had each other, Tad, and their babies until their men came back from war. They did what women have done for centuries. They kissed their men goodbye, cried and prayed for their safety as they marched off to war.

Chapter 35

"All right men, prepare for departure," Will called to his company as he and Jeff rode into the camp. "We leave in ten minutes."

"Looks like your speech done some good, Captain," a middle-aged man in dirty buckskins with a floppy brown hat and a toothless grin yelled as Will rode past. "We got some more riders this morning."

Will continued riding through the camp, speaking to men here and there, observing their condition as they packed their gear and prepared to ride.

"Time to mount up," Will called. "Fall into formation in four columns. Jenkins, help the men get information. I need to address the troop."

The toothless man who had greeted Will earlier limped to his black gelding, swung a stiff leg over the saddle and started helping the men and their mounts line up.

"All right, boys, start linin' up right here. Yeah, you beside him, that's right. Come on, boys, shake a leg. We ain't got all day." Soon Jenkins had arranged the men in four lines facing Will.

Will spoke loudly. "First, I want to thank you men who joined us this morning. I know you hated leaving your families as much as I hated leaving mine, but you answered the call of your country. Thank you for that. How many new men do we have today? Let me see your hands." Will counted as men started raising their hands. He counted nine new men.

"All right. We're seventy-three strong. That's a good sized company. For the benefit of the new men, I'll go over our daily routine. We march two abreast and make one rest stop in the morning, one at midday and one in the afternoon. You best take care of your business before we start because we won't stop for you if you break ranks. I shouldn't need to tell you to take care of your horses. See that they graze and get watered whenever we stop for a rest. We'll send four men out every morning to hunt and scavenge for food. We don't have the luxury of supply wagons traveling with us, but we haven't gone hungry so far. Now that we're in Texas, I advise you to seek out abandoned cabins if it's your day to provide the food. You may find some livestock, maybe a hog or some chickens, maybe even a cow. There might be some cornmeal, or maybe some cured meat in a smoke house or sweet potatoes in a cellar. I expect the owners would support our mission if they were home. If you don't run across a farm, you'll find plenty of wildlife.

"Men, you all know why we're here. I don't know what to expect anymore than you do. Our orders are to join up with General Houston when we find him. I don't know whether we'll run into any Mexican soldiers before then, but if we do, we've got to be ready. I know you're all volunteers, but you're also now soldiers. For soldiers to fight and win effectively there have to be a few leaders and there have to be a few rules. I haven't selected any additional leaders until now because, as you know, we've been picking up good men all along the way. Now we have to be ready to fight, so we have to know who'll be giving the orders, and you must all have the discipline to follow orders. Any of you who have ever been in battle know that you've all got to work together or you might get your whole company killed. Does anybody here have a problem following orders? If you do, we need to get it out in the open right now." Will hesitated a moment to see whether anyone would respond. After he got no response he continued.

"Anybody who has ever been in any kind of war or battle, major or minor, with Indians or anybody else, ride forward, up here with me." At first there was some hesitation, then several men spurred their horses forward. Then several more rode to the front of the formation. A total of eleven men rode forward, including Jeff. Two other Texans who had joined them that morning were among those who circled around Will in the group of experienced fighters. One of them was a young man about eighteen dressed in a homespun shirt and leather britches.

"What's your name?" Will asked the young man.

"Bob Abbott, Captain."

"How long have you been in Texas?"

"Me and my family been eight years at the north end of the DeWitt grant. Me and my pa had to run off some Comanches a couple of times. They killed my brother, though."

"Abbott, do you feel like you know your way around Texas?"

"Reckon so. Been all around with my pa, tradin' wild cows for hogs and such."

"All right, Abbott, you're a scout. You'll ride up front with Jefferson here." Will motioned to Jeff.

Some of the men looked scornfully at Jeff. Nobody said anything, but Will read their thoughts. "This man has been with me in Texas for six years," Will said." He knows his way around better than any man here. I know he knows how to scout. I taught him."

Will continued to question each man as to his battle experience. Only Jenkins, the toothless man with the wrinkled face in the floppy hat, had actual, organized battle experience. Will learned that he had fought with Andy Jackson in the Indian wars years earlier. He later learned that Jenkins still carried an arrowhead in his leg from those wars.

Will made his leadership assignments after getting a brief understanding of each man's background. He assigned a sergeant and a corporal for each group of eighteen men and promoted Jenkins to sergeant major. He then returned to face his troops and flanked his leaders on either side of himself, facing the men.

"All right, men, these are your leaders. You have a sergeant and a corporal assigned to each column. Jenkins here is the sergeant major for the entire company. He's my second in command. If anything happens to me, he's in charge. Is that understood?"

No one questioned his selection.

“Abbot and Jefferson, there, are our scouts. They'll ride well ahead of our main body and report back any sign of the enemy. Now, about the rules. There are some things that are very important to a military operation. Discipline and obedience are two of them. I will have a meeting with the sergeants every night to discuss and plan strategy. What I say is what we do. Your sergeants are in charge of your smaller groups. They will assign guard duty and other jobs. From here on out we will have guards posted every night, all night long. The rules of war apply starting now. Any man sleeping on guard duty will be shot. Does every man here agree to follow the rules I have stated?"

Hearing no response, he walked Baron to the front of the column of men. “Scouts, take your positions.”

Jeff and Abbott spurred into a lope and continued well ahead of the company.

“Sergeants and corporals, take your positions.”

Will watched as the sergeants and corporals established their positions at the head and tail of each column.

“Sergeant Major, give the order to march.”

Jenkins took his position beside Will, “All right, boys, let’s move out. Column of twos, forward . . . march!”

Chapter 36

Will led his company along the same road that Jeff and their families had just traveled. There were still hundreds of refugees on the road traveling eastward, toward safety. It seemed that with each group of people they passed, they got a new and more devastating account of the events of the war and the whereabouts of both Santa Anna's and Houston's armies. They learned that Santa Anna had split his forces into five different divisions and ordered them to conduct a massive sweep through Texas. Their orders were to burn every town, plantation and farm in their path. The Anglo's presence was to be eliminated in Texas.

They also learned that Houston had moved his six hundred or so still untried but motivated troops eastward from Gonzales, across the Colorado to the Brazos in what appeared to be a retreat before the Mexican troops.

Will and his company camped for the night beside a creek, within a day's ride of San Felipe. They were just setting up camp and starting their fires when a sentry brought a wagon with women and children to Will. He watched in the fading light as the sentry led the worn-out team and wagon to his camp. A flash of recognition crossed Will's mind as the old woman on the wagon bench spat tobacco juice on the ground.

"Captain, I met these folks on the road," the sentry said. "When they learned we was here, this woman said she had some news for us. Said she wanted to talk to the man in charge."

"Aunt Bess!' Will exclaimed, "What are you doing here? I thought you'd be off in Louisiana somewhere by now."

The tired old woman looked directly at Will, first with a blank stare. Then her wrinkled face softened slightly in recognition. "I know you."

"Yes ma'am, Will Bowman. You might remember Jeff here too." Jeff had joined Will after building the fire. "We stayed over with you and enjoyed your cooking when we first got to Texas."

"I 'member now." The stress and exhaustion of her difficult journey under such terrible conditions was evident in her voice. "Surveyors . . . from Virginia or somewheres like that. My 'ole body mighta give out but I can remember . . . Oh, Lordy, there's some things I wish I could forget."

"From the looks of all of you, you folks need a rest," Will said. "Please camp here tonight. I believe we can round up enough to feed everybody. It won't come close to matching your cooking, Aunt Bess, but Jeff does pretty well with venison."

"Mama, let's stop," the woman on the bench beside Aunt Bess said. "You and the girls can't go on much further."

"Guess we ought to," Bess said. "It's nearly dark anyway. Help me down, would you Mister Bowman? Ole busted up hip gets mighty stiff ridin' up here all day. I don't walk too good neither. It might take both you and your boy there to lift me down an' help me over to that tree over yonder."

Will and Jeff gently lifted the heavy woman out of the wagon and carried her to a place where the younger woman had spread a quilt under a hackberry tree. Will wondered how the young woman and three girls had managed the old woman on the muddy road by themselves.

After they got Aunt Bess settled onto her pallet, Jeff went to tend to the guest's horses, and Will introduced himself to the woman traveling with Aunt Bess.

She worked up a slight smile. "I'm Emily Styles. These are my daughters, Rachel, Ruth, and Rose," the travel weary and dirty woman said. She turned to the oldest, a thin blond girl about ten years old. "Rachel, y'all go get the things we'll need for the night out of the wagon." She looked at Will again. "I'm so glad to see you and your men. They'll need you when Houston starts fighting, if he ever does. Seems like all he's done so far, from what we hear, is just push his men east ahead of the Mexicans."

"Where's Houston now?"

"The last we heard, he was at the Groce plantation, about twenty miles north of San Felipe, trying to gather more troops and train them."

Will nodded. "I know the place. How far back are the Mexicans?"

"We're not real sure. Everybody we talk to has something different to say, but we believe Santa Anna is leading a group of about a thousand or so toward the new Texas government headquarters at Washington-on-the-Brazos. But I imagine President Burnett and the rest of the new Texas government will be gone before the Mexican Army gets there. I don't know where the rest of the Mexicans are . . . spreading out and burning everything they come to, I guess. We barely got out ahead of them at our place down in the DeWitt grant. My mother-in-law has been real sick, and we couldn't move her. We waited till she got a little better, and we've been on the road ever since."

"That's the first I've heard of a new Texas government," Will said. "How did that come about?"

"I don't have all the details, there's been so much turmoil in the last several months. But from what I was told, a convention of delegates was called in San Felipe just a few days before the Alamo fell. The delegates had come together to draft a declaration of independence from Mexico and a new constitution for the republic. It was all approved in mid-March and they elected David Burnett president. A fellow named Zavala was named vice president and Sam Houston was elected Commanding General of the Army. They immediately moved the government down the river to Washington-on-the Brazos and Houston started putting his army together."

"Thanks for the information. I can't say that I'm surprised after all we've been through."

Will looked at the figure on the pallet and saw that Aunt Bess had fallen asleep from exhaustion. The three girls were preparing their bedding beside her.

Jeff took care of the Styles' horses and got back to his

cooking. Before long he had a supper of venison and baked sweet potatoes for them and their guests. Emily Styles shook the old woman awake, and they all gathered around Aunt Bess to eat their supper.

After they finished, Jeff fished a bottle out of his saddlebags.

"Ma'am, this isn't near as good as what you offered Will and me to celebrate our becoming citizens seven years ago. It's local whiskey — not too bad though. I keep it mostly for snakebite but I guess there's not much chance of getting bitten with all these men tramping around all over the place. We don't have anything to celebrate tonight, but I'd like to return your kindness and ask you to join us in a drink."

"Boys, even though Emily is a little embarrassed by my ways at times, I'll just take you up on it. Besides, it might help me sleep better."

Jeff poured a shot of whiskey into three cups and offered some to Emily, which she declined.

After they tasted the whiskey and Aunt Bess nodded her approval, Will asked, "What are you doing down here in the middle of this mess anyway?"

"Well, I fell off my porch and broke my hip a couple years ago. Got to where I couldn't get around to do much of nothin', so my boy come got me and brung me home with him. I been there makin' a burden of myself ever since."

"Oh, Mama, you have not," Emily said. "You've been a lot of company, especially since Tom left and . . ."

Emily put her hand to her mouth and looked away, unable to continue as she quietly choked back tears.

"That's the news we come to tell you about, if you ain't heared about it already, about my boy Tom and all the others at Goliad with Colonel Fannin."

"No Ma'am, Will said. We haven't heard anything about Fannin at Goliad. I've been collecting these men back east and have heard very little of the war except the fall of the Alamo and the fact that the Mexicans are burning all the families out of Texas. What happened?"

"Well, Tom went and jined up with Fannin when the call for arms came. Some of the men in Fannin's army were goin' to take the war south of the Rio Grande to Matamoras, but they never really got their campaign off the ground. They ended up protectin' the fortress at Goliad while Travis, Bowie and a bunch of other fellers were defendin' the Alamo. In the meantime General Urrea crossed the Rio Grande, marchin' toward Goliad with orders to wipe out the Anglos there. Anyway, the long and short of it is that Fannin lost a battle and surrendered all his men to the Mexicans, with a promise that they would be treated honorable.

"Then them sorry, cutthroat, murderin' bastards ended up shootin' almost four hundred unarmed men, includin' my Tom. Slaughtered 'em after they done surrendered!" Bess lost control and had to stop for a few moments to choke back her sobs before she could continue. After she gained control of her voice, she said, "Only a handful escaped. We heard the story first hand from one of the few men who got away durin' the commotion. We found him on the road, yesterday, half-starved, lookin' for Houston's army. He knowed Tom; seen him shot dead like a sick dog in the street." Aunt Bess stared off into the darkness.

"My condolences, ladies," Will said, searching for the right words. "If it gives you any comfort, my men will do everything we can to avenge your loss." He got to his feet and stood next to Bess' pallet. "It's getting late and we all need our rest. We'll wake you for breakfast."

Will and Jeff left the grieving family to deal with their loss among themselves.

That night by the firelight, Jeff wrote in the small journal he carried in the pouch on his belt.

April 8, 1836

Met an old friend tonight with tales of terror from the war. So much death and destruction already. The Alamo, Goliad, all the suffering families being driven from their homes, many dying on their way to safety. This madness must be stopped. Should meet Houston tomorrow. Hope we can add the strength that he needs. My thoughts and prayers are with Libby, Anna, Tad and the children every day. I know they pray for our safety too.

Jeff

The next morning Will and Jeff treated the Styles family to a meager breakfast and saw to it that Aunt Bess was as comfortable as possible in the Styles' wagon. Jeff gave them enough food to last several days. Then he and Will wished them well before sending them on their way. Both men knew this would not be the last grieving family they would see.

Chapter 37

After Will had Jenkins assemble the men for what he hoped would be the last day of their march before joining Houston's Army, he told them of the butchery at Goliad. The men spent their morning in a hard ride with a grim determination to somehow turn the Mexicans back and put an end to the death and destruction.

Since they were only a few miles from the Groce plantation, they pushed on instead of taking a mid-morning break to rest. Before noon, Jeff came racing back to the troop with word that Houston's army was ahead.

They were met with shouts of welcome as they rode into camp. Men ran to greet them when they approached the plantation house where Houston made his headquarters. Word of their arrival had preceded them, and Houston met them in the yard, in front of the large house.

"Captain Bowman, reporting with volunteers from the States," Will said to the small knot of men with Houston. "I'm to report to General Houston."

"I'm Houston," the tall, stout looking man said as he took Baron's reins while Will dismounted. "Glad to see you, Bowman."

"Yes sir, glad to see you too," Will said shaking hands.

"Looks like you've brought us the right kind of help." Houston was eyeing the men in Will's command. "Austin told me he'd sent you to the states to bring back some fighters. Looks like you've done well, very well indeed. Go ahead and have your men set up camp. Anywhere over east of the house will be fine. Join me for lunch and I'll bring you up to date."

Will passed his orders on to Jenkins and followed Houston into the Groce plantation house for lunch.

“I'm not able to offer you anything very fancy,” Houston said as they sat at the table. “Groce pretty much cleaned everything out when he took his slaves back east before we got here. I’m just glad to have a roof over my head, for a little while anyway. We eat about what the men eat. Whatever they can forage.”

As they ate, Houston questioned Will about the men he’d brought. He also told him of the events that had brought them to where they were and where he hoped they would lead. “I've been severely criticized by everyone from my own men to President Burnett for not challenging Santa Anna in a major fight before now, especially since we got word of the massacre at Goliad. But I'm just not willing to send untrained and undisciplined boys off to their slaughter.

“I'm much more willing to bide my time, continue to gather troops, train my men, take my criticism, and wait for Santa Anna to make a mistake. He will soon, and when he does, I want to be ready. One of my major concerns is with my own troops. These men have been separated from their families who have been driven away from their homes to who knows what. They've seen their homes destroyed and their friends slaughtered. They’re ready for a fight. I don't think they'll stand for much more drilling and delays. They want revenge.”

Houston continued. “I received a report just this morning that Santa Anna with less than a thousand men have split off from the other divisions to chase the new Texas government south toward Galveston Bay. Our new government leaders are on their way to Galveston to be ready to take a ship to sea if need be to escape from the Mexicans. I think we'll just head out in that direction and wait for Santa Anna’s next move."

The next day, on April 12, Houston gave marching orders. They headed south toward Santa Anna's splintered forces. The roads were still in terrible condition from the heavy rains and the travel was slow, but by April 18 they were camped near the burned-out ruins of the town of Harrisburg.

Deaf Smith, one of Houston's most effective scouts, brought in a Mexican courier as a prisoner. When the documents in his pouch were translated, Houston learned of Santa Anna's plans and movements. The intelligence was just what Houston needed to make his long-awaited move.

He'd retreated and drilled his men enough. If he pushed back any farther or drilled any more, his men would revolt. He had just the fighting force he needed — tired, but not so exhausted to have the fight drained from them. They'd been spoiling for a fight for so long, they were neither nervous nor fearful.

Santa Anna finally made his mistake. He placed himself close to Galveston Bay in terrain that, when confronted with Houston's forces, prevented either side from executing an effective retreat. Houston knew that as he crossed Buffalo Bayou and positioned his army so that it appeared to be trapped near Galveston bay.

Buffalo Bayou lay to Houston's rear. The San Jacinto River lay to his left and open prairie extended to swampland on his right. Santa Anna and about eight hundred troops were directly ahead, beyond a slight rise. Houston and his army of slightly more than nine hundred men and two cannon were ready.

Santa Anna was in no hurry to attack Houston. He intended to move on his own terms. He and his troops were tired and needed rest. Three-quarters of a mile lay between his and Houston's armies. The Mexican soldiers hastily put up some breastworks made of saddlebags and brush they had cut nearby.

Late in the morning, Houston was surprised by the arrival of General Cos at Santa Anna's camp with reinforcements of four hundred additional troops who were tired and in need of rest. His arrival brought the Mexican strength to over twelve hundred.

Angry with himself for not doing so sooner, Houston sent Deaf Smith and a few others to destroy the bridge across the Brazos to eliminate the possibility of further reinforcements joining Santa Anna and to block the last avenue of escape. He was not the first, nor would he be the last general to burn his bridges behind him. At noon, he called his officers together for a war council.

"Men, we missed a good opportunity to attack early this morning before Cos and his men arrived, but what's done is done. Our men are ready, but they're tired. I suggest we plan our attack at first light tomorrow, after the men rest. We will have the rest of the afternoon to plan. Go on back and tell your men to rest today, and we'll attack tomorrow. Meet me back here in an hour to review our battle plan."

Will returned to his men to relay the orders. As soon as he told them, he was met with a groundswell of resistance.

"We didn't come all this way just to wait around!" One man shouted. "We want a fight!"

Another added, "We got 'em where we want 'em, Captain! Let's get 'em now!"

Then another, "Ain't no use a'waitin'. They ain't expectin' us now. They's expectin' us to do just like the general plans. Let's get 'em now while they's a nappin'. What do you say, boys?"

The entire Bowman company shouted their agreement.

Will stood in the midst of his men, listening to their disapproval of the orders for another delay and their eagerness to fight. He reached for the stirrup and swung into his saddle.

"Jenkins, you hold the men right here. I know they're fired up, but nobody leaves before the rest. I'm going to gather the rest of the officers and meet again with the general." He turned back to his men. "Men, just stay put. I'm going to talk with the general again. You'll have your fight."

As Will rode through the companies, gathering the other officers for another meeting with Houston, he heard the same attitude. No one wanted to wait another hour, much less another day to reap their revenge against the Mexicans.

Soon Will and the other officers were again at Houston's camp.

Will addressed Houston. “Sir, I believe we'll have a rebellion on our hands if we make our men wait ‘til tomorrow to fight.”

“That's right,” said Lamar, another cavalry captain. “General, some of those men are itching for a fight so bad, I believe they'll break ranks and go on their own if we don't lead them — today.”

“How about the rest of you?” Houston asked. “Is that what all the men want?”

The rest of the officers agreed that their men had universally agreed to attack without delay.

Houston stood, stone faced, staring at his officers. A smile slowly spread across his face. “All right, boys, that's what I wanted to hear. We've got ourselves a motivated fighting force.” Houston drew his sword and strode over to a bare patch of ground. “Now, here's what we'll do.”

He spent the next few minutes defining the specific responsibility and position of each company as he scratched the development of the line and its advancement toward the enemy in the dirt. Will's company of horsemen was to take the right flank to contain the enemy and prevent them from escaping into the prairie or the swamps beyond. They were also to close in on the rear of the Mexican camp and block any possibility of retreat.

Will and the other officers were soon back among their troops, preparing for battle.

The slight rise in the landscape that separated the Texan and Mexican forces acted as a cover to hide the formation of a one thousand yard line. A lack of pickets during the Mexican afternoon siesta also failed to warn the sleeping Mexicans of the line of revenge-seeking, battle-ready freedom fighters before them.

Will's men shared the appearance and determination of every other man on the line: tired and dirty, outfitted in their dirty and stained buckskin or ragged homespun; hats of all descriptions, some wide-brimmed straw, some sweat-stained, misshapen felt, and some made from animal fur. They also shared the memory of the misery and terror they had seen in the eyes of those fleeing their homes. They remembered, too, the brave men cut down at the Alamo and at Goliad.

Houston waited until every man was in position along the line. He walked his white stallion forward between the ranks, drew his sword and raised it high over his head. Looking first to his right, then to his left, he hesitated a moment, then quickly brought his arm down, pointing the sword toward the enemy camp. Spurring his mount, he shouted, "Forward men! Make every shot count!"

The line started moving. The cavalry on the right and left flank spurred into a trot. They eventually lead the straight line into a bow. The twin cannons pulled by thirty men were in the middle.

The Mexican sentries soon alerted the camp with a few scattered musket blasts. The Texan's line started weaving and breaking as the men rushed toward the panicked Mexican soldiers.

No one knew for sure where the battle cry started, but "Remember the Alamo!" and "Remember Goliad!" surged from the Texan's mouths and resounded that day as the cannons blew away the flimsy breastworks and the men charged into the compound. Mexican soldiers ran in all directions, some attempting to follow confused, conflicting orders. Others dropped their weapons and broke to run in any direction they could, only to be cut down by musket fire or long knives.

Deaf Smith shouted, "Take prisoners like the Meskins do!" as he chased down and clubbed a running soldier with his rifle butt. Many of the Mexican soldiers ran toward the back of the encampment, seeking an escape route away from the main line of attackers, only to find Will's and Lamar's men approaching from the rear on horseback, blocking their way and cutting them down.

The battle lasted only a few minutes, but the raw and raging

Texans continued shooting, clubbing and slashing much longer in the screaming death trap. When the killing frenzy was over, the officers finally managed to bring the men under control and some prisoners were taken.

Will found Jeff kneeling over a fallen Texan, bandaging his arm where he had taken a copper ball. Satisfied that Jeff was all right, Will took his first real look at the death and devastation around him as he walked his horse over the battleground.

The stench of burnt powder and death hung in the air like a fog. Hundreds of gray-uniformed Mexican soldiers lay in every imaginable position where they had fallen. There were several places along the edge of the bayous where they had fallen in piles as they were cut down. Other bodies were floating in the water where they drowned. There were over six hundred enemy dead, he was told later. Wounded men were moaning and pleading in Spanish. They would count over two hundred of them. They would be tended to after the wounded Texans were treated.

Will saw many of the young Texans sitting on the ground or leaning on their weapons, drenched in sweat, heaving to catch their breath. He also saw several men on their hands and knees, retching—sick in mind, spirit, and body from their participation in the carnage.

Will had not seen many injured Texans. He learned later there were only three Texans killed and about thirty wounded.

One of the injured was General Houston. Will found him propped against a large oak tree with several men around him, treating his wound and relaying orders. His leg had been shattered by a rifle ball above the ankle after two horses were shot from under him.

"Bowman!" Houston called through the pain when he saw Will. "Go find Lamar. You two get your men on horseback, and go round up everybody who got away. Nobody has been able to find Santa Anna. I want him brought back here alive. You understand me, Bowman? Alive!"

"Yes sir." Will rode off in search of his men and Lamar. He soon found Lamar and within a few minutes had their companies spread out looking for Santa Anna and other fleeing Mexican soldiers. Their men brought in small groups of prisoners they found hiding in the tall grass and along the edges of the swamp, but by nightfall Santa Anna still had not been found.

Jenkins and a group of men brought in a handful of prisoners after dark and told Will, "Captain, it's just gettin' too dang dark out there to see anything."

"I agree. Put these with the others and post guards for the night. See that the men get some rest. We'll take up the search again first thing in the morning."

Will and Jeff were both uncommonly quiet that night as they each recorded the events of the day in their journals.

"Do you think this is the end of it?" Jeff asked as he put his small journal back into his belt pouch.

"I don't know, but I hope that's the last killing I ever see."

The next morning Jenkins and Jeff were forming several search teams as the sun came up. "Captain," Jenkins said, "I thought I'd take some boys and make another sweep along the swamp area out there. Jefferson and a few more are heading out along the prairie toward the bay to see what they can find."

"That's fine," Will answered. "I'll send another group of men out toward Vince's Bayou."

Will found a man from another company who could speak Spanish, and the two of them went to the compound to question the prisoners to see whether they could get any information as to the whereabouts of Santa Anna.

About mid-morning, Jeff and two other men rode into camp with another prisoner.

"Found this one hiding out in the high grass on the prairie," Jeff called as he approached the guarded compound.

Most of the able-bodied Mexican soldiers sprang to their feet when the soldier came into view. All the soldiers in the compound were watching the new arrival.

"Hold him where he is," Will called to Jeff.

Will sought out a young, scared-looking Mexican boy about fifteen years old with a wounded leg and motioned for the interpreter to join him by the boy's side. "Ask this boy who that man is out there."

The interpreter conversed briefly with the young man.

Will understood the answer before he got the translation. Grinning, he turned to Jeff and the others who had ridden in with the lone Mexican. "Boys, you just brought in President Santa Anna."

"Well, I'll be!" Jeff grinned. "He just looked like any of the rest of them to me. Looks like he ordered somebody out of their britches to get their uniform." Jeff laughed as he, Will and the interpreter walked behind Santa Anna toward Houston's camp.

They found Houston still reclining under the tree as they approached with their prisoner.

"General Houston," Will said, making the introduction. "This is Santa Anna. Some of my men found him out on the prairie, hiding in the weeds."

A smile spread over Houston's face as he looked over the new arrival. "Thank your men for me, Bowman. They've done good work."

Houston and Santa Anna quietly glared at each other. President Santa Anna and General Sam Houston were facing each other at last.

Even with a shattered leg, victory was sweet for Houston, but he knew he must make the most of this moment, with several thousand Mexican troops massing only a few miles up the Brazos.

Santa Anna was also developing his strategy as he stood at Houston's feet. His goal was to stay alive by whatever means necessary. He would agree to anything Houston asked to keep from swinging at the end of a rope, as some of the Texans were already demanding. He initially took an humbling position by bowing slightly at the waist to Houston. Then, straightening himself to his full height, dressed in an ordinary soldier's uniform, he took the position of the President of Mexico. Standing tall in a military stance, he said, "*Mi General, ha derrotado el Napoleon del Oeste*!"

The interpreter quickly translated his words. "My General, you have defeated the Napoleon of the West!"

"You dern tootin' we have, you murderer!" a bystander shouted. "Let's string him up, General! Remember the Alamo! Remember Goliad!" There was a chorus of agreement among many of the men who had followed Will and the prisoner to Houston.

"Just calm down!" Houston shouted. "There won't be anybody strung up today. Now you boys get on back to your camps. This man and I have some talking to do. Bowman, you and your men have guard duty here. Your job is to protect this man. Everybody else get out of here. Now!"

The audience drifted away as Will, Jeff and several of Will's men formed a protective circle around Houston, his doctor, his prisoner and the translator.

Houston and Santa Anna commenced discussions on the conditions of Mexican troop withdrawal and an armistice. Their morning-long parley resulted in Santa Anna's agreeing to all of Houston's demands. Santa Anna then drafted a letter to his generals, advising them of his defeat and giving them orders to withdraw their troops south, to beyond the Rio Grande, and to cease all hostilities.

That evening, with Santa Anna safely tucked away under guard, Will once again returned to Houston's bedside. "Sir, today, while you were talking with Santa Anna, I was talking with the doctor. He tells me your leg is in pretty bad shape, and you need to go to New Orleans to have it fixed."

"Yes," Houston said. "I'm afraid if I hang around here much longer, I'll be stumping around on a peg. We're going to put Tom Rusk in charge of the army, and I'm leaving tomorrow by ship for New Orleans to try to get this thing patched up."

"Sir, now that we have Santa Anna captured and his army on the run, I'd be honored if you would allow Jeff and me to be part of your escort to New Orleans. We'll make sure you get there safely and receive the care you need along the way."

Houston thought a moment. "Bowman, I haven't even had time to think about an escort, but I believe I owe it to the men who brought me Santa Anna to take them on a little boat ride. Go find Lamar and turn your command over to him. You and Jeff meet me back here first thing in the morning, and we'll go meet the ship."

"Yes sir. Thank you, sir." Will grinned as he left Houston to find Jeff and tell him the news.

Chapter 38

Will and Jeff joined Houston at the railing as the steamer slowly moved toward the New Orleans docks. They had been drawn to the railing by a commotion on the docks. As the ship got closer, they were surprised to see a huge crowd cheering and waving to them.

“Look at all the people," Jeff said. "What's all the ruckus about?”

“I don't know,” Will answered. “Can’t make out what they're saying.”

The captain of the ship approached them from behind with a sheepish grin on his face.

“General, it looks like your arrival hasn't gone unnoticed. I'm afraid I might be partially responsible for your reception there.”

Houston shot an incredulous look at the captain. “You mean all those people are there for us?”

“Yes sir, it kind of looks that way. You and your men are the heroes of San Jacinto. That's what the newspaper was calling you yesterday when they put out a special edition about your victory. Seems they just heard the news and got it out on the street yesterday. Last night, when the harbor master came aboard to give us docking instructions for this morning, he told me all about the newspaper account of your victory at San Jacinto. I guess what you and your men did has been the biggest, and for sure, the best news, since they got word of the fall of the Alamo and the massacre at Goliad. There were a lot of New Orleans boys with the volunteers who fell at both the Alamo and Goliad.”

“Since you and that harbor master had so much to talk about last night, what else was said?” Houston asked.

“I had to tell him who my passengers are. That's a requirement, you know. That man got all excited and scurried back into his small boat, saying something about getting handbills plastered all over town."

Houston looked at Will and Jeff, who had broken into wide grins, barely able to contain their laughter. When he saw their expressions, he erupted into a hearty laugh with them. "Boys, there ain't no reason why an old soldier shouldn't enjoy the fruits of his victory. Wave at those folks out there. I'd dance a jig for them if I could."

As they watched the crowd, they saw two men, one sitting on the other's shoulders, nailing banners to the warehouse walls alongside the docks. One sign declared in bright red paint, *Welcome Sam Houston*. Another said *Hero of San Jacinto*. The third was painted *Champion of Texas Independence*.

When they got close enough to start recognizing faces in the crowd, Will excitedly grabbed Jeff by the arm and squeezed it as he shouted above the crowd, "Jeff, do you think they might—"

"I sure hope so!" Jeff waved his hat at the crowd, carefully scanning the hundreds of faces for the few that mattered to him.

Anna and Libby pushed forward into the crowd. Tad, carrying a child in each arm, followed closely behind. "Excuse me! Please let us through!" Anna shouted above the din as she elbowed and shoved her way through the people. With a handbill announcing the arrival of Sam Houston in one hand and clutching Libby's hand in the other, she led the way toward the front of the crowd. "Even if we can't talk to Houston, maybe we can talk to someone who has seen them and find out if they're all right," Anna yelled in Libby's ear as she pulled her through the mass of people.

They broke through the crowd as the ship slid alongside the pier. Pushing her way between two tall men, Anna looked up to find herself no more than thirty yards from the ship's railing as the mates threw the thick ropes to the dock workers, who tied the vessel to the pier.

Looking up to the deck to see whether they could determine

which man was Houston, Anna and Libby saw Will and Jeff leaning against the rail, standing tall and handsome even in their stained and dirty buckskins. They were smiling, waving their hats and hands high over their heads, carefully scanning the faces in the crowd beyond Anna and Libby.

While Anna was startled speechless to see her husband, Libby screamed, clutching Anna's arm, “It's them, Anna! It's them!”

Anna, Libby and Tad were all shouting to Will and Jeff and waving their arms frantically to get the men's attention.

Will saw them first, and a look of amazement and sheer joy came over him. The women saw him punch Jeff and point them out as they screamed their welcome and felt a flood of relief at seeing their men safe.

Will and Jeff were waving with both hands at their families. Finally, after all they had all been through, they would be back together again.

Tears of joy streamed down Jeff's face as he mouthed *I love you* to Libby. No longer trying to hold back the tears herself, Libby was half-crying and half-laughing as she took Billy from Tad and pointed out his father to him, high above the crowd.

Will noticed that men were preparing to attach the gangplank when he turned to Houston and excitedly told him that his and Jeff's families were in the crowd. “Sir, we'll be back in just a few moments to get you to the hospital. We'd just like to kiss our wives and babies first.”

“You boys go on and look after your families,” Houston said, extending his hand to shake with Will and Jeff. “There are plenty of others to see that I'm taken care of. You two take your families and go on back to Texas. You've got a lot more to be concerned about than fretting over an old soldier. I'll run into you boys again some day, I'm sure.”

“I hope so, General,” Will said. “If there's ever anything, and I mean *anything*, we can do for you, you can find us at Virginia Point on the Brazos. We'll come for whatever you need."

"The day might come when I'll hold you to that," Houston said, grinning. "Now get on down there and hug those babies."

Jeff and Will grabbed their weapons and saddlebags and scrambled off the ship as soon as the gangplank was secured.

Within seconds they were reunited with their families. After the initial hugs and kisses, Will took Texanna in his arms and took Anna's hand to pull her away from the noisy gathering. He turned to Jeff, who was still hugging Libby, and called above the noise of the crowd, "Come on! Let's go home!"

They stayed in New Orleans for two weeks with Will's cousin, Sarah, resting and making plans for their return to Texas. Will closed the account at the New Orleans bank that his father had opened for him and booked passage for them all back to the mouth of the Brazos.

By early summer, Will, Jeff and their families were again back on Texas soil. Will and Jeff retrieved Baron and Buck from the man they had paid to look after them and purchased a wagon and team for their families' return trip home. They had no trouble finding a wagon and team for sale, since so many had been sold by families eager to flee Texas during the "Great Runaway."

They did not find Texas as they'd left it. Santa Anna and his troops had been true to their plan. Almost very farm, cabin and plantation they passed had been burned.

As they traveled northward, they passed many families like themselves. At first there were dozens, then hundreds, returning to their homes to find them devastated. Like the Jeffersons and the Bowmans, they were determined to make a new start and rebuild from the ashes an even stronger and greater Texas than before. They would not only rebuild their homes; they would build their own, new, independent nation.

They saw signs of new building and development as they continued northward. Some people had already started rebuilding their homes. Others had returned to live under the stars while they attempted to work their ground to get in a late planting. Still others were bringing in businesses.

When they arrived in San Felipe, they found that a few commercial buildings were already going up. They also learned that Texas' independence had spurred a renewed surge of immigration. Settlers were streaming in, looking for farmland and business opportunities. Sam Williams was busy in a temporary land office, issuing head rights to new families. After declining an offer to again take up surveying, Will and Jeff visited friends in town who had returned and started to rebuild.

They met a man from Georgia named Adams who was waiting for his saw mill equipment to arrive. He would be putting his mill up river from San Felipe, less than a day's ride from Virginia Point.

“With all the people coming in and filling up the open land and all the other folks rebuilding, it just looked like a good place to put a saw mill,” Adams said as he and Will discussed opportunities along the Brazos.

“When will you be setting up your mill?”

“I just sent off my order for equipment a few days ago. Didn't know where I would settle till I got to these parts and got to looking around. Looks to me like this whole Brazos River valley offers a wide-open opportunity for a man like me and the sawmill business. Plenty of timber and plenty of demand. The order for the parts has to go all the way to Pennsylvania. It will probably be late fall or early winter before we get it running. We'll be cutting timber in the meantime.”

Eager to continue their trip, they left San Felipe and continued northward. They hoped that with their places so far north, they’d be spared the destruction that they’d witnessed along the way. But as they turned onto the lane leading to Jeff's and Libby's cabin, they learned it wouldn't be so. The cabin and all the out buildings they had worked so hard to construct had been burned to the ground.

Tad pulled the wagon to a stop in front of what used to be the Jefferson cabin and Will and Jeff dismounted. Libby and Anna sat staring at the ashes for a few moments before they climbed down from the wagon seat. Jeff walked through the ashes, kicking at the remains, looking for anything that resembled home. He found nothing.

Will and Anna stood holding hands, watching Jeff. Libby then slowly walked to Jeff and slipped her arm around his waist. “We'll just build a bigger and better house than this old place,” she said, holding her head high. “This place was too little anyway; we need a whole lot bigger place than that to raise all the babies we’re going to have." She embraced her husband.

“Let's not even go over to our place today” Anna said. “I'm sure ours looks about the same. Let's just stay here and decide how we're going to rebuild.”

That night, around the fire next to the old tent, the Bowmans and Jeffersons formed their plans to rebuild.

Chapter 39

Will and Anna decided to delay the building of their home, opting instead to work with Jeff and Libby on theirs. Will had always promised Anna a big house on the hill surrounded by live oaks. He could now afford to fulfill that promise and the eventual construction of the saw mill would soon make the materials available. It was too late to consider planting anything for the year, so they resolved to put their energies into their new homes.

The next morning they got started. Jeff and Libby liked the location where their old cabin had been, so they cleared the rubble from the old site and scraped the ground clean to make a fresh start.

During the next few weeks, everyone developed a routine around the Jefferson homestead. Will and Jeff worked together cutting, trimming and hauling the timbers to the building site while Libby and Anna looked after the children and gathered stones along the river for the foundation and fireplace. Tad spent most mornings hunting or fishing and gathering berries, roots, honey and fruit for their meals. In the afternoon, he helped the men with their chores.

By mid-September they'd finished the new Jefferson home. Although it was made of logs, it had only a faint resemblance to the original house.

Jeff and Libby's new home consisted of two major structures: a large room with ample space for cooking, dining, and sleeping, connected by a breezeway to a two-story building for more sleeping space.

Will and Jeff spent the fall and early winter making furniture while they waited for the arrival of the sawmill parts and construction of the mill.

Finally, in late November, Will made a trip specifically to

check the mill’s progress, and found that Adams had received his parts and would soon have the mill operational. He was already taking orders and would be able to have the first lot of Will's material ready in two weeks.

Will and Anna had worked for weeks by firelight at night developing the plans for their new home, high on the rise, overlooking the prairie and shaded by large live oaks. While they waited for their first lumber order, Will and Jeff started leveling the building site and collecting the river rocks for the foundation and chimney. By the time the first load of lumber was ready at the mill, the large rock foundation was almost completed.

Will and Tad each took a team and wagon and set out early on a crisp December morning to get the first load of lumber, promising to be back sometime after nightfall. Jeff planned, with the women's help, to finish laying the last rocks of the foundation while Will and Tad were gone. They worked most of the day and progressed well. Anna handed Jeff the rocks as he troweled them into place with the mortar mixture. He was pushing himself because of the change in the weather.

The wind direction changed, and the temperature had been falling all afternoon. It looked like the first cold spell of the season was upon them. A light snow had started falling. Jeff hurried to finish the job and get the women and children back to his house before it got too cold.

It was late afternoon, and Jeff was almost finished with the last course of rock. Suddenly, Anna let out a small, almost inaudible gasp. Jeff looked at her and saw that she was staring beyond his shoulder frozen in fear. Turning quickly, he saw five mounted Comanche warriors no more than a hundred and fifty yards away, north of the building site. They had quietly walked their horses to where they stood and were waiting for Jeff and Anna to make a move.

Libby was playing with the children and Jake, down the hill, south of Jeff and Anna, and out of the sight of the Indians.

Jeff's mind raced, thinking of how to protect Anna, Libby

and the children. He glanced toward the tree where Buck was tied with his loaded rifle in its scabbard and his handgun in his saddlebags. The horse was no more than twenty paces from him, in the direction of the Indians.

Anna was now behind him as he faced the Indians.

"Anna," he said in the coldest, sternest voice she had ever heard. "Don't move yet, but when I say go, you run and get Libby and the babies. Get to the root cellar as fast as you can. You get in there, and you stay until I come back to get you or Will comes. You stay there, you understand? No matter what happens, you stay there until either me or Will and Tad come looking for you. But wait till I say go. I don't want to force anything. If they want a fight, they'll make their move."

Jeff continued to stand his ground, staring straight at the Comanches. He didn't have to wait long. Suddenly, the Indians let out a series of loud whoops and kicked their horses into a gallop toward the building site.

Before they were into their first stride, Jeff yelled, "Go!"

Anna raced down the hill, gathering up Texanna and Billy as she ran. The startled Libby read the terror in Anna's eyes and ran after her and the children with the dog on her heels.

Jeff raced to the horse and stripped the tied rein from the bush with one hand as he fished his handgun from the saddle bag with the other. Stuffing the single shot handgun into his belt, he mounted the horse in an instant and took off at a dead run — directly toward the Indians. He pulled his rifle from its scabbard, took aim and fired. The ball struck one of the startled Comanches in the chest, knocking him off the back of his horse.

Flipping his rifle to his left hand, Jeff pulled his handgun. By then he was only sixty feet away from the four advancing horsemen. Two of them had drawn their bows and were ready to let their arrows fly. Jeff shot one of them with his pistol when he was no more than thirty feet away. An instant after the ball left the barrel of his pistol, he felt an arrow slice deeply into his left shoulder. He thought he heard his collar bone break with the impact.

Now, with two on the ground and only feet away from the three others, he attempted to shove the handgun back inside his belt but missed his mark and lost it. He flipped his rifle back to his right hand and used it as a club as he rode past the Indians, catching the one closest to him on the chest, but the blow didn't knock him off his horse. Jeff knew he had a horse race on his hands. He looked back after a few moments and saw the three remaining horsemen chasing him. Wounded as he was, he had accomplished his immediate goal. He wanted to draw their attention to himself.

He had confused them by riding directly at them, and pursuing him had made them angry enough, for the moment. He had to get them far enough away before losing them so they wouldn't go back for Libby, Anna and the children.

He frequently looked back, gauging the distance between himself and the Indians. He seemed to be pulling away from them. His horse was fresh. He had no idea how far or hard they had been riding before they had come upon him. Several times he saw arrows flash past him as he pushed Buck as hard as he had ever pushed any horse. He soon realized he was out of their arrow range, but they continued to press on. He knew his horse wouldn't last indefinitely and started thinking of ways to elude them.

He knew he had at least one advantage over his pursuers. He knew the area. He had hunted many times in the woods they were approaching. He decided to try to lose them in the thickets of the deep woods along the Brazos shore. When he crashed into the woods, he was three hundred yards ahead of the Indians. *These are plains Indians*, he thought. *Maybe they'll be slowed even more in the thickets and big trees.* As he rode into the thickets he realized his injury was more serious than he first thought. He had already lost a lot of blood. His shirt was soaked on the left side, the stain extending beyond his waist. By the time he got well into the thicket, he was far ahead of the Indians, but he knew he must stop and take care of the wound or he would bleed to death. He started looking for a hiding place.

He knew the Indians would search the ground thoroughly. *The trees. Take to the trees*, he thought. *Maybe one of these big ones. Just maybe. Yes! I know just the one!* His mind raced. *I don't think even Will knows about this one.*

Jeff spurred Buck toward the river until he came to a huge oak tree, then lunged for a limb just within reach of his good arm. He pulled himself onto the branch. With Buck still standing under him, he squatted on the tree limb, swung his foot forward, gritted his teeth, then brought it back as hard as he could, sinking his spur into the horses flank. The horse screamed and lurched forward, blindly running in a panic toward the river's edge. Buck would travel a good distance along the river before finally tiring and coming to a stop. Jeff began climbing the massive tree.

Slowed by pain and loss of blood, he struggled, climbing toward a large hollow at the top of the thick trunk.

A squirrel had toyed with him here a year before, first hiding in the hollow, then popping up, until Jeff brought him down with a well-placed rifle ball. If he hadn't seen the squirrel retreat to the tree hollow, he would have been unaware that it existed.

He heard the sound of the riders crashing through the brush as he reached the top of the hollow. He managed to swing his legs into the hole and fall into the heart of the tree as the Indians came into view. He almost screamed out in pain as the shaft of the arrow caught on the top edge of the hollow and broke off as he dropped into the hole. He bit his lip until it bled to muffle the scream.

Enduring that instant of intense pain, Jeff was oblivious to the fact that the broken shaft of the arrow had fallen outside the hollow and tumbled to the dead leaves at the base of the tree.

The hollow was much deeper than he'd imagined. He expected he'd have to crouch down inside the hole to stay out of sight. As it was, he was in a deep, narrow chamber with his legs totally extended beneath him and the top of the hole beyond his reach.

Jeff hung there quietly, afraid even to breathe as the Indians followed his trail to the tree, hesitated there for a few moments in quiet discussion, then moved off in the direction Buck had taken. Had they circled the large tree, they would have seen the feathered shaft on the tree's north side, but they followed Buck's trail along the south side.

Jeff continued to rest in the cramped position, expecting them to double back when they found Buck. True to his prediction, he heard sounds from the river about a half-hour after the sun set. He listened carefully to the sounds of horses' hooves rustling through the leaves toward his tree. The sounds continued as the Indians passed under Jeff's position and headed away from the tree and south, back toward Will's home site.

Oh God! Jeff thought. *Please don't let them go after the women and children!* He strained to listen as the sounds faded once again to silence. He thrashed about inside his cramped cylinder, trying to free himself until lights started flashing behind his eyes in the darkness and the ringing in his ears grew louder and louder.

The three Comanches had found Buck, finally calmed and grazing almost a mile upriver from Jeff's tree, and led him back into the woods to look for Jeff. Retracing their trail, they spread out through the woods, looking for any sign of Jeff. Failing to find any, they headed back toward Will's rock foundation to collect their dead brethren and their horses and then look for other whites. They had two dead warriors and no scalps to show for their efforts.

Jeff realized he must have passed out from the loss of blood when his shivering woke him up. It was dark. His head was damp, and he was cold all over. He had no idea how long he had been unconscious. The pain in his shoulder was throbbing and he was shivering, from chills or the cold, or both.

He tested his left arm and found that he couldn’t move it at all. It was pinned to his side. The broken arrow was embedded in his shoulder and the broken collarbone precluded any use of that arm. Although the space was cramped, he did have limited movement of his right arm. He could reach over his head toward the top of the hole but he couldn't reach the top. He tried his feet and legs. He had much less mobility there. He could wiggle his feet a little, but his legs were pressed against the side walls so tightly that he had no flexibility in his legs at all.

Jeff stared up at the cloudy, black sky that loomed beyond the naked branches and realized that his head was damp from snow. Although he tried to put the thought from his mind, it kept flooding back.

I’m trapped!

Chapter 40

Anna and Libby watched the crack in the door above them. The only light that penetrated their small world was the thin sliver that entered through the crack where the door closed against its frame. It wasn't much, but it was enough to tell whether someone was moving above the door.

They huddled in the cramped, dark chamber next to the bins Will had constructed to store potatoes and other root crops. They clutched their children tightly, trying to calm their fear of the crowded cellar while trying to tame their own fears of the terror outside.

Jake had followed them when they ran to the cellar. The women knew he could be both an asset and a liability. He would do whatever he could to protect them, but he might also give away their position if the Indians came back looking for them. He occasionally whined, but obeyed when he was told to be quiet.

Minutes seemed like hours as the late afternoon turned to twilight and their little sliver of light faded to total darkness. Libby and Anna whispered to the children, trying desperately to keep them calm and quiet in the darkness. Both women shed silent tears as they rocked their children in their arms, hoping to see Will or Jeff when the door opened, but fearing they would see Comanches. The two young women prayed quietly together, but both separately devised plans of what they would do to protect their children if they were captured by the Indians.

Will and Tad pushed their teams on the return trip to Virginia Point, but the heavy loads of lumber slowed their journey.

The clouds continued to build as the north wind blew colder in the late afternoon. Will fastened his coat around his neck and pulled the collar up to protect his ears from the cutting wind as he led the two wagons on the now well-worn trail toward home. He had been hoping the winter weather would hold off just a little longer until he could get a good start on framing his house, but the first few flakes of snow dampened his hope of fair weather for several days. The closer they got to home, the heavier the snow fell.

He had been reviewing the house plans in his mind and had lost track of the time, but as he turned into the lane to Jeff's cabin he estimated it was almost an hour past sundown.

The three Comanches rode out of the wooded area, leading Buck onto the prairie toward the site of the short, but deadly battle with Jeff. They stopped to collect the two ponies, no longer needed by the riders lying lifeless on the prairie. After tethering the ponies to Jeff's horse, they went to collect the bodies of their fallen comrades.

As Will's and Tad's wagons approached Jeff's cabin, Will knew something was wrong. The house was dark. There was no smoke from the chimney. The dog didn't greet them as they pulled toward the house. He whipped the sluggish team to a full run for the last hundred yards, panic building in his throat. Will pulled on the reins to stop the team, shouting names as his and Tad's wagons stopped in front of the house. "Anna! Jeff! Libby! Where are you?"

He jumped from the wagon and ran into the house, finding it untouched since they had all left that morning. He raced from the house. "Tad, nobody's here!" He vaulted back onto the wagon bench. "We've got to find them! Come on, put your brake on and ride with me!"

Tad ran toward Will's wagon, trying to keep his voice calm. "Where are they? What do you think happened?"

"I don't know, but it doesn't look good." As soon as Tad scrambled up onto the seat, Will was punishing the team with the reins to get them started again. “We’ve got to get to my place. Whatever happened, happened there.”

Within seconds, the team of horses was kicking up fresh snow as they raced across the prairie, pulling the burdened wagon toward the Bowman farm.

The grim-faced Comanches were finishing tying the bodies of the dead warriors to the backs of their mounts with lengths of horse-hair rope when they at first felt, more then heard, the horses pulling the rumbling, heavily laden wagon across the prairie at break-neck speed. With the single-tree chains jingling, the wheels complaining against the heavy load and the yet unseen horse’s hooves charging through the thin coating of snow, the Indians couldn’t tell how many whites were rushing toward them. They hurried to finish securing their gruesome cargo, mounted their own ponies in a single leap and within seconds were galloping through the light snow to the north, leading the other horses into the trees and toward the river before the wagon reached the top of the rise at the house foundation.

“Look, Will!” Tad said excitedly, jumping from the wagon as they reached the rock foundation. “Here's Jeff's tools! Left where he was using them!” Tad brushed the snow away from the small, short-handled spade that Jeff had modified into a mason's trowel. He found it lying on the rock wall, still dirty with frozen mortar on the blade.

They both grabbed their rifles and quickly walked around the foundation, looking for evidence of what might have happened to their families. Will extended his view across the prairie from the vantage point of the hill. The moonlight between the clouds reflected by the snow intensified the light and dark contrast of the oak trees, cedar bushes, mounds and crevices scattered across the prairie. He first looked to the west, seeking anything that would give him a clue to the events earlier in the day. He then focused his gaze to the north.

“Tad, look out there,” Will pointed across the prairie and started running in the same direction Jeff had taken almost two hours earlier.

Within seconds, Will and Tad were examining signs of activity in the snow.

“Looks like two or three men in moccasins.” Tad said, comparing the different footprints.

“I agree, but they’ve got extra horses, and one of them’s shod.” Will squatted beside the prints, looking at the distinctive prints left by the steel-shod horse. “Tad, these are really fresh. They were here just a little while ago. There’s no snow on top of the prints.”

Tad quickly scanned the landscape around them to make sure they were alone.

“I think I understand part of what happened here,” Will said. He had been staring at a larger spot of grass not covered with snow, next to the human and horse tracks. “Look at the shape of that bare spot, and that big dark spot—that’s blood. A body was loaded here onto one of the horses.”

“These tracks all came and went back north,” Tad said, looking beyond the cluster of tracks surrounding them. Looks like they stopped up there too.” Tad pointed farther north.

They hurried toward the area of tracks Tad pointed out, clustered around another bare spot in the snow soaked with blood. A few feet before they reached the second cluster of tracks, Tad’s foot slid off a rawhide battle shield, partially concealed by snow.

Will was examining the large blood stain in the second bare patch of grass when he looked up at Tad, who was holding the thick rawhide shield, painted red and black with a patch of long, black hair hanging from the center, the same color of Anna’s. “That’s Comanche, isn’t it?” Tad asked.

“Oh God! I’m afraid so!” Will spun around and raced back to the foundation wall with Tad following at his heels.

“The last trace of Jeff was at the wall, here.” Will picked up the trowel, grasping it tightly in his hand as he frantically looked around the foundation for some evidence of his and Jeff's families. "But there's no sign of the women or kids. Tad, they've got to be around here somewhere!" *Lord, please let them be all right!* "Tad, we've got to find them." Will's mind was spinning. *Which way to go? What to do next?*

"Let's turn this place upside down," Will turned to Tad to give instructions for the search and hardly recognized the boy from the terrified look on his face. Will, forcing calmness upon himself, grasped Tad by the shoulders and looked directly into his eyes. "Tad, we *will* find them! If they're not here, we won't give up till we get them back. We'll get the neighbors to help us find them wherever they are. You understand?"

Tad nodded his agreement.

"All right, here's what we'll do. You go check that old brush arbor, the one upriver aways. Anna and I talked about that being a good hiding place once. I'll meet you back here."

Tad took off running for the river. Will walked around the building site one more time, trying to decide where to look first. He didn't want to call their names loudly because he feared Indians might possibly still be in the area. He walked over the snow-covered ground, heading down the hill toward, the burned-out old buildings, looking carefully to his right and left for any sign of life. He looked around the burnt corn crib and the remains of the old cabin and found nothing. He then headed toward the cellar.

The snow muffled his steps as he approached the cellar. He reached for the door. As he grasped the handle to pull it open, a strange sound came from the darkness behind the door. He started to call Anna's name but was knocked off his feet as he got the door halfway open.

Jake was on him, snarling and snapping like a demon from hell before he caught Will's scent. Will threw his hands over his face as he was knocked backward by the force of the lunging dog. Jake suddenly realized from Will's startled cries whom he had attacked and his attack turned to licks and whines. Will managed to get to his hands and knees to see Anna and the baby emerging from the cold cellar.

"Will, we were so scared!" Anna cried as she embraced him, both of them on their knees in the snow. "We thought the Indians had come back."

By then Libby and Billy had climbed out of the cellar. Will wrapped his arms around all four of them, and they cried together as he asked about Jeff.

"We don't know." Libby cried between sobs. The pent-up emotions that had swirled for so long in the darkness of the cellar erupted now that they were safe with Will. He was still holding and comforting them when Tad ran up. Libby lost control again when she hugged Tad.

Finally they calmed enough for Will to get what little details they knew of what happened to Jeff.

"All we know is that there were five of them. When Jeff told me to run, I took off and got Libby and the children and went for the cellar like he said. We really don't know what happened from there. We heard a couple of shots, and that was all. We've been here ever since. Jeff told us to stay here until you came after us, and that's what we did. Will, we were so scared!"

"You're all fine now," Will said as he kissed her and the baby again. "Come on Tad, let's get them home and warmed up. Then we'll go out and get some neighbors to ride with us to find Jeff."

Will, Anna and Libby all crowded onto the wagon seat, with the baby in Anna's lap. Tad and Billy scrambled to the top of the load of lumber for a sorrowful ride back to the Jefferson home.

After they arrived home and had a fire started in the fireplace, Will and Tad were preparing to go back into the cold. "I know it's late," Will told Anna. "But at least we'll alert the neighbors and have them here at daylight. Those Comanches have a good start on us already, and if it snows any more, the tracking won't be any easier, so we can't afford to waste any time."

It was almost daylight when Tad and Will arrived back at Libby's place. Four men rode in with them, and eight more had promised to be there at dawn. Libby and Anna cooked breakfast for the men while they waited for sunrise and the other riders. Libby also packed several sacks of jerky and other provisions for the men to eat on the move.

Shortly after daylight when the others arrived, Will and Tad reached for their coats. Libby approached Tad and put her hand on his arm and grasped his sleeve, bunching the fabric in her hand and, holding on tightly.

"I'm going, Libby." Tad said, looking into his sister's red, tear-rimmed eyes. "You can't talk me out of it. This is my fight, more than anybody else's. He's been like a papa to me."

"I know," Libby said. "You understand that you might be all I have now besides my son."

Tad nodded, buttoned his coat, embraced her quietly for several seconds, then headed out the door.

"Men," Will said, looking at his neighbors through tired eyes after they'd mounted in Libby's yard, "I'm confident they headed northwest. Probably followed the course of the river. The tracks I saw last night headed for the river. I don't know how far they are ahead of us. A far piece, I guess. I don't know how long we'll be gone. I don't even know whether Jeff is alive, but we've got to try to find him no matter what it takes. This is the only way we'll ever have safety here for our families."

"We're with you, Will," one of the men responded.

"Whatever it takes," another called out.

"All right," Will said. "Six of you men follow the river north at the water. They might have tried to cover their tracks there. The rest of us will spread out across the prairie and follow the timberline north trying to pick up their trail. I can't believe they would have gone into the thicket. It would have slowed them down too much. They're in a hurry to put some distance between us. Let's come together along the river before dark if we don't find anything. We'll make further plans then."

Jeff spent a fitful night fighting nausea and chills. His left arm had become numb, but whenever he thought about it, he wiggled his feet to keep the circulation going in his legs. So far his legs or feet hadn't gone numb like his arm. He tried not to think of the cold, but at times he awakened with his teeth chattering, or shivering as a chill ran through his body. He was glad to see dawn so he could assess his situation and find a way out.

He soon realized there wasn't much to see—just the wall of the hollow in front of his face extending to the top of the hole. He tried to wedge his right elbow against the wall in front of his face and pry himself loose but each time he tried, he almost fainted again from the pain in his shoulder. He examined his shoulder to find a nasty looking wound underneath the dried blood. The skin was hot and puffy, and the color around the puncture was beginning to look strange. He had no idea how deep the arrow was, but he thought he felt it almost protruding from his back when he tried to free himself with his right elbow.

He hadn't thought much about food or water, but he realized the loss of so much blood made him thirsty. He had tilted his head back and tried to catch some snow during the night but finally gave up the fruitless effort.

He hadn't realized how weak a man could become in such a short time after an injury like his. He was surprised at how much effort everything took. After learning that he couldn't free himself by wedging his elbow against the wall, he again lifted his right arm and felt all around the wall of the hollow above and behind his head. *If I could just find something to grab hold of,* he thought. He found nothing.

He managed to reach his right hand along his belt to try to retrieve his Bowie knife. After struggling for several minutes, he finally managed to free it from his belt. He clutched the bone handle of the knife in his fist and drew it alongside his body until he finally held it over his head. He tried to stab it into the face of the tree wall over his head. Several times he slashed at the wall trying to get the blade tip to penetrate enough to hold while he tried to pull himself up. Each time the blade gave way. Exhausted, he tried to catch his breath, listening to the wind above the rim of the hollow.

The morning was clear, with a bright blue sky overhead. As he listened to the wind blow through the tree branches, he occasionally heard the screech of a distant hawk and the chatter of a squirrel. He'd listened to the sounds of the woods for a while, when suddenly there was a different, strange sound. An unusual sound. Jeff closed his eyes tightly so he could identify the new, intrusive noise.

Splashing . . . The river . . . Horses in the river. That's what it was. Men were looking for him. Will had put a search party together to look for him.

"Here! I'm here!" he yelled, realizing he was projecting only a feeble cry from his dry, cracking lips. He knew the tree was no more than sixty feet from the water's edge. They could hear him if he was loud enough, he thought. "Here! Right here! Please don't go away! Don't go! Please . . ."

His voice faded to a whisper as the sounds became fainter. He visualized the men splashing through the shallows, focusing on looking for tracks, the noise of their horses' hooves splashing in the water drowning out any other sounds of the forest.

Jeff tried to hold back the tears as a wave of helplessness flooded over him. *I'm not going to die today*, he finally told himself. *We'll just take this a day at a time, but I'm not going to die today.*

Jeff spent most of the midday struggling to retrieve his small journal, quill pen and ink bottle from the pouch on his belt. He was determined that if he was going to be stuck in this tree, he would record some of his thoughts while he still had the strength.

He found that he could keep the open bottle of ink in his belt and wedge the open journal between his ribs and the side wall of the hollow, allowing him to write for short periods of time. He slowly and painfully wrote

> December 9, 1836
>
> Killed two Indians yesterday. Knocked them off their horse anyway. First day in tree today. Could have found better place to hide. Arrow in shoulder. Heard riders in river today. They didn't hear me. Cold last night.
>
> J. Jefferson

Chapter 41

Twenty-three days later Will, Tad and the other riders returned to Virginia Point. The other riders split off from Will and Tad at the lane to Jeff's cabin, and the two of them rode to the house by themselves. Anna was reading one of Jeff's books by the fireside and Libby was at the window, peering into the twilight like she usually did when she was done with chores. She saw the riders slowly walking their thin, worn-out horses toward the house. Her heart jumped when she first saw the riders, then sank when she didn't see Jeff with them.

"They're back, Anna."

"What?"

"They're back. Will and Tad are back."

Anna dropped her book and ran to the door.

Will and Tad slid out of their saddles when the horses approached the porch. Anna almost didn't recognize them from the dirt, whiskers and weariness they both wore like a cloak.

Anna met Will in the yard and threw her arms around him. He kissed her on the cheek and looked beyond her at Libby. He stepped onto the porch and reached for her. "I'm sorry, Libby," he said as he embraced her. "We looked everywhere. We finally caught up with the bunch we were chasing way up by the Red River and killed them and some more we found in other places, but we never found Jeff. We criss-crossed this country all the way between here and the Canadian, along both sides of the Brazos and found no trace of him."

"Y'all get those horses unsaddled and tended to and come on in," Libby said. "You're tired and hungry. I'll start heating some bath water, and we'll get something for you to eat. You get cleaned up and fed, and then we'll talk. There's some things I want to tell you."

Later, after dinner, Will and Anna sat at the table. Texanna sat in Will's lap, and Billy sat in Tad's lap across the table. The women had cleared the table.

Libby sat down and took a deep breath. “I guess I knew after about the first week that Jeff wouldn't be coming back,” she said, looking directly at Will. “Of course I hoped he would, but I think I knew he wouldn't. Will, he died doing what he lived for. He sacrificed himself to protect his family and friends. You would have done the same thing if you had been in his place. He was a good man, and he accomplished so much for himself, his family, and his country. He gave me more than most women could hope for in a lifetime. He gave me love, protection, a home, a son, an education and freedom. I know Mister Bell gave us our freedom, but I've always wondered if he ever would have done it if he hadn't known Jeff.

“But one of the most important things he gave me, he got from you, Will. That's something I'll always have, and Billy will have, and Tad, and their children will have — always. They have the ability to dream for a better life, and the ambition and drive to act on those dreams. You gave him that gift, along with his freedom, and you showed him that he could strive for better things for himself and his family. You showed him how to make those dreams happen.

“Well, sir, he passed that on to us. He not only left us his memory and all the love that goes with it, he left us a legacy. He left us a legacy of dreams. He, like you dreamed of being a part of making Texas great. And he did that. Both of you have done that together. But there's much more to do. I know you're not finished making things happen here and making Texas grow.” She paused for a moment.

“There’s one thing I want you to know. Will, don’t you ever forget that your very good friend Jeff Jefferson will be right there with you. His spirit will be riding double with you all the way. He'll be looking over your shoulder as you do all the rest of the work you'll do for Texas. He'll also be looking over my shoulder and Tad's and Billy's as we work to fulfill his dreams.

"He labored and dreamed of making this farm produce and grow and be a success. Tad and I, and all our friends will make that happen. He dreamed of providing a good education for his son. His son will be one of the best educated men in the country, black or white. I'll see to that. And he needn't be concerned about our welfare, because we have the best, most loyal friends anyone could ask for. I know that if there's ever anything we need, we can count on you."

Libby leaned forward in her chair, took Will's hand in hers and looked him in the eyes. "Will, I want to thank you for both Jeff and myself for everything you've done, but most especially, for giving Jeff his dreams. I don't know how he died, and I may never know. But I believe he died satisfied that his dreams will live on."

EPILOGUE

SUMMER, 1879, VIRGINIA POINT, TEXAS
Forty-Three Years Later

Will Bowman was up early, but with more purpose than usual. He typically didn't leave the house until well after breakfast, but this morning he was out early. He had already caught Prince, the sorrel gelding that he had been riding for the last few years, and had him saddled and tied to the post by the back porch by the time Texanna had breakfast ready. Will prided himself on the fact that he was still riding at his age. Most of his friends had taken to their rocking chairs—those who were still alive, anyway. He tried to ride a little every day. He told Anna it kept him young.

Anna worried about him riding since the blackout spell several months earlier when he fell off his horse. He hadn't broken anything, but since then she'd demanded that he not ride too far away from the house and barn or working pens by himself.

He enjoyed riding out to watch the hands work the stock. Most of the time he stayed out of their way and didn't try to help them any more than he felt necessary. But he just couldn't give up keeping an eye on things even though his sons had been running the ranch for the last several years.

He had something on his mind that morning other than checking the cowboys' work when he headed back into the kitchen for breakfast.

“Papa, look at your boots!” Texanna caught him as he started to come in the door. "If you're not going to scrape that mud and who knows what else off those boots before you come in the house, at least take them off on the porch. Here, just sit on that stool there and I'll pull them off for you.” Will patiently sat while Texanna straddled one muddy boot, then the other, and pulled them from his feet.

"What are you doing tromping around out there in the mud before breakfast anyway?"

Will seated himself at the table and took a sip of the coffee she had poured.

"I've got to ride up north into the thicket up there by the river to see what kind of damage that lightning did last night. Sure glad it was raining as hard as it was. If it hadn't been pouring down rain, that big ball of fire would have set the whole prairie ablaze."

"I know. I kept lying there listening to the storm, waiting for you to holler for everybody to go get in the cellar."

"You know how your mama is about that cellar. We've just about got to have a tornado coming in on top of us before she'd consider getting in that old cellar."

"You're right about that," Anna said, walking into the kitchen. "I heard you talking about that cellar. I'll take my chances right in my bed. I've got some bad memories of that old cellar."

After breakfast, Will pushed himself away from the table, complimented Texanna on her cooking and headed for the door.

"Papa, get Taylor and take him with you."

Will let a deep sigh escape his lips. "Texanna, I don't need a keeper."

"Papa, he is not your keeper. You just might need a hand out there. You might find a calf caught in a bog in the river or something. You never know. Just take him with you."

Will shook his head and mumbled under his breath as he pulled his boots on. "Not only do I have two women telling me what to do, now my grandson's my keeper."

In a few minutes, Will was mounted up and riding toward the corral, looking for Taylor. He found him cutting out a green colt from the herd of unbroken horses.

"Save him till later, Taylor. I need you to come with me."

Taylor started coiling his lariat as he rode to meet his grandfather.

"Where we going, Grampa?"

"Aw, I just want a little company to ride up into the thicket up there where the river cuts back west. Want to see what happened in the storm last night."

Taylor rode through the corral gate and latched it without dismounting. Then he and the old man turned their horses north and walked them back up the hill, beyond the house and out onto the prairie. They rode through the thick grass, checking the longhorn stock as the clusters of cows with calves by their side moved out of their way.

"I never did go back to sleep last night after all that thunder and lightning," Will said. "Don't know why, but I just kind of got a strange feeling, watching that storm out there. Kind of an uneasy feeling. Just thought we'd ride out this morning and see if some stock got struck by lightning."

As Will and Taylor approached the edge of the grassland and rode into the quiet, deep shade of the thicket, the air took on a heavy scent that reminded Will of the smell of a hot campfire that had been quenched with a bucketful of creek water. The leaves on the ground, shaded from the bright morning sun by the canopy of summer foliage, were still wet from the heavy rain the night before. As they got closer to the river, they could hear the water rushing downstream from the run-off.

"My God!" Will said as his horse pushed its way past a clump of brush and exposed the view in front of them. "I saw the lightning hit something over here last night, but I had no idea it had done anything like this. That tree must have been at least three hundred years old."

Will and Taylor continued toward what was left of the huge oak tree. The part facing them was still standing but the back side was blown away and scattered across a seventy-foot radius around the tree. Will sat on his horse, staring at what remained of the old tree for a few moments, then continued walking his horse toward the backside looking at the charred and splintered pieces that littered the ground.

Something caught his eye among the burnt fragments on the ground. *What's that light color over there?* As he moved to get a better look, a glint of sunlight bounced off the white bone handle of the Bowie knife lying among the remains of the tree.

Will's gaze shot upward from the base of the tree and saw that it had split down the middle, blowing away half the trunk and leaving the other half intact, including the long-dead human skeleton still wedged in what was left of its tomb.

Will and his grandson stepped onto the Jefferson front porch and knocked on the door.

Soon, the door was opened by a middle-aged, well-dressed Negro man, holding a book and removing his glasses.

"Why hello, Senator," Billy Jefferson said as he opened the door and shook hands with the two men. "What a nice surprise to see you and Taylor. Mama was just mentioning you this morning."

"I'm surprised to see you here too, Billy," Will said, shaking the man's hand. "It's been a long time. To listen to your mama talk, I didn't think they could run that college back east without you."

"We're still growing, that's for sure. There seems to be no end to the number of bright young people wanting an education. And we're enrolling almost as many older, former slaves as the young folks, even this many years after the war. We've added several new professors in the last two or three years. As the founder of the institution, it seems that I spend much my time these days exploring new funding options, which leads me to do more traveling.

"But I'm on a special trip out here now to look after Mama. I think she needs me more right now than the college does. I just got in last night. Took the new train to Dallas, then the stage the rest of the way. Been away too long.

"You know how Mama is. She never would complain in her letters. I guess I never would have known just how frail she was if Uncle Tad hadn't written and suggested I come home for a while."

"How's she doing?" Will asked. "I was just over here a couple of days ago. She seemed fair then. She hasn't taken a turn for the worse, has she?"

"No, she seems to be holding her own. Come in and sit down. I'll tell her you're here."

"No, wait a minute. Come on out here to the yard. There's something I've got to tell you first, since you're here."

Billy and Taylor followed Will to his horse where he untied his saddlebag. "Billy, what I've got to tell you, your mama needs to know too, and I need to be the one to tell her. I think she's strong enough to handle the news, but I wanted you to know first, just in case."

"What's the matter, Senator. It's not Mrs. Anna, is it?"

"No Son. It's your papa."

"What do you mean, my papa? He died over forty years ago!"

"We found him today, Billy. I'll tell you all the details when I tell your mama, but I just wanted you to know before we broke the news to her. I've got the pouch he always carried, and his journal is here in my saddlebag."

Billy stood looking at the saddlebag for a moment, then took a deep breath and said, "Let me go get Mama. Come on in and sit down. Help yourself to some coffee. I made some fresh a little while ago."

"Why hello, Will. Glad to see you brought Taylor with you this time," the frail and wrinkled Libby said as her son helped her to a soft chair. Didn't Anna come with you? I was kind of looking for her today."

"No, she didn't come with me this time . . . Lib, I've got something to tell you that's going to upset you pretty badly. Do you think you can handle it?"

"What's the matter? Something hasn't happened to Anna, has it?"

"No, Anna's fine."

"I haven't seen you this long faced in a long time, Will. Tell me what's wrong."

"Lib we found Jeff today."

Libby sat straight in her chair, not taking her eyes off of Will but maintaining her composure. "Tell me about it," she finally said after a long silence.

Will continued, watching Libby carefully as she received the news, making sure she handled it all right in her condition. He told her of watching the storm the night before and the strange feeling and chill that came over him as he saw the lightning strike the tree from his bedroom window. He then told how he and Taylor had found the remains still in the tree that morning.

"Some of my men will be bringing him home in a little while, but I wanted to give you this now." Will reached into his saddlebags and brought out an old, hardened and cracked leather pouch. "The thread has rotted and the pouch is falling apart now since I've handled it, but it stayed intact all these years, protecting its contents." He reached into the pouch and pulled out a small journal. He opened the cover to find a fragile, faded piece of paper lying between the cover and the first page of the journal. Will reached into his pocket and pulled out his spectacles.

He sat there for a moment, looking at the paper. He glanced at the faint script on the single piece of paper, then took his spectacles off and put them back in his pocket. He swallowed hard and wiped his eyes as he handed the paper to Libby.

"I didn't have to read it to tell what it was. That's my writing. That's his freedom letter that I gave him when we were on our way to Texas. I guess he carried that scrap of paper with him in that old pouch every day of his life."

"Will, that one little piece of paper meant more to him than anything else in the world except his family," Libby said, clutching the paper.

Will looked at the journal in his hands. "Libby, I can't read this now, and I'm not going to ask you to. Would it be all right with you if Billy reads the last few entries? Billy, can you do this?"

"I'll try," Billy said, reaching for the journal.

"Yes. Please, Billy, read it for me," Libby said. "And Will, thank you for being here with me for this."

Billy carefully opened it to the last several handwritten pages, read a few lines to himself and then started reading aloud. Although it was Jeff's son that was reading his father's words, Will heard Jeff's rich, deep voice resonating from the words on the paper.

> "December 9, 1836
>
> Killed two Indians yesterday. Knocked them off their horse anyway. First day in tree today. Could have found a better place to hide. Arrow in shoulder. Heard riders in river today. They didn't hear me. Cold last night.
>
> J Jefferson

> "December 10, 1836
>
> Pain in shoulder, but no feeling in arm. Getting weak today. Lost a lot of blood. Guess I really got myself stuck here. Wish I had Libby's biscuits and fried chicken now. Dreamed of Billy last night. I'm so thirsty.
>
> J Jefferson

"December 11, 1836

Sun's bright. Snow's melted. No feeling in legs today. No pain anymore. Cold, hungry. Think of Lib and Billy. Love them.

Jeff

"D 12

Somebody find. Thirsty. No strength. J"

Billy sat staring at the faded page. He took a deep breath, then removed his glasses and slowly and carefully closed the book.

Will stood tall by Libby's side as the preacher finished his message about a man being laid to rest many years beyond his time. After the closing prayer, Will gave Libby a long, silent embrace. Then Anna and the rest of Will's family followed Libby, Billy and Tad and Tad's family down the hill from the graveyard to the string of wagons, buckboards and carriages waiting along the trail next to the Negro church. Will watched as everyone made their way down the hill. Finally he stood alone at the top of the hill, next to the grave.

The light summer breeze tousled his white hair as he stood there for the longest, turning his hat in his hands, staring at the freshly spaded brown Texas dirt. He slowly lowered himself to both knees, put his hat on the ground, and reached for a handful of the rich earth. Turning the soil between his fingers, his thoughts went back fifty years to some of the earliest days after he and Jeff came to Texas.

Kneeling beside the grave, the memory of his first ownership celebration flooded his mind. He saw Jeff smiling at him, holding hands with the Bigelow and Cartwright children on the other side of the circle of new settlers. He smiled as the vision became clearer. He closed his eyes and saw himself, Jeff and all the Bigelow and Cartwright family squatting in the circle. Will slowly dug the fingers of both hands into the fresh mound of dirt, filling his hands with as much as he could grasp as his vision continued to unfold before him.

He saw Jeff as he, along with the others, sprang into the air, flinging dirt and bits of grass and twigs above them. He saw Jeff, laughing and yelling in his youth and exuberance, hurling himself high, freeing his handfuls of dirt.

Will pushed himself to his feet. Standing tall and erect, he flung his hands high above his head, discharging into the summer sky handfuls of dirt from Jeff's grave. He blinked away the dirt, raining on his upturned face while the memory of the yelling and laughter lingered and echoed through his mind. He picked up his hat from the ground and carefully straightened it on his head, and thoughtfully nodded his satisfaction, finally able to say goodbye to his life-long friend.

THE END

As a sixth generation Texan, Dan Vanderburg grew up listening to tales of his ancestors as they worked to build their farms, ranches and way of life on the Texas frontier. Those accounts lit a spark in Dan as a youngster to learn more about the people and events that built the American Southwest. He enjoys developing strong characters with their own stories to tell, then placing them in and around critical events in history. Dan Vanderburg lives and writes in Arlington, Texas.

If you enjoyed Legacy of Dreams, please consider leaving a review on Amazon. Thank you for your interest in the Texas Legacy Family Saga.

More books by Dan Vanderburg:
Trail of Hope (Texas Legacy Family Saga Book 2)
Freedom Road (Texas Legacy Family Saga Book 3)
The Littlest Hero

Coming soon: Little Old Ladies and Larceny and Other Humorous Short Stories and Captivating Poetry

You can find out more about Dan Vanderburg on Facebook, Instagram, Goodreads or Amazon

Read on for a peek at the continuing saga of the Bowman and Jefferson families in ***Trail of Hope (Texas Legacy Family Saga Book 2)*** available now on **Amazon.com**

TRAIL OF HOPE

CHAPTER 1

Central Texas, Along the Colorado River, March, 1836

My lungs heaved, begging for air. My heart pounded as I raced along the river's edge, ignoring the mesquite thorns ripping snags in my homespun shirt. I fought panic trying to focus on reaching the cabin in time.

I first saw them as I worked my traps along the shallows

where the wagon trail veered close to the river. Crouching in the water behind a growth of cattails, I heard bits of their Spanish conversation and occasional laughter filtering toward me from no more than fifty yards away. Their muskets repeatedly thumped against their canteens as they marched along the trail toward the cabin. Sunlight glinted off their weapons through the cottonwoods and tangled undergrowth. A dry, high-pitched squeal emanated from some of the wheel hubs of their heavily loaded ox carts. The three officers in blue high-collared jackets with gold trim rode in front of the marching soldiers, their saddle leather squeaking beneath them. Tobacco smoke from the pipe of the bearded one permeated the air. I knew who they were and why they were here. Oh God, my nightmares were coming true.

I'd been waking in a fit every night since the man from the Smith settlement came galloping up the road to the cabin three days ago on a heaving, frothy stallion. He was spreading the word about the fall of the Alamo in San Antonio and Santa Anna's sweep through the Texas countryside burning out all the white settlers. The man's final warning to Papa was still etched in my memory: "Mister, you take your family and get on outta here right now! Everybody's headin' east to get beyond the Sabine River, out of Meskin territory. They done killed almost two hundred good men at Fort Alamo. They ain't stoppin' till they run everybody that ain't Meskin outta Texas. They're burnin' ever cabin they find and ain't takin' no prisoners." I'll never forget the fearful look on the lanky man's face as he turned to me before he spurred his bay to warn more settlers to the north. "Boy, you help your pappy get the family outta here."

I remembered the vacant, faraway look on Papa's face as the man rode away from the cabin. Papa stood in the yard, his arms at his sides, staring at the ground for the longest time. Then, head still bowed, he walked back into the cabin to take care of Mama.

Papa had lost interest in everything but taking care of Mama. It seemed that he had lost touch with reality since Mama had gotten so sick. He didn't talk much to me or Rosie any more.

He spent most of his time in the cabin, ignoring the planting that needed to be done, just looking after Mama. For the last couple of weeks he hadn't left her side.

Mama had pushed to take care of the things that needed to be done for all of us as long as she could. But she collapsed on the floor of the cabin two weeks ago and had been in bed ever since. I rode the mule to the Smith settlement to bring back the doctor, but was told he was in Galveston. Nobody knew when he would be back.

Rosie tried to talk to Papa sometimes but her questions usually went unanswered. She spent most of her time with me outside the cabin for the company, sometimes just following me around like a puppy. But on this day I was glad I'd told her to stay home when I went out to check the traps along the river.

I was confident the Mexican soldiers hadn't seen me. I was separated from the soldiers moving up the road by the boulders alongside the river and the thicket between me and the road. I grasped my side in pain as I ran, pushing harder, trying to put more distance between me and them.

Tears stung my eyes and rolled down my cheeks as I ran, remembering how I tried to get Papa to agree to load Mama and Rosie in the wagon and go east with the rest of the settlers. That was the first time I ever yelled at him and the first time I had seen him cry. I even tried to lift Mama from the bed and carry her to the wagon myself, but Papa overpowered me and pushed me away.

"Son," Papa said through his tears, "she won't last overnight in that wagon traveling cross country. She talked a little this morning. She might get well, Andy, she might . . . ."

Before Mama got sick, she was stronger than Papa in many ways and he depended heavily on her during all the years they were married. He told me once that he considered himself a lucky man to have attracted the beautiful, intelligent school teacher when they were younger. She had been courted by several men with better potential, but she had chosen him.

Now Mama looked nothing like she did before. She'd lost so much weight, I hardly recognized her. Her thin, putty-colored skin was draped over the angles of her face and her eyes were sunken into her skull. She hadn't been able to talk to anyone for over a week. Sometime she made noises in her pain, but most of the time she just slept.

Papa wouldn't listen to me when I tried to make a plan for what we would do if the Mexicans came. He just brushed me away. "The Lord will deliver us. The Lord will provide," he said. Papa was never a religious man, but now I guess it was his way to cope with Mama's illness and his inability to reason.

I startled Rosie from her play when I broke through the brush and into the cabin clearing. She was squatting, barefoot, in her threadbare cotton dress next to the rain barrel at the corner of the cabin, rolling out mud pies. I couldn't hide the look of fear on my face. It frightened her.

She forgot her mud pies and stood when she saw me. "What's wrong, Bub? Why you running?"

I bent over, resting my hands on my knees trying to catch my breath. I scooped a handful of water from the barrel and wet my mouth so I could speak. "Rosie," I gasped between breaths, "we gotta leave. We gotta get Mama and Papa outta here!"

"But Papa already said he's not leaving." She followed me as I headed toward the cabin door. "Are the Mexicans coming?"

"They're on the trail right now. There's not much time. Come on!" I burst through the door into the dimly lit cabin, shattering the silence of the room. "Papa, we gotta go." I was almost yelling. "The Mexicans are just down the hill! Must be thirty of 'em! We don't have more than a few minutes! You grab her up by her shoulders and I'll get her feet! We'll hide out in that cave back up on the hill behind the house." I threw the covers off Mama's legs, grabbed her feet and started dragging her off the bed.

Papa glared at me, his sad eyes red-rimmed and blood-shot. "Leave her be, boy."

"But Papa, we gotta go! We don't have time to talk about it!"

"I said leave her be!" He returned his gaze at Mama's face. His face softened, his voice barely above a whisper, "I talked to your Mama again this morning. She said we'd be fine right here." He swabbed her neck with a damp cloth and looked at me with a blank stare. "You take your sister and go up on the hill. Come back after they pass us by. Me and Mama ain't goin' no place."

"Papa, please!" I pleaded, snatching the cloth from his hand.

He ignored me, smoothing Mama's hair. "Every thing's gonna be all right," he whispered and kissed her on the cheek. "You'll be feeling better soon."

I stood beside the bed, helplessly looking from Mama to Papa, trying to make a decision. Rosie held Mama's hand and cried softly.

"Rosie," I was desperately trying to choke back tears, "give Mama and Papa a hug and tell them bye."

I reached for Papa's rifle, checked the load and leaned it against the foot of Mama's bed, then kissed her on the cheek and hugged Papa. "Papa, here's your rifle." I grabbed Rosie's hand, took another look at Mama over my shoulder, and then pulled Rosie reluctantly out the door.

Rosie was too confused and scared to fully understand. She only knew she was leaving her Mama and papa. "Wait . . . My baby." She pulled away from me to pick up the rag doll she'd earlier dropped in the dirt.

"Okay. Come on, let's go. Hurry!" I again took her hand and led her running toward the cedar breaks behind the cabin. Both of us wiped tears from our eyes.

We dodged the low hanging cedars and live oaks and avoided the jagged rocks and prickly pear as we started climbing the rise behind the cabin.

I knew the rugged hill country well. I'd explored the river and hills for miles around the cabin. There was a vertical cave covered with low brush near the top of the ridge, about a quarter-mile away. It would be a good hiding place.

I continued to pull Rosie up the hill, pushing our way through the small cedar brush. Twice her long skirt caught in tangles in the mesquite thorns. Once as I yanked her skirt loose it tore, causing her to cry harder.

I stopped and knelt, pulling her close, wrapping her in my arms, trying to calm her. I looked in her frightened, blue eyes. "Rosie, you've got to be quiet. If they hear you crying, they'll find us." I wiped her tears with my finger as she tried to choke back her sobs. Soon we were again running up the hillside.

"Here it is," I said, pushing aside a clump of brush on the rock-strewn ground. I parted more of the cedar bush, exposing the lip of the cave.

"I'm not going down there!" She looked down the dark hole in fright, struggling to pull away from my grip. "It's dark and scary. Bub, there may be snakes in there." She started crying again.

"Look, I've been here before. It's all right. Here, I'll go in first to show you it's safe."

"Oh, Bub! Don't let the snakes bite you!" She grasped her rag doll to her chest with both hands and watched me lower myself into the hole.

"Shhh! Be quiet!" I scolded. My feet touched the bottom of the pit and I stood still as my eyes adjusted to the near darkness. "Come on down," I called quietly. "There's nothing down here but me. Just grab hold of those roots and climb down."

"No. I'm scared." She stood at the edge of the hole, looking down into the darkness holding her doll tightly.

"Rosie, listen to me." I hesitated briefly before continuing. "I don't want to scare you any more than you already are but . . . if the Mexicans find us, they'll kill us. Do — you — understand?"

She didn't answer for a few moments. Then in a quiet voice she answered, "Yes."

"Look, I'll climb back up part way. Just grab the base of that bush up there and lower your feet to me. Please, Rosie, we've got to get out of sight."

"Here, catch my baby." She leaned over the hole and dropped her doll into the darkness. "Will you catch me if I fall?"

"Yes, I'll catch you. Now come on."

I cushioned her body as we fell the last couple of feet to the floor of the small chamber.

"There better not be any sna—"

I clamped my hand over her mouth and cocked my head to listen to the faint rattle of gunfire from the valley below. It lasted only a few seconds, but there must have been at least twenty shots fired.

We huddled together at the bottom of the pit, watching the light fade from the small opening at the top as clouds moved in. For the longest time neither of us said anything. Rosie broke the silence. She looked at me and in a quiet voice asked, "Bubba, what do you think happened to Mama and Papa?"

I knew what had happened, but I didn't know how to share it with Rosie. I struggled to get the words out as tears welled in my eyes. "I, uh . . . I don't know, Rosie. I just don't know." *Oh God, how can I do this? How can I tell my seven-year-old baby sister that Mama and Papa have just been murdered and we're totally on our own in the wilderness? All the other families left days ago and we're hundreds of miles from safety — in the middle of a war.*

Made in USA - Crawfordsville, IN
33094_9781523447329
03 15 2022 1148